Written by: Konn Lavery

Second Edition Edited by: Will Gabriel

First Edition Edited by: Robin Schroffel

ISBN-13: 978-0-9958938-3-2

Published in Canada by Reveal Books.

Book artwork and design by Konn Lavery of Reveal Design.

Photo credit: Nastassja Brinker.

Printed in the United States of America.

Second Edition 2017. First Edition 2014.

Find out more at:

konnlavery.com

THANK YOU

Thanks to everyone who has supported me in pursuing the re-releases of the Mental Damnation series. This novel that you hold is the second iteration of my second novel, Dream, originally released in 2014. Mental Damnation's storyline has evolved greatly since the reissue of Reality in the spring of 2017.

The feedback received and experiences gained from the project since its conception in late 2016 has been astonishing. I'd like to extend my thanks to you, the reader for picking up this book and willingly dive into the depths of Mental Damnation.

I'd also like to thank my mother, Brenda Lavery for supporting my creative outlets even before I could walk. Thanks to Meghan Cooper for encouraging me to follow my dreams and spark my writing career. Thanks to my brother, Kyle Lavery who always eager to read the new work. A thank you to Will Gabriel and Robin Schroffel for working on each edition of this book.

Also thanks to my father, Terry Lavery and my sister, Kirra Lavery. Lindsey Molyneaux, Nastassja Brinker, Suzie Hess and all of my friends and fans who continue to show interest in my writing. It would have been a much more difficult journey without all of you. Cheers to you!

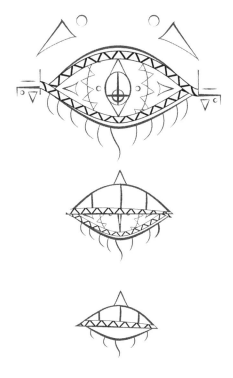

MENTAL DAMNATION
DREAM

Thought to be banished to the underworld by the humans, Krista mysteriously finds herself as the first of her kind to walk on the surface in centuries. This was caused by one of the underworld's corrupt leaders, Danil, who uses her in an unholy ritual to set their people free. Danil's infectious touch gives Krista the nightmarish disease known as Mental Damnation.

She becomes the key interest of two men, Paladin and Dr. Alsroc, who struggle to make sense of her sudden appearance and how it relates to Mental Damnation. Her friend back in the underworld, Darkwing, abandons his gang to begin his search for her.

Krista finds herself torn between two worlds, gaining acceptance among the humans while experiencing inner turmoil from hallucinations caused by her disease. These visions paint a hellish dream world known as Dreadweave Pass where the realm's ruler, a corrupt god known as the Weaver, is on the hunt for her. Krista's blood is believed to be a key component for the Weaver's retribution against the Heavenly Kingdoms that once banished him!

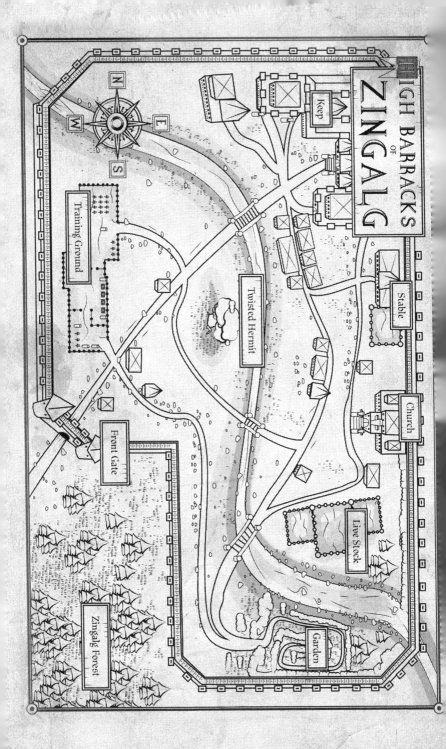

TABLE OF CONTENTS

CHAPTER I

An Era Ends

 itting cross-legged, the motionless man exhaled steadily from his dry mouth. Eyes closed, he gradually followed the action with an inhale. His eyes remained shut, his full concentration on his breathing cycle. He ignored the cool floor and the subtle deep rumbling ambience that echoed throughout the chamber. His goal was to keep his mind as empty as possible.

Silence, he thought to himself. The man's bottom eyelid twitched slightly, realizing that a word had entered his mind. *No thoughts,* he thought. *Wait!*

"Damn it," he muttered to himself. His eyes slowly peeled open as he came to the realization that he had broken his moment of bliss. The concentration he'd invested into clearing his head of thoughts was now gone. A surge of frustration coursed through his veins: the slight burning sensation of anger. The same anger he'd concentrated on suppressing over his years of training as a paladin—a warrior of the light.

As descendants of a holy bloodline known as paladins, his kind had abilities that matched the angels. The power given to the paladins was from another era; an era when God believed man was worthy of such gifts. Paladins had to meditate daily to retain a connection with their lord, heightening the holy ability fused to their physical being.

When one could not focus on their meditation, it was more than frustrating.

The man scanned the surrounding space, a chamber that served as the primary meditation area in the Temple of Zeal. Large marble columns stretched from floor to ceiling in the four corners of the square room, supporting the intricately carved illustrations of winged men above. The flooring had three circular designs overlapping one another painted in the centre where he sat. He gazed straight toward the stained-glass windows filled with varying shades of beige, yellow, and red. The sun beamed into the chamber and tinted the area with the hue of the glass.

Through all my years in the temple, even with the holy gifts blessed upon me by our lord, I still can't master something as simple as meditation. He shook his head and stood, staring directly at the centre stained-glass piece: an image of a shirtless man with a crown of thorns piercing into his head.

Despite following the practices of my mentors and the words of God, the Creator . . . the man thought to himself while marching out of the chamber. He walked beyond the circular painting toward two large wooden doors reinforced with black painted steel. He pushed the handle plates open with one hand on each door, moving them aside so he could enter the hallway beyond: a long, narrow passage with marble sculptures lining either side.

If only the temple's spiritual training came as easy as using a weapon, he thought. Physical tasks were something the man had always preferred. Using his mind to master his consciousness seemed to be a waste of time. He had his foundational beliefs and didn't understand the need to meditate to find anything more.

"Brother Zalphium." A masculine voice came from down the hall. Zalphium looked up; a man was marching toward him, clad in the same matching gold-plated armour that he himself wore.

"Brother Franch." Zalphium returned the greeting with a nod. The two of them converged, stopping merely a foot apart.

"I hope you were able to come to some sort of epiphany through your meditation," said Franch.

"Unfortunately, no. I find my mind is unable to quiet itself enough to find what it needs to. Especially in a time like this."

Franch brushed his red beard with his hand and sighed. "I am sorry to hear that."

"The blade is something that I identify with far easier than delving into a mental foundation that is already seamless. It's essentially running my mind around in circles."

"You raise a good point. Keep in mind, though: unless you challenge your mindset, you will never broaden your consciousness. We may already out-live any normal man by several centuries, but that doesn't mean you can brush aside any training of wisdom."

"Yes, as our mentors have told us," said Zalphium. "I feel it serves no purpose to me, though. I am far better off perfecting my combat skills so I can further serve the Paladins of Zeal on the front lines, spreading the word of God and cleansing the world of Dega'Mostikas's evil."

"If meditating is difficult at a time like this, that is precisely why you need to meditate. Eliminate your weaknesses. You must seek answers about why you remain so disturbed by it."

Zalphium folded his arms. "Perhaps because all we did during the Drac Age was fight. I think that is all I know."

"You're not a soldier, Zalphium. You're a paladin. The days of battling the draconem with swords and blood are over."

"I'm not a soldier anymore, but I was. It becomes difficult to remove that mindset from one's head. During the war, we had to be certain of who we were when fighting those monsters."

"Hence why you need to meditate," said Franch. "Face the inner demons that trouble your thoughts so they do not corrupt you."

"You know what troubles me? Even through all the struggles we went through during the Drac Age, ending their tyranny and bringing the world out of the darkest era it has ever seen, we are still following the draconem's steps in every way."

"Are you referring to the vazelead exile? You do recall Saule found evidence of the reptilian people serving the last Drac Lord, Karazickle? They are not worthy of being anywhere in the charted world."

"I know this, but is exile to the underworld really necessary?"

Franch extended his hand while turning back the way he came. "Walk with me, brother."

The two began to move farther down the hall, strolling side by side while passing numerous closed doors on each side of the path.

Franch kept his hand behind his back and sighed. "I understand what you are proposing: that our actions mimic the harsh tyranny of the Drac Lords. Their goal was to eliminate all other life. I disagree that we are following their ways. We are only exiling the vazelead people to the underworld, not annihilating them."

"How is exile to that harsh environment any different? You know the stories as well as I do—the heat, the winds, and the utter darkness. We both know that Saule and the Council of Just chose the underworld because they knew of its conditions, how it mutates people into fiends. No one comes out of there the same. There is something otherworldly down there."

"The vazelead people will never return from underworld, so we do not have to worry about what they will become from the metamorphosis fumes in the air. We are preparing a banishment ritual."

Zalphium's eyes widened. *A Prayer of Power.* "But that will keep them shackled there for eternity!"

"Yes. The vazelead people are not like us; they pose a threat that must be addressed. You cannot deny that."

"Perhaps they are an opposition, but I do not believe that this is morally any different than the actions of the Drac Lords. Do you really think God approves such actions?"

Franch shrugged. "We tried to convert the vazelead people when we enslaved them decades ago. Now that they are free, they retain little of what we taught them about the civilized world. They're animals, not human."

The two pushed open a set of wooden doors leading out onto a stone balcony that extended along the outer wall of the marble temple. Beyond the balcony's cylindrical stone railings was a vast and steep mountain-scape, covered in snow and dark charcoal rocks. The sun overlooked the clear blue sky, shining down on the ice and reflecting a bright white light directly at the temple. A single dirt path in the distance led to the base of the Temple of Zeal, directly below where Zalphium and Franch stood.

I never tire of the view of Mount Kuzuchi, Zalphium thought briefly. Through the debate with his comrade, the mountain-view provided him a moment of peace.

Franch extended his hand. "The Council of Just wills the banishment of the vazelead people, and we must obey. They led us out of the Drac Age and are responsible for ensuring such a threat never arises again."

"They also traded for witchcraft from the nymphs to do so."

"The politics with the kingdoms and nymphs is a whole other discussion. Regardless of the technicalities, you need not question the will of the Council of Just." Franch grinned. "You were the one telling me that you don't want to challenge your intellect, so why question clear instructions?"

Zalphium frowned. "I don't want to challenge my mind's moral foundation—not my critical thinking. This action does not follow the Paladins of Zeal code of morality that the Creator has given us. I may have followed orders without question during the Drac Age, but now that the war is over I do not agree with the Council of Just's choices. We would be better off sending out missionaries once more to convert the vazelead people to the light."

"Not if they are serving the Drac Lord Karazickle. If this is the case, they have chosen their side and we must take the opportunity to prevent another war."

"With a banishment to the underworld? It's practically sending them down to Dega'Mostikas's Triangle!"

Franch shrugged. "It is a devilish landscape, I will agree with that. Not that I've seen it personally."

"Subjecting them to the mutation is murdering them."

"The Council of Just is wise, as is Saule, who was chosen to lead the council. They would have thought about conversion as well. We simply cannot take the any chances."

The two continued to walk on the balcony, following it along the outer rim of the temple. Franch kept his gaze to the floor as Zalphium stared out at the mountains.

Zalphium brushed his dirty blond hair from his face and looked over to his comrade. "Do these questions ever haunt your mind,

Brother Franch?"

"No. I put my trust in Saule's leadership."

"How did he discover this knowledge about Karazickle and the vazelead people, though?" asked Zalphium. "Where is the proof? I've never seen a vazelead champion the Drac Lord's winged-moon symbol."

"True, but they spoke a weak form of Draconic before we discovered them. There's one link."

"How do we know Saule's sources regarding Karazickle are credible?"

Franch stopped in his tracks and turned to face Zalphium. "I am your temple brother, and you're lucky I am also your friend. That kind of talk amongst the other paladins would be met with rehabilitation."

"I know." Zalphium folded his arms. "That is why I am asking you. I know you are on my side."

"To answer you, no we do not. I don't think anyone knows how he found that information."

"That is what makes me sceptical of the whole thing. Which is also why I do not want to be a part of it."

"It's already in the process as we speak. From what I heard, the last tribe was gathered at the base of Mount Kuzuchi, near Kuzuchi Forest. The rest of the paladins in the temple will be joining our brothers and the Knight's Union at the top of the mountain."

"I will pass."

"This will not look good to the others, Zalphium. You should include yourself in the ritual. We need all the manpower we have to channel the banishment prayer."

"I have full faith that our brothers are capable of finishing it on their own. I cannot fully invest in something that I do not believe in." Zalphium gestured to the far end of the temple, where they were headed. "I'd rather practice my agility in the chamber of endurance."

"That will be there any other day."

"I am sorry, brother. I cannot join you. I must stick to my beliefs."

Franch stopped in his tracks and nodded. "You are bold, Zalphium. I admire that greatly—but it makes you a fool at times."

"As I said, I have my core principles from God. I will not stray from them. I believe this banishment is against everything we stand for."

Franch smiled. "As any paladin must do. It is why we were blessed with divine powers from the Father."

Zalphium placed his hand on Franch's shoulder. "Indeed."

Franch patted his brother's arm. "I must prepare with the others. We leave on horseback within the hour."

"Go now. I will see you when you return."

The two bowed before each other and parted ways, Zalphium continuing to the chamber of endurance and Franch returning to the doorway they'd come through.

He sees my view but doesn't understand it, Zalphium thought to himself while marching down the pathway. His hands were clenched. The discussion had upset him, knowing that he could not convince his friend of the error of their ways. If not Franch, he would be unable to convince any of the Paladins of Zeal that he was right. And by not participating in the vazelead people's banishment, he would prove himself to be an outcast amongst his own kind.

I'll be a reject. The thought made him sick. He simply did not understand how they could not see what he saw.

Zalphium turned to look at the mountain landscape, feeling a cool breeze pick up, blowing gently against his face. He inhaled through his nostrils, letting the brisk air fill his lungs. He understood the paranoia amongst the humans and why they would want to banish an entire race if they potentially posed a threat. The world was a beautiful place, especially the Kingdom of Zingalg, the home of Mount Kuzuchi

It's why we fought so bravely during the Drac Age . . . for this.

A part of him felt a duty to join the other paladins in the banishment, but he had to stand his moral ground. If he didn't, where would the line be drawn? He could only pray that his fellow paladins would understand his justification.

Directly below the balcony, Zalphium spotted several dozen cavalry on the base level of the temple. The horses of various colours were clad in steel-plated armour with saddles on top of their backs. They were prepped for the journey up Mount Kuzuchi where the entrance to the underworld stood.

Beside the horses were paladins in golden armour and deep red tunics, polishing their weapons and making last-minute adjustments to the horses' armour.

My fellow paladins, readying themselves to perform a banishment

prayer.

Zalphium had never performed a Prayer of Power of that size on his own; these special prayers required a lot of mental strength. He was only good at simple tasks like healing and casting light. It was a weakness of his. He knew that paladins who could master the banishment prayer were capable of constraining a person—or a group of people—into a location for eternity. If they got enough paladins together, all channelling their prayers, they could banish an entire race.

If the banished person or people attempted to leave the area, they would be dragged back by glowing shackles. To the untrained eye, one would think that the spontaneous appearance of shackles around the beings' limbs pulling them back was some sort of witchcraft. It wasn't, though; it was simply the power of God channelled through the divine abilities of the paladins. These powers were what separated paladins from the rest of the mortal world—a direct link to the heavens.

Our power doesn't change the fact that we are still human. We sin individually and in large numbers, Zalphium thought while pulling open a wooden door before entering a chamber twice the size of the meditation room.

The chamber was filled with rows of marble columns extending to the opposite end of the room, where target dummies made of linen and stuffed with hay were lined up. There were fewer windows in this room than in the meditation chamber, which made the room much darker. Only small stained-glass windows ran along the top of the walls, providing a gradient of light that dimmed progressively from floor to ceiling.

Each row of columns had unique obstacles such as pits, walls, spikes, and pillars. All were used by the paladins for their training exercises. It was the endurance chamber of the temple, where Zalphium preferred to spend his time.

This will keep my mind off all this banishment nonsense. To Zalphium, the banishment was a dark time for humanity and he was frustrated in his inability to change the course of events. He felt it was best to keep his focus on something else. Something simple that would not frustrate him.

No more meditating today, he thought.

Zalphium stepped farther into the chamber, walking along the side so he could look down one of the rows of columns to inspect the obstacles. He wanted to find a challenge that would require all his focus so he could forget about the worldly events that were taking place.

After a couple of rows, he paused at one with a series of smaller pillars scattered in between the columns.

This will do, he thought while stretching his legs as a warmup.

After a couple of minutes of stretching, he took a deep breath while extending his left leg and prepared his muscles.

Focus. Breathe in . . . and out, he instructed himself. Without further waiting he dashed forward, lifting his entire body from his left leg to enter a daring sprint.

Within seconds he rushed into the series of columns, approaching the first pillar directly in his path. Only about half an inch from the pillar he leaped to his right, preserving his momentum. He continued to dodge upcoming pillars as he ran, maintaining a constant speed through the row.

The whole dash took well under the time any normal human could achieve even without the heavy plated armour that Zalphium wore. This was his specialty: agility and combat. As fast as the eye could follow, he dashed to the opposite end of the room, shifting past the last pillar and stomping his foot just past the series of columns. No sweat ran down his face and his breath was steady and measured as it was before he started.

One down, he thought, turning to face the row of columns again. This was a task he would spend hours doing. Running the pillars once was nothing to him. He had started doing these exercises from an early age and had grown used to building endurance. He didn't start feeling fatigue until he reached a hundred repetitions, minimum.

Once again, he prepped his dash and charged down the hall. Zalphium pushed himself to move more nimbly than the previous run, constantly challenging his own best. The second run proved no different than the first; he showed no signs of tiring.

He continued to repeat this task for several hours, running back and forth, dodging the pillars and increasing his speed with each sprint. After about sixty sets back and forth Zalphium stopped on the far end of the chamber with the combat dummies. Sweat ran down his forehead as he brushed his wet hair aside, exhaling heavily.

That will do, he thought to himself while exiting the chamber into the connecting hallway. He marched down the hall toward the bathing pool as he always did after training. It was a natural hot spring on Mount Kuzuchi that they used to clean themselves and spend leisure time.

Reaching the door, he stepped into the humid room. Despite the white mist covering most of the details, he could still make out the general shape of the square pillars, the cavern ceiling, and the rectangular bathing area where bubbles rose to the surface of the water from the heat. Off to the side of the entrance was a rack with fresh towels.

Often paladins would come to the pool to lounge, chat with one another, or simply take a break from their hard training and duties. The bathing pool, along with the Temple of Zeal, was a haven for all paladin kind.

After I wash off this mess I will return to my study, Zalphium thought while unbuckling his armour, placing it beside the edge of the pool. He carefully removed his necklace, placing the leather-laced golden cross on top of his armour.

When Zalphium was not on duty—as he should have been that day—he spent his days following a strict routine of meditation, intense physical training, and research in the temple's library. Each of the paladins specialized in a form of study. Some of them focused on prayers, biblical history, politics, or in Zalphium's case, draconem. His fellow paladins questioned his choice of study considering that the Drac Age was over.

They tell me that my studies are obsolete now—that no one studies draconem anymore. He shook his head while dipping his naked herculean body into the hot water. He washed himself from head to toe, trying to keep his thoughts off the vazelead banishment. It was difficult for him to do; the act the paladins were about to commit went against all the morals they had been handed down by God.

I shouldn't overthink it; there's nothing I can do now. What's done is done. I should accept what I cannot change, he thought while washing the remaining dirt from his skin.

After washing himself clean, Zalphium got out of the pool and dried himself before putting his clothing and armour back on. The last item he put on was his cross necklace, placing it over his head and letting the pendant drape across his chest plate. It was the symbol of his saviour and offered him reassurance of God's presence, as it did for all paladins.

He moved back through the entrance to the bathing pool chamber, returning to the cool, bright hallway. The sun shined directly into the hall, casting sharp shadows as it lowered in the west; the day was coming to an end. His steps echoed as he marched toward the study. Never had the temple been so vacant. It normally buzzed with paladins moving between chambers or standing and chatting amongst one another.

The quietness is rather welcoming for a change, he noted while examining the vacant space.

The walk came to an end with an open doorway leading into the library. Every wall was covered in shelves that reached the ceiling, so tall that a ladder was needed to reach most books. Few shelf spaces were empty; most were packed with books ranging from leather-bound to simple stacks of paper, all organized alphabetically by topic and author. Several oak tables were also set up for studying, prepped with chairs and lanterns for when the sun set. It was the smallest of the chambers, but this did not mean it was the least useful. It happened to be one of the most valued rooms in the temple. Through their crusades, the paladins collected every book they found, keeping and preserving as much knowledge as possible.

What to focus on in a time like this? he wondered. It hadn't occurred to Zalphium what he would study. He was too preoccupied with his frustration at the unprecedented event taking place. He stepped to the nearest bookshelf to examine some of the spines to see if anything could catch his attention.

Draconem has always been my study of choice. But is it truly relevant to our current path? Ideally, he wanted to find something that was related to the vazelead banishment. *What do we have on dictating the fate of an entire race?* The thought amused him, as he knew the topic was too specific for the library to have anything of the sort.

Zalphium strolled deeper into the library, looking at each bookshelf carefully to locate a topic that sparked his interest; anything that would offer some sort of insight into what his brothers were about to do.

Zingalg Botany . . . Zingalg Tribal Regions . . . A Guided History of the Nymphs . . . Origin of the Trolls . . . Wait! He stopped in his tracks when he noticed a book titled *Draconem: Before the War*. It had a black leather-bound cover with steel-reinforced edges.

How have I not seen this book before? he thought while squinting. It was odd considering he had visited library for years and had studied most of the books about draconem.

It might give some insight, he thought while recalling his conversation with Franch about vazeleads speaking Draconic. Perhaps there was a link between the two species after all.

Zalphium pulled on the book, but it remained fixed in the shelf. He tightened his grip and yanked firmly. The book tilted forward and the sound of grinding stone reverberated throughout the library.

Zalphium stepped back, eyes wide, and watched the book slide back inward as the shelf retreated to the side, revealing a passageway.

"What?" he said aloud in pure surprise. The Paladins of Zeal were transparent with one another, so a hidden passageway in the temple was quite unusual. If he did not know about it, surely the others did not either. Zalphium had to find out where it led.

The hidden hallway was pitch black, making it impossible to see what was inside. Zalphium rushed to the nearest study table to grab one of the lanterns. It had a candle inside, yet no flame.

Zalphium opened the lantern and extended his hand directly over the wax. He closed his eyes and exhaled slowly, calming his breathing from the excitement of discovering the mysterious hallway.

"God, our Saviour, help us to follow the light and live the truth. Grant me flame so I may reveal what lurks in the shadows. Amen." He opened his eyes as a surge of light pulsated from the cross pendant on his neck, channelling through his chest plate and into his skin. He could feel the tingling warmth run past his torso and through his extended arm down to his fingertips.

A small spark of flame ignited from the palm of his hand, shooting onto the wax candle and projecting light from the lantern.

Zalphium smiled while closing the lantern and taking it by the handle. Casting light was one of the more simplistic Prayers of Power—one he had no trouble performing.

He marched back to the hidden passageway, gripping the lantern tightly while eyeing the darkness of the hall.

"Here we go," he muttered to himself while stepping beyond the bookshelves and into the darkness.

The candle wasn't exceptionally bright, but it did provide some light as he entered the passage. The flooring, walls, and ceiling were made of the same stone as the library. It was a little dusty, which made it difficult to breathe, but that was of little importance to Zalphium—he had to learn what this hallway was for and report it to the temple.

Paranoia stuck Zalphium briefly as he realized perhaps he should have brought some sort of weapon for facing the unknown.

Nonsense, he thought. This was the Temple of Zeal; there wasn't going to be any beast or foe—or so he hoped.

The hallway seemed to extend forever at a gradual downward slope. He walked with caution, keeping the lantern facing ahead to light the way. The light only provided a couple of paces' worth of sight; he was still practically walking blind. What he could see, though, he scanned intensely. He eyed the flooring for cracks and the walls for any holes—potential booby-traps. It all remained sealed, marking the path as safe.

After several dozen more paces from the passage entrance, the hallway came to an end where a staircase led deeper into the unknown. He persisted onward, descending the stairs until he reached the bottom where he encountered a closed stone door. A circular copper doorknob was attached to the far right.

Glancing at the floor, he saw there were curved scrapes from the edge of the door to the wall—signs of the stone door moving. Zalphium concluded that the door could be opened with ease.

This hallway has been used recently, he realized while reaching outward with his free hand to twist and pull the handle. It was far heavier than the book leading into the hallway, but he was able to grip it tight enough to move it.

The sound of grinding stone filled the air as he pulled with all his might, forcing the stone door open. Once there was enough space to move through, Zalphium stopped and stepped through the doorway and into an open, dark space. On the left and right side of the doorway there were unlit torches.

He took the candle from the lantern and carefully leaned the flame onto the first torch, causing it to light up within seconds—he noted the smell of burning oil.

Oil? This room was used too recently, he thought while turning to light the second torch.

After both torches were lit, enough light was provided so he could see the whole room under a warm yellow tint. The light revealed several suits of armour mounted in steel and glass cabinets off to the far end, one shoulder of each suit draped with a deep red cape. In front of the armour was a large black wooden desk with papers and stones scattered across it.

What is this place? Zalphium wondered while placing the candle back into the lantern, closing it, and stepping deeper into the room.

Shelving lined the top of the wall all along the room, holding trophies made of metal, gold, and colourful gems. Several large claymores and a shield were mounted just below the shelves. Each one had engravings of crosses, eyes, and other markings Zalphium recognized as symbols of paladin kind.

"I know some of these weapons," he spoke aloud while brushing his sandy blond hair aside. He had seen their leader, Saule, sport the gear during the Drac Age. *What are they doing down here?* he thought, stepping deeper into the room. *Does our leader have a chamber hidden from his brethren?*

Instantly Zalphium's eyes were drawn to the far-right wall where a painting hung. It portrayed a moon and draconic wings erupting from behind it. Just below the painting was a deep blue robe decorated with a moon-shaped symbol on the chest.

"No . . ." he muttered to himself while staring directly at the moon icon on the robe. The icon was clear as day to Zalphium. It was the memorable moon of Karazickle, Drac Lord of the night.

This doesn't make any sense. Zalphium was flabbergasted, yet his eyes did not deceive him. His countless years of study did not make him a fool who would not recognize draconem symbols, especially the Drac Lord Karazickle moon.

There's got to be an explanation for this. Zalphium turned his back to the robe and the painting, trying to justify their presence to himself. He brought his attention to a bookshelf that housed hundreds of old, worn scrolls. On a desk near the shelf were linen paper, a quill, and a red ink bottle. One of the papers was unrolled and pinned down with bright, polished, blue and green rocks.

Zalphium leaned closer, feeling the veins in his body tingle. The scroll had swirled lines of varying weights, outlined with dots and straight lines. He gasped, recognizing the Draconic alphabet. He took another deep breath and read the glyphs of the scroll in more detail. He recognized the words from his studies: It was a formula which granted draconem shape-shifting abilities. From his research, Zalphium knew draconem could retain their new shape—whatever shape they wished—for as long as they pleased, but once they morphed back to their natural body, the shape-shifting ability ended.

The paladin felt ill as he put the pieces together in his mind. He wanted to believe it was a hoax, but seeing Saule's armour, the moon crescent of Karazickle on the painting, the robe, the scrolls, and the shape-shifting formula was too much. It all added up: the paladin leader was truly Karazickle, the last of the Drac Lords, in human form.

"It cannot be," he muttered. Turning his head, he saw a jar of human teeth on the bookshelf with the scrolls. Draconem that consumed humans vomited their skeletons back up for easy digestion, and many were known to take teeth as trophies of their kills.

Zalphium clenched his jaw and snatched up one of the coloured stones, hurling it at the glass jar with all his built-up fury. The rock smashed into the jar, shattering it into hundreds of pieces. The teeth poured out on the floor, scattering.

The Drac Lord has deceived us, he thought while grabbing the scroll from the desk and storming out of the hidden chamber.

It was most dreadful news that he had ever discovered. Their leader was a fraud. Zalphium was certain that God had led him there; how else could have he found the chamber? Regardless, the discovery ignited many more questions in his mind: Had Saule always been Karazickle? Or did the Drac Lord kill Saule and take his place? He suddenly remembered the vazeleads. Why did Karazickle want to banish the vazelead people? Saule coincidentally happened to be the leader of the Council of Just—did they know of this exploitation?

How could have we foreseen this? Zalphium thought to himself. His mind was burning with questions about the discovery that he knew would not be resolved anytime soon.

None of the questions could be answered at that exact moment. Right now, Zalphium had to leave the Temple of Zeal and reunite with his brethren atop Mount Kuzuchi, where the banishment was taking place. He had to show the Paladins of Zeal and the Knight's Union proof regarding Saule's identity.

Zalphium rushed out of the hidden passageway and back into the library. He hurried through the Temple of Zeal to gather his belongings and prepare to leave on horseback. He glanced out the nearest window while he ran down the hall. The sun was nearly set, meaning it would be dark soon. The travel to the top of Mount Kuzuchi would take several hours.

After sprinting through several hallways, the paladin burst through the door into his quarters. He tucked the scroll into his belt, then placed the lantern on the nearby nightstand. Hastily, Zalphium snagged his sheathed sword from the wall and tied it to his belt then grabbed the shield beside it, strapping it over his shoulder so it rested on his back.

Wasting no time, he blew out the candle in the lantern and exited the quarters so quickly he left the door open. It didn't matter; if he didn't get to the mountaintop to expose the Drac Lord in time, the Paladins of Zeal might do something that morally wrong at the hands of Karazickle.

Zalphium hurried down to the base level of the temple from the long staircase that led to the entryway, the largest room in the temple. The doors had been left open when his brethren left, allowing him to rush out to the horse stables. He made it to the wooden shelter to find that there were still several horses left behind, though they didn't have their armour or caparisons. Most likely they were spare horses.

The paladin opened the gate to one stall that housed a black horse. He rushed to the far end where he could grab its saddle that rested on a wooden bench. As quickly as he could, Zalphium harnessed the horse and mounted.

"Go!" he shouted while lashing the reins, encouraging the horse to dash out of the stables.

Zalphium felt the cool wind on his face, blowing his hair out of the way as the horse rushed down the dirt path, leaving the Temple of Zeal behind.

There was little time to spare. Considering how long Zalphium had spent in his sprinting exercises and bathing, he knew the other paladins were most likely at the top of the mountain already. The Temple of Zeal was built high up the rocky landscape far from other civilized areas in Zingalg. It provided the paladins a sense of isolation so they could focus on their training and not be bothered by worldly affairs. *Not this time, though,* Zalphium thought. It appeared that they had corruption from within all along.

The path split into a fork: the left led down the mountain and the right led farther up, inclining drastically.

Zalphium spurred the horse to go faster, to the point he could hear it wheeze to catch its breath. He felt sympathetic for the animal as he knew he was pushing it to its limits. However, this was not a time for the horse to enjoy an easy stroll. The fate of an entire race was at stake.

The paladin and his steed continued ascending, enduring the progressively colder climate and sharp winds up the mountain. The terrain transitioned from rock and snow to pure snow. Zalphium could see the footprints of thousands of beings on the ground. A mixture of boots, hooves and claws—claws being, he knew, from the vazelead people.

Even blotches of black blood could be seen on the snow, most likely due to the humans aggressively driving the reptilians to move faster. Farther up the road he spotted a few corpses littering the pathway. Passing them he could see the brown scaly tails and clawed hands and feet of the bodies—vazeleads that could not keep up with the humans' forced march.

This must end, he thought.

Zalphium began to feel the snow build up on his eyebrows and eyelashes as they went even higher. The feeling of the cold air biting at his cheeks and nose became prevalent.

Keep going, he urged himself, ignoring the cold, the blood on the ground, and the horse's desire to slow down. He had no other option;

this had to be done.

Time seemed to be a blur for him rushing up the mountain; what was over several hours of horseback riding felt like mere minutes. The paladin was too focused on his goal to pay attention to details such as impatience of time. The only indicator he had of how much time had passed was that the sun had set. He had ridden well beyond the clouds, revealing a pure night sky and countless stars accompanying the moon.

The steep climb gave way to flatter travel at the top of the mountain. Zalphium was high enough now that a faint chanting could be heard from above through the sharp winds. This was common; it was only the angels in the heavens singing their continual tune.

"Faster!" Zalphium urged the horse as they approached a wide pathway. Rock formations created sharp walls on both sides, forming a passageway leading to a wide-open area at the centre of the mountaintop. Beyond the path, mass groups of humanoids seemed to writhe en masse, some panicking and others taking aggressive actions to push the others toward the centre.

"No!" Zalphium shouted, realizing that the humans were already forcing the vazelead people toward the massive pit in the middle of the mountain that descended into the underworld. *There is still time,* he reassured himself.

Rushing through the passageway, the paladin could fully grasp the scene at the summit. A massive pit about a third of the total area was in the centre of the landscape. Glowing gold chains ran all along the rim of the hole, channelling from the far end of the canyon where a group of hundreds of gold-plated men stood in a circle, chanting to one another. They were too far for Zalphium to hear but he knew that they were performing the banishment Prayer of Power. The glowing chains were the result of their prayer.

Screams erupted from the scene as silver-plated men—Knight's Union—and other gold-plated men lashed their spears and swords at the horrified reptilian humanoids. The vazeleads hissed and cried for help as they fumbled over top of one another due to the shackles and chains that bound them in pairs.

The vazeleads that moved too slowly were pierced by the weapons and left to bleed, forcing their shackled comrade to drag their dying corpse with them to avoid being next.

This is madness! Zalphium thought while shaking his head.

Scanning the scene, the paladin's eyes widened when a commanding voice echoed through the chaos, shouting. "Continue to round them up toward the pit!"

Zalphium glared off to the side of the chanting paladins. There was a large boulder, upon which a gold-plated man stood, his billowing red cape blowing in the wind. He grinned wickedly as his wavy hair flew into his face—Saule, the Paladins of Zeal's leader.

"This ends here. Hiyaa!" Zalphium spurred the horse forward, dodging the stray vazeleads and humans who were on the outskirts of the chaos so he could get as close to the paladins as he could.

Taking a deep breath, the rogue paladin shouted, "Karazickle! Drac Lord of the night!" His voice was so strident through the all the noise, so devastating, that it even silenced the distant angels.

Zalphium brought his horse to a halt and glanced around to see that, for the moment, the fighting had stopped. Many of the humans and vazeleads glanced around to see where the shout had come from. He snatched the scroll from his belt and held it high in the air. "Brothers! Saule is a fraud! He lied to us! He is the Drac Lord Karazickle!"

"This is absurd!" Lord Saule's voice echoed over the summit.

Zalphium scanned the faces that watched him; humans and vazeleads alike seemed more confused about his statement than anything else. Even two young vazeleads not too far from him, chained together, had faces painted with confused expressions at his bold statement.

"Banish Brother Zalphium with the vazelead people!" Saule ordered.

Within moments several men approached Zalphium; one of them was a paladin while the other two were knights.

Damn it, Zalphium thought. He'd been too caught up with his discovery to formulate a legitimate case to argue against Saule. "Brothers," he spoke while unrolling the scroll. "We have all learned to recognize the symbols on this scroll! Behold—a formula for transmogrification, found in a secret chamber belonging to Saule!"

"Zalphium!" an approaching paladin shouted while taking off his gold helmet, revealing his red beard and brown hair. It was Franch. "What are you doing?" he asked, sheathing his sword.

The two knights beside Franch continued to march toward Zalphium with their weapons drawn.

Franch slammed his gauntlet into the nearest knight's head. "Stop for a moment, fool!"

One of the knights shook his head and spoke in a hoarse voice. "Paladin, you did hear Saule's orders?"

Franch shook his head. "Give me a moment with Brother Zalphium." He stepped forward and nodded. "I warned you not to oppose Saule's will. Everyone obeys him; see how mindlessly these two knights were complying without question?" He glanced back to see the knights had stepped closer, gripping their weapons tightly and ready to strike.

"Let me see the scroll," Franch demanded.

Zalphium extended his hand, giving him the document.

Franch sighed. "I will be in disciplined for disobeying a direct order and looking at this." He unrolled the scroll and his eyes widened while they scanned back and forth. "My God. . ." He lowered the scroll. "Zalphium, how?"

"I don't know." He pointed at the oncoming knights. "Let them know. We have to stop this senseless banishment!"

Franch turned around and raised the scroll. "He's right! Brother Zalphium has indeed found a formula of transmogrification!"

The two knights in front of them stopped in their march and glanced at each other.

"What do we do?" the hoarse-voiced knight asked.

"Warn the others. Hurry!" Zalphium shouted. He glanced back up at Saule, drawing his sword in the process. "Karazickle, Drac Lord of the night! Reveal yourself at once!"

Franch pressed the edges of his hands against his mouth to amplify his voice while ordering, "Cease the banishment!"

"Stop, men!" shouted the hoarse-voiced knight.

Deep maniacal laughing slowly rose from the depths of Saule's throat. Its frequency was so low it caused the ground to vibrate as the laughter boomed throughout the canyon.

"Well done, young paladin," Saule sneered in the same deep, unnatural voice, exposing his teeth as sharp fangs. "But the banishment cannot be stopped!"

Zalphium scanned the scenery to see that most of the knights and paladins had not heard them and were too invested in their task. The large herds of vazelead people were round up like cattle, forced by the humans to leap into the giant black pit or be stabbed to death.

"We can't stop them!" Franch shouted.

Zalphium wiped his face, feeling a deep level of defeat while watching the last few hundred vazeleads around the rim be pushed into the underworld's entrance. Their screams dwindled in the distance as they fell into the unknown. The glowing chains from the Prayer of Power unnaturally snapped open to bind the vazeleads by the ankles as they fell. The gold chains then disintegrated as the reptilians dropped deeper into the pit.

Zalphium's heart felt heavy with the knowledge that he had been unable to rescue the vazelead people in time. Now that they had leaped beyond the rim of glowing chains—the banishment Prayer of Power—and into the underworld, they would be trapped there for eternity.

"This ends here," Zalphium snarled while turning to face Saule.

The paladin leader waved his hands in various formations and patterns, moving faster and faster until he extended his hand into the air with a boom of thunder.

Black and grey clouds quickly rose to swarm the skyline, shrouding the stars as a heavy wind picked up. Snow and ice began to rain down from the darkened clouds at high speeds in an aggressive blizzard.

"That's not possible! We're far higher than the clouds. We're practically near the heavens!" Franch exclaimed, eyeing the blackening sky.

"It is possible for the Drac Lord of the night." Zalphium spoke while extending his hand. "Brother Franch, we must stop Saule."

Franch grabbed Zalphium's hand and leaped, joining Zalphium on his tired steed.

"We may have lost the war, but you haven't rid the world of the Drac Lords!" Saule shouted just before his neck cracked, forcing his head to violently swing back and forth, hair flailing. His skull extended forward, forming a wide, reptilian muzzle. The man's arms and torso tensed, curling inward while his body grew drastically, forcing the gold-plated armour to shred like paper from the immense force. A bulge ripped through his behind, forming a black-spiked tail that swayed side to side. His ever-hardening skin began to morph and re-shape around the skeleton jerking violently inside. The motion caused his torso and limbs to twist in unnatural positions. His skin shred open and white scales tore through, his fingernails and toenails extending into black claws. The shoulder blades rose outward, skin stretching to form giant bat-like wings. The newly morphed white-scaled being stomped on the ground, crushing the boulder Saule previously stood on to rubble as if it were made of snow.

"You certainly weren't lying." Franch exhaled heavily. "That's the bastard, Karazickle."

Zalphium couldn't help but smirk at his comrade's choice of words. "Bastard indeed." He lashed the reins, forcing the horse to pick up the pace.

The paladins' armour clanged as ice shards hit their plating, some so sharp that it dented the armour.

"Christ!" Franch shouted.

"Brace yourself!" Zalphium replied.

The Drac Lord stood on his hind legs and spread his giant wings, flapping them several times and leaping into the air. The sheer size of his wingspan obscured the moon. Between the draconem, the clouds, and the thick blizzard, the entire scene was left in darkness.

Franch extended his one hand high into the air shouting, "Our father, help us to follow the light and live the truth. Grant us sight in the darkest of times. Bless us with your eternal light!" Franch's armour lit up and his entire body glowed brightly, casting a soft light that projected for about two hundred paces around them.

Several other bursts of light were spotted throughout the canyon—other paladins following his lead, providing some light in the darkness.

Karazickle let out a fierce roar, loud enough to cause human ears to ring uncomfortably. "Your kind will pay for the destruction you have caused draconem kind!" he snarled while soaring down toward a large group of knights and paladins.

The draconem flew down past Zalphium and Franch, toward the centre pit where most humans stood. Karazickle built up enough wind that the horse wobbled and tripped over its own legs, throwing the two paladins into the air.

Zalphium fell, colliding into the snow head-first, still holding tightly onto his sword. He got himself up and glanced around at the scene to see Franch had landed on his knees and was able to regain balance quickly. The horse was not so lucky and remained motionless on his side.

Near the centre pit, Karazickle extended his hind legs and landed with a heavy thud into the snow, colliding with several dozen humans in the process. His force crushed them instantly on impact, splattering their blood across his sharp claws and spraying red-stained snow into the air.

Through the mist of snow and blood, the knights began to charge at the draconem, projecting their spears into the air in hopes of penetrating his scales. The closer ones lashed their swords at the draconem. Regardless of their method, the steel weaponry only rebounded off his rock-hard scales.

The paladins nearby began to chant to themselves, clutching the pendants around their necks, performing Prayers of Power. Before they could finish their words, the blizzard increased in speed and density. The hailing ice rained down like a volley of arrows, piercing through the armour and flesh of any human it came in contact with.

The thin mountain air was now filled with screams of pain as men collapsed to the ground with ice shards puncturing their heads, limbs, and chests. They fell in rapid numbers, staining the snow with their blood.

Zalphium's eyes widened as he unbuckled his shield and placed it over his head.

Franch rushed over to him, taking shelter under the shield. "I'll cast a protection Prayer of Power! May God guard and protect our senses. So that this misfor—" Before he could finish his sentence, an ice shard pierced through the shield and punctured right through his skull, splitting it in two. Blood and brain matter splashed across Zalphium's face and the glowing light from Franch's body dimmed to nothing, leaving him in darkness.

"Franch!" he shouted. His mind raced, trying to figure out what to do next. He did not know enough Prayers of Power to shield himself, and the shards of ice were shredding through the knights and paladins at an incredible rate.

He glanced up to see Karazickle was lashing his giant claws at oncoming paladins. Some of the golden-plated men glowed blue—a sign that they had activated a protection Prayer of Power. The ice shards that hit them shattered on impact, leaving no sign of damage on them or their armour. Other paladins that were unable to perform the protection Prayer of Power followed the fate of the Knight's Union and were pierced repeatedly by the ice shards.

Karazickle's tail swung violently, throwing the few remaining men behind him in the air.

An ice shard pierced through Zalphium's shield, ramming into his ankle before he could make any sort of decision. The sudden penetration caused him to yelp in pain as a body, sent flying by Karazickle's tail, collided directly with him. The blow sent him into the air, skidding across the snow until his head slammed directly into a rock. The body that hit him remained on top of him, covering his wounded leg.

Zalphium grunted, trying to shift the body off him before he was penetrated with an ice shard. *This is it*, he thought. *I am about to meet the Father. I have failed.*

Before his fears were proven true, the ice shards stopped falling from the sky and the clouds began to dissipate, leaving only the clear, starry sky in front of him.

A part of Zalphium wanted to get up, but he was too dazed by the impact with the rock to focus. His senses were still somewhat intact but he could no longer hear screams, shouts, or shredding flesh. There was only silence.

The moment passed quickly as a deep, colossal roar echoed through the canyon.

Karazickle, Zalphium thought as the whooshing sound of wings filled the air and the breeze from the draconem's take-off fanned his face, leaving him defeated in the snow.

CHAPTER I: AN ERA ENDS

.

CHAPTER II

Stitch Me Up

Upon a battlefield, where I lay.
Blood on my breath, soon to see death,
Dark tunnel with blooming light.
This was all that was to stay.

Judgment from above, seen me unfit.
Sought unworthy from the holy.
Awaken in hills of bone.
Body of two, one of spirit.

Born anew from my found master.
His will, mortals' minds I drill.
Serving without question.
So his vengeance will be achieved faster. . .
. . . Here I am,
in the land of the damned.

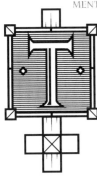hree silhouettes stood cast in the dim light of an icy cold stone room. Twin fiery torches mounted on opposite walls lit the chamber, exposing two human-like figures while the third—the one in the middle—was almost unrecognizable. A discoloured torso with no arms, its skin was being peeled back by shiny hooks. The face of the character to the left was hidden in shadow, but they wore leather gloves and held a knife, the polished blade reflecting the torchlight.

The figure to the right brushed his bone-thin hair from his pale, wrinkled face. He could feel the scraping of his polished gauntlet against his flaky scalp. The protective glove was just one piece of a blood-red-and-black armoured suit, pointed and sharp at every edge. The breastplate had a crest with a large reptilian eye in the centre and stylized jaw lines branching down to the waist where sharp teeth were molded to the metal, creating the illusion of a horrific cycloptic face on his torso.

He was General Dievourse, and he commanded the army in the hell known as Dreadweave Pass.

Ironic for the land of the damned to have a room so cold, the general thought. He ran his tongue along his pointed teeth and hocked a thick lump of saliva to the ground. *However, it is not much of a surprise that my master, the Weaver, would have a chamber of this temperature. Being the ruler of Dreadweave Pass, he must plan every detail of this hell to ensure he has full control of it—even creating bizarre, unexpected features like this ice-cold room. The cold is needed to properly stitch together his puppets from the flesh of mortals.*

The being with stretched skin grunted, his lipless mouth dangling open and the exposed muscles flexing. Dievourse looked down at the humanoid's shoulder to see the surgeon wedge his knife deep into the bone. This was normal; a part of the upgrading process for the Weaver's minions, who were often referred to as the Weaver's 'puppets.' A term their master had coined which was now commonly used throughout his army.

The surgeon was busily removing scraps of flesh and bone where the left arm used to be, prepping the area for the installation of a new, more robust arm.

Dievourse glanced at a wheelbarrow parked to the surgeon's side. The edges were stained with blood and it was piled with numerous limbs, pieces of skin, and bones. These were the parts that were to be grafted onto this puppet to make him faster, stronger, and deadlier in combat. The puppet was going to have numerous layers of skin stitched onto it, making it more resistant to piercing weapons.

My master's power to give life after death is supreme. He can bring anything dead back to life with a single thought, transmitting his will into the dead. The power of a god. I can only be envious of such awesomeness.

The surgeon placed his knife in the sheath strapped to his belt. He reached for a spare arm in the wheelbarrow. With one tug, the arm pulled free. Tendons dangled from where it had been torn off and the hand clenched its fingers, briefly convulsing like a fish out of water.

Dievourse grinned while thinking, *having the ability to give life to the unnatural.*

The arm calmed down and lay limp. The surgeon pulled out a needle from the pouch on the left side of his belt.

The general watched while the surgeon carefully placed the sliced end of the arm against the newly-carved shoulder socket. He folded his arms while watching the surgeon work.

Surgeons have such a detail-oriented profession. Patience and care . . . Characteristics shared with my master, which is why he has been able to create as much as he has in this hell.

The general let his gaze linger on the surgeon, passing over the leather boots, black trousers, bloodstained linen apron, and bare chest covered in pale, dead skin that was stitched together and reinforced by staples to keep the limbs attached. The surgeon's six eyes were intent upon the operation he was performing: affixing the loose muscle tissue to the torso. The surgeon's face had no mouth—he didn't need one to modify minions for the Weaver—but he did have small earholes so he could hear any unusual sounds during operations and nostrils so he could smell for rotten parts. 'test'

Our master is wise to know that not all puppets must be crafted for war; some are needed for other purposes. I myself was his first creation.

He created me to manage his soon-to-be army and force his power on the mortals whom had been doomed to Dreadweave Pass.

Dievourse nodded to himself, recalling how he was in a similar situation to the puppet the surgeon operated on. *The Weaver was meticulous in my construction, exploiting the strengths of two men. One was wild and uncivilized but had the might to outmatch a dozen men. The second held my mind, still filled with the strategic experience of my previous life. The Weaver bound my head to the body of the brute, making the barbarian nothing more than an instrument for my actions.*

The merging of his head onto the barbaric body was a gift unlike any other. Most puppets the Weaver created were slaves to his will. Dievourse was one of the few puppets granted the gift of free will. The Weaver did this knowing of Dievourse's life in the mortal realm.

The puppet on the operating table roared, emphasizing its lipless face with exposed teeth rattling. The surgeon sealed the last gap in its new arm and the puppet grunted. The limb burst to life, thrusting forward and grabbing for the surgeon's neck.

Dievourse snatched the wrist a fraction of a second before the puppet snapped the surgeon's spine.

"Easy, now," Dievourse spoke, his deep, raspy voice bouncing off the bare walls of the hollow chamber.

The puppet glanced over to Dievourse. His eyelids had been stripped away, leaving bloodshot eyes staring right into Dievourse's bright white eyeballs that seemed to float in the middle of his oversized, pitch-black eye sockets.

"Your time will come to inflict pain, but now I need you to remain still," said Dievourse. He set his ghostly eyes on the surgeon. "Can you add the intelligence unit now?"

The surgeon nodded and put the needle away as he leaned toward the wheelbarrow, sifting through the pile of flesh.

"I can't have an inept warrior roaming so close to the Weaver. We just dealt with enough incompetence from the destruction Sporathun caused." Dievourse ground his teeth and let go of the puppet's newly-installed arm.

Sporathun, another prime example how the Heavenly Kingdoms use Dreadweave Pass as a dumping ground for their rejects. Then it is up to me to neutralize the situation. The Weaver instructed Dievourse to govern Dreadweave Pass and ensure it remained stable. When angels and mortals are banished to this hell, they often become enraged. Sporathun was one case where Dievourse had to stop the fallen angel from causing too much havoc in anger with his expulsion from the Heavenly Kingdoms.

The surgeon stood again, this time holding a third of a brain. The action caused the general to perk up.

"Excellent," said Dievourse, stepping back to allow the surgeon to proceed with his work. *I am fortunate that the Weaver has allowed the creation of my own personal servant. This addition to his intellect will make him a powerful servant and give him complete loyalty toward me.*

The general began to walk around the puppet, watching the surgeon lift the top half of its skull and tear the loose skin, revealing its brain tissue. "He will be a fine addition to the Weaver's army. This puppet will be my one and only lieutenant, executing any command given by me—a loyal minion that serves without question."

The surgeon nodded, steadily holding the skull with one hand while the other carefully placed the chunk of brain into the puppet's head.

General Dievourse stroked his jawline and nodded to himself. "You will be the lieutenant, serving me without question."

The puppet being operated on, identified as the lieutenant, grunted while the surgeon dug his hands into his open skull, placing the brain matter in the correct place.

"You will listen to every command I give, even those above the Weaver."

The lieutenant kept its eyes dazing at the general, breathing intensely.

Dievourse began to pace back and forth in front of the lieutenant, staring at each side of the room as he walked by.

"You must be rather confused as to why you are here. As the surgeon installs the intelligence unit, you will start to become self-aware, like I am. This is a rare gift for our kind, the Weaver's puppets."

The general stopped and gestured to himself. "We have the ability to think for ourselves, despite feeling the thoughts and emotions of the other beings bound to us. The Weaver has given us primary control of these bodies."

The surgeon stepped back and nodded at Dievourse, acknowledging that the intelligence unit had been installed.

"Good work." Dievourse nodded back at the surgeon. "Finish with his lips, then we will seal up the remainder of his skin." Dievourse brought his gaze to the lieutenant as the surgeon leaned over to sift through the wheelbarrow, looking for spare flesh to substitute as lips.

"Lieutenant, I'll be blunt with you: You have died and the Heavenly Kingdoms have deemed you unworthy of entering their golden gates."

The lieutenant growled while glancing upward.

"I'm not sure how much you can recall of the incident. I remember every detail of my denial at the golden gates. Believe me, I too was furious when they forced me to descend into Dega'Mostikas's Triangle. The gods in the Heavenly Kingdoms weren't entirely heartless with us. You see, Dreadweave Pass was designed for mortals to pay for their sins in the mortal realm; it is written by the gods that mortals who enter Dreadweave Pass are supposed to suffer a secondary life of agony, leaving it up to the individual to better themselves."

The surgeon dug a rugged flap of skin and flesh from the wheelbarrow. Once he held it out with both hands, it was easily identifiable as half a face that had been torn from a skull. He walked over to the lieutenant, pulling a needle from his operating pouch.

Dievourse extended his hand. "Stay still, lieutenant. Let the surgeon finish his work so you may talk." The general took a step closer. "Before our master, the Weaver, was banished to Dreadweave Pass, this hell used to be a simple barren wasteland for souls given a second chance at redemption. It was not until the Weaver was exiled from the Heavens that it was given a real name."

The lieutenant groaned as the surgeon pierced into his flesh with the needle, stitching the flap of face-skin onto his skull. The dead skin twitched with life as it came into contact with the lieutenant's skull.

"You are probably gaining new senses as the surgeon affixes your mouth. What you are experiencing is the Weaver's power first hand. The very same power that banished him from the Heavenly Kingdoms. You see, the Weaver's practice of taking mortals against their will and dissecting them to forge his own soldiers did not give them a fair chance to repent their sins. Once they became puppets, they were compelled to obey the Weaver's bidding. Even when these mortals were torn to shreds and fused with other flesh, they were still able to watch, sense and feel what their new body was experiencing. How can one repent when they cannot control what they do?"

The lieutenant began to groan and his partly-attached mouth moved, making the noises of, "wah-oo-I-conchrol-mah-body?"

Dievourse was able to comprehend the statement as the phrase: why do I control my body? He raised a finger to his head. "Because the mortal with the most willful pieces holds custody of the body, like you and I with the mind."

The surgeon stitched the last bit of the mouth to the lieutenant's face and stepped back, nodding at Dievourse.

"Why am I chosen to control this body?" came the slightly slurred, croaky voice of the lieutenant.

Dievourse pointed to the stretched skin, ordering the surgeon. "Finish sealing up his flesh." He eyed the lieutenant. "The Weaver knows all, able to read minds and develop complex relationships with each of his puppets. He chose you because of your history, as he chose me to command his army."

The lieutenant pressed his hands onto his new face and shook his head. "Unbelievable. I . . . did not ask for this."

"Of course not." Dievourse put his hands behind his back. "We all want eternity in the Heavenly Kingdoms. However, they do not accept everyone; they punish those they judge unworthy. They did this to our master, the Weaver. He feels our pain and has offered us an alternative. His power grants us eternal life."

The lieutenant clenched his teeth as the surgeon carefully took one of the many stretched skins off a hook and wrapped it around the flesh of the lieutenant's torso.

"Why would a powerful god offer such gifts?" he asked.

"The Weaver is generous and needs an army. Before our existence, or even the existence of Dreadweave Pass for that matter, our master lived in the high tiers of the Heavenly Kingdoms where he was accompanied by the other gods and angels. The Weaver differed from the other gods; he believed in the recycling of damaged souls into new. He took mortals that could not redeem themselves from sin, the souls that would only fill up space in hell, to practice on. He did not think Dega'Mostikas's Triangle should be used as the Heavenly

Kingdoms' dumping ground."

"So how does this involve us?"

"Good question, let us take a step back and I will explain to you why our master is here. The other gods referred to the Weaver's recycling of souls as unholy arts or necromantic rituals. They were tied up on the idea that all mortals should have free will to repent for what they had done, even if it took them an eternity to redeem themselves. The gods met with an elite group of angels from all the tiers of the Heavenly Kingdoms to discuss the Weaver's arts and made a final judgment to banish him to Dreadweave Pass, where he could repent for his actions. After making their judgment, the gods summoned the Weaver to their council. In that moment, they surrounded him in a circular fashion shouting the words 'punishment', 'impure', and 'encase.'" Dievourse clenched his fist and paused for a moment. "These divine words caused the ground to crumble beneath the Weaver and he descended to Dreadweave Pass. The words of power confined him to the realm, trapping him in a prison inside Dreadweave Pass where he was unable to use his necromantic practices and could only reflect on what he had done."

"So, the Weaver offers us eternal life in exchange for serving as his army for revenge?"

"I see the intelligence unit has made you a quick learner. That is his offer in the simplest form. There are more complications to his desire of revenge. The gods had never mentioned anything about him returning to the Heavens or if he was permanently banished to the prison they'd forged within Dreadweave Pass. But our master took this imprisonment personally. He swore revenge upon the Heavens and vowed he would find a way to continue his necromantic studies. For centuries, the Weaver had been forced to watch other immortals and mortals alike be condemned to the hell, suffering for their sins. This captivity boiled rage in the mind of the Weaver, motivating him to formulate a plan for escape. He examined his prison in great detail to find a way out. Ultimately, he discovered that the prison was not perfect. He found a small crack in the structure, meaning that the words of power had been corrupt from the beginning; there was an immoral angel amongst those who had condemned him."

"Who?" the lieutenant asked.

Dievourse shook his head. "This I do not know. It was a blessing for the Weaver, though. He was able to exploit this fissure and use it like a funnel to channel his power out into the plain of Dreadweave Pass, using his necromantic ways to recycle the sinful mortals into his army of what are known as puppets."

Dievourse extended his hand to the room. "Of course, this is not all he had done. The Weaver was able to further explore the realm and strengthen his own necromantic knowledge. Quite recently, he learned to project his will onto the physical space of the realm, tearing the space that makes up reality. This torn area, or rift, allowed the beings of Dreadweave Pass to cross into the mortal realm."

"We can leave hell?"

"If only. The Weaver has strict rules regarding who can enter and leave Dreadweave Pass. He could not simply let any being here escape. To maintain full control of Dreadweave Pass, the Weaver created a unique kind of servant known as a gatekeeper. These powerful mortals are hand-picked by the Weaver to watch over the rifts and only allow beings chosen by the Weaver to pass through."

"Why is he building these rifts? Can he escape back into the Heavenly Kingdoms?"

"No, unfortunately. Their words of power protect the Heavenly Kingdom. The Weaver is still bound to his own prison. He can only project his will into Dreadweave Pass."

"Then what is the purpose of these rifts? Are we to slay the gods' creations in the mortal realm?"

Dievourse chuckled. "I admire your desire for destruction. War is something that I also crave. The army is large enough, and we have the tactical abilities to overthrow the mortal realm. But regardless of what we think, the Weaver has given explicit instructions to the gatekeepers to not allow anyone through without his word."

"Why? It seems like a waste of time."

"The Weaver is no fool. Arrogant, perhaps. He wishes to be a part of his vengeance firsthand. Being trapped in the prison does not allow him to taste the blood of the gods. Therefore, the Weaver has devised the second part of his plan: destroy the holy prison he is trapped in."

"Elaborate." The lieutenant let out a groan while the surgeon continued to seal the remaining slabs of flesh to his body.

"His necromantic arts are said to come from the Book of Consulo."

"What is this book?"

"It contains rituals to counter everything created under the Heavenly Kingdoms. The book's origin goes beyond the Weaver's time, or even the gods'. It is said the book was designed by the Creator."

"Why would such a book exist? Seems to be a flaw."

"The Creator is wise and as old as time itself. His reasoning is beyond what we can comprehend and at times he seems more like an idea or myth than anything else. Regardless, it is believed he is the one who made the gods, the Heavenly Kingdoms, and Dega'Mostikas to watch over the mortal realm. The Creator made the Book of Consulo as a fallback in case his creations in the Heavenly Kingdoms went too far beyond his vision; with the book, everything could be reversed."

"The Weaver took this book from the Creator?"

"The book was believed to be a myth—a tall tale about ways to counter the gods' powers and the knowledge to alter time and space. The Weaver believed in it, though. Before his banishment, he spent centuries trying to find the book, obsessed with the power it was said to have. Ultimately, he found the Book of Consulo; proof of it was the puppets he created. The gods never caught the Weaver with the book because he did not bring it back to the Heavenly Kingdoms in fear of it falling into the wrong hands—and he refuses to tell anyone its whereabouts or how he came to obtain it. He memorized as much of the book as he could when he found it. The complexity of the text is beyond most beings' comprehension and to decipher the entire book would take multiple lifetimes."

"So he used the knowledge from this godly book to alter life and create the realm we are in."

"Precisely. This leads to his second half of his plan. One of the rituals the book is rumoured to contain is a method to break free from divine words of imprisonment. The gods do not know this for certain, and no one knows what the Weaver has memorized from the book or what he has discovered through experimentation."

Dievourse continued, "The key is this: The divine words only imprison those that have been targeted. The book speaks of drenching yourself in a fountain of blood. Blood found in pure and innocent souls, which behaves as camouflage. The divine words will then disintegrate, thinking they have wrongfully captured a child—the purest of lives."

"The Weaver requires us to obtain blood?"

"Not us. The gateekeepers. They enter the mortal realm and explore the various worlds to find the innocent blood he needs by reaping the children into Dreadweave Pass. After all, it's not like innocent children are ever sent to hell by the gods."

The surgeon finished attaching the last few flabs of flesh onto the lieutenant's body and removed the hooks, nodding at his completed work.

The lieutenant stood from his chair and examined his body, feeling it with his hands. "This body . . . it is implausible. I can feel the others stitched to me . . . their senses and feelings."

"It takes time to get used to. You will adapt to the new form."

"The Weaver's necromantic arts, the crack in his prison . . ." He raised his hand and shook his head. "His puppets—it is demonic. How can all of this activity that the Weaver is performing go unnoticed by the Heavenly Kingdoms?"

"One would think they'd find out. To the Weaver's benefit, politics is not just a mortal affair."

"The immoral angel you mentioned?"

"I'm sure that they play a role in it. Luckily for us, the Heavily Kingdoms and Dega'Mostikas's Triangle try to sort their differences through words, letting certain actions slip by. This has been known as the Truce of Passing."

"So where does this leave us?"

Dievourse smiled. "You are of action, lieutenant. We will get along well." He extended his hand to the doorway of the chamber. It was sealed with a stone door with a circular shape carved in the centre. "We must drape you in weapons and armour of destruction. As the gatekeepers reap the children, we must prepare the army for the Weaver's freedom and the war upon the Heavenly Kingdoms."

CHAPTER III

The New Life

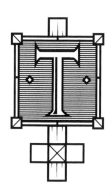

he loud crack of a leather whip echoed throughout the red sandy streets. The noise muffled out the other surrounding groans, chiseling stone, and footsteps with its strident sound. The leather material lashed down onto the bare, charcoal-scaled back of a bony humanoid, splitting the scales aside and exposing black blood that oozed down the spine.

The humanoid hissed, flickering his tongue as his tail perked straight up reflexively to the sudden strike of pain. He dropped his chisel and hammer from the impact and glanced back to see the attack came from a well-built reptilian draped in gunmetal armour from head to toe. The assailant's scowling face could be seen under his helmet; its metal frame formed two horns that extended past the jawline. A third point arched over the head and past the back of the skull. His armour had a glimmer from the distant molten lava that projected light onto the otherwise black environment, creating a sight orange hue over the scene. The armoured being raised his whip to the dark sky, ready to strike again.

"Work faster, scum!" he shouted with a scowl on his face. The mesmerizing red, smokeless flame that surrounded his eyeballs flickered rapidly, highlighting his grey skin. "You've been dragging your scaly ass around all day. This district won't build itself. Put your back into it." He lashed the whip again, striking the poor being in the outer thigh and collapsing him to his knees, limbs shaking.

The being let out a yelp as he fell, glancing around to see the other 'scum' around him work faster and avoid eye contact with him. "Please!" he cried. "No more."

"Put some effort into your work and we won't have an issue," the armoured reptilian hissed while marching down the row of dirt-covered reptiles.

About a dozen workers were lined up along a clay wall, each one using their own chisel and hammer. They carved away at the rock, forming simplistic shape-based designs on the exterior of an incomplete building; planks of wood were still being nailed together above, creating the frame of a roof.

"Damn Renascence Guard," the whipped reptilian muttered to himself while retrieving his tools with one hand. He used his other hand to brush his black scalp-feathers from his face.

Beside him, a young girl—also a reptilian—kept her head lowered while ignoring the scene and working quietly. Her long black and blue scalp-feathers draped down past her bare shoulders, hiding her face.

"They are supposed to help us regain order after our banishment by the humans. Instead they behave the same. Seem like a bunch of hypocrites if you ask me," the whipped reptilian continued to complain.

The girl swallowed heavily and kept her focus on the task of carving her portion of the building's exterior design. She chiseled faster with the tools, raising some dust in front of her face.

"How can you work so peacefully here?" he snarled, glaring over at the girl.

"Hey!" came a young, stern voice, one over from the girl. "Leave her alone."

The reptilian leaned over to see that a boy, a little older than the girl, stared directly at him. He snarled while exposing his pointed teeth.

"Oh, so I can't I talk to who I want? It's enough to have the Renascence Guard suppress us and now some random street scum thinks he can stop me?"

The girl stopped chiseling and turned to face the boy. "Darkwing, please." She swallowed the thick built-up saliva in her mouth from the lack of water before speaking again. "Let's just work."

"Krista, he's not well received by the guards—he's going to get you into trouble too," the boy identified as Darkwing spoke. His tail perked up while eyeing the older male. "Let's just do our duty to pay for what we did."

"Your duty to pay?" The reptilian snorted to himself. "They never let me go after my arrest. What makes you think they'll do any different for you?"

"We don't murder families," Darkwing said.

The male roared and rushed toward the young boy, flickering his tongue as the smokeless fire that unnaturally surrounded his eyes shimmered intensely. He raised his hammer and attempted to make a swing at the boy.

The girl shrieked and covered her face, curling up into a ball while the two males engaged.

Darkwing hissed and dodged as the sloppy blow slammed into the wall, cracking the clay. He dropped his tools and exposed his sharp claws, lashing them at the male who was too slow to dodge. The attacks sliced into his arm, causing him to whelp while backing away. Darkwing followed his attack with a swift kick to the kneecap. The blow snapped the reptilian's leg on impact, causing the bone to shred through his skin and poke out the other end, exposing the marrow.

The male collapsed to the ground while crying in pain, dropping his tools and clutching his mangled leg. His misery caught the attention of the other workers beside them, causing them to stop and watch the scene with wide eyes.

Darkwing stepped forward, snarling, and raised his claws for a second strike. His long scalp-feathers vibrated from the blood pumping to his head, forcing them to stand straight up.

"No!" the girl shouted while stepping in front of her friend, placing her hand on his chest.

"Move!" Darkwing attempted to nudge her aside gently, but she grasped onto his tense forearms.

"No! This isn't you. It's the mutation. Darkwing, please!"

Before Darkwing could reply, the sound of clanging metal filled the air and the armoured reptilian returned to the scene.

"The Renascence Guard, Darkwing. Calm down." Krista clutched the boy's arms with her hands.

"Scum! Back away." The guard lashed his whip into the air, causing it to crack while he hastily approached the three. "What happened?" he demanded while eyeing the male who clutched his bleeding leg.

"Darkwing." Krista said softly, keeping her orange fiery eyes on his face.

Darkwing lowered his arms as his scalp-feathers gradually lowered, the blood returning to the rest of his body. He kept his gaze on his defeated opponent, breathing heavily through his nostrils.

The Renascence Guard pulled a knife from his belt and pointed it at Darkwing. "You cause this?"

Krista looked behind to face the guard and said, "It was an accident. He didn't mean to."

"I wasn't talking to you, whore," the guard hissed.

Darkwing growled while clutching his fists. Krista stroked his arms lightly. "It okay," she whispered to him.

"Looks like I wasn't the only one who had it in for you." The guard lightly kicked the wounded reptilian and chuckled. He turned to face Darkwing again. "If you had done this to anyone else I would have taken the proper measures to assure you were disciplined for your actions. However, I have been waiting for someone to give this scum what he deserves for a while." He leaned down, placing the dagger around the throat of the wounded reptilian. "With a wound like that you can't serve your time for your criminal history. Punishable by death." The guard sneered while pressing the knife into the reptilian's throat.

"No! Wai—" Before the reptilian could make his defense the blade sliced into his neck, tearing through the flesh and spewing blood out from the open wound. The knife cleanly moved from one end to the other, exposing the innards of his throat while the fluids rapidly oozed down his neck and clavicles.

Krista kept her head turned to Darkwing, eyes closed while avoiding the horrific scene. She could still hear the gargling of the other male as he collapsed onto the sand.

The guard got up and wiped the blade on his black kilt before putting it back into its sheath. "You are not to go unpunished. Clean this mess up," the guard ordered before turning around and marching back down the row of 'scum.' "Back to work! Nothing to see here." The prisoners hastily returned to chiseling away at the clay, eyes wide with fear.

Krista opened her eyes and let go of Darkwing's arms. "You are so lucky that guard had it in for him." She shook her head. "You could have been executed on the spot."

Darkwing sighed and looked to the ground. "I know. I mean, I knew that the guard would be easy on us. He hated that one."

"It still doesn't make it right for what you did." Krista folded her arms. "Did you really mean to hurt him? Or was it the mutations?"

The boy scratched the back of his head. "I think a bit of both. I don't know."

Krista sighed and opened her arms, stepping close to hug him. She tightly squeezed him and buried herself into his chest.

"I just want to protect you," Darkwing said while placing his arms around her. "Whatever is in the air of the underworld is taking a toll on my thoughts."

"I know," Krista mumbled. "I am just glad you did not turn into one of the Corrupt. I would have lost you forever."

"No, not with you around. You give me something to fight for now that our old lives have been lost."

Krista looked up at the boy and smiled. "As you do for me. I couldn't imagine trying to survive if you didn't find me in my home—after the humans did what they did to my family." She let go of the boy and turned to face the fresh corpse whose blood now soaked into the red sand. "Or if you weren't around during the decent into the underworld." Krista could only imagine herself ending up like the body in front of them.

"I wouldn't leave you, Krista." Darkwing stepped forward while leaning down, grabbing hold of the corpse's arms. "Grab the back legs, will you?"

Krista obeyed and in a single feat of strength, they lifted the body from the ground. It sagged slightly on Krista's end as the girl did not have the same strength as Darkwing. He walked backward, making it easier for her to lift and move at the same time.

She was beyond grateful for having the boy with her, her one and only friend she had since the banishment atop Mount Kuzuchi. He was able to defend her against their people while they endured the mutation caused by the bizarre air in the underworld. It scorched most of the scales off their bodies, leaving them with smooth grey skin and a heightened night vision. The mutation caused some of their people to go mad, reduced to animals who craved flesh: the Corrupt.

The males of their people were naturally stronger and much larger than females, making it easy to overpower them. With Darkwing around, Krista was safe—and that was all she needed in her life. They were family and while he protected her. She helped him maintain his sanity. Their relationship was simple amid their complicated lives. Lives that, at that moment, included an order to remove a corpse from the line of workers who were all paying for their crimes against the Renascence Guard.

"Do you think the guard will tell the others about this?" Krista asked.

Darkwing shook his head. "No, I cannot see that happening. He has no reason to. As long as the mess is gone, no one is going to care." He looked behind him to see where he was going, ensuring that he led them down the right path. "Besides, the guards have more important duties, like ensuring this district is completed."

Krista nodded while eyeing the path they walked on; the sand gradually faded and was replaced by gravel, forming a road that split into several side streets. Each street was filled with more incomplete buildings. Many of them had workers performing tasks surrounding the structures with the Renascence Guard watching over them. There were several buildings where the reptilians were not watched by the guard. They happened to be dressed in cleaner clothes, were well groomed and worked calmly. Some painted the walls various colours such as blue or green. Others installed windows and still others nailed shingles to the roofs.

"Why aren't those people being watched by the guard?" Krista asked.

Darkwing looked over to see the group. "They're paid to be here."

"What?" Krista exclaimed.

"Yeah, not everyone is a street scum—a slave. Some people are actually paid for their skills."

"Paid? With dracoins?"

"Yep." Darkwing took a turn down one of the side streets, carefully stepping over a small sand dune that formed from the winds. This street was more barren than the others, with less buildings and more fences nailed together with barbed wire and planks of wood. Inside the fences there were workers who organized various goods such as planks, clay blocks, and gravel in wheelbarrows in preparation to build more structures. Each section was observed by a Renascence Guard who watched sternly as the workers hustled about.

At the far end of the road was an open excavation that had one entrance, the rest surrounded by a black metal fence. Behind the site was a large pile of sand and dirt a couple storeys in height. The entryway was watched by a Renascence Guard who eyed them as they approached.

"We should get a skill—or something. Then we won't have to constantly steal."

Darkwing smirked. "Trust me, if I was good at anything else other than tracking and killing, I would. Unfortunately, my dad only taught me survival—and a little history."

"Why not joint the Renascence Guard? They would at least offer something. I could learn to clean or cook. You'd vouch for me!"

"Don't be silly. There's no way I'd join those fascists."

"Why not?"

"You see how they treat us? Or what they did to this guy here?" He nodded at the corpse they held.

Krista frowned. "We aren't exactly giving them many reasons to go easy on us. Maybe once we're done our duty? Stop stealing and take a chance."

"I already said no. I don't believe in what the Renascence Guard is doing to our people." Darkwing slowed his pace while they approached the large excavation site.

The rotting smell of flesh filled the air the closer they got to the site. Krista's nostrils flared, recognizing the familiar stench of decaying corpses.

They reached the open entrance of the excavation where the Renascence Guard stood, clutching the spear he held tightly. He impassively eyed the corpse that the two of them held.

"Throw it in with the rest," he ordered.

Darkwing continued through the entryway, guiding Krista onto the dirt ramp leading into the pit. The two of them stopped just before the decline, standing near the sheer drop that had to be about several storeys deep. The walls were supported with planks of blackwood—a type of plant that grew in the underworld—to ensure their stability. At the bottom of the pit was a mound of reptilian corpses. More rotting, mangled corpses lay near the mound.

Krista gagged at the foul smell and dropped the legs of the freshly-deceased to cover her nose. The feet landed with a thud and forced Darkwing to adjust his hold.

"Thanks." He rolled his eyes.

"Sorry. It smells so bad," Krista replied while plugging her nose.

Darkwing shifted his hands under the body's armpits and chucked it over the ledge, letting it cartwheel in the air and collide with the pile of corpses below. It made a thud while the head crushed into the open stomach of a rotting carcass.

"If the Renascence Guard supports this, I want no part of it." Darkwing spoke quietly while motioning at the pile of corpses.

"They're trying to regain order since the banishment."

"More like establish order in their favor. They're just exterminating anyone who opposes them so they only have weak-willed followers." He placed his hand on her back. "Come, let's go."

The two retreated through the entrance and walked back to the primary road, moving past all the fence-divided sectors. Other reptilians moved out of the fenced areas pushing wheelbarrows filled with various building materials.

"I think you might be jumping to conclusions," Krista said while eyeing the workers. "How else would our people be able to build one unified city? Look at how quickly we're building the third district."

"Building it against our will. You should know that we didn't need one mega-city back on the surface. Our people functioned in tribes; we aren't meant to exist like this. This lifestyle is for the humans."

Krista frowned. There was no convincing Darkwing when he made up his mind on something. He was so sure that the Renascence Guard were out to destroy their people and not aid in their recovery. There was no telling him otherwise.

The two turned down to the main road leading back to their working station.

"Hey!" came a raspy monotone voice from a side street.

Darkwing pushed Krista behind him and the two turned to face the dark alley where the sound originated from. It was between two completed buildings, leading into the finished portion of the district.

"Who is there?" Darkwing asked. It was difficult to tell where the voice originated from. The alleyway was covered in boxes and sand dunes, providing many hiding places.

"I saw the way you took care of that shit-bag," the voice spoke again.

Darkwing glanced back at Krista and she shrugged at him.

"What's your point?" he asked.

A male emerged from behind a pile of boxes. He fashioned a unique hairstyle by plucking the black and bronze scalp-feathers from the sides of his skull and slicking back the top portion. He wore an open vest and had a red cloth wrapped around his arm.

"I like what you got—killing that useless scum as a distraction so you could get away." He peeked out of the alley and eyed down the street both ways. "Come in here. Quickly."

Krista glanced back at their station. The guard was at the far end, lashing his whip at one of the workers. "He'll see us."

"Not if you hurry. Come on! Do you want to keep working under the Renascence Guard's thumb or do you want freedom?"

Darkwing snatched Krista's upper arm and marched into the alley without further hesitation.

"Darkwing!" Krista hissed. She turned her head to check behind them—nothing but busy workers and the Renascence Guard watching the reptilians as normal. No one saw them slip into the alley.

"Well done." The male smirked while stepping back. "Come. We can get back into the completed portion of the Lower District."

"Wait. How? They have this development fenced off."

"Above ground, yes. But below? No." He waved at them to follow as he turned around.

"Hold up." Darkwing held out his hand and shook his head. "Who are you? We appreciate the help, but why are you out here if you're not working?"

"The name is Draegust." The male turned around and extended his hand. "Draegust Bronzefeather."

Darkwing shook it with his own and nodded. "Darkwing Lashback. This is Krista."

Krista stepped forward. "Kristalantice Scalebane."

Draegust's eyes moved from her boots to her tail and all the way up to her black and blue scalp-feathers. Quickly he turned to face Darkwing in the eyes and smiled. "Pleasure to meet the two of you." He released his hand and pointed down the alley. "Now, shall we?"

"What's on your arm?" Krista asked.

Draegust touched the red band on his arm. "This? The marking of a Blood Hound."

"What's a Blood Hound?" Darkwing replied.

"Come. We can chat about these things as we walk. We'd best get a move on before they start looking for you two." Draegust turned and swiftly moved down the narrow street, navigating through the rubble.

"Do we follow him?" Krista whispered. "This seems a little weird if you ask me."

"Let's go, he clearly isn't Renascence Guard with that gang mark."

"That's what makes it weird. What is he doing here?"

"Recruitment?" Darkwing gently pushed Krista forward, encouraging her to move.

She obeyed and picked up her pace to follow closely behind Draegust. She stared at the male's red cloth band during their run.

"Do you mind elaborating what a Blood Hound is?" she asked.

Draegust turned back and eyed her with a devilish grin. "Something you're not quite ready for yet, darling. He nodded at Darkwing before turning back to watch his front. "Your friend here, on the other hand, might be interested."

"Why is that?" Darkwing asked.

The three of them crossed an intersection and continued down the same road, reaching the other end of the street where the buildings on both sides were taller, darkening the alleyway. They slowed their pace while Draegust walked toward a closed blackwood door of one of the buildings. Gently, he pushed the door open and stepped inside. "We're a lot like you, that's why."

Darkwing and Krista stepped into the dark building to see that the large room was empty. It was covered in dust, sand, and splintered wood. None of the interior had been polished, making it dry and filled with cracks. There were two doorways leading into opposite sides of the building. Draegust led them off to the right.

"Like me in the sense that I killed a shit-bag?"

Draegust chuckled. "That is one way to put it. What you did was a public service to our people by removing that waste of breath."

"I think most people would do the same."

"Not so. Notice how the rest of those scum just buried their heads into their work and did not bother to intervene?"

"He didn't have to die," Krista muttered.

Draegust shook his head while leading them into a secondary room. "No, that individual did. I've watched him for days and he wasn't worthy of living. He looked out for himself and was a hazard to those around him. Darkwing did the right thing getting him killed—to protect the others."

"Murder is never the answer," Krista added.

Darkwing nudged her slightly and shook his head, clearly implying for her to be quiet. "I'm pleased you took notice to why I injured him in the first place. So you were watching that whole time. Why?"

"We're looking for people to join our cause. Those that are strong enough and bold enough to fight against our oppressors."

"The Renascence Guard?"

"And the Five Guardians." Draegust stopped when they entered the second room.

Two reptilians stood beside a pile of large wooden planks and a hole in the centre of the room. The hole had a dirt ramp descending below the building. One of the reptilians was as wide as he was tall while the other was lean-muscled, keeping his hands behind his back. Both had the same red band around their arms.

"Snog and Shoth, this is Krista and Darkwing," Draegust spoke, turning to face them.

"Hello!" Shoth said with a toothy grin.

Darkwing stopped slightly in front of Krista, making sure she was standing behind his arm. He nodded at them and turned to Draegust. "You built a tunnel?"

"My men and I have built several passageways throughout the new district. This one will take us back to the southern side, away from all the construction."

Darkwing and Krista smiled with excitement.

"I had no idea this existed," said Krista.

Draegust grinned. "Most don't—and we want to keep it that way, sweetheart."

Darkwing licked his lips. "Hold on a minute. You're forming a revolution against the Five Guardians?"

"Indeed. Those self-righteous pricks have suppressed our people long enough. Just because the mutations affected them differently doesn't mean that they have the right to rule over us."

Darkwing folded his arms. "It's not like we had much of a choice. Their size, strength, and stamina make them near-impossible to take head-on. What do you have against that?"

"Fair question. We are working to build a strong enough force—a network, if you will—inside the city." Draegust spread his hands. "Imagine what we can do once we get Blood Hounds into every district. The Commoner's District and the High District—this is something no other rebellion has been able to do. They stick here in the Lower District, fighting one another like fools."

"You have those connections?" Darkwing asked.

Draegust smirked. "I'll be transparent with you, kid. We're new to this game. It started with myself and Shoth once we heard about the Law of Unity."

Krista and Darkwing exchanged looks and shook their heads. "What is that?" Krista asked.

Shoth folded his arms. "It's disgusting."

Draegust nodded. "A new law that the Five Guardians will soon put into effect. The law is straightforward: no being is to publicly show their face or express any form of individuality. They've got tailors crafting cloaks in the marketplace to have us all dress the same."

Krista scratched her head and said, "that makes no sense. Why?"

"They say it is to help unify us as a people. Show that we are strong in numbers, unlike on the surface world where we were scattered in small tribes." Draegust raised his finger and gestured to himself. "I will tell you what it is really about. It is to hide these hideous mutations that we went through. While the Five Guardians mutated into elegant beings, the rest of us look like hell-bound."

"Another way to oppress us," Darkwing added. "If we all dress the same, we'll start acting the same. Control through assimilation."

"Like an army," Draegust confirmed. "Unification destroys independence. The Guardians settled on the matter over a month ago."

"So it's done? We've been working the third district for months; outside news has been hard to get."

"They've got this place locked down. Once Shoth and I heard, we had to take matters into our own hands. We're stuck in this underworld and it is only getting worse with the Five Guardians in control." Draegust folded his arms and puffed out his chest. "That is why we formed the Blood Hounds. Since then we've already accumulated twenty members."

"That's quick," said Darkwing.

Shoth nodded. "That's because people are pissed off. We just need to find the right people."

Krista fiddled with the tip of her tail with her index finger and stared at Darkwing nervously. She wasn't too fond on their new allies. Yes, Draegust helped them escape, but he clearly had an agenda: recruitment for his gang. It wasn't simply a noble deed.

A part of her wanted to speak up and question him further, yet in the back of her mind she knew it would be best if she just stayed quiet and wait until they were out of this dark building.

Darkwing nodded. "Say you overthrow the Five Guardians and the Renascence Guard. What do you want?"

"To live the way we are supposed to: in tribes! Our people's behavior is changing to the way the humans had us behave when they enslaved us."

"That was before our time," Krista objected.

Draegust shrugged. "Not mine. Let me tell you, living in that culture was sickening. They tried to fit us in a box they called society, make us talk their language, pray to their god, and learn their history while they burned ours," he hissed. "Now you must understand my hatred for the Five Guardians when they are behaving the same way."

Darkwing's eyes narrowed. "I feel the same."

"I'm glad to hear we are on the same page." He brought his hands back down and stared at Darkwing keenly. "Is this something you are interested in?"

Krista lightly touched Darkwing's arm, stopping him from answering.

He looked down to her and mouthed the word *what*.

She swallowed heavily and quickly glanced at Draegust then back at her friend.

"This, it's just . . . moving too fast," she said softly.

"How so?" Darkwing asked.

"We just got out of months of slavery. We were talking about starting a new life away from thievery."

Darkwing shook his head. "No, *you* were talking about that. Believe me, I would love to live a normal life. But hunting is all I really know."

Krista felt her heart sink and her lips trembled. "Darkwing, I don't want you to join a gang."

"It's a rebellion."

"Whatever!" She swallowed heavily. "I don't want you to get hurt."

"You seemed so keen on me joining the Renascence Guard."

Draegust held out his hands. "Hold up. It looks like you two have some things to sort out." He regarded Darkwing. "It isn't going to be a simple recruitment either. We screen our members carefully before they can join; make sure they truly want to follow the Blood Hound way."

Darkwing smiled at Krista. "See?"

Krista pressed her lips together tightly. She felt her hands shake from the intensity of her emotions. She didn't think she would get so upset, but she dreaded the idea of losing Darkwing. He was all that she had and couldn't risk losing him.

Draegust waved his hand. "Come. Let's get you out of here." He turned to join the other two Blood Hounds. They grabbed the planks of wood in preparation to cover their hidden passageway.

Darkwing and Krista hurried to catch up with Draegust.

"That's it?" Krista asked Draegust.

"That's it what?" Draegust turned to look at her.

"You're not going to force us to join or murder us?"

Draegust let out a laugh while they stepped into the tunnel. "Then I would be no better than the Renascence Guard. I rescued you two because you're unlike the other scum. You're just caught up in the wrong mess and I am willing to offer Darkwing another way."

The sound of the wood planks piling over the entryway bounced off the walls, followed by the footsteps of the five reptilians.

"Why not me?" Krista protested.

"Perhaps when you're a little older and have experienced some of the ugly aspects of life."

"I already have, thank you. But I don't want to be a part of it."

"Sure." Draegust stepped forward, leading the way and leaving Krista and Darkwing to walk behind him. The other two Blood Hounds kept watch on the rear.

"You're not really going to join them, are you?" Krista whispered.

"I don't know. I like what they have to offer and it would be a life I could be proud of: fighting for what is right."

"Darkwing, please. Let's just try and live a simple life. I don't want to lose you."

"You won't lose me, Krista." Darkwing slipped his hand into hers and held it tightly. "I've always been here with you. I always will."

CHAPTER IV

Two Centuries On

etal clanged as the long sword blades smashed against each other. Sweat flew into the air with each devastating blow. Dust rose as two pairs of leather sandals skidded on the dirt.

Hardy hands held the worn, deep-red-stained leather grip of each evenly balanced sword. The blades were longer than the sturdy arms that held them—a type of great sword known as a claymore. Both sets of arms shook, veins bulging, pressing their weapons forward against each other. The sharp edges scraped together, filling the void with the sound of grinding metal.

It was difficult to make out who was stronger as the two pushed with all their strength. Who would win the blade lock? They seemed so evenly matched—but perhaps not.

There was a pair of greater arms, older and more muscular. These arms pushed against their adversary's sword with immense force, throwing the younger wielder back.

The victor of the clash stood tall awaiting the next attack, his sword pointed to his opponent, calm, fearless, and aware. His light sand-coloured hair reached his broad, bearded jawline and blew in the wind as his sky-blue eyes stared down at his young challenger, a thin teenager.

The teen struggled to gain his balance. He pushed the blond, sweat-drenched hair from his eyes while adjusting his stance, shifting his breastplate.

"Never rush your opponent," the older man said, his voice dry and scratchy from the dust.

Young men dressed in double-breasted red-and-white uniform tunics stood on the grass surrounding the large dirt patch. The front row watched eagerly, waiting for the next move.

The boy—only about 17—panted heavily, lifting his sword so the blade pointed to the sky.

"Approach them with caution," the old man continued, eyes on the boy's stance.

The boy's arms shook as he held the sword up—a sign of his weakness. He nodded and gripped the sword tighter, taking his first step, dust rising.

"Remember what you learned today. When you are on the battlefield, you cannot make mistakes."

The boy slowly closed in on the man, who remained still, eyeing his every move.

It was only a demonstration of skill, the older man being a tutor to the crowd of boys, expressing the importance of defensive tactics in a close-range battle. Some of the boys watching from the outer rim of the circle showed little interest in the demo; they were clearly sidetracked by thoughts of the annual festival that would take place that night.

As for the older man, he did not concern himself with parties. For him, the evening only meant more training. More meditation.

His young opponent yelled and rushed toward him, swinging his blade aggressively.

The older man spun to the side, avoiding the youth's reckless attack.

The boy's sword cut into empty space and he glanced over to track his adversary. He skidded in the dirt, stopping his charge. Dust clouded the air as he changed directions and rushed his opponent again; this time, he aimed high, leaving his torso wide open.

The older man thrust his sword at the boy. The claymore slammed into the boy's armoured breastplate, stunning him and pushing him back.

The shock from the attack left the boy open for another assault. The older man could quickly end the demo with one swift blow to the boy's ribs. Instead, he decided to humiliate him—make him learn the mistake of rushing opponents once and for all.

The man swung the blade again with ease. It whooshed past the boy's torso and struck downward on the boy's knee, throwing him to the ground.

The man lifted his sword and stepped to the side, slamming the flat side of the blade down on the boy's backside with a loud slap. The blow threw the kid down on his hands and knees.

The crowd laughed hysterically as the man rested the blade on the boy's bare neck.

"Your patience is weak," the man said.

"Sorry, Master Paladin," the boy replied, hanging his head low in disgrace.

The man nodded and lifted his sword. "Class dismissed," he announced, walking away from the dirt patch and onto the road.

The boys moved aside to let their instructor leave. The man could hear them laughing at the scene that had just taken place and joking amongst each other. It was sickening to him. Here he was, in the Kingdom of Zingalg by direct orders from the king to train these boys to become men. Train them to be the most courageous warriors the land had ever seen. But the truth was, it was nothing more than a disaster. These boys were immature and obviously didn't understand the seriousness of their training. They didn't even grasp why they were there.

It was humiliation at its finest. He was the last surviving Paladin of Zeal, and he was forced to train children with wooden swords. Today's use of steel blades was an exception; he'd wanted at least one of them to know the touch, the weight, and the feel of a real sword.

Based on the attention span of the boys and their laughter at their blond friend, not one of them understood what he was trying to teach them. He wanted to express the focus and intensity of a one-on-one duel. The boys were ungrateful to be chosen to be trained as the kingdom's best. It only made Paladin wish his former comrades from the Paladins of Zeal were still alive—even one. Just one!

His body was aging faster than his mind and he longed for the former days of great crusades, bringing word of God to foreign peoples and cleansing lands of draconem and Dega'Mostikas's evil. Unfortunately, that time had come and gone, and he considered his current existence laughable . . . a pure disgrace to paladin-kind. He was a warrior, not a nursemaid.

Paladin returned to his quarters in the light red brick keep inside the High Barracks of Zingalg. The room was made of sandstone brick walls, left bare, and the floor was grey. He put his claymore gracefully in its glass cabinet and closed it shut. It was the same weapon he used when the Paladins of Zeal were prominent. He admired the wide base of the blade, the finely crafted feather design of the silver guard, and the sharp steel talon of the pommel just underneath the worn leather grip.

Each paladin forged their own sword; it was the final exercise of their training. They designed their blades to fit their fighting style and symbolize their strength.

The eagle—their freedom of flight, speed, and fortitude. These are characteristics I honor. His sword wasn't the only one he treasured; he also kept a second, belonging to a former comrade.

She based her weapon on fire, he thought while turning to face the secondary sword in its own cabinet. The guard was carved into the shape of flames and the blade's curved shape ended in a hook. *I couldn't dispose of it; the fine craftsmanship was stunning. It would be a dishonour to my kind, even though she fell from the light.*

The lonesomeness that Paladin experienced was new. Just over two decades ago, there were still two paladins left. They'd been the only two for over a hundred years, but she—the other—had died.

I fear I grew too fond of her, it made me blind to her corruption, he thought while swallowing heavily, recalling the memory of her fine features. Paladin often replayed the events leading to the death of the red-haired female paladin in his mind. She had to be slain at his own hand. She was courageous and had a fiery passion for her beliefs. This fire of hers had made her impulsive and unpredictable. She couldn't control her sinful human nature, and she fell from the light. Paladin was forced to execute her.

To his advantage, when she lost her faith, the powers from God that she was blessed with refused to obey her. As with every paladin, their lack of faith caused their holy gift to weaken, making them unable to perform Prayers of Power.

Her losing the light gave me an upper hand in the battle we had before I ended her life. Now I can only hope that the Heavenly Kingdoms' judgment was kind on her soul.

It was a tragic event for him to go through. He knew as soon as he struck her down that he would be the last of his kind. No one else in the mortal realm would be able to relate to him. It was a deed that had to be done; he could not risk having a fallen paladin run rampant in the Kingdom of Zingalg.

Although, that's the trouble with giving humans such power. We cannot appreciate the responsibility. Eventually we become blinded by greed and fear, which is why God no longer gifts humans with heavenly abilities.

It pained him to remember such scenes, and to feel the desire for his former days with the Paladins of Zeal. He was supposed to be a bringer of justice—fearless, remorseless to evil—and envy no man. But Paladin was older now, and age was showing in his thoughts, words, actions, and his face.

In an odd way, I envy the boys' excitement for their festival. They get to be with friends who they relate with.

He turned to his wooden nightstand where he kept a bowl of fresh water and washed off the dirt and sweat from the day with a fresh white cloth. He'd worn minimal body armour for the demonstration and the sun had been bright. It baked his skin, darkening the parts left exposed around the breastplate he wore.

His body was still in prime condition, well-molded with lean muscles. Paladin owed it to his intensive training and the meditation that kept his mind from falling victim to the sins of man. For Paladin, there was no secret to his health; he kept his mind honest and his goals pure, and nothing more was needed.

He found it easier to keep this clarity now; times were easier. Only simple folk and creatures populated the world. The Drac Age had come and gone and any potential threats, such as the vazeleads, had been dealt with.

Paladin shook his head, thinking about the banishment of the vazeleads. *What a tragic disaster.*

Every so often, Paladin contemplated this. He'd been present on Mount Kuzuchi when the reptilians were rounded up like animals and thrown into the pit of the underworld. He recalled how the Drac Lord Karazickle rampaged through the closely-packed groups of men like a moving death machine, lashing his claws at them and splitting their bodies into pieces.

"That was another time, and there's been no sign of Karazickle since." Paladin muttered to himself, lost in his own haunting memories. *I should not fixate on what won't change.*

Several paladins survived the brutal attacks of Karazickle, wounded and hidden underneath the corpses of their brethren. They were able to recover through healing Prayers of Power and attempted to recover their kind from the attack, Paladin included.

It was on that fateful night atop Mount Kuzuchi that the Paladins of Zeal's dynasty began to crumble. With their false leader revealed, and most of their kind killed, the paladins found it challenging to maintain their old ways. Some retired. Others lost their faith and resorted to a sinful lifestyle. More still were murdered by people with grudges against paladin-kind. Paladin was one of the few who remained faithful to the old ways, and now here he was: the last.

I am the last. Because of this, I keep the name 'Paladin' so the world knows the Paladins of Zeal are still alive. He dried his face with a second cloth and put on a simple tunic similar to those worn by the boys.

He strolled over to the large window of his quarters that looked over the High Barracks of Zingalg. The camp was the size of a small town, complete with livestock and a church. It sat among rich green hills and a river that split the barracks in half. The base was surrounded by massive brick walls that encased it entirely. Night was quickly consuming the day and the yearly party that celebrated the founding of the High Barracks was soon to begin.

Paladin would have banned the party if he could order it, but he only trained the boys during the day and couldn't tell them what to do at night. Besides, no one within the barracks would approve of cancelling the party. It only came once a year and was the one time when the people of the barracks could truly let loose and relax.

To Paladin, those reasons were just poor attempts to justify getting drunk and acting like hooligans. Paladin grew up in a time with different beliefs, long before this day and age. It was a world where you thought a party was through launching your blade through a foe's heart. You'd get drunk off the bloodshed of their slit throats and the hooliganism was heard through your fierce battle cry.

His time had come and gone, and it was obvious to him that the paladins were no more. They were no longer needed, and this new generation of men would never grasp what hardships his generation went through or the world he came from.

A knock at his door echoed through the chamber, breaking his longing thoughts.

Paladin took a deep breath. "Come in."

A man dressed in black entered the quarters and bowed before Paladin.

"Smyth. What brings you to me?" Paladin asked, turning to face the man. He knew that it could only be Smyth; no one else would dare knock on his door. Others simply waited for him to leave his chambers.

"Paladin, the yearly celebration of the barracks is to begin, sir." The man stood stiffly, face emotionless. The lighting from Paladin's candles in the quarters gave a high contrast view of Smyth's freshly-shaven face. The sharp shadows revealed a series of scars that spread across the right half of the man's lip and the curly black hair covering his forehead.

Smyth is a courageous man, having to live with that constant reminder of his cousin's downfall. But he knew his duty to God and his kingdom well, and did not waver, even when she attacked him; for that I give him the utmost respect. She was my fellow paladin, and so lost from the light, he had to expose her secrets to me. To slay one of my own—one of our last—was unfortunate, but there was no other choice.

Paladin blinked a couple times, trying to break free from his haunting thoughts. "Yes, I know," he sighed, shaking his head in disgust.

Smyth moved closer and looked through the window. "Perhaps we should take a walk?" he suggested.

Paladin nodded.

The two left his chamber, exiting the keep through a door leading onto the walkway atop the tall brick walls that surrounded the barracks. The walkway followed alongside the dirt-patch training fields, which were now littered with tables and benches. Men and women were setting up various party activities that Paladin did not bother to familiarize himself with.

"It disgusts me," Paladin said, frowning as they watched the celebration get started.

"Excuse me?" Smyth asked.

"Parties should not be accepted within the High Barracks of Zingalg."

Smyth shrugged. "The adolescents enjoy it, the cooks like a change in their regular routine, the maids can have a chance to be outside . . . everyone loves our yearly celebration except you, Paladin."

"That's because our people have grown weak." Paladin's nostrils flared at his own words. He did not mean to be so cynical, especially in front of Smyth. The man was probably the only person he could relate to.

Smyth squinted. "How so?"

"Look at them; tell me what you see in the people down there."

Scanning the party, Smyth answered, "I see our soldiers who are on guard duty all year long finally relaxing, and our trainees laughing and playing games."

"Is that all?" Paladin asked.

"Should I see more?"

"These boys look forward to this meaningless celebration every year, and it sickens me. They only see what each year's party brings them and they don't focus on the greater picture."

"What greater picture?"

"Justice. Their king. Their people. Something with more depth than a simple gathering where they behave like fools."

Smyth shook his head and stared out beyond the walls of the barracks, into the vast forests and mountain range that surrounded them, stretching on for miles and disappearing into the dark sky.

The two stood in silence, seeing that they would never come to an agreement about the party. Smyth was only a man and Paladin saw himself as much more. He *was* much more.

Paladin hated thinking so highly of himself, but it was too obvious to ignore. He thought logically and worked effectively at any given task. Paladin was far more intelligent than men from this age and he was physically superior thanks to his heavenly blessing. He had not been able to test his power against a worthy foe in decades.

A flicker of lightning appeared in the sky, breaking their conversation.

"What's that?" Smyth exclaimed, wide-eyed and staring out into the distance.

Paladin peered into the thick pine forests. "What is it?"

"I saw a lightning strike in the trees," said Smyth.

The two looked up into the sky but could only see stars; no clouds or signs of violent weather.

Another lightning strike appeared, and this time Paladin saw the white bolt of light spring from far into the forest and disappear into the sky, as if the bolt had erupted from the ground.

"There!" Smyth pointed excitedly. "Yet not a raindrop in sight. Do you figure that it is the wicked ways of the trolls?"

"No . . . trolls try to manipulate the weather. The lightning bolt spawned from the ground. This is abnormal." *Only God's resources come from the ground; anything coming from below it cannot be good news.* He looked at Smyth. "Meet me at the stables, we're going to investigate. Inform Captain John, too."

"Yes, sir," Smyth replied before jogging off.

Paladin was uncertain what the light beam was, but it was too strange for him to simply brush off. Besides, it was a chance to leave the barracks and not have to deal with the noise of the party.

Paladin returned to his quarters to get his claymore from the glass cabinet. Removing it, he held the sword with both hands and eyed the scuffs on it.

"It's possible I may make use of you tonight," he muttered. Paladin sheathed his sword and tied it to his back. *Or maybe I am simply wishing so.* He barged out of his quarters and left the keep.

By the time Paladin got outside, Smyth and Captain John were already waiting at the red wooden stables at the keep's edge.

Paladin greeted John with a nod, noticing the deep red hair that extended past the man's shoulders, draping over his breastplate.

"Ready, gentlemen?" he asked.

The three took their black horses from the stables and rushed onto the gravel road, following it up to the main gate leading out of the barracks. The two gate guards on duty weren't about to miss out on the celebrations: they already had several empty bottles scattered on the ground, some tipped to the side. The guards exchanged glances at seeing the oncoming horses. They wobbled over to the locks on each side of the large wooden entrance. After a couple attempts to unlock the bolts, the guards succeeded and the gates flew open.

The horses' hooves raised dust from the gravel road. Paladin's horse trampled over a pile of vomit. He was disgusted that it was so early in the night and already there was such a level of carelessness at the party. Clearly, no one at the party had noticed the lightning. Paladin, John, and Smyth seemed to be the only ones aware of it.

All three riders kept their heads low, their bodies bobbing up and down while the horses trampled down the road, passing into the large forest that surrounded the High Barracks of Zingalg for miles around. The forest was dark and the sky was barely visible through the massive amounts of foliage. The horses stomped over the dark path, raising more dust behind them as they sped through the thick undergrowth. John and Smyth rode behind Paladin as he led them deeper into the darkness. It was uncertain how far away the lighting had come from, but Paladin had a feeling that if they kept heading south—in the direction it had originated—they would come across the source. He kept his ears keen on listening for any unusual sounds, his eyes sharpened to detect any movement, and his sense of smell heightened for any abnormal aromas.

"How far do you suppose it is?" John asked, red hair blowing as his stallion surged forward.

Paladin glanced back before answering; John had not even undressed from his armoured uniform for the party. The other men in the High Barracks often took their heavy armour off after a day's work to enjoy the evening, but John was captain of the barracks and ensured safety for all who lived there. He took his position as seriously as Paladin did, and Paladin respected the man for it.

"It's tough to tell," he replied.

"Do you smell that?" Smyth interrupted.

Paladin sniffed the air and picked up on the scent of burning metal.

"Aye," John said.

"We must be close," Paladin said, slowing his steed to scan the forest more closely.

He knew it must be what they were searching for because the barracks were surrounded by nothing but nature. No small villages or towns were nearby, which made the smell of burning metal unusual.

The acrid odour grew stronger as they rode further down the path. A light breeze brought the scent closer and led the three off the main track. They dismounted their horses and guided the animals through the thick vegetation. All three drew their swords and cautiously examined their surroundings.

Several minutes passed with only the sound of their footsteps and the branches brushing against their armoured legs.

Paladin could see the thick forest was nearing an end; a bare patch was visible, seen through the vegetation several feet ahead. He looked back at his comrades and, their eyes wide, all three stepped forward. They emerged into the open area; a large patch of scorched earth with smoke rising from what appeared to be a recent fire. The clearing was obviously not natural. Patches of fire still burned on some of the vegetation. This was no doubt where the lightning had come from.

Paladin got down on his knees and sifted his hands through the burnt soil, feeling its sandy texture. The scorched earth covered the whole open formation, creating a perfect circle. He stood and looked to the centre of the patch to see that the earth got darker until it was deep black. A bright red light near the centre of the circle caught Paladin's attention. There was a set of glowing runes in the centre, encircling a body.

John and Smyth stepped beside Paladin.

"It's still alive, but it looks hurt," Smyth observed.

"Twitching, too," John added. "Either the skin is burnt grey or this is not a human."

Paladin sheathed his sword and moved toward the body. As he got closer, he could make out details: the curved waistline and thin frame suggested it was female. She had smooth grey skin and youthful cheeks that made him guess it was a young girl of some kind. Her face ended in a tiny muzzle and her scalp was covered in long black and blue feathers. They were tattered and extended down to her shoulders. She had a tail with scales along the top that was curled up alongside her. She wore a short black dress, a deep red robe, and black boots.

The glowing runes around the girl formed a circle that was half the size of the open patch. The runes consisted of rectangles, swirls, arrows, and other simplistic shapes, each group spaced out evenly. An inner circle of glowing runes—slightly dimmer—was made up of small circles. The surface of the runes appeared to be stone, and the light beamed from inside them. Paladin felt a warm heat radiating from them as he got closer. All the shapes and their alignment seemed outlandish to him; they certainly weren't created by anything in the known world.

"Don't touch the runes," Paladin warned. "They may be quite hot."

Paladin got down on one knee and felt liquid splash against his leg. Looking down, he saw he was kneeling in a small pool of black fluid flowing from the girl's body. It had to be blood—but blood was red, even in the other races like trolls and nymphs.

Black blood? That is something seen in demons—or draconem. Paladin squinted and ran his eyes along the girl's body. She was soaked in the blood, her frail figure visible through the drenched material. Her red robe had been rolled up over her elbow and exposed a long, deep gash across her limb. There was a circular burn mark visible on her open palm, and it too was covered in blood.

Paladin lifted her cold arm gently and examined it more closely. He could see that the cut was no battle wound: it looked deliberate and done with care. The cut's position was such that the girl's major arteries were avoided, greatly reducing the blood loss—also a sign of an expert's knowledge of her species anatomy.

He brought her arm down and looked over her physique, noticing how scrawny she was. She must have not eaten much in weeks.

The girl's scalp-feathers was spread wildly on the grass, exposing her neck and clavicle. One side of her neck had another mark, a scar in the image of circle and two triangles—one smaller and encompassed by the other. It had an eye in the centre and was surrounded by glyphs that were strikingly like the glowing runes around the scorched earth.

Smyth walked to Paladin's side, sword sheathed and arms folded. "What is it?"

Paladin lifted the girl's head and, with his fingers, opened one of her closed eyelids. Smyth gasped. They were yellow, with a bright red iris and a reptilian's slit-shaped pupil.

"Could it be an angel that fell from the Heavens?" John asked, approaching his comrades.

Paladin opened the girl's mouth to see a thin black tongue and sharp-looking fangs. "Remember that this beam came from the earth," he said. "Fallen angels come from the Heavens, not rise from the ground."

He ran his hand along the back of the girl's neck, feeling leathery scales embedded into her skin.

"Could she be a demon?" John asked.

Smyth laughed. "Does it look like one to you?"

John shrugged. "I thought so."

Paladin shook his head. "No, she's not a demon. Demons always come to our world in human form first, and not unconscious." He lifted the girl in his arms and stood. "We'll take her back to the barracks and see what we can do for her."

"What of this scene?" Smyth asked, looking around.

"And the glowing runes?" John added.

Paladin hesitated. There must be meaning or message in the glowing stone symbols, but he knew that the girl's condition meant her life was in grave danger. "I'll study more of this on my own time. For now, we must work to save her life. She has lost a lot of blood." Paladin marched back to his horse and lifted the girl into the saddle. Once she was safely up, he examined his arms and chest, now smeared with the black blood from her body.

He was uncertain what the child was, but he wasn't simply going to leave her to die. He did not sense evil from her, but the scene was undeniably disturbing: the scorched circle, the runes, and the smell of burning metal. Sighing, he mounted the horse with the girl in front of him and they rode back to the barracks. Knowing their destination, the return trip was faster. Paladin made haste as it was unclear how bad the girl's condition was.

As they approached the red brick enclosure protecting the barracks, the guards atop the walls saw them and immediately opened the gates. Still on their horses, the three rushed into the sea of people. The party was in full swing, and the drunken laughter was loud as large groups of people clumped together, covering the road and grass. They sloshed their drinks while wobbling from person to person, patting one another on the backs and talking loudly. A group of five boys stood on wooden tables, banging on cow-hide drums, strumming guitars and shaking tambourines to create a cheerful tune. Men and women alike crowded around the tables dancing with one another, clapping and stomping to the beat. The three horses were on course to trample the outer rim of the crowd.

"Move!" Paladin shouted.

"What is that?" asked a man in the crowd, pointing to the girl draped over Paladin's saddle.

"It's a monster!" howled a middle-aged woman with brown hair, dropping her full mug of ale in shock.

Paladin looked back at Smyth and John. "Deal with the crowd."

The people parted into groups, whispering to one another while the three horses marched forward to the front of the keep.

When they reached the stairs to the keep entrance, Paladin dismounted his horse and took the girl into his arms.

"There's nothing to see here, people!" Smyth shouted, waving his arms at the crowd to leave. "Enjoy your evening."

Smyth and John had worked with Paladin for so long that they knew who was best suited to handle the orders he gave out without explicit instruction.

John dismounted his horse and followed behind Paladin. The two walked up the wide staircase leading to the keep.

"Any news on when Dr. Alsroc plans on returning?" Paladin asked as John moved ahead to open the keep's large oak door.

John shook his head as he pulled the round door handle, allowing the entrance to creak open. "It is uncertain. He sent a letter about a week ago, so he should be arriving any day now."

Paladin moved into the massive foyer of the keep where large columns were set up on both sides of the walkway and the vast ceiling formed an archway. Green running boards lined the bottom of the bricks.

"We'll keep her in the doctor's office while he is gone."

John rushed ahead of Paladin so he could open any doors they approached. They both knew the keep inside and out and moved swiftly down the halls without pausing. After several turns through the dark halls, they arrived at Dr. Alsroc's office. John grabbed the gold handle and threw the door open, allowing Paladin to step through.

Paladin entered the office and placed the girl on the operating table. He knew the office by heart as he had brought many trainees into the room after accidents during their exercises.

The girl shivered on the table and her limbs twitched.

"Do you think she was poisoned?" John asked, walking to the side of the operating table.

"No, I don't. There's something unearthly going on with all of this."

John nodded. "We could try and mend the wound but I think we would need Dr. Alsroc to ensure there wouldn't be a long-lasting infection."

Paladin cracked his knuckles and took a deep breath. "I can try to at least seal her wound with God's aid to prevent the bleeding, through a Prayer of Power."

John stepped back as Paladin leaned over the girl and held her bleeding arm in the air with one hand. He waved his free hand over her wound; closing his eyes, he focused his mind on renewing her body.

For I will restore health unto thee, and will heal thee of thy wounds, sayeth the Lord; oh Father, I pray to thou who forgives all iniquities, who heals all disease. Lord in Heaven, I come to you. Paladin repeated the verse in his head several times.

It didn't bother him to attempt the ancient arts of healing on the grey girl. If she were a demon, the holy words would have an opposite effect on her body and burn her skin instead of healing her. The words of God would ignite anything unholy to eliminate it from existence. This was something Paladin had learned from experience.

Paladin spent several minutes concentrating and chanting the verse in his head, waving his hand back and forth along the girl's wounded arm. Soon, the wound began to seal itself. The skin stretched across the gap and joined together, preventing any more blood from escaping.

Paladin opened his eyes and lowered the girl's arm. "Amen."

He stepped back from the table to stand beside John.

John shook his head. "Amazes me every time."

Paladin nodded. "For with God, nothing is impossible."

John scratched his head. "Seems we know she isn't a demon. What do you think she is?"

Paladin shook his head. "I don't know. But from the strange place where we found her, I fear it could be something much more than just a girl materializing in the forest. Glowing runes don't appear for nothing. I need to do more research into them."

He took the girl's tail in his hand and felt the texture of her skin. It was just as cold as the rest of her body, hairless and smooth. "We'd best get her some blankets."

"Yes, sir," John said and began searching the doctor's office.

Paladin leaned closer to the girl. He saw that the blood that covered her body truly had no hue to it; it was pitch black. He carefully ran his hands over her body, patting her down to feel for any items stashed in her robe or underneath. Nothing, pockets empty; he could only feel her bony frame.

The girl kicked in the air and groaned.

Her movement didn't startle Paladin. He figured that the girl was dreaming and wasn't near waking. The kick brought his attention to her boot: he could see that the front was worn out almost completely and there were two holes.

Curiosity overcame him and he unbuttoned her tattered boot, carefully slipping it off her leg, making sure the claws that poked out from the front end of the boot did not get caught. The boot came off easily and revealed a two-toed foot with three sharp claws, one sprouting from the sole of the foot and one from each toe. The same leathery scales that ran down her neck covered the top portion of her foot to her ankle.

John came back to the operating table with a stack of blankets and his eyes fell immediately on the girl's bare foot. "Good Lord!" he exclaimed, passing the blankets to Paladin.

Paladin took the blankets from John and softly tucked the girl in under the thick sheets, muttering to himself, "What are you?"

CHAPTER V

Reflection

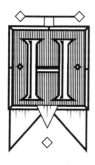 is eyelids opened, fiery pupils looking up at the low red ceiling then around the scarlet stone room to see an empty cot across from him with the sheets kicked to the side. It was expected—typical behavior of Krista who liked to explore on her own—but nevertheless, he found it unsettling that she was not there. Where could have she gone? There wasn't much to explore beyond the underground temple. There was nothing else but sand dunes and Magma Falls in the nearby area.

Darkwing rose from his bed, still wearing his deep red robe belonging to the Eyes of Eternal Life; he had fallen asleep immediately when they'd arrived back at their cell the day before. Their long travel away from Renascence City was tiresome. Not to mention they had spent their time at the temple listening to the ramblings of cult lunatics, who believed in a savior called the Risen One.

It's complete garbage. Our people are so gullible, he thought.

Sniffing the air, he could pick up a faint, sweet scent. It was Krista's and he adored it. However, it was weak. She must have been gone for quite a while.

He was unsure where she had run off to and he wanted to find out. They already went through enough struggles escaping their fallen leaders, guardian Danil and guardian Ast'Bala, who took a bizarre interest in her. Krista said they wanted to 'reap her innocence'. She was a delicate girl and did not know how to handle herself in dangerous situations, which made her vulnerable.

Her safety is what matters.

It had never occurred to Darkwing how dear she was until the recent events that led them to the Eyes of Eternal Life. However, that was the past. He was here now, and uncertain where she was. But he had a hunch that the albino, Saulaph, might know. Krista had worked with Saulaph in a group meditative task the day before and they seemed to have gotten along well. It was possible that she was with him now; she got attached to new people quickly.

Darkwing had met the albino vazelead along with a red scalp-feathered girl named Alistind just outside of Renascence City at a farmstead while trying to find a place to hide Krista from guardian Danil, who was on the hunt for her. Saulaph and Alistind were about Darkwing's age and wore deep red robes—the uniform of the temple. The two spoke to him about the Eyes of Eternal Life, hidden beyond Magma Falls, underground and secluded. They were a group of vazeleads that resented the Five Guardians. Their initial offer was too good to pass up and Darkwing took Krista to hide until the fallen guardians were taken care of by the Renascence Guard.

At least we both have that in common.

The temple members—or as Darkwing thought of them, cultists—performed group prayers and meditative tasks in hopes of waking the mysterious Risen One from his deep slumber. To Darkwing, the idea seemed insane, but he saw these vazeleads were desperate to believe in anything other than the Five Guardians.

It's not like I prefer the Five Guardians. They oppress our people and treat civilians like cattle. Only difference I have from these cultists is I would rather take down the enemy rather than pray to some sleeping being that probably doesn't exist.

Rising from on top of the soft sheets, Darkwing looked over at Krista's bed to see if she'd left any sort of message. No such luck. There was only the black blanket and pillow. Would it be so hard just to leave some sort of indication where she had gone? Instead, he would have to rely on his tracking skills to find her. Darkwing had become a good tracker in his youth, using his skills to hunt animals for their fur. Tracking people was just as easy. He always marveled at how one's tracks could tell such a descriptive story.

I'm sure I have nothing to worry about; I just want to know where she is.

Darkwing rose and left the cell through the single black door. His movements were sluggish from the heavy sleep as he moved down the dark stone halls. The walls were covered in canvas paintings—abstract characters in vibrant colours, humanoid in shape but difficult to tell which race. They were littered with crude black glyphs aligned in columns. Tiled patterns of eyeballs, triangles, rectangles, and circles framed each painting.

Alistind and Saulaph are the only two Krista knows here. She has got to be with one of them, he thought while wandering the temple.

He walked through the halls for several minutes in hopes of passing someone he recognized—anyone at all. But all the faces looked the same to him: expressionless drones. All the cultists in the underground temple acted the same and spoke the same. They might as well be the same person. Darkwing realized it could take forever to find someone he knew, and he'd have better luck asking strangers.

He reached his hand out and waved at the nearest cultist in the hall. "Have you seen Brother Saulaph?"

It was a male cultist. He was wearing the same red robe as Darkwing and was walking alone. Like all cultists, his hood was down, revealing his long black scalp-feathers.

He raised his head to look up at the ceiling; his yellow eyes had a blank gaze to them. "No." He shifted his gaze to Darkwing. "I have not, brother."

"What about Sister Alistind?"

"No."

Darkwing nodded. "Aren't there any prayer sessions that they might be in?"

The male smiled. "Brother, do you not recall it is a silent day? They are free to do as they please."

"Right, thanks." Darkwing had forgotten about the silent day. There was no telling where Alistind or Saulaph were, or Krista for that matter.

The cultist nodded, slowly turning his head and walking away.

Useless, Darkwing thought while continuing to wander the halls, slowly making his way to the main lobby of the temple. If Krista was not with one of the cultists, she had probably left the underground structure—which greatly concerned him. The only other place she could go is Magma Falls. Despite being the one source of water in the underworld, it provided its own series of dangers.

The left side of the mountain—closer to the underground temple— housed the water factories that farmers used to harvest water and export to the City of Renascence. They weren't friendly to strangers and were willing to kill trespassers on sight.

The right side of the mountain was native to the Corrupt and other beastly creatures found in the underworld, making it equally as hostile.

Krista, please be smart, he thought, feeling his stomach tense up from the idea of her wandering Magma Falls on her own. He knew she had visited Magma Falls by herself before, but it didn't reassure him of her safety. Darkwing could only hope that Krista did not leave the temple after all.

After several minutes, Darkwing reached the square entrance hall of the temple, having seen no sign of Krista, Alistind, or Saulaph. From what he could examine of the temple, it housed several hundred cultists and had two main halls. If no one he saw could say where the albino or red scalp-feathered girl was, he had no choice but to leave the temple.

Knowing Krista, she probably got bored of the cult members' rambling. He couldn't blame her, it was quite tedious to listen to.

Magma Falls is not far. I can go look for her there then return to the temple. If I haven't found her, then I'll search every room here.

Darkwing reached the temple's entrance door leading up to the surface level of the underworld. It was made of stone with a circular centrepiece carved into it. The centrepiece was engraved with glyphs, much like the paintings on the walls of the temple. Triangles and rectangles created rings in the circle leading to the centre of the door where there was an eye surrounded by fire.

"Are you leaving, brother?" came a monotone female voice.

Darkwing turned to face the girl, hoping it might be Alistind. Unfortunately, it was not. The female had dark brown scalp-feathers unlike Alistind's bright red feathers.

I've never see her before. What could she want? Darkwing casually glanced at the door then back at the girl. "Yeah, I want to go to Magma Falls."

"Fair enough, brother. You're one of the new members, correct?"

"Correct."

She smiled and reached for a keyring on her belt. "You might not have a key yet."

The locked door, Darkwing thought, recalling the outer door at the top of the staircase he and Krista passed through when they first entered the temple. Alistind and Saulaph had unlocked it, then.

The cultist pulled a skeleton key from her keyring and handed it to Darkwing. "Here. You can have mine. I can get a new one from the elders."

Darkwing smiled. "Thanks. You are kind."

The female bowed. "Of course, brother. Every follower of the Risen One needs access to the temple."

Darkwing smiled then turned to face the stone door. He squinted with confusion before asking, "How does this work?"

The female nodded and stepped forward, pushing the carving's pupil inward. The eye retreated and the sound of grinding stone filled the air as dozens of gears moved in sequence to pull the door aside. Beyond the temple entrance was a stone staircase spiraling up to the surface of the underworld.

Darkwing nodded at the female. "Thanks again."

"Of course, brother. We will see you when you return."

Darkwing marched up the stairs to the main level that belonged to a cavern. At the top was the locked blackwood door. He placed the skeleton key into the door's lock and twisted it. The lock clicked and he pushed forward, stepping through into the limestone cavern.

There were two directions: To his left was a pathway leading to the cavern's main entrance and to his right was a secondary path he had not explored. Darkwing guessed it was another entrance into the cavern based on the size of the cave. He had no desire to explore it at this time. He had one goal—find Krista—and the familiar entrance was his best bet to leave the temple entirely.

He began his hike to the front of the cave, moving through the winding path and eventually reaching the entrance. The cavern narrowed the closer he got to the exit, where he could see a shine of orange light project into the cavern—the distant magma that illuminated the underworld's landscape.

He checked behind him before taking off his robe, causing his thin, black scalp-feathers to sway in front of his eyes, brushing against his jawline.

I don't want them seeing me take off their colours, he thought while tying the garment around his waist so he could move through the sandy dunes more quickly. As he removed the robe, a red square of cloth slipped from his belt. He picked it up; it was his Blood Hound sign, given to him by the leader, Draegust, when he was accepted into the gang.

'Welcome to the Blood Hounds, Darkwing Lashback.' Draegust's smile, teeth razor-sharp, spread across his bony face as he handed Darkwing a finely knitted red cloth with a firm hand.

Darkwing remembered it like he was just there—the sense of acceptance, accomplishment, and oddly enough, regret. He wasn't completely satisfied with his choice to join the Blood Hounds. He'd had to sacrifice Krista's trust to get into the gang. It tore him apart inside to remember her cries when he'd abandoned her in the elixir shop.

As his initiation into the Blood Hounds, he had to obtain a certain elixir from an elder who owned a potion shop. It would have been easy to steal the potion if it hadn't been for the old vazelead's pet shade.

A pain in my ass. Darkwing thought, recalling the first time he tried to take the potion and the shade caught him—resulting in jail time.

Shades were four-legged beings that fed on mortals' emotions. It sounded like a far-fetched concept to Darkwing, but shades were believed to live both in the physical realm and in the afterlife—a realm Darkwing was not convinced really existed. That was the reason shades could supposedly feed on your soul. But regardless of how they did it, they could sense emotions. If you were scared or anxious, they would be able to pinpoint your exact location.

The elderly shopkeeper kept a shade as security and for company. They made excellent guards and were loyal to those who offered dedicated companionship, despite being illegal as decided by the Renascence Guard. Shades could not speak with their mouths, but could send their thoughts to one or more people at once. It had something to do with their bodies existing in two realms.

Either way, this is what made obtaining the elixir so challenging and why Darkwing had decided to break into the shop using Krista as both a lookout and, unknown to her, as bait.

I really could have treated her with more respect.

What made Darkwing sick today was he had been confident she'd be all right; the old shop owner was softhearted and would pity her. But, it did not change the fact that Darkwing had abandoned her, simply using her to get the elixir so he could join a group she disapproved of.

So stupid of me. I couldn't look past her faith in the Five Guardians at the time.

Darkwing stepped out of the cavern and into the open sand—nothing but dunes for thousands of miles around, disappearing into the darkness of the underworld. Not far from the cave entrance was a large misty mountain that disappeared into the black sky—Magma Falls. Technically it was a giant pillar that connected to the ceiling of the underworld—or so it was believed. No one had actually seen the top of Magma Falls because it is too steep to climb and too high to see beyond the darkness.

Magma Falls' unique source of water was believed to come through numerous cracks from the surface. These cracks seeped water down and through Magma Falls and down an enormous waterfall into a lake of lava, causing the mist to rise.

Darkwing always questioned how long the water would last. Where did it originate from? His concerns were shared amongst many of the vazelead kind.

I hate being at the mercy of something I do not understand. It makes me uncomfortable, he thought while taking his first few steps onto the red sand.

A burst of wind shot by him, making him nearly let go of the red Blood Hound band he still held. He clutched it tightly and stuffed it back into his pocket. The underworld winds were notorious, which was why the people of the City of Renascenece built large wind-breaking clay towers.

The construction makes sense, but the Five Guardians are just fools, building a unified city. He couldn't help but smirk to himself at the thought. *We're tribal people. We don't function well in large masses.*

Darkwing had proof of his concept. It was seen through the gangs that were revolting against the Renascence Guard. Not to mention the Five Guardians themselves had now collapsed after one of their members, Ast'Bala, murdered guardian Cae and freed the city's prisoners. He also managed to infect guardian Danil with some sort of madness which set him on a hunt for Krista.

And here we are, hiding among a cult, hoping that the fallen guardian won't find us.

Darkwing scanned the sandy ground for any signs of recent footsteps but found none. It did not help that the constant wind covered up even his fresh tracks. Tracking Krista would be a little more difficult than he first anticipated.

He started marching up the first large dune that separated him from Magma Falls. It was steep, causing the sand to trickle down the hill with each step he took. It was challenging to keep his balance while fighting the wind's constant push.

Darkwing let out a wheeze once he reached the top of the hill, glancing back to examine the vast distance he had just hiked. He shook his head while muttering to himself. "I just wish Krista would take some responsibility and keep a low profile. I don't want to go hiking through the dunes to try and find her."

Would have it been so hard to leave some sort of message? he thought.

Darkwing was only doing what he thought was best. The Eyes of Eternal Life was their most suitable option to stay hidden until the recent events with the Five Guardians corruption and escape of the prisoners blew over. Eventually the Renascence Guard would regain order and Danil and Ast'Bala would be dealt with by the two remaining guardians, Zeveal and Demontochai.

I'll give her a piece of my mind when I find her, he pledged while gradually stepping onto the sharp slope of the hill, carefully gliding down the other side of the dune. *She's got to work with me if we are to survive together.*

After several more climbs and descents, the sandy landscape shifted to large boulders and rocky ground at the base of Magma Falls. Mist obscured much of Darkwing's view, making it difficult to see the details of nearby objects. What he could make out were silhouettes of water factories moving up and down as they harvested the water that descended into the lake of lava. To the far right, dozens of worn-down paths and sharp rocks could be seen leading into the mist.

Krista wouldn't be by the water factories; the farmers do not tolerate strangers. She might be in one of the caves. It was what Darkwing and Krista had initially done when they first left the City of Renascence, after Danil's corruption. There were plenty of hiding places in Magma Falls, which is why the Corrupt used it so frequently.

He took a deep sniff of the air hoping to get some sense of Krista's soft scent. It was unlikely considering the overwhelming sensation of heat from the lake of lava. With no luck, Darkwing continued to hike toward the far side of the mountain away from the water factories.

He hiked up the right side of the mountain and entered several of the nearby caverns, examining the entryways for tracks and any smells he could pick up that resembled Krista. Nothing; any smell beyond the burning magma was difficult to detect. After several caverns he had no luck, feeling discouraged.

Darkwing continued to hike higher up the mountain, recalling the paths they had initially took days ago before joining the Eyes of Eternal Life. He ultimately found the cavern where they had first rested. He scanned the ground to try and find any fresh tracks but the ground was solid rock. No dust or sand was present to make imprints.

"Krista!" Darkwing shouted, hearing his own voice rebound off the rocks. "Krista! Let's go!" It was a long shot but he thought he might as well give it a try. He didn't want to shout too much to cause unwanted attention.

At that moment, the idea came to him: perhaps she was nowhere near Magma Falls. What if the cult had done something with her?

Saulaph and Alistind were gone, too; it was possible that they had taken Krista somewhere. The idea sounded plausible at first, but upon reflection, Darkwing had to admit it was highly unlikely. There was nothing logical about it. The cultists were crazy, but they were peaceful.

Maybe I jumped to conclusions about her being at Magma Falls. For all I know she has been in some prayer chamber inside the temple this whole time. He thought she might even be searching for him. Maybe he was just being paranoid.

Darkwing turned back from the cavern entrance and hiked back down the mountain, retracing his path. While walking down, a rotten stench filled the air. He recognized the smell: it was decaying flesh. The odour that usually meant the Corrupt were near. Considering how little he could smell on the mountain, it probably meant the Corrupt were *very* near. The strength of the smell only amplified his worried state of mind.

Great. This could be more than I bargained for, he thought while glancing around the nearby rocks. He tried remain optimistic, but he knew he was quite high up Magma Falls, which was common ground for the Corrupt. Then again, most creatures of the underworld eventually wandered to the mountain, when they needed to quench their thirst.

The smell wasn't prominent when he first climbed the mountain, meaning that the Corrupt were either stalking him or they happened to be wandering near the same path. Either way, chances were that they could pick up his scent, too.

Darkwing drew his dagger and tucked it inside the cuff of his coat, hiding the weapon in case someone found him. He walked along the rough path moving down the mountain slowly, watching every rock, slope, and path for signs of life.

An arrow shot by Darkwing without warning, pinging off a nearby rock a couple feet away from him.

He spun around to locate the attacker. The arrow had to have come from above, but no one could be seen higher up the mountain whence he came.

"Show yourself!" Darkwing demanded, drawing his dagger free.

Corrupt can't use weapons, he thought.

"Are you lost, scum?" a throaty male shouted.

Two reptilians leaped from opposing rocks, somersaulting down over Darkwing's head and landing on both feet in front of him, raising dust. One was male, the other was female; they both appeared to be his age and size but wore masks on their faces made from stitched vazelead scales. They had sharp metal blades drawn and were prepared to kill.

"Let's strip him!" the female hissed.

"I'm not looking for trouble," Darkwing said, keeping his dagger pointed at them.

"You're rather far from the City of Renascence. Clearly you want something," the throaty male said, his eyes widening.

Darkwing scanned the two reptilians closely, taking note of the glassy reflection off their eyes and lack of pupils. *Or perhaps they are Corrupt,* Darkwing thought. The eyes were a clear identifier that the metamorphosis fumes had mutated them into savages. Oddly enough, the two were still capable of handling conversation, wearing some form of clothing, and carrying weapons. They mustn't be fully converted into the Corrupt. The metamorphosis fumes affected their people in varying degrees, some harsher than others.

Maybe I can reason with them, Darkwing thought, hoping that the two Corrupt were not completely mad. He lowered his guard and raised both hands. "I'm looking for a girl."

The two laughed.

"You found one." The female flicked her tongue at him.

Darkwing was desperate; he wanted to find Krista, even to the point he was going to try and reason with two Corrupt. It was insane but he had to give it a try. "She's about a head shorter than you, and quite frail. Short black dress, high boots."

The male grinned, showing his grimy teeth. "Sounds tasty."

"Indeed. In fact, this scum looks rather appetizing," the female added.

This is a waste of my time. Reason isn't going to work. Darkwing wasn't a fool; he knew that this conversation wouldn't end in his favour. Drastic action had to be taken to escape.

He lunged forward without further hesitation, throwing his dagger at the female. The weapon spun once in the air and plunged through her eye socket.

She screamed as the fire in her eye sputtered a couple bursts of flame and extinguished. The girl fell to the floor, trying to pull the dagger free from her face, but it was in too deep.

The male rushed Darkwing, tackling him with both hands. They collided into a boulder and tumbled on the gravel floor with a thud. He sat upright and locked his hand into a fist.

The male's fist descended on Darkwing's face. Darkwing snatched his attacker's arm with both hands and redirected the blow into the ground. The fist hit the dirt with a crunch and the male roared, trying to break his hand free from Darkwing.

Darkwing let go and threw a swift punch to the Corrupt's ribs, hearing a bone crack while knocking him clear. Their similar size made it easy for Darkwing to push the male aside and leap to his feet.

The Corrupt was still on the ground; Darkwing took the opportunity and lashed his tail at the male's neck, coiling it around his throat.

The female managed to pluck the blade from her eye and got herself up, black blood oozing down her face.

"Leave him alone!" She sprinted toward Darkwing. Her eye injury unbalanced her depth perception, though, and she was closer to him than she thought. Darkwing curled his hand and slammed a fist in her face. His knuckles crushed her nose and he could hear her cartilage collapsing. Her nostrils began to ooze black blood, and she clutched at her face.

Darkwing noticed a dagger tucked in her belt. He pulled the male closer to him while reaching to grab the weapon from the female. Snatching the dagger, Darkwing uncoiled his tail and thrust the blade into the male's neck. His victim gargled while blood squirted from his throat. The male's hands twitched as he fell to the dirt trying to grab the handle of the blade.

Darkwing pounced on the female, throwing her to the ground. Her hands broke free from her face and Darkwing slammed a fist at her wounded eye, then landed a second punch to her mouth and a third to her nose. Her body twitched, with blood spurting from the seams of her mask and drizzling down her neck. Blow after blow, Darkwing could feel her skull crack and crush inward. He continued to beat her face until her limbs fell limp.

He panted, holding both fists in the air as they dripped with blood. He licked his lips and looked at the aftermath of his violent defense against the two reptilians.

The male lay on the ground with blood pouring from his body, still twitching from the knife in his throat. The female, pinned to the ground by Darkwing's weight, was beyond recognition.

"Oh shit," Darkwing muttered to himself, realizing the chaos he had just caused.

Killing the male had been necessary; they were equal in size and he was a major threat. But the female . . . If he was merciful, he could have let her live. She had a broken nose and had lost an eye, and couldn't have done much damage. But he didn't show mercy; he'd kept beating her with an uncontrollable urge to kill—the same desire he'd felt as the metamorphosis fumes mutated his body when his people were banished to the underworld.

The same urges that make the Corrupt who they are. Darkwing swallowed heavily.

It was an unexplainable surge of primal satisfaction that developed during their people's transformation after being banished. He didn't like killing and wanted to consider himself civilized, but sometimes, like now, it was too difficult to hold back when he could feel the oily texture of blood on his hands.

"No!" Darkwing rose from the girl's corpse. "I'm not like them." He looked over her body again and saw that she was only a kid—just like Krista.

He hissed and shook his head. She wasn't anything like Krista; she had none of her features. *Krista's skin is lighter, her smell is sweet . . . her body . . . mesmerizing. Something I long to dominate.*

Darkwing hit the side of his head. *Get your shit together. Krista is more than that. She's my family.*

It was only his mind playing games. His frenzy had made his thoughts so primitive, he found it disgusting. He could keep himself under control when Krista was around, but when she was gone, he found it challenging to keep the savage within him at bay.

Darkwing closed his eyes and took a deep breath. Trying to calm himself, he could feel his heart pumping fast, the blood flowing through his body, and the tenseness of his muscles. Opening his eyes, he looked around the path to see it was empty—just him and a couple of fresh corpses.

"I'm not like the Corrupt," he reassured himself.

Darkwing glanced around, remembering the dagger, and saw it was still lodged in the corpse's throat. He walked over and pulled it from Corrupt's neck then wiped the blade clean on his boot. He smeared his hands on his pants, trying to remove the blood from his hands.

"I've got Krista."

CHAPTER V: REFLECTION

CHAPTER VI

Compassion or Disgust?

Child . . .
Blind and Blameless.
Child . . .
Naïve and New.
Child . . .
Innocence fills you.

Child . . .
Curious and Cute.
Child . . .
Such a bane.
Child . . .
I welcome you to my domain!

You won't lose me, Krista. I've always been here with you. I always will.

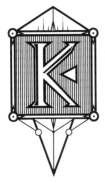rista sprung up from her prone position, panting heavily; blankets fell from her torso and onto her lap. Being exposed to the room's cool air made her aware of how cold and dry the scales were on her neck and down her backside. The icy chill caused her entire body to shake and the sides of her head throbbed with each heartbeat. Her vision swayed and it was difficult to maintain a sense of balance. The area was bright—blindingly bright.

A deep voice shouted. "It moved!"

Krista looked around for the source of the voice, but the brightness of the room still overpowered her sight like she was gazing directly into a torch. Her eyes burned as she squinted, trying to see.

"Her eyes are on fire! I'll get Paladin," squealed a higher-pitched voice.

"She's not burning, though," the deep voice replied.

Krista kept moving her head: up, down, left, and right. Her eyes were adjusting to the light ever so slowly and she could now see the brick walls and stone floor. Krista looked over her shoulder and saw the rough outline of a humanoid watching her. Their arms were folded and their face, neck, and hands were of a light tone.

Who is that?

She sat straight up and kicked the blankets off to get a better look at the being. It was still challenging to make out the rest of the room; she could not see the walls but her eyesight was becoming more stable. She could make out some of the humanoid's details. Yes, the skin was a light tone and its figure masculine—red hair down to his shoulders, a beard, and a suit of armour. The sight of him made her feel uneasy for some reason.

Pale skin . . . hair?

He unfolded his arms and stepped closer, his brown eyes locked on her palms.

Krista swallowed heavily and clutched her hands together, body still shivering from the cold. "Back away," she snapped.

The male kept approaching her.

"Back away!" she shouted as the blood pumped to the roots of her scalp-feathers, causing them to stand up.

"My God," the male muttered.

"Back!" Krista jumped backward on the soft sheets covering the cushioned surface she rested on, putting pressure on her wounded arm. The weight on the injury caused her arm to collapse and she yelped. Losing her balance, she tumbled over the edge of the cushion. Krista landed on the stone floor with her wounded arm absorbing the impact. She cried out in pain and lashed her tail in the air, trying to scare the humanoid away.

"Stay away from me!" she hissed.

"What did you do, John?" a stern voice demanded.

"I didn't do anything! It started to act irrationally when it woke," the deep voice replied.

Krista shivered on the floor, skin rubbing against the smooth stone surface. She crawled toward the platform she'd been on—it was clear now that it was a metal table with a mattress and a woolen blanket on top—trying to hide from the beings.

A humanoid with dirty-blond hair stepped forward and blocked her way under the table. He was muscular in build and was dressed mostly in red with black pants and leather ankle-high boots.

"It's okay," he said gently while reaching out to her with his large hands.

Krista shook her head and leapt to her feet using her good arm as support. Her balance was unstable as she bolted in the direction of the most open gap in the room.

I'm getting out of here!

Before she knew it, she ran into a green wooden shelf, knocking down some books. She stumbled to the cold floor as a couple more books—luckily, lightweight—fell on top of her.

The coldness of the room was unbearable and the brightness made it difficult to see. The situation fueled her headache. It was challenging to maintain her thoughts, no matter the effort she made. Her instincts were in charge and she only felt the overpowering need to run.

The dirty-blond-haired humanoid rushed over to Krista's slumped body and looked down. "She's not well." He kneeled and gently picked her up, tightening his grasp to prevent her from squirming. "She's cold as ice," he observed, bringing her back to the table.

"Leave me alone!" Krista tried to wiggle free from the humanoid's arms, but it was no use—he was stronger than her.

"She speaks perfect English!" the high-pitched voice exclaimed. Now that Krista's vision was clearer she could see that it belonged to another pale male with curly black hair.

"Rather loud, too," remarked the deep-voiced male—the one that had been identified as John, with red hair and a beard.

The dirty-blond-haired male gently placed her on the cushioned surface of the operating table. "We're not here to hurt you, girl," he said calmly, covering her with the soft blankets. "Your arm is deeply wounded and you seem to have a fever, so you need to rest."

Krista relaxed her muscles and admitted to herself that the male was probably right. *He knew of my injury. How was I hurt, anyway?* She shifted her body to a more comfortable position and closed her eyes.

"It's so bright," she complained.

"Tell me, girl," he began, kneeling to her eye level. "What's your name?"

Krista turned her head toward him and opened her eyes. He was so close she could make out the wrinkles on his face. The being seemed so familiar, like something from her distant memory.

"Krista," she said, shivering. "Kristalantice Scalebane. What's yours, sir? What are you?" Krista asked.

The humanoid smiled. "Simply call me Paladin."

Krista gasped and sprung back up, frantically trying to get away from him.

Paladin? These are humans! Krista scooted backward on the table, this time making sure she did not fall off. "Soft-skins! Someone, help!" she shouted.

How did I end up here? she thought. Between her semi-conscious state and the headaches, she found it difficult to recall her recent memories.

Paladin stood and displayed his empty hands. "We are not going to hurt you."

Krista noticed a pendant around his neck in the shape of a cross. She felt her lip tremble and she shook her head. "Don't tie me up like an animal. Don't hurt me—don't kill me!" She took the blankets and covered her face with them. *Please be a dream.*

Maybe the men were imaginary and they'd go away if she hid. The last time she saw humans was when her family was slaughtered and her people were gathered like cattle. They were forced to march up Mount Kuzuchi nearly two centuries ago.

The memory of her last encounter with humans was also her first memory of her dear friend. *Darkwing, you saved my life then when the humans caught us, and when we were in the underworld running from the Renascence Guard.* A tear rolled down her face. "I'm so scared," she whined. "Darkwing, where are you?"

"What's she saying?" the high-pitched voice asked. "Who is Darkwing?"

"We're not here to kill you," Paladin said. "Or hurt you, at that. Tell us, Krista, why do you think we'd do such horrible things to you?" He supported her back so she wouldn't slip off the table again.

Krista brought one eye from under the blankets and looked at him. The long-ago memories of the remorseless, ruthless knights and paladins capturing her people, and Darkwing's bravery, played back in her mind. *The humans were so heartless—these memories I can recall. Why can't I remember how I got here?*

Paladin took the blanket in his hand and gently tugged on it. "Why don't we start by you telling us what you are?" He folded his arms and raised an eyebrow.

Krista squinted and let go of the blanket. *This isn't a dream. The soft-skin doesn't know I'm vazelead. The metamorphosis fumes did change us a lot. Maybe I have an advantage.*

She took hold of her tail and started fidgeting with the end of it. *Darkwing would do something clever. He's good at negotiating.* "Can you answer questions for"—she paused, thinking carefully about her words—"for me first?"

Paladin smirked. "All right, girl. Ask your questions."

"Are the Paladins of Zeal and Knight's Union still controlling the world?"

John laughed. "Is she joking?"

Paladin remained motionless, his eyes focused on the ground. "How old are you?"

Krista folded her arms. "Not answering. Are the paladins still in charge?" she demanded.

"Frisky," the high-pitched man commented.

Paladin glared at the man. "Smyth, you're not helping." He turned back to face Krista. "No." Paladin brought his eyes to meet hers. "They were massacred by the Drac Lord Karazickle two centuries ago. Few survived, and with our culture destroyed, we slowly vanished."

"Okay, but you're a paladin? What about the Council of Just?" Krista asked.

Paladin smiled. "Not answering. One answer for you and one answer for me."

Krista frowned. "All right, fine."

"How old are you? To look so young and ask such a question—"

"Nearing three hundred."

"Three hundred what?" The man referred to as Smyth stepped closer and Krista could see his curly hair and scarred face. "A number means nothing to us without a measurement."

"Years," Krista added, looking at Smyth. "Three hundred years."

"As in three hundred sixty-five days in a year?" Smyth asked.

Krista smiled. "Not answering." *They're not so smart.*

Paladin sighed and nodded.

Krista unfolded her arms. "Same question. Are you really a paladin?"

"I am the last."

Smyth leaned over and whispered into Paladin's ear. Despite her superior vazelead hearing, Krista was unable to pick up on his words. Her ears were ringing and her headache had diminished her naturally keen senses.

"I know how to handle this," Paladin said.

Smyth nodded and backed away.

"Now Krista, you speak perfect English. Do your years follow the traditional three hundred sixty-five days like in the Kingdom of Zingalg?"

"Yep," she replied. "Am I in Zingalg right now?"

The men looked at each other.

"Three hundred years . . ." John scratched his chin.

Paladin looked at Krista. "That is correct. We are in Zingalg."

The surface world. Krista's eyes widened while she glanced around the room. Was it true? Was she really on the surface? But how?

"That's not possible. I don't understand."

"Nor do I, Krista. That is why we are speaking."

"This can't be Zingalg."

"I assure you it is."

Krista bit her lip while thinking, *there are humans here. That says something.* "I used to live here," she said, gently rubbing her wounded arm. "It's so cold now, and bright."

"Krista, are you from the underworld?" Paladin asked.

How did he know that? Oh gosh, he knows what I am, doesn't he? Should I tell him? He's a paladin—one of those who banished my people. She felt her muscles tense thinking about the question, like an invisible force pushing against her back.

"Krista? Are you reptilian?" Paladin said.

She bit her lip. "I'm vazelead."

"Vazelead?" Smyth exclaimed. "You show no resemblance to the depictions I've seen."

"It wasn't our fault!" Krista hissed and slammed her hands on the table.

Paladin put his hand on her shoulder. "Easy, girl, you're not well. It's no one's fault."

It surprised Krista to see that Paladin was so calm after her revelation.

"Any more questions for me?" he asked.

"No. This is just happening too fast. Too many questions from everyone," she said, keeping her eyes on the other two men as the flame around her eyes flickered intensely. *I don't like these other humans here.*

"All right, I'll continue." Paladin let go of her shoulder and put his hands behind his back. "You show no resemblance to the vazelead people. What happened to you? You said it wasn't your fault."

Krista nodded and began to coil her tail around her finger. "My head is fuzzy, but it's clearing up . . . I was only a small child at the time. Our people were quickly changed; something in the underworld air mutated us. It made us adapt to the environment." She swallowed before continuing. "Every gulp of air changed us. A little at first—our colour; our size. Then at one point it rapidly altered how we looked and even changed our thoughts. Some of us went crazy and became cannibals."

The two men leaned closer, intent on listening to the story.

"The ones that went too far and fed off our own kind were banished by those of us who remained sane. We call them the Corrupt. They crave anarchy and the flesh of vazeleads. The Corrupt wander the outskirts of the city feeding on whatever they can find in the underworld."

"How did your mind handle the mutation?" Paladin asked.

"I stayed normal. Well, as normal as I am now. I couldn't control the pains in my body and I changed like the rest of my people. The underworld is much warmer and darker than the surface, so I guess the mutations saved us in a way." She dropped her tail and looked up at Paladin. "You're still not going to hurt me, right?"

Paladin shook his head. "No, girl. Though I do need you to tell me how you came to be on the surface world. It is of great importance."

Krista looked to the ground. *It's coming back,* she thought. The more they discussed the more her memory gradually returned. *I don't remember much. I know I was in a temple . . . Darkwing and I were hiding from all the chaos in that cult, the Eyes of Eternal Life. There was the high council, and now I am here. Why does this human want to know, anyway?* It was a tough situation. She didn't know who these men really were, or what they would do with her information.

"It's a rather long story, sir," Krista said, trying to buy herself time.

"Share it with us, then." Paladin folded his arms.

"I don't know where to start. I'm ashamed of it now, Paladin, but I joined a cult to have shelter over my head and food in my stomach. Things got ugly and I learned my lesson. My friend forced me to see the high council of the cult. Something was wrong with him—he wasn't himself." She inhaled and exhaled heavily. *Saulaph.* "I don't think I want to talk about it." She spoke, recalling the albino vazelead's death.

Paladin took her hand gently. "You need to tell us, Krista. It's only a memory now."

"Saulaph is dead!" she shouted and yanked her hand free. *And I have no idea what happened to my dear Darkwing.*

Paladin shook his head and folded his arms.

"Who's Saulaph?" John asked.

Krista brushed her scalp-feathers backward with both hands. "My friend—" She swallowed. "Saulaph was my friend and another vazelead tore off his head, and . . . then . . ." She looked down at her clothing to see it was covered in dried black blood. "He sprayed the blood all over me!" Krista began to scratch at her dress, trying to scrape the blood off.

Paladin grabbed both of her wrists. "It's okay, Krista! We will have your dress washed."

"She clearly needs more rest," Smyth observed.

"Krista, focus!" Paladin ordered. "Anything else you can tell us?"

Krista breathed heavily and stared off into the bright room. "I think he carved into my arm." She shook her head, thinking about the pain. "He chanted, 'Blood of the innocent blinds the Just.'" She closed her eyes. "He chanted so many words. It was all a blur."

Paladin let her go and walked toward the other men. Krista opened her eyes and watched as they talked amongst each other. Her hearing was returning to proper levels while her body adjusted to the new conditions. Her head still throbbed and it was a challenge to focus in on their conversation.

"What do you think, sir?" John asked.

"Clearly, she is a spy," Smyth said.

Paladin shook his head. "I fear the girl was forced to take place in a necromantic ritual of blood."

What is that? Krista thought. *Did Danil take me to the surface world?*

John glanced at Krista. "Poor girl."

"Which would mean she is not a spy, Smyth."

Smyth frowned. "You said 'forced'. What do you mean?"

"Whoever knew of this ancient ritual understood its power and used it to break the shackles over the vazelead people."

John folded his arms. "How do we know if the shackles have been broken? Maybe they just got her through."

Paladin shook his head. "The holy shackles are designed to only affect the target or targets. The Prayer of Power works on everyone or no one. There are no exceptions, which can only mean that the shackles don't work at all."

Smyth scratched his head. "Her blood was used in the ritual to trick the holy shackles to release all the vazeleads? Then the vazeleads are free to leave the underworld as they please?" he said, grinding his teeth.

"Correct. A ritual that can counter a Prayer of Power that binds can only come from a very evil place. The vazeleads probably don't know about our false leader. This is grave news for us. The kingdom could be at war and not even know it."

"False leader?" Krista asked, raising her voice. "What do you mean?"

Paladin nodded at Smyth. "Smyth, send word to the king of this. It is vital that he knows immediately."

"Yes, sir."

Paladin turned to face Krista. "The accusations against your people were false, Krista. We were unknowingly led by the last Drac Lord, Karazickle, who mastered the arts of shape shifting and posed as the paladin leader, Saule. I am sorry"—he lowered his head—"for I was there when your people were banished."

Krista's jaw dropped. *A draconem was responsible for our banishment?* It made no sense, because it was man who forced them into slavery and the draconem had set them free. Plus, as time went on, the vazeleads began to learn how to use the humans' tools, which seemed to her like a valid reason for the banishment. Why would a draconem banish her people?

She shook her head. "I really don't know what I should be saying to you." She forced a small smile across her face, trying to be friendly, but she felt helpless.

Paladin walked over to the table and sat down beside her. "I didn't expect you to; you're only a girl. It is only to ease my own pain for your people's punishment."

Nodding, Krista relaxed her muscles. She was exhausted and just wanted her headache to go away.

Paladin looked over to John. "Captain John, keep two men outside this office. I want her watched."

"Yes, sir." Captain John left the room.

Krista grabbed her scalp-feathers and stroked it gently. "You're not keeping me as a prisoner, are you?"

Paladin looked to the ground and stood. "Try to stay warm. Get some rest." He marched to the door of the room.

Krista still found it hard to see the door in the light but she heard Paladin's footsteps exit the room and the door close behind him. She looked around the room. With the door closed it diminished the lighting and she could see slightly more. It was unclear whether she was at ground level, underground, or above the ground. Either way, she saw several small barred windows as high as the ceiling of the room that let light in.

Krista felt her headache swell again. *You'd think I would have more questions about all this. I am on the surface after two centuries.* She rubbed her head. The headache made it impossible to focus on anything. She crawled off the sheets so she could grab hold of them. *It's so cold. I should try to sleep.* She tugged on the blankets and brought them over her.

I forgot how bright and chilly the surface is. She closed her eyes and sighed. *But right now it doesn't matter. I need sleep.* Her mind felt like it had incomplete thoughts running through her head. *I'm on the surface world . . .* Darkwing, where are you? The words echoed in her mind and dissipated her thoughts, allowing her to drift off into a slumber and forget about the humans for one quiet rest.

CHAPTER VII

The Crossover

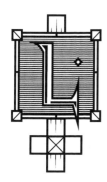oud wind roared throughout the desert, blowing the red sand into the air. It caused the lone vazelead to cover his face with his arms while marching through the landscape.

Travel seemed to pass instantly, lost in his thoughts. In what seemed like only a few moments, he had hiked all the way down Magma Falls and across most of the desert toward the limestone rock formation. He was pondering his slaughter of the two Corrupt back on the mountain. He felt shame; he let his recklessness get the best of him.

I'm not like them, Darkwing repeated to himself.

He kept trying to reassure himself that the Corrupt were simply savages and that their lives did not matter. But in the back of his mind, he could only think about what Krista would say: that the execution was ruthless.

I acted out and fed my animalistic behavior, he thought while staring at the sandy ground. Normally he would be paying a great deal of attention to his surroundings, ensuring that he wasn't being stalked by animals or other vazeleads. This time was different, though. He was distracted. Sulking, he mechanically hiked over the dunes. All he wanted was to get back to the temple and take a moment to gather his thoughts in his quarters.

The boy slid down the last dune leading to the main entrance of the cavern.

If Krista had just been in our sleeping quarters when I woke up, I wouldn't have had to go on a wild chase to find her, he thought to himself. *She is naïve, but I know she wouldn't have gone far. Magma Falls is all there is out here and she knows guardian Danil is looking for her.*

Darkwing's hike back finally came to an end when he reached the rock formation housing the temple entrance. He stepped inside of the narrow cavern while wiping off sand specks that stuck to his feathers.

Time to blend in, he thought while untying the cultist robe from his waist, slipping it back on. He walked through the winding path of the cavern back to the blackwood door and unlocked it with the skeleton key. He trudged down the spiral stairs until he reached the bottom where the large stone door rested. He pressed the pupil of the carving and the door slid open, allowing him to enter the temple.

Exhausted from his battle, Darkwing kept to himself and moved through the halls to his quarters. A pair of scrawny female cultists smiled at him with their wrinkly faces when he passed. He forced a smile and tucked his hands in his robe, hiding the dried blood.

When he entered his cell, Darkwing sat down on the bed and buried his face in his arms, frustrated. He took his dagger and threw it to the ground, not wanting something so hostile near him. He had spent all day looking for Krista and found nothing. Hope seemed lost to him.

Maybe Danil found her and took her to that Dreadweave Pass she spoke of—or maybe she is still in the temple. His thoughts were jumbled but he felt he needed to keep looking. Still, he needed time to settle; he couldn't take his mind off what he did to the Corrupt. It disturbed him that he lost control of his ability to remain civil. What would Krista think? The stress of keeping Krista and himself hidden was getting the better of him.

Interrupting his thoughts after what felt like hours, he noticed three cultists walk past his still-open door. One was pure white from scalp-feather to toe.

"Saulaph!" Darkwing felt his heart race as he sprang from his bed.

Now maybe he could get some answers.

He dashed out of the room to catch up with the three cultists. The albino was in the middle of the two hooded ones.

"Where is she?" Darkwing demanded.

Saulaph looked to the floor and the other two cultists remained silent, ignoring him. "Saulaph!" Darkwing shouted and moved in front of the three.

The cultists pushed him aside and walked onward.

Darkwing ran to catch up with them. "What's going on?"

Silence.

"Any of you?"

Darkwing noticed a quick movement from Saulaph's tail: it jabbed backward several times, pointing.

"I don't know where she is. Sorry, Brother Darkwing," Saulaph said. "Have you taken a walk out and around the cavern? The winds are less violent today."

That's a lie, but an odd statement, Darkwing thought, knowing from his journey to Magma Falls that the winds weren't soft.

Darkwing stopped in his tracks. "No. I have not, brother."

The three moved on, leaving Darkwing behind. Something was off about Saulaph's behavior. It was not normal, even for this temple. Darkwing knew he'd been given a message: Krista was not in the temple.

With that in mind, Darkwing rushed down the hall. Krista must be elsewhere. How had he missed her? There was nowhere else to go. He ran back down the hall in the direction of the lobby to see it was now cluttered with dozens of cultists; they must have just finished a group prayer.

On a silent day? he thought. *Shit. I don't have time for this nonsense.* Darkwing brushed his scalp-feathers back quickly, eyeing the large crowd that blocked the entire hallway. He knew the temple's primary halls well now and decided to take a sharp corner down another hall, a roundabout way to the entrance of the temple.

After a couple of turns he made it to the entrance where the large circular door rested. He glanced over at the crowd of cultists to see them slowly retreat down the hallway.

That would have taken way too long to push through, he thought.

Darkwing turned to once again press the door carving's pupil.

The door moved aside and he ran up the spiral stairway toward the cavern. At ground level, he tore the skeleton key from his pocket and frantically unlocked the door. Darkwing pushed the door open, only to be confronted with four Renascence Guards, armed head to toe with their gunmetal armour. His heart sank as he scanned past the four to see over a dozen more lingering in the cavern.

Darkwing froze.

The tall guard directly in front of him cradled his black spear with both hands. "What were you doing down there?"

Darkwing glanced around to see if there were any cultists or possibly Krista in the room. No. Darkwing was alone.

How did the Renascence Guard get here? Where is Krista? he thought, confused by the whole scenario. Did Saulaph set him up? They were a good day and a half away from the City of Renascence. Darkwing had not seen anyone else when he travelled back to the temple. Maybe he had been inside his cell for far longer than he thought.

"Answer the question!" the guard demanded, moving closer.

"Nothing," he lied.

"Don't toy with my patience, boy!" the guard shouted. He pushed Darkwing aside and marched down the stairway. "You're beyond the City of Renascence. Nothing good can be found here."

The guard was certainly going to the find the cult.

This is going to be utter chaos, Darkwing thought.

Regardless of how the Renascence Guards found this place, it surprised Darkwing that their hands weren't full enough within the city. But unity was something the Guardians took seriously, and the cult was not aligned with their people's beliefs. Things were not going to end well for the Eyes of Eternal Life. Truthfully, it didn't matter to Darkwing if he could find Krista and get her out of there.

Two other guards followed the tall one down the staircase.

"You're coming with us," one said. This guard was female with an almost masculine tone of voice.

"No, wait! Krista!" Darkwing shouted and tried to push past the guards.

They both grabbed hold of his arm and forced him to move with them down the spiral staircase. He stopped fighting; guards were dangerous and aggravating them was a death wish. At the bottom of the stairs, the tall guard waited by the closed stone door.

"Open this"—the tall guard tapped the door with his spear—"and your life will be spared."

Darkwing obeyed without question. What other choice did he have?

"Do I have your word?" Darkwing asked, eyeing the tall guard closely.

"You do."

Darkwing did not trust the Renascence Guard, but he had to put his faith in them. He was out of options. He stepped ahead of the two guards toward the stone door. He looked at the centre pupil of the fiery eyeball and pressed it inward, opening the entrance to the temple. Cultists could be seen wandering slowly up and down the hall, paying little attention to the newcomers.

The tall guard hissed as he shoved his way past Darkwing to enter. "Brilliant." He eyed the corridors filled with cultists walking through the chambers and nodded at Darkwing. "Well done, boy. I am pleased to see your loyalty to the Five Guardians is greater than whatever this abomination is."

"Wait! Have you captured a girl?" Darkwing asked.

The guard shook his head. "Excuse me? No, not yet—and nor will we. Their disloyalty can only be met with execution."

Krista mustn't be caught yet. This was a promising sign for Darkwing. "Can I retrieve my belongings?" Darkwing asked. He realized he had forgotten his dagger in the excitement and would need to keep hunting for Krista, wherever she was.

"Get moving. Fast," the female guard warned. "We will show no mercy to anyone in our way."

"Of course." Darkwing bowed and rushed into the temple. While he ran down the halls he could hear some of the cultists scream; the Renascence Guard was already killing.

He sprinted through the halls turned to where his cell was located. The door was still open as he left it earlier. This time, he spotted two cultists at the entrance.

From the white tail, he could tell one of them was Saulaph. He was dragging a girl out of the room. She was small, with a pointed nose, and black and blue scalp-feathers parted to one side.

"Krista!" Whatever Saulaph was doing, Krista didn't look pleased. Darkwing rushed toward her in a mighty sprint.

I won't lose you.

Krista opened her eyes and shouted, "Darkwing!"

"Saulaph! Let her go or I'll rip your throat out with my teeth!" he roared, feeling his scalp-feathers stand upright.

Anger boiled inside him and he could feel that primitive rage heighten once more. Did Saulaph lead him away so he could take Krista? She could have been down there the whole time. Darkwing's feelings blinded him. He was unaware of the two cultists approaching from down the hall until they were closing in and about to block his path.

Darkwing had no choice but to break through them to get to Krista. The two cultists were only a couple feet away. He could do it; he had the momentum to push past them.

Using his shoulder, he tried to barge past the two, but the cultists dodged his charge and grabbed hold of his arms firmly, preventing him from escaping.

"Darkwing!" Krista cried again, arms lashing while Saulaph dragged her away.

The cultists brought Darkwing to a stop, and he could see tears trickling down Krista's cheek as she was pulled out of sight. He was close enough to hear her dress drag against the stone floor—close enough to smell her sweet scent.

"Evil found us, brother," one of the cultists stated calmly, every bit as monotone as usual.

"Let me go!" Darkwing roared, trying to break free. He tried to throw a punch at the nearest cultist but together they were stronger and held his arms back.

"Sister Krista was summoned to meet with the elder council, as was Saulaph. They'll take care of her. She is blessed now," the other cultist said.

A spear whizzed past Darkwing into the skull of the nearest cultist, pinning his hood to his head. The cultist let out a grunt as the force threw him forward. His head hit the floor first and rebounded once off the ground. Blood leaked out around the spear. Darkwing's strength outmatched the remaining cultist and he managed to extend his claws, lunging them upward into the male's jaw. The claws pierced through his flesh, causing the cultist to release Darkwing's arm. Darkwing swept his foot in an arc, tripping the reptilian. As the cultist's head pulled loose of Darkwing's claws, blood sprayed over the floor.

The familiar sound of clanging metal rang through the halls nearer and nearer: the sound of marching Renascence Guards.

"Enough, boy!" a guard shouted.

Darkwing looked up to see the tall guard from earlier. He had not noticed in the dark before, but the guard wore bronze-plated armour: the marking of a captain.

"Is that the girl you mentioned?" the captain asked.

Darkwing nodded and pointed down the hall. "They took her that way. We have to find her; the cult wants to do something to her. Let's go!" Darkwing began to run.

The captain's gauntlet collided with Darkwing's chest. "I'll send my men through the chambers." He lowered his hand. "You're not like the others. You were so willing to betray the cult to help your friend. Every other cultist has been blindly loyal to it."

"I never claimed to be loyal to this temple," said Darkwing.

"I do not blame you, boy; our people face dark times. We'll do our best to find your girl. But I don't want you wandering these halls. My men don't know you and they will kill you."

Darkwing bit his lip, agitated. He knew the captain was right.

"Before you go, show us her room. I'll send a first set of guards to find her. If they fail, I can send a second squad after her scent."

"Of course." Darkwing found it odd he'd spent so much of his time battling the Renascence Guard and now they were working with him. He was not going to complain, though. They were better equipped to find Krista than he was on his own.

The captain silently pointed three guards down the hall where Krista had disappeared. The three nodded and moved in sync to find her.

Darkwing led the captain and a couple of his men to the small quarters. The captain looked at Krista's bed then took the sheet from the cot.

"I'll find you at the surface, where Demontochai and the rest of the squad remains. I will bring news as soon as I can," the captain said, rolling up the sheet. He handed it to one of his men.

"Guardian Demontochai is here?" Darkwing exclaimed.

"Yes. We caught word of guardian Danil being here. Go now! We mustn't waste time," the captain shouted before exiting the cell.

Danil. Darkwing swallowed heavily. *What is going on here?* The Renascence Guard, Saulaph capturing Krista, and guardian Danil— none of it added up.

Wasting no time, Darkwing picked up his knife from the ground and took one last look at his bed, briefly considering taking the sheets to sleep on later. Lying on the bed was the necklace he'd given Krista, orange pearl as fiery as ever.

Why would she leave this behind? I thought she would have kept it around her neck as a reminder of me. He walked over and grabbed the necklace, his hand shaking as he held it in the palm of his hand. He felt an unusual emptiness in his stomach. His heart was heavy, and he was unsure if he could obey the captain. If Danil was present, there was a chance the necklace was all Darkwing would have of left Krista. He knew what hall Saulaph had taken Krista down; he could try to find her before the guards did.

Aggravated at the cult, he hissed violently, tore off his red robe off, and threw it across the room. He tucked the necklace into his pocket.

Darkwing exited the cell and scanned hall to see cultists running in fear in all directions; some were screaming and others were bleeding. Still others were slain, their bodies left on the ground, black blood filling the cracks in the stone floor.

I could look for Krista . . . It was a foolish thought; he would certainly be killed, whether by cultists, the Renascence Guard, or possibly Danil. *I need to take the chance.*

He began moving to his left, toward where he'd seen Krista being dragged, when a gentle hand grabbed Darkwing's arm, trying to tug him into the quarters to his side. He looked over to see it was the red-feathered girl, Alistind.

"Brother!" she exclaimed, waving for him to come in.

Darkwing glanced down the hallway to see if he was being watched before slipping into the room.

She rushed him in and quickly closed the door, backing him up to the nearest wall with her hands pressed against his chest. "I thought I was alone!" She began to cry, pushing herself against him. Her fine narrow face clenched up, resisting the urge to sob. "They're killing everyone." She burrowed her head into him in a way that reminded him of Krista.

It was hard for him to feel pity for her when he was fixated on a single thought: Krista.

Alistind mumbled, "The elders took Saulaph and your Krista. The elders will ensure their safety."

Alistind's words were angering Darkwing. Each of the cultists always seemed to say the same thing: The elders would make sure they were safe, and the Risen One would protect them. Their stupidity was beyond his understanding.

Darkwing pushed her back and lightly slapped her face. Shaking her shoulders, he hissed, "Are you completely brain-dead like the rest of these cultists?"

Alistind's big eyes widened in shock, and she looked up with her mouth open. "Brother, I . . . I'm unsure if I follow."

Darkwing shook his head. "I'm not your brother." He let go of her arms. "Tell me, do you actually believe in this faith?"

Alistind thought about the question. Her eyes looked off into space; it was as if Darkwing could see the gears in her mind trying to work but nothing was going through her head.

She pushed her long scalp-feathers from her eyes and blinked before answering, her long spikey brows catching Darkwing's attention. "You mean free from the Risen One's whispering words?"

"Whispering words? What words? This temple is a sham. Listen, what I mean is, can you live without this cult?" Darkwing didn't want to waste too much time with her; he had better things to do than deal with a mindless cultist.

I must find Krista. At the same time, he wasn't ruthless like the Blood Hound leader, Draegust. He didn't want to see Alistind be butchered by the Renascence Guard, nor would Krista. He had wasted enough time talking to the girl; the three Renascence Guards were ahead of him in searching for Krista, and he wouldn't even know where Saulaph went. Alistind had ruined his chance to find her.

The girl looked down and squinted. "I've relied on the Eyes of Eternal Life so heavily that I have not questioned or seen anything on my own in decades. The temple has been my home, my thoughts . . . How would I survive?"

"Listen to me. The Renascence Guard is killing everyone wearing a red robe. Come with me and we can get out of here alive."

"Leave our brothers and sisters to die?"

"They had their chance to escape, but they'd sooner die with their beliefs."

"I'm scared!" she cried, grabbing Darkwing's hands.

The words rang in his head. 'I'm scared' were the two words Krista most often used whenever they were in tight situations. That's all he could think about; he had to get his mind out of this rut where everything reminded him of her. He had to focus on where he was right now and trust that the captain would find Krista. Besides, he couldn't leave Alistind here alone now. The guards would surely show no mercy.

"All right." Alistind let go of Darkwing and untied her robe. "I'll do it." She slipped the robe off, revealing her simple tunic, tight leather pants and lean figure. "The Risen One will not forgive me for this, but I don't want to die. Not now."

Darkwing smiled. *Guess there is still hope for her.* "Let's get out of here."

He opened the door, keeping Alistind close to his side. They hurried through the hallway, keeping to the walls and out of everyone's way. The Renascence Guard stormed by them several times, ignoring them. Darkwing hadn't known for sure if removing their robes would get them through, but it appeared to work.

They were left alone all the way to the entrance. Darkwing took Alistind's hand and led her up the spiral stairway to the cavern.

"Thank you," Alistind said, tightening her grip on his hand.

Upon reaching the surface, they could see that about a dozen Renascence Guards still waited beyond the blackwood door.

Darkwing took the lead, keeping Alistind behind him. When they stepped beyond the door, a guard hissed, raising his spear to block their way. "Who are you?" His voice was hoarse and his grip on the spear was shaky.

"We escaped the cultists." Darkwing used his free hand to wipe his face, also exposing his bloody palms. "They had us captured down there," he lied.

The guard nodded. "Do not fear. They will all pay for this."

"We are waiting for our friend. She is down there and your captain said they'd try to find her."

"All right . . ." The guard lowered his spear and stepped aside, letting the two pass. "Outside is windy. You best wait in the cavern with us."

"Thank you," Alistind whispered to Darkwing.

"It's fine." He led her past the guards and through the winding cavern toward the main entrance. The two kept their heads down low while moving around the group of Renascence Guards. The closer they walked toward the entrance, the more guards they could see. A particularly tall reptilian stood in front of a group of six. He wore a metal human-like mask and a black kilt.

One of the guards spoke, "We've cleared the surrounding area. This is the only entrance into the lower level."

The tall being hissed. "Excellent. Danil has nowhere to go. Soon I will be face-to-face with my blood brother."

Guardian Demontochai, Darkwing thought.

The guardian pointed back toward the blackwood door. "We must do what we must and put an end to him. Put our units in formation."

The Renascence Guard marched away from the guardian and the squad positioned themselves in front of the door, still allowing a clear walkway for the other guards to come through.

Demontochai looked down toward Darkwing and Alistind, now the only two in front of him. "Now, who are you?"

Alistind's eyes widened, unsure of what to say.

Darkwing stepped in front of her and cleared his throat. "We escaped the cult. Your captain is trying to rescue our friend down there."

Demontochai nodded. "We will protect you, as it is my duty to our people. Stay near the cavern entrance in case we confront Danil."

"Is he here?"

"He told me so himself."

Darkwing and Alistind exchanged glances, unsure what Demontochai meant by his words.

Demontochai marched toward the blackwood door. He stood about twice as high as the door, making it nearly impossible for him to fit through the entryway. Darkwing knew that Danil was of similar height, making him wonder how he could have fit through the door to begin with—unless there was a secondary hidden entrance to the temple.

"What are we to do now?" Alistind asked Darkwing.

The 'we' in her sentence surprised him; he had not expected her to stay. Darkwing was certain that she had family somewhere, and figured she would go away after they escaped. However, it was clear she didn't plan on leaving.

"We'll wait for the captain. He'll bring Krista back here."

Alistind combed her scalp-feathers with her fingers. "No one has ever returned from meeting with the elders. How are we to know the Renascence Guard will find her?"

"They will."

Time crawled as the two sat by the cavern entrance, watching Renascence Guards stand in formation, motionless. They must have spent several hours waiting while the remaining guards massacred cultists in the temple.

Worry filled Darkwing as more time passed and no guards re-emerged from the spiral staircase.

It was unlikely that the captain would spend long looking for Krista. He was still a part of the Renascence Guard, and they didn't waste time on useless tasks such as finding a girl. He felt it had been stupid of him to trust the Guard when he'd never trusted them before.

I should have stuck to my instincts and looked for her myself! I keep making mistakes with Krista's wellbeing. Darkwing sulked, thinking back to the elixir shop.

The blackwood door flung open and the captain walked out with the sheet from Krista's bed in his arms. He was followed by a couple of his soldiers.

The other Renascence Guards relaxed their positions and glanced up at the guardian.

"Well? What did you find, captain?" Demontochai asked.

"Nothing but scrolls, books, and the cultists themselves."

Darkwing and Alistind stood, carefully listening.

"What of Danil?" Demontochai spoke in a stern tone.

"No sign of him. We checked both levels of the temple."

"He has to be there!" Demontochai slammed his fist into the wall.

"We did venture into the lower level in search of a girl. She was easy to find from the screams but she was behind a closed stone door." He stopped. "Four of us tried to push the stone door aside but it was sealed shut."

Krista. Darkwing bit his lip, eager to hear more.

Demontochai shook his head and spoke, "And?"

"We heard her cries, and another voice—much darker and evil." The captain shook his head. "Whatever happened in there wasn't natural. Some sort of ritual was performed. We heard her screams, the other voice chanting, and more screams. The hallway began to shake and the smell of melting metal seeped from the room. Then there was silence. Did you feel the vibrations? They were intense."

No. Darkwing felt a force hit his chest hard, as if someone had punched him.

Demontochai shook his head. "Nothing was felt from up here."

"We were able to get through the door once there was silence. We found an altar dripping with blood. No one was in the room, except for the corpse of an albino vazelead. His head was severed from his body."

Alistind wrapped her arms around Darkwing, hugging him tightly. He barely noticed her affection, in shock from the captain's news.

Demontochai growled. "Unusual . . ."

"It is, but I assure you, Danil is not down there."

"Have your troops destroy the books and artifacts and ensure everyone else down there is dead. We'll head back after."

"Of course." The captain nodded. "You heard the guardian, men, back into the temple!"

Demontochai looked to the ground. "What are you trying to tell me, brother?" he muttered to himself.

The Renascence Guard marched one by one through the blackwood door and down the spiral staircase. The captain moved past the guards and toward Darkwing, who remained motionless. He was unsure what to do; he was in complete awe.

The captain looked to the ground while approaching. "I'm sorry, boy. Like you heard, some sort of ritual was performed in there. But there was only one body. I wouldn't give up hope, boy. She's alive, somewhere."

The captain held out the sheet. Darkwing did not respond.

Alistind took the sheet and smiled. "Thank you."

"You can return to the City of Renascence with us. It's safer in numbers. We won't be much longer," the captain said before turning around, returning to Demontochai.

Darkwing was unsure what to think—unsure what to do. The captain's words painted painful visions in his mind of Krista screaming, her blood drenching an altar. Then there was the dark, evil voice. Who was that? Was it Danil? If it was, then through the ritual, he must have taken her to that place—Dreadweave Pass.

The captain had said she was most likely alive and he couldn't give up hope yet, but he had no idea where to begin. What made the captain so sure, anyway? The disappearance of her body made him sick to his stomach.

Where are you, Krista?

CHAPTER VIII

Curious Kid

Child!
Time goes by quickly.
Where are you?
Awake you must be.
Tell me, what keeps you?
Release your mind and body . . .

. . . Child!
Wake up, this is enough.
I'm eager to meet you.
Each night you cough.
Tell me, what are you?
You wake each day in a huff . . .

. . . Child!
Clear your mind.

Who are you?

You're so confined.

Tell me, scared are you?

The nightmares won't end . . .

. . . I pain for you.

ising from her bed, Krista gasped for air with her body burning with warmth. The fever-like heat mixed with the dried blood on her skin and her clothes felt uncomfortably sticky.

A gust of wind blew in through the open windows, making her shiver from the coolness of the air. She glanced around to see the blankets had fallen to the floor, leaving her vulnerable to the icy-cold breeze.

Where is everyone?

Krista shielded her eyes from the heavy light shining through numerous windows on the wall opposite to the door. She looked at the radiating sunbeams, squinting. They gave her an odd sensation—a strange warmth much like the underworld, but different.

It's like my veins are working in overdrive. She ran her hand down her right forearm, feeling the veins throb. She then examined the healed skin where Danil had cut her open, running her hand down to her palm where she noticed a circular burn mark.

What?

Blood caked over her skin and it was difficult to make the mark out in detail. Krista tried to wipe the dried blood from the burn but the moment she touched it, her palm flared up.

"Ouch!" She bit her lip. *This is all too familiar.* The burn, the circular mark; it all had striking similarities to what had Ast'Bala did to Krista before Danil found her. Guardian Ast'Bala had initially burned a mark into Krista's neck when he found her with the escaping prisoners from the citadel. *He held me off the ground with his tail and gave me the mark after he saw me cry. I was so scared.*

Innocence of a child, Ast'Bala's deep voice had murmured. The hulky guardian's eyeballs had been plucked out and he'd wrapped his face with a black cloth to soak up the blood from his eye sockets. His normal vazelead figure had mutated: giant draconic-like wings sprouted from his back, his muscles had grown beyond anything earthly, and his feet set fire to the ground he walked on.

Even without his eyes, it was like he could see me.

Ast'Bala had felt Krista's tear fall from her face and spoke: *However, my new master has not assigned me to this world. I have been chosen to serve elsewhere.*

Krista remembered gasping for air, feeling her neck burn underneath Ast'Bala's tightening grip. Her body twitched and her muscles tensed until the guardian let go and threw her to the stone pavement in front of the doors of the citadel prison, where the prisoners were running free all around and out into the streets of the City of Renascence.

The burning sensation sank deeper into Krista's skin, moving into her bloodstream and making her body convulse aggressively.

Before Krista blacked out, she heard Ast'Bala's words: *My master assigned me to seek a gatekeeper for this world. Once I've converted a guardian for this task, they shall reap you to Dreadweave Pass, young one . . . As the Weaver commands.*

Krista shuddered, recalling the horrific memory. When she woke, the mark was on her neck. Darkwing had told her that it was a circle, with two triangles, one inside the larger one with an eyeball in the centre.

Later that day, Ast'Bala infected guardian Danil with what she now knew to be Mental Damnation. It caused Danil to go insane, just like Ast'Bala.

Danil was obsessed with finding me. The half-breed, Abesun, said it was Mental Damnation. The mark that Ast'Bala gave me somehow called Danil to where I was. Did Danil make a mark on my palm, too? What would that mean? Ast'Bala, Danil and Abesun all talked about being sick with Mental Damnation, and about Dreadweave Pass. Krista shook her head. "I must not be better yet, I'm totally overthinking this in detail." She slipped from the bed and moved unsteadily away from the windows, gently rubbing her shoulders as another breeze blew in. She felt dizzy and it was challenging to keep her sense of balance.

Krista walked to the closed door and sniffed the air. She could pick up the strong scent of humans—a disgusting smell of dirt, meat, and sweat—far more powerful than her people's smell.

Humans, she thought to herself. It was difficult for her to grasp that they were all around her. She hadn't seen or smelt one since before their banishment to the underworld. She felt like this was some sort of dream. *Vazeleads can't leave the underworld. Darkwing said so.*

Despite the dizziness, her mind was clearer than the first day she awoke. Now she could use her senses better. Her vision was a bit difficult still, due to the brightness.

Darkwing . . . how would you handle suddenly teleporting to the surface world? He'd keep his cool. He always does, she thought while examining her surroundings.

There was a small window on the door with three metal bars to prevent someone sticking their hands through. Krista got up on her toes and peeked through the small opening. She could see two human guards wearing metal breastplates and red tunics standing by the door. "Hello?" she called.

No response.

She knocked on the door, hoping they'd notice her. "Hello. I'd like to leave now." Her legs felt numb from the cold. "It's freezing in here!" she complained.

Footsteps came from the other side. Krista decided to call one more time.

"Someone let me out!" she cried.

The footsteps stopped.

Krista bit her lip and hugged herself tightly, trying to warm up.

I think they heard me.

The footsteps picked up again, this time moving closer to the door. They got louder and louder until a man brought his head to the window and looked at her with a scowl. It was the curly-haired man from the first time she awoke. She remembered he'd been identified as Smyth.

Krista got down from her tiptoes and backed up. "Hi." Her focus was sucked into the man's white skin. *So, so pale.*

"You're awake." He eyed her from her bare two-toed feet upward. "How are you feeling?"

Krista rubbed her head. "I'm cold, but my headache has gone down." Smyth stopped at her shoulder, seeing she was coated in blood.

She motioned at the blood. "I'd like to wash."

"I'll get Paladin and see what he says." The man's head disappeared from the window and his footsteps echoed as they trailed off.

Krista desperately wanted to clean the blood from her body. It smelled bad and it reminded her of Saulaph—the poor boy's blood, drenched over her skin. At the moment it was her fixation. The thought of someone else's bodily fluids coating her skin was disgusting.

It's not fair. Why did he have to die? Krista clutched her scalp-feathers, pulling at the roots. The memory of Danil tearing off the albino's head replayed in her mind.

I just hope I never see something so horrific again.

Krista sniffed the air and picked up on some new smells, but they were hard to classify. The clash of so many unknown odours was overwhelming—yet she only wanted to smell more, to pick up and identify every new scent.

I don't recognize any of these. It's all so foreign. What are they?

She walked around the room, trying to identify the smells. Krista saw a large range of linen-covered books on the oak shelves kept against the wall with the narrow windows. They were higher than the bookshelves but equal in length. She got closer to the shelves and looked at some of the titles down the spine. It was difficult to try and understand what they were about; she was not a good reader to begin with and making out words was tough. Plus, the humans used a slightly different style for the English alphabet, which made it even more challenging to read.

Forget it. Krista continued walking to the opposite side of the operating table she slept on. There sat a chair, a desk, and more shelves—all made of the same oak wood. There was also a cabinet with closed drawers just behind the desk.

What's in there?

Curiosity got the best of Krista and she walked over to the cabinet. The wood was stained with a green finish and the handles were metal, coated in gold paint. She put her hand on one of the knobs, feeling the smooth, cool, plated handle as the palm of her hand ran along its surface.

Krista tugged on the knob to open the drawer; it was locked.

She looked over to the desk and saw a couple books, along with papers that were scattered on the surface.

One book caught her attention because the oil-tanned leather cover had an illustration of a human face with its brain exposed and strange black tentacles reaching out from one side of the brain.

She walked to the table and picked up the book. It was heavy and had at least a few hundred pages. Krista began to skim through the volume; it was filled with illustrations of skulls, eyeballs, brains, and more black tentacles. One illustration in particular caught her eye: it was of a pale man with thin hair, wearing blood-red armour with a reptilian eye in the centre of the chestpiece. Most of the book seemed filled with statistics in the strange human-based English alphabet: numbers and labels and what she assumed to be measurements. The writing was scribbled—besides, she couldn't read the words anyway. She could piece together some of the larger chunks of words, however.

I think it has something to do with brains, but his writing is all weird. I can't read it well. Frustrated, Krista closed the book and put it back on the table. She walked over to her bed where the blankets awaited. *At least I can try to stay warm.*

The sound of locks rattling caught her attention and the front door swung open. Two men walked in; one was Smyth, wearing a long black shirt, and the other was Paladin, who wore the same tunic and boots as the first time Krista saw him.

"Good morning, Krista. I hope your rest was better than the night before. You've slept for just over a full day." Paladin's robust voice echoed in the room.

Krista nodded and put on a weak smile.

"We've prepared a bath for you, and a maid will take your clothes to be washed."

"Thank you," Krista said, sliding from her bed.

Paladin smiled and led Krista out of the office. Exiting the room, she soaked up the scenery. It was a large stone-floored hallway that seemed to extend forever. The red brick wall trimming was covered in planks of wood painted a forest green. On the bricks were mounted a range of wall scrolls, armour, weapons, and highly detailed paintings of clouds and humans with feathered wings. The ceiling was finished with green wooden archways that ran down every hall.

Krista's eyes were wide. *This puts the High District to shame.*

Paladin led her down the hall and Smyth followed behind her. She wasn't sure why, but he made her uncomfortable. Maybe it was his scarred face, or maybe it was the way he scowled when he looked at her. But what could she do? Tell Paladin? They were kind enough to escort her to a bath, let alone allow her to bathe in the first place. She recalled the humans being a cruel race that were unaccepting of other species; after all, they exiled her entire race.

Krista did her best to make a mental map of the path she took, in case she had to escape. She took note of a suit of armour they passed, which was plated from head to toe and had red paint along the rims. Paladin took her straight down the long hall for at least a minute, then they took a right, which led to a wide stone stairway up to the second level.

I wonder how many floors there are.

Paladin didn't go as far down the second-floor hall; they stopped by a door about 50 paces away from the stairs where a blonde human female, pale as a sheet of paper, stood smiling as they approached her. She was wearing a black dress and a white apron.

Paladin stopped by the door and gestured to the woman. "Give Lady Marilyn your clothes and you may use the tub inside. Your clothes will be brought back when they're clean."

Krista made a curtsy. "Thank you, Paladin."

"Inform me when she's done," he instructed the female, then nodded at Smyth. "Come, Smyth."

The man followed behind Paladin and the two returned to the stairway, leaving Krista with the woman.

"Hi." Krista waved.

The human seemed young and she nodded at Krista, averting her green eyes. The lack of eye contact and biting of her lip made Krista wonder if the woman was scared of her reptilian physique.

Krista scratched her head. "Let me slip out of these clothes." She pushed the door open, seeing it was not closed.

The door creaked open and she stepped into the room. Inside, a metal oval-shaped bathtub waited. There was a mirror, a small stool, and a window. The floor in this room was made of wood and it also creaked as she walked on it.

Krista moved behind the door and removed her clothes, leaving herself bare. She glanced at the blue tattoo on the lower left portion of her stomach. It was given to her as initiation into the Eyes of Eternal Life. She admired the simplicity of its design, the outlined oval with pointed ends, the single line inside the oval, and the triangles along the outer bottom curve. *It looks like an eye with teeth.*

Krista folded the garments, and then, with both hands, she passed them around the door and handed them to the maid.

The human took the clothes and Krista shut the door. "Thank you." She turned the lock on the knob and made sure it wouldn't open. *Just in case.*

Moving toward the tub, she sniffed it, making sure the liquid inside was water. Perhaps she was being paranoid, but the humans made her uncomfortable. Krista remembered all too well what they did to her kind and it was hard to trust them so easily again. Being back on the surface was such a drastic change. Her people had a whole new culture, a new life in the underworld and now the surface felt like a foreign land. Krista tested the temperature with her toe to feel the water was hot; it was soothing on her frozen body.

Pleased with the temperature, she slid herself into the metal tub and embraced the heat of the water. Krista rejoiced in the returning feeling of warmth. In the underworld, she always bathed at Magma Falls, where the water was cool. Krista knew that the vazeleads who lived in the Commoner's District heated their water for warm baths such as this, but never before had she experienced it. Even before her people's banishment, her mother would simply scrub her in the cool river just to get the dirt off. Washing was not something vazeleads normally used for relaxation.

The moment she immersed her limbs in the tub, the dried blood began to wash off and revealed the mark on her right palm.

Krista felt a stinging sensation and raised her hand in the air, looking at the circular burn. *It can't be . . .*

The mark looked exactly how Darkwing had described the mark on her neck given to her by Ast'Bala: a circular formation with an eye in the centre, surrounded by two triangles, one slightly longer than the other. Had Danil given her the full dose of Mental Damnation? *Abesun had a mark just like this one on his palm too.*

She swallowed heavily and brought her hand down in the water again. *It really is it.* Krista felt her stomach turn. Abesun had informed her it made you go into a hell called Dreadweave Pass when you're dreaming. She had no idea what that meant and did not want to meet the being known as the Weaver that Ast'Bala and Danil spoke about. *Am I going to start going to Dreadweave Pass when I sleep?*

She took her time bathing, washing the blood from her body and focusing on the change in temperature, trying to keep her mind off discovery on her hand and the fact she was now on the surface world.

None of this makes sense. I just want to go home, but I have no idea how to get back to the underworld and find Darkwing. Do I try and find Mount Kuzuchi and climb to the top and jump in?

The thought of Darkwing made her heart sink and she swallowed heavily. He was all she'd had during their transformation in the underworld. Darkwing had helped her fend off the Corrupt and rebellious vazeleads while the Five Guardians struggled toward unity of their people and to build the City of Renascence. She was certain she would not be alive today if it was not for Darkwing.

I'm sure he is okay; I often got in his way, anyway. Some time alone might be good for him.

Krista looked around the room; it was about a third of the size of the office she'd been in earlier. A window was above the tub, keeping her hidden from the outside world.

I wonder what outside looks like. I haven't seen the surface in so long.

She had to see. Slowly, Krista stood to try and look outside. Even climbing onto the rim of the tub, the window was too high. But she had to know what the surface world looked like. Krista slid down into the water and cleaned the rest of her body just as a knock came at the door.

"Your clothes are washed. I'll leave them here for you," came the maid's voice.

"Thank you!" Krista said with a smile.

She was excited that the humans were taking such care of her. It reminded her of her childish dreams of a luxurious life in the City of Renascence's citadel: being able to decide what she wanted, having servants cater to her needs. She used to fantasize about falling in love with guardian Cae, the youngest and most handsome of the Five Guardians.

But that was before Ast'Bala tore his head off.

Ast'Bala claimed that Cae had gone mad with Mental Damnation first and the two then fought to the death. With Cae dead, living the dream of luxury didn't seem as important, and she knew she had to be cautious about these humans.

They banished my people from the surface. But I guess there's no reason why I can't enjoy a little bit of luxury right now.

Krista lost all sense of time in the bath; soon, another knock came at the door.

"Krista, are you all right?" Paladin's voice came.

She got out of the tub. "Yes, I'm fine."

"You've been in there for well over an hour."

"Oh, I didn't realize. It was just so peaceful," Krista said, glancing around the room. A towel was folded on the stool for her; she took it and started to dry herself off.

"Don't hurry yourself, then."

Krista felt rushed anyway, and folded the towel around her body before unlocking the door. She opened it to see Paladin standing to the side of the entrance. He looked down at her and smiled.

She smiled back and pushed her wet feathers aside. "Thank you again for the bath," she said with a toothy smile.

"You're most welcome." He took a bow.

Krista saw her clothes neatly piled by the doorframe, so she leaned down and took them in her arms. They were mostly dry, with just a few damp spots.

"I'll be back." Krista stepped into the room and closed the door behind her.

"I came by and checked on you during the night," Paladin said. "Your sleep seemed as restless as the night before. Are you sure you're feeling better?"

Krista began putting on her clothes, enjoying the clean fabric against her tingling skin. "I don't know."

I remember a voice whispering in weird wording, but didn't see anything.

Putting on her dress, Krista noticed her arm that Danil had carved into. There was a now a large scar running down it.

So ugly.

She opened the door and fixed the top of her dress. "I don't recall anything, really."

"Whatever is happening in your sleep, we'll figure it out. A doctor is on his way back from a previous patient, and he'll be willing to examine the situation more closely."

A doctor? I don't need one. Nothing is wrong with me. She began to play with the tip of her tail with her fingers, an old nervous habit. "What do you plan to do with me?"

Paladin smiled. "I am a paladin. I want to ensure you're healthy."

Krista squinted, uncertain if he was lying or telling the truth. She vividly remembered how ruthless the paladins were to her people.

Paladin pointed down the stairs. "I'm currently training some lads to become soldiers. Would you care to join me?"

"Outside?"

"Of course."

She smiled. "I'd love to."

"Right this way, then." Paladin led Krista from the second level to the first floor. He walked straight across the hall from the stairway where two closed doors reinforced with steel plating were at the end.

Outside, on the surface world, Krista thought in awe. She was going to step on grass. She couldn't even remember how it felt.

Once they reached the doors, Paladin pushed them open with both hands and Krista followed close behind him. As she took her first step past the door, a beam of light blazed in her eyes. She stopped in her tracks and squinted, trying to adjust to the change in brightness.

Paladin looked back at her and brought his hand on her back. "Come, the trainees are this way." He moved her forward beyond the door into the outside world.

She could feel his warm, rough hands on her scaly back. Krista kept her eyes shielded from the brightness of the sun. Her eyes adjusted slowly and she could see a dirt road with green grass on both sides. Far in the distance, she could make out large walls surrounding the terrain. The sky was light blue and the sun bore down on them. Its heat was soothing on her body, yet the strange feeling in her veins perked up again.

"You're sure you are fine?" Paladin asked as he continued to guide her down the road.

Krista nodded. "It must just be the sun; the underworld has little light. Where are we?"

"We are in the High Barracks of Zingalg. A place where the most impressive warriors of the kingdom train and rest."

Paladin took Krista down the dirt road that trailed off into a fork. He led her off to the right, where the road branched off to a picket-fenced area. Inside the fence, there was a large dirt patch where about a dozen human boys fought one another with wooden swords. They kicked up dust in the air as they swung their weapons at each other. The sound of wood splintering echoed repeatedly.

"These boys here are to become the greatest soldiers the kingdom has ever known."

"They're learning to fight with sticks?" Krista asked, watching the boys fight. Their attacks seemed clumsy and they swung their wooden blades wildly. The boys were not the type of warriors Krista was used to seeing.

The Renascence Guard are way more impressive.

Paladin chuckled. "Training swords. Later, they'll be given real swords, then eventually I will send them on missions. They're young and overconfident, and they need time to mature."

Krista lost her attention on Paladin's words. He continued to talk about the training techniques used to turn the boys into warriors but the sun was too much for her to keep focused. The light felt as if it was piercing through her skin and slowly baking her innards.

It's just me overreacting. I've been on the surface before.

A blond boy glanced at Krista as she and Paladin got closer to the training ground. His glance caused him to lower his guard and his opponent swung at him ruthlessly. The blond was struck in the chest, throwing him to the ground.

"Focus on your fight, boy!" Paladin shouted.

"Don't they ever get tired of fighting?" Krista asked.

"Tiredness is a weak emotion. Whether they like it or not, they fight."

"Why?"

"It builds up endurance."

"No, I mean, why do they want to fight? And become warriors?"

Paladin thought about her question before responding. "I'm afraid they weren't given much of a choice. Their parents sent them off and we inspected them to see if they were suited. Parents send their children here in hopes that they will bring honour to their family name."

The two stopped at the end of the dirt road and kept close to the picket fence.

"They seem pretty focused." Krista folded her arms.

"Not quite. Less than half of these boys would have made it in here if I had tested them for acceptance into the barracks."

Krista leaned against the fence; her eyes were squinted while looking up at Paladin. "So why do humans need such warriors? Isn't the Drac Age over? It's not like you have big monsters to worry about."

"The world has changed, Krista." Paladin sighed. "Man split their unity after the destruction of the draconem and the banishment of your people. No one was able to retain order and the kingdoms that were once friends became foes."

"You fight amongst yourselves?"

"Yes, it is most unfortunate."

The two watched the boys fight in silence. It was depressing to hear that the humans now fought one another after they had banded together and brought an end to the draconem.

They're no different than my people now.

"Poor attempt!" Paladin shouted. He shook his head and looked at Krista. "These boys need a lot of work." He leaped over the fence and approached a pair of them.

One had dropped his sword and leaned down to pick it up.

"None of you put any effort in fighting one another." Paladin glared into the eyes of the two boys. "I expect you to work harder."

The boys kept their heads lowered, saying nothing.

Paladin raised his hand. "Your lunches are ready; be gone!" He waved his hand and returned to the fence where Krista watched.

She examined the boys tucking their swords in their belts and leaving the training ground one by one. They walked out onto the dirt road leading back to the building Krista had come from.

As the blond boy walked past the fence, his bright blue eyes locked with Krista's.

Paladin leaped over the fence again and put his hand on Krista's shoulder. "Keep moving," he ordered.

Being around these boys sure changes Paladin. One moment Paladin was friendly and caring to her, then the next he was directing her much like the Renascence Guard did.

Maybe he isn't happy with the boys' progress. Krista didn't know much about fighting, but it was obvious that they were sloppy swordsmen even compared to the convicts that escaped the City of Renascence's prison.

The blond boy rushed to catch up with Krista and Paladin. He cut in front of them. "Who's the girl?" he asked with a bright white smile.

She felt a surge pulsate from her heart at the sight of him, making her scales stand up on her back. Seeing him up close, Krista could truly admire his soft blond hair, bright blue eyes, and his charming grin. Even a rush of his scent entered her nostrils. It wasn't as potent as the other, older humans which made it far more appealing.

Paladin kept walking and pushed the boy aside. "None of your concern."

Krista looked back at the boy and smiled while waving at him.

"I'm not a bastard!" came a shout.

She brought her attention to the yell to see two boys brawling on the grass, one viciously pounding the other boy's face.

"Take it back!" the boy on top yelled.

Paladin let go of Krista and rushed to the side of the dirt road. "Enough!" He pushed the boy on top off into the grass. He started yelling but the words were quickly muffled as the other boys swarmed around, chattering to one another.

"So, are you from around the forest?"

Krista spun around to see the blond boy smiling at her. She took hold of one of her scalp-feathers and began to brush it with both hands. "No, not really."

The boy put his hands on his hips. "I can't say I've seen your kind around here before."

Krista put on a soft smile. "No, I'm not exactly from around here."

"Well I'd like to know more about you; we don't get visitors too often."

I don't really want to get into my crazy past, especially in front of this nice human. Krista decided to casually change topics. "From what Paladin said, you train all the time. You must get really tired, training here all day."

The boy smiled and put his hand on the hilt of his sword. "Ah well, it's all part of our duty to the kingdom."

Krista giggled. She felt nervous being alone with the boy; he was friendly, charming and confident, characteristics not seen in vazeleads. "It must be exciting having a meaningful duty to your people."

Nodding, the boy agreed. "It is, but also plenty of work. Not just anyone can be here, you know." He brushed his sweaty hair from his face. "What's your name?"

"Krista. My name is Krista."

"I'm William," he said as he held out his hand.

Krista shook it. "It's nice to meet you." She liked the feeling of William's hand better than Paladin's. It was still firm, but softer.

"What brings you here?" he asked.

"Sorry?" Krista asked.

"To the barracks. I haven't seen you around here before."

I should have known what he meant! She felt an unusual headache burst into the frontal portion of her skull. "Oh, yeah. I think I've been here for only a day." *I'm just overwhelmed.* At that moment, her innards felt like they were being squeezed.

A slap was heard in the distance and the two looked over to see Paladin had hit one of the boys.

"Paladin is so uptight." William shook his head.

Krista looked back at the blond boy and he gasped.

"Krista!" he exclaimed.

"What?"

"You're bleeding!" He moved past her and waved at the crowd. "Paladin! Something's wrong with her!"

Krista glanced at her arm to see her scar was fine; no open wounds. She swallowed and felt the taste of blood fill her mouth. Then she realized that the blood was oozing from her nostrils.

Paladin left the boys and rushed to William and Krista. "What did you do?" he demanded.

"Nothing!" William shot back.

"Go have your lunch," Paladin ordered, taking Krista into his arms.

She cupped her nostrils, trying to stop the blood.

William nodded. "Yes, sir."

Krista watched as the boy slowly walked away, returning to the group of trainees. He looked back at her as Paladin marched her past the boys to the building they'd come from.

Paladin rushed down the dirt path and pulled open one of the doors with a single hand.

"What's happening to me?" Krista asked. Her vision was blurry and her brain felt like it was spinning around. She kept her head close to Paladin's chest and her hand against her nose.

"I'm not sure," Paladin said. "Your skin feels warm; you might have a fever."

He walked across the hall and up to the second level. Krista tried to watch where he was taking her but she was too dizzy.

Paladin took a couple turns until he stopped at a door. It was open and he pushed it aside with his shoulder, revealing an empty dark room with a metal bed and a small maple dresser.

He placed Krista on the bed, and got down on his knees so he was eye-level with her. "How do you feel?"

Krista let go of her nostrils and saw her hand was now covered with blood. She rubbed her arm with her clean hand. The feeling of her organs being squeezed did not go away. "It's hard to explain," she muttered. "At first my veins felt like they were boiling and now it's like I am being crushed from within."

While she spoke, she felt her strength slowly returning and the pressure from her organs decreasing. The throbbing veins slowed down and began to function as normal.

Paladin took a cloth from his pocket and wiped the blood from her lips and nose. "The bleeding seems to have stopped," he observed as he opened her mouth.

Krista gently broke free from his grasp. "I think outside had something to do with it. The light," she sniffled, feeling that there was still some blood in her nostrils.

Paladin placed his hand on her forehead. "Your temperature is returning to normal."

"Do you think the sun had something to do with it?"

"Possibly, which is rather odd—you told me that you were cold in the dark."

"The heat from the sun is soothing, but the light that it radiates is something different. It's not like fire or the molten surface light that the underworld has. It's like I'm being scrutinized."

Paladin rose and folded the towel into his pocket. "Perhaps it's best if you don't expose yourself to the daylight for now."

"Okay." Krista nodded.

Paladin spread his arms out. "This will be your room for the time being."

"Thank you." Krista smiled.

"Don't thank me. The door will be kept locked during the night. I don't think the night watch would be kind if they found you wandering about."

Krista nodded.

"Get some rest, Krista. You're not well yet," Paladin said, turning to leave the room.

Just as Paladin was at the door, Krista blurted, "William is a nice boy."

Paladin stopped. "Excuse me?" He looked over his shoulder.

She swallowed. "I mean, I'd like to spend more time with him."

"He doesn't concern you. He's merely a boy." Paladin turned away and closed the door, locking her inside.

CHAPTER IX

Alpha Male Tide

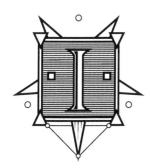t didn't take the Renascence Guard long to finish their raid of the Eyes of Eternal Life's temple. Following guardian Demontochai's orders, they tore and burned all the found artifacts and books that were related to the teachings of the Risen One. Any remaining reptilians they found in the underground chambers were slaughtered. Their screams could be heard echoing all throughout the cavern. If there was one thing that the Renascence Guard despised most, it was disloyalty to the Five Guardians.

After the slaughter, guardian Demontochai and his guards returned to the City of Renascence. The long day and a half journey was draining on the reptilians, having to endure the heavy winds and fine sand in their armour. Their leader, Demontochai, remained silent for the trip, displeased that they were unable to find his brother, Danil. Their two additional travelers—Darkwing and Alistind—stayed in the rear of the group. They had both lied to the Renascence Guard about why they were in the temple and felt like outsiders amongst the guard.

Particularly Darkwing was most uncomfortable. He couldn't help but feel his long-standing grudge against the Renascence Guard and the Five Guardians for the reality they had created for their people. Not to mention he kept a Blood Hound insignia in his pocket.

The two walked in silence for most of the journey; there wasn't much for them to say after the horror they had just experienced. Darkwing's closest friend, Krista, had vanished and Alistind's home destroyed.

Darkwing was at a complete loss what to do with himself.

I'm such a fool, he thought, playing back the events that led to seeing Krista be dragged away down the hall. Her screams played in his mind over and over. He knew he should have done better at protecting her.

I should have just gone after her. Why did I stop for Alistind? He thought to himself while looking over at the girl.

Alistind kept her head low. Her scalp-feathers draped down past her face, hiding her expression. The girl was likely pondering her own thoughts on what had happened.

I pitied her, Darkwing thought. It was the only explanation. Especially after his barbaric execution of the two Corrupt atop Magma Falls, he was vulnerable and easily sympathized with the girl when she pulled him into the cell.

It was at Krista's expense, though. I am such an idiot. Darkwing turned to face the pathway ahead. The group had covered a great deal of distance. The lights from windows and lanterns in the City of Renascence were finally coming into view.

"Darkwing?" Alistind gently spoke.

He blinked and looked over at the girl.

Her eyes still had the same ditzy blank glare that she had when she first met him. The difference was this time they were wide open, the spikes on her brows tilted; she was sad. "It's not over, Darkwing. The captain said she's alive. We'll find her."

Darkwing nodded, knowing he wasn't willing to give up. He couldn't give up. His life would be empty without Krista's pretty smile or her soft scalp-feathers. "I don't understand, though. I've been running this through my head during the trip back: Saulaph is dead, yet I saw him take Krista away. He never struck me as one to take his own life."

Alistind squinted. "I didn't think he was, either. I've known him for years. It's unlike him to do such a thing. There had to be someone else in that room. Demontochai said that Danil was there; do you think that had something to do with it?"

"Perhaps. If so, why would Danil tell Demontochai he was going to be in the temple? None of it adds up."

"No, it doesn't. I agree with the captain. It had to be some sort of ritual. What better place to perform one than in a sacred temple?"

"Yeah." Darkwing bit his lip. He didn't quite agree with her statement. There was nothing sacred about the Eyes of Eternal Life in his mind. They were simple naïve fools fantasizing about a better life. Alistind had a point: there was more going on in that temple than what appeared.

The group's travel led them back onto the Great Road in the outskirts of the Lower District. The Great Road acted as the main artery through all three districts of the city. The road was about three times wider than the rest and was used mainly by farmers shipping their goods to the city for sale.

Darkwing was all too familiar with the Lower District from his life as a 'scum' and his involvement with the Blood Hounds. It was the poorest-kept of all the districts. The roads were mostly flattened sand, with the occasional gravel road. In the thick of the district, most of the buildings had been abandoned due to the gang wars on the streets, and many civilians migrated to the Commoner's District. Some vazeleads remained in their homes in the Lower District but often maintained ties to the gangs to keep their houses. You could tell which homes were occupied by their locked doors. The abandoned buildings had no doors; gangs had smashed them in looking for supplies or food. They had chipped paint and shattered windows. Roofs had collapsed and walls had crumbled, making most of the Lower District uninhabitable by common folk. Darkwing did not find the environment disconcerting; it was where he spent most of his time with the Blood Hounds.

On the outskirts of the city, where the group walked, the buildings were scattered sparsely; clay structures with flat rooftops in varying degrees of completion. Darkwing recalled some of these structures being built by himself and Krista many years ago when they were being punished for thievery by the Renascence Guard. It seemed just like yesterday they were constructing the buildings, before they had met Draegust.

That was simpler time, Darkwing thought.

Off in the distance a loud bell was heard, ringing twice. The sound was faint but distinguishable: the Citadel Bell.

"Midnight!" Alistind's eyes widened.

"Appears that way." Darkwing had truly lost track of the days during their stay with the Eyes of Eternal Life. Without the Citadel Bell, it was difficult to judge what time it was.

"We've been traveling nonstop." Alistind rubbed her neck. "We'd best get some rest—especially you."

"Probably," Darkwing replied, eyeing his blood-crusted hand. He looked up and eyed the guards who kept marching up the Great Road leading deeper into the city. "We should ditch now that we're in the city." He stopped in his tracks.

"Should we tell them?"

Darkwing couldn't help but smirk at her comment. "No. They don't care. Come on. Traveling with them has me ill at ease." Darkwing snagged her arm and hurried her away from the Renascence Guard. He led her further away from the Great Road and into the side streets. The girl linked her arm with his, allowing her to keep up with his pace. Even though he felt physically sick that he'd failed to rescue Krista, it was nice to have Alistind around for comfort. She was oddly affectionate toward him, considering they barely knew each other. Then again, physical actions were often expressed more than words in vazelead social behavior.

"We're just going to leave them?" she asked.

"The last thing we need is to stay within the grasp of the Renascence Guard."

"Why? We haven't done anything to them."

"You haven't, but I have."

Alistind nodded while reaching into her pocket, only to pull out lint. "I have no dracoins for an inn."

Darkwing rubbed his forehead. "An inn? You really have been sheltered, haven't you? I know of a place we can get some rest."

"Where are we going?" she asked.

"To the Blood Hounds."

Alistind gasped. "Are we safe? The Blood Hounds are ferocious."

Darkwing shook his head, astonished by her words. *She doesn't get out much.* "We're going to take shelter at the Blood Hounds' hideout." He figured they'd sleep there for the night and then try to find out more about the ritual Krista was forced to take part in the next day.

But where to look? Darkwing thought, wondering where they could information on what happened at the temple.

It didn't take long for them to reach the familiar hideout of Darkwing's gang on the southern side of the district. He knew the Lower District well and could weave in and out of alleyways until they reached the side street leading to the hideout.

The two stepped off the side street in front of the Blood Hounds' lair—or, at least, the pile of rocks, metal scraps, and wood splinters that concealed it. Darkwing led Alistind through the debris—remnants of an old store. Navigating through the maze of wreckage, he sought out the stack of wooden boxes that masked the entrance to the hideout.

A few small box lids were tied together to form one large one. The stack of small boxes was clever camouflage: inside was a stairway leading beneath the ruins. The boxes were nailed together at the sides, forming an empty façade that concealed the stairs. Darkwing stopped abruptly. The lid was already cast aside, exposing the staircase leading down. That was unusual; the gang rarely left the door open.

Darkwing shrugged and leapt over the boxes, holding out a hand to assist Alistind. She smiled and gripped his palm to step over the boxes and into the hole. They watched their step, making their way down the steep stairs.

Darkwing drew out his dagger and moved Alistind behind him while he scanned ahead. "We've got to be careful," he said, creeping closer to the hideout entrance with his knees bent and dagger ready.

The wooden door at the bottom of the stairs was wide open and he peered ahead into open underground space that had been dug out from the dirt. The walls were mostly earth, and wooden poles were spread throughout the hideout to brace the wooden-plank ceiling. But the space was empty.

Alistind took Darkwing's hand when they entered the room. He looked around, realizing that the place had been abandoned.

"Darkwing!" a voice shouted, followed by a loud cough that sounded wet with mucus.

Darkwing didn't even have to look; he recognized the voice of Draegust. The Blood Hound leader lay on the ground just to the side of the wooden door inside the large hideout opening, waving his one arm in the air to get Darkwing's attention.

Sheathing his weapon, Darkwing rushed toward Draegust and helped him sit up. "What happened to you?" Darkwing asked.

Draegust coughed and brushed the scalp-feathers on the top of his head back, exposing the plucked sides. "I tried to make it into the hideout but I couldn't. I'm wounded."

"What happened to you?" Darkwing repeated.

"Our attack on the citadel . . ." He glanced at Alistind and back at Darkwing as he leaned against the wall beside him. "Guardian Demontochai is a monster . . ."

"Demontochai?" Alistind spoke up.

"We just saw him, though," Darkwing added.

Draegust's eyes widened. "Where?"

"He just returned to the city, when did you see him?"

"Days ago, after we last spoke." Draegust coughed. "We made it into the citadel without any problems. Their defenses are weak . . . We planned to kill the guardians and take the city for our own. As you know, I gathered the Blood Hounds after the prisoners were set free from the citadel."

"Yeah, after guardian Ast'Bala ripped guardian Cae's head off and made Danil loony."

". . . Ast'Bala battled Zeveal and now those two are nowhere to be seen. All that was left was Demontochai. We thought we could take him."

Darkwing folded his arms. He had been there when Draegust was mustering the gang members to overthrow the citadel, but refused to join the attack against Demontochai. He knew he had to hide Krista from Danil.

"That's a big task!" Alistind exclaimed.

"Demontochai tore us apart; he's nothing but a beast. His attacks were effortless but overwhelming, far more than guardian Cae ever was. We didn't expect such power." He shook his head. "One by one, he tore our spines from our backs and hearts from our ribcages, showing no mercy."

"Did anyone survive?" Darkwing asked.

"I was the only one. He butchered the other Blood Hounds. He tore their limbs off, forced them to eat their own fingers. Demontochai is not the noble guardian he's led everyone to believe. He enjoys torture."

"How'd you escape?"

"I don't think I did escape. I think he let me go," Draegust grunted as he stood.

"Your wounds don't seem to be so bad." Darkwing stood with him.

Draegust's attention landed on Alistind. "No, they're not. A broken rib and some bruises—nothing that won't heal." He slowly limped toward her and reached out to touch her face, leering. "Who's the new gal?"

Darkwing slapped Draegust's hand aside. "Don't touch her," he hissed.

Alistind moved to hide behind Darkwing.

"I'm not strong enough to fight you, boy"—Draegust said, eyeing Alistind's body—"so I'll just ask you: why do you defend the weak? Specifically, females?"

"They're our own people." Darkwing was furious, tired of how Draegust objectified females.

Draegust shook his head. "How's your whore doing?"

Darkwing charged at Draegust, throwing him to the floor, knowing he was referring to Krista. He landed on top with his hands clenched around the gang leader's neck. "Insult her again and they'll be your last words." His tail stood straight while the tip wiggled intensely.

Draegust had never treated Krista with respect in the past. He had known he could get away with molesting her because Darkwing looked up to the Blood Hounds, believing they offered the answer to a brighter future. Draegust had pushed it so far, he'd attempted to defile Krista while she was alone in the Lower District.

Before losing her, Darkwing would have shrugged off an event like that. He would have believed it was for the greater good, but not now. Now, he had to defend her honor. *I owe her that.*

"All right, get off me!" Draegust struggled.

"Why should I? You're nothing now; the Blood Hounds are dead!"

He pushed Draegust into the dirt and exposed his fangs, flicking his tongue at the downed thug.

"Please don't kill him!" Alistind pleaded. "No more blood!"

"Remember why you joined the Blood Hounds?" Draegust spoke through his teeth. "You wanted a better future for our people!"

Darkwing squeezed harder. "I couldn't care less about our people. I only joined so Krista could live in a better tomorrow!"

Draegust let out a choking cough as his skin started to turn white. Alistind tried to shove Darkwing away. "You're killing him!"

Darkwing let go, realizing the primal urges were affecting him again. He sat down beside Draegust.

Draegust gasped for air and sat up. "You really care for that girl, don't you?" he asked, rubbing his neck.

"Yes," Darkwing said. He stared at the ground, ashamed of his primitive actions. *I did it again. I can't control myself without her.*

Alistind sat beside the two. "We'll find Krista."

"What happened to her?" Draegust asked.

Darkwing shook his head, remembering what the captain had told him. "We hid in a cult temple, and she was taken away from me. The Renascence Guard raided the temple and couldn't find her. They told me she was forced to take part in a ritual."

"Ritual?"

"Yeah. The Renascence Guard captain said she's most likely alive, but I have no idea where to search now." Darkwing kicked a small rock, frustrated.

Draegust grunted as he relaxed his posture. "Any idea what type of ritual it was?"

"No."

The three sat in silence. Each one had lost something dear to them that day: Darkwing lost Krista, Draegust his gang, and Alistind, her faith.

It was oddly amusing to Darkwing that they all had nothing to do now that their obsessions had been taken away from them. Darkwing often considered the idea that a greater being—a god—simply toyed with their lives and saw dark humour in situations like this. It made life easier when he could blame something, a force that could not be seen, instead of blaming himself. Even though he knew he *was* to blame.

"I've got nothing left, Darkwing." Draegust sighed. "The Blood Hounds are dead; we're the only ones that remain. Witnessing Demontochai's strength made me understand that he's far superior to any vazelead. No one can overpower him. I'm on my own now."

Darkwing looked over at Draegust. "What are you getting at?"

"I have a few hunches that may lead you to Krista." He looked down to the ground. "If I can join you in your quest to find her, I'll share them with you."

"You want to help find her?" Darkwing scowled. "So you can try to rape her again? You're no less of a monster than the guardians."

Draegust nodded slowly in agreement. "I've got nothing good to say about myself, kid."

Alistind blinked and brushed her scalp-feathers back. "Darkwing, do you have any plans to find her?"

He shook his head no.

"Then why don't we let him help? We have nothing else to go on."

"I'll prove my loyalty." Draegust looked over at Darkwing. "I thrive on adventure and danger. Shit, it's all I know." He picked up a pebble and threw it against the nearest wall. "If you don't let me find her with you, I'll be no different than the others in this city. Scum, leeching from the streets."

Darkwing could not help but smirk, amused by Draegust's words. "You want me to feel pity for you? The same way you felt pity for Krista when you tried to force yourself on her?"

Draegust rose from his seat. "I said I'd prove my loyalty!" he hissed. "I can start by taking you to someone who understands rituals."

"It's a good idea, Darkwing," Alistind offered.

Darkwing glanced at the two. Clearly, Alistind had bought into Draegust's side of the debate. She obviously didn't understand what he had done to Krista—but then again, no one ever did in this city. Vazeleads were barbarians, rapist, murderers, and robbers. It was the reason why he'd joined the Blood Hounds in the first place: to change things. It was clear to him now that Krista had been right from the start. The Blood Hounds weren't the answer. Draegust was the same as the rest of their people; no less power-hungry than the Renascence Guard.

However, things were different now. The Blood Hounds were gone. Draegust was aware of that and it seemed he wanted to move on with his life. But what was the benefit for him in finding Krista?

Darkwing spat on the ground and rose to his feet, eyes locked with Draegust. "You'll prove your loyalty?"

"Yes."

Darkwing put out his hand. "Then prove it."

Draegust gripped his hand, keeping eye contact. "I will."

CHAPTER X

Two Vazeleads?

epentance: a word that holds a heavy weight on one's psyche—that is, if they understand the sensation of guilt from an action. Even if one isn't the direct cause of the situation, one can still feel a sense of accountability for what occurred. They may feel they could have prevented the affair or felt powerless in its wake. How long does one hold onto these negative emotions until no longer haunted by them?

"Paladins have been known to act quickly before processing a scenario. What happened in the past is not your fault," a high-pitched yet manly voice spoke while he stared at a bronze cup filled with water. The man brushed his black curly hair out of his face while keeping a cold gaze on the cup. His scarred lips were expressionless.

The cup rested on an oak table, gripped tightly by another man's large hands. He stared at the liquid inside, seeing a faint reflection of the dirty-blonde hair that draped down past his face. The other details of his figure were shrouded in the darkness; only the silhouette of his face appeared.

I am simply a reflection of a time that has come and gone, the man thought.

"Paladin?" the curly-haired man asked.

"Yes, Smyth?" Paladin asked as he looked up to his companion, who sat on the opposite end of the table.

"I was saying you cannot hold yourself responsible for what happened on Mount Kuzuchi all those years ago. There were much larger events at play than what one man can control."

"I disagree with that. The whole event was orchestrated and executed by Karazickle, one draconem. A man and a draconem are still each a single individual." *I could have prevented it, if I had known sooner.*

Paladin looked out to the window behind Smyth where he could see the sun begin to set, projecting an orange hue onto the landscape. They sat on the second level of the keep, in one of the study rooms. The two of them had taken some books from the nearby shelves. The manuscripts were filled with information about rituals and tribal species in the Kingdom of Zingalg.

Paladin looked down to his open book where some illustrations of swirls and circles were accompanied by brief descriptions. "Nothing explains why the Drac Lord was disguised as Saule, or why he wanted to be rid of the vazelead people to begin with."

Smyth closed his book. "Whatever the Drac Lord Karazickle wanted out of the vazelead people had little to do with us, therefore it has little to do with you."

"That is why he slaughtered my comrades? That is why he destroyed the Paladins of Zeal and dissolved the Knight's Union?"

Smyth sighed, clearly agitated at Paladin's negativity. "Yes, he possibly held a grudge toward the humans for ending the Drac Age. Who knows, if Zalphium had never exposed him for being the Drac Lord we may be living in a very different time. Karazickle would possibly still be disguised as Saule—a wolf in sheep's clothing."

"I wouldn't call us sheep." Paladin folded his arms.

"I beg to differ. At the time? Humanity obeyed the Council of Just without question. It was because of the events on Mount Kuzuchi that humanity began to question themselves. As tragic as it was, that event woke our people up."

"Which also led us to fight amongst one another. We simply cannot live without war."

Smyth nodded. "That is beside the point. There has been no sign of Karazickle since. What's done is done. You followed your duty to the Paladins of Zeal that day and you're simply lucky to be alive."

"Perhaps luck, perhaps God's will. I cannot simply let go of the guilt that weighs down on me. I can only pray that the Drac Lord will return."

"Pray that he returns? What for? Revenge? That is not in the paladin code."

"Retribution for my brethren and the vazelead people's banishment is worthy of the code."

"It has been two centuries since the event on Mount Kuzuchi. Karazickle succeeded in banishing the vazelead people and has been in hiding ever since. Karazickle and the draconem are no longer a threat. Merely shadows of our past."

Paladin tightened his fist. "He better pray I do not find him."

Smyth gestured at Paladin's open book. "We're getting sidetracked."

Paladin released his grip and looked back down at his open book. "That event strikes a chord with me, a wound that has yet to be mended. I'm simply trying to figure out how this whole thing is connected."

"Connected with the vazelead girl spawning in the forest?"

"Yes. If we trace our steps back to the origins of this event, it may shed some light on how Krista appeared here." Paladin stroked his beard.

"You may be looking too far back." Smyth placed his index finger on the table. "I am willing to place my bets on this girl and Karazickle being unrelated. The underworld is a vast and mysterious landscape that we know nothing about. The vazelead people could have learned unthinkable powers down there that broke the holy shackles the paladins placed."

"You raise a good point. Prayers of Power cannot be broken by anything in the mortal realm, but . . ."

Smyth folded his arms. "Plus, you mentioned on the day we found her that you think it has to do with some necromantic blood ritual? That has no relation to draconem."

"It is just a hypothesis. Like I said, a Prayer of Power comes from the Heavenly Kingdoms. So it would take something of equal ability to counter it—something from Dega'Mostikas's Triangle perhaps. Which would mean you are right, it has nothing to do with the draconem. They are power-hungry but do not utilize demonic power."

"Precisely."

Paladin sighed and closed the book in front of him. "Perhaps I am letting my past haunt me and simply wishing the two could be connected. Krista's arrival in the forest is far too obscure to be of this world."

"Despite our political differences with the other kingdoms and the occasional war, we haven't had anything this troublesome since the vazelead banishment. If it is related to Dega'Mostikas, what does that mean? Are the vazeleads working with the afterlife? With demons?"

"I don't know." Paladin let go of his cup and stood from his seat. "This is why I must return to the ritual site tonight. I'll see what other knowledge I can gather from where we found Krista."

Smyth stood and turned to eye the window. "I will join you."

"No need for that. You are better to continue our research here, in the study. See if you can find anything useful."

"We've been through these books," said Smyth. "No records are even close to what we saw there."

"You won't understand the ritual site any more than the first time."

"Perhaps, or perhaps not. But I want to understand this as much as you. The burden need not rest on you alone. Besides, I have had a fair share of exposure to demonic practices."

Paladin nodded. "Of course. Your cousin. Let us go."

"Don't you have any more courses to instruct today?"

"Not tonight. I've decided to reduce the time I spend training the boys throughout the day. At least until we get this under wraps. Krista's arrival is significant and may signal trouble for the kingdom."

The two marched quickly from study room, walking side by side. Paladin kept his gaze forward, eying the exit they strolled down the hall. He wanted to find some answers about the summoning circle before anything else occurred. There were too many variables at play here that left him ill at ease. A part of him wished that the draconem were involved; he could come face-to-face with Karazickle after two centuries since their last encounter.

Focus, he thought to himself, slightly surprised at his fixation on the draconem. *I suppose I am only human.*

Smyth and Paladin stopped by Paladin's quarters before heading to the first level of the keep so Paladin could grab his claymore. The two then exited the keep through the front entrance on the main floor, maintaining their pace while they headed for the stables. The sun still peeked over the horizon.

Paladin didn't want to the ritual to be an unknown any longer. The sooner they revisited the site, the sooner they could resolve their situation.

The two mounted their black horses and barged out of the stables, riding straight for the main gate of the High Barracks. Paladin and Smyth rode side by side while the two guards quickly released the locks on each side of the large wooden gate.

"Surprising how efficiently they open the gate when they aren't intoxicated, isn't it?" Paladin shouted to Smyth as they dashed through the entryway.

"It was the yearly celebration!" Smyth called back.

Excuses, Paladin thought to himself. He understood that the men looked forward to the yearly celebration to unwind from their serious lives. However, if there was an emergency, their inebriated state made them less effective soldiers. They were lucky that two nights ago it was only a reptilian girl that arrived. What would have they done if something else spawned from the ritual site? The intoxicated fools would have been unable to fight.

It didn't matter now. Unfortunately, that was one debate Paladin was never going to win against Smyth or anyone in the High Barracks for that matter. They were all too invested in the yearly celebration to ever agree, despite the facts he provided.

The two bobbed on their horses, riding swiftly along the dirt road, retracing the steps they took mere nights ago when they first discovered Krista. The sun had now retreated beyond the horizon, leaving them in an ever-darkening environment. They rode in silence for a good portion of the trip until Paladin slowed his horse, Smyth doing the same.

"I believe it was here," Paladin said while sliding out of the saddle.

"Are you sure? We really should have left a landmark last time." Smyth got off his horse and held onto the leather strap, leading his animal toward its comrade. "I can't smell the burning metal from the previous night either."

"Nor can I, but listen."

Smyth stopped next to Paladin. There was a slight breeze that caused some leaves to rustle while the horses snorted.

"Nothing really," he replied.

"Exactly. Where is the wild life? No activity around here. They've strayed from this area, meaning the ritual site must be near. If the ritual is related to Dega'Mostikas's Triangle, then this is unholy ground."

Paladin stared off into the dense foliage. The forestry darkened until it was pitch black and impossible to see through. Their view was drastically limited as the sun vanished, leaving them in pure darkness. They could see barely a couple feet in front of them, leaving them to wander in hopes of going in the right direction.

Smyth stroked his neck. "I don't remember it being this dark."

Paladin ignored his comment while stepping forward, drawing his sword instinctively as he did. "It's this way."

"How can you be so sure?" Smyth replied, following behind.

"God leads us, my friend." Paladin slowed his pace but continued into the thick vegetation. He knew that Smyth would quit talking if he referenced their lord. What else could he say to that? Truthfully, he was taking an educated guess based on timing and the surrounding area—and putting his faith in God to guide them. But Smyth didn't need to know that; he needed only to follow.

Smyth grunted while his face collided with a branch. "I can't see a thing," he complained

"We'll fix that." Paladin extended his free hand. "Father, grant us sight in the darkest of times. Bless us with your eternal light." He closed his hand and pressed it against his chest, causing a spark of white light to ignite from his breastplate. The spark expanded and dimmed to create a soft white light radiating from Paladin's entire body. "Amen," he added.

"Thank you," Smyth said while drawing a short sword from his belt. "We can at least see what is ahead of us, in case we run into trolls."

"They will leave us alone."

"What makes you so sure?"

"If the animals are nowhere to be found, the trolls won't want to be involved with this place either."

The two continued to walk through the thick forestry with Paladin leading the way for several minutes. They brushed branches aside and stepped over thick roots until they finally broke through a set of bushes, stepping onto a bare, open patch. The size and scorched earth made it easy to identify as the ritual site.

"My God," Smyth muttered while eying the scene. "It is just as chilling as I remember."

"Less animated, too." Paladin sheathed his sword and handed his horse's leather reins to Smyth. "Hold this. I'm going to investigate," he said, and cautiously moved toward the ritual circle. The smoke and glow were gone, leaving nothing but dark, scorched ground.

Smyth stepped forward, pulling the horses with him. They huffed and jerked their heads back, forcing him to stop. "Woah!" he exclaimed.

Paladin looked back at his friend who struggled to calm the animals. "Tie them up, like last time."

"Whatever this is, they want nothing to do with it," Smyth said while leading the horses to a nearby tree.

Paladin walked toward the ritual circle, examining the ground as he did before. Now that the smoke had cleared, he was able to see the burn marks in the barren patch clearly. It appeared to be a blast that originated from the centre of the circle—where they found Krista. The scorch marks forming the ritual circle and the runes were still clearly visible. They weren't glowing anymore but they were pitch black, proving they had once burned much hotter than the surrounding blast.

Paladin got down to examine the surrounding scorch marks again—nothing unusual about them. For all he could tell it was caused by a fire.

An unnatural flame from a necromantic ritual.

"Find anything?" Smyth asked, walking over.

"Nothing yet." Paladin's eyes wandered ahead toward where they found Krista's body. The blood from the previous night had dried up, staining the ground in the central point of the surrounding scorch marks that formed the runes.

"There's no heat here either," Paladin said. "Not like last time." He marched over to the nearest runes to examine them. They were not ones he recognized in any ritualistic practices he had seen before. Each rune was simplistic in design on their own but combined in groups of four or more, they ranged in size and orientation. It was as he hypothesized: this was something otherworldly.

"This certainly doesn't look like what we found in the books," Smyth said, stopping beside him.

"Not at all."

"Still think it has to do with draconem?" Smyth sarcastically smirked.

Paladin shook his head. "I know my fixation on vengeance can blind me and encourage wishful thinking. These runes: they're the key to this ritual. Remember what Krista told us? She was with another vazelead?"

"Yes. Two others, if I recall. One was forced to shed their blood with her."

"And another vazelead made them do it. This other performed the necromantic ritual of blood. The odd part is he let Krista live. Her wound was carefully made; it avoided her major arteries. That takes precision." Paladin scanned the ground around them, examining everything within his projected light. "How did this vazelead come to such knowledge?" Paladin touched one of the scorched runes, feeling a depression in the dirt as if someone had used a rod to draw the lines.

"That is why we are here, is it not?"

"Keep your eyes out for anything else." Paladin stood and continued to examine the site.

"Like what?"

"Why would this other vazelead perform the ritual and send Krista here?"

"As a message, perhaps? The vazelead people might know that the shackles to the underworld are broken."

"It is a possibility. If so, they would be storming from the entrance at Mount Kuzuchi."

Smyth's eyes widened. "We should be preparing for their arrival then."

"Not yet. You've sent word to the king as I've instructed. We will wait for his order." Paladin stopped in his tracks when he passed the central point of the circle, stepping over Krista's dried blood. "As I said, it is a possibility that she is a message. But I think it is unlikely."

Paladin squinted while staring down at the dried blood in closer detail. The stained ground dented inward where Krista's body once lay. Around the rough indent of her form was the imprint of Paladin's knee. On the other side of where her body once rested were two footprints, twice the size of a man's, pressed into the dirt. They had two large toes; the indent merged into the one made by Krista's body, making it difficult to see how long they were.

"Smyth. This may be our answer."

Smyth hurried over to Paladin and his jaw dropped, staring at the footprints.

"The other vazelead that performed the ritual must have used Krista and her friend to return to the surface."

"And break the shackles over their people," Smyth added.

Paladin scanned the surrounding ground. No other large footsteps were visible: only the pair overlapping Krista' form. It is as if he vanished into thin air. Paladin turned his gaze to the stars, which had taken full form in the night.

Did they take flight? he thought.

"The tracks disappear," Smyth pointed out.

"Which is unsettling. They may have taken to the sky."

"A flying vazelead?" Smyth exclaimed.

"Based on the surroundings here, I would have to say so. The footprints indicate they and Krista were both at this site. Yet the other vazelead shows no other signs of being here."

"An airborne vazelead. The girl, Krista, looks nothing like the vazelead people written in the history books either. The underworld changed them far more than I could have imagined."

"I remember what vazeleads were," said Paladin. "Simple, brown-scaled humanoids with yellow eyes."

"Yet from what we saw of Krista, they have burning eyes and scorched skin, like spawns of Dega'Mostikas's or something."

"Now they can fly."

"What are we really dealing with here?"

Paladin rubbed his face and exhaled heavily. "I do not know." He was hoping that the ritual site would give them more answers when in truth, it only brewed more questions. Who is this flying vazelead? How did they know how to perform this ritual? Where are they now?

Smyth folded his arms. "We could possibly ask some of the surrounding villages if they've seen anything flying in the sky."

"It is a stretch—but worth an attempt." Paladin turned to face Smyth. "I'll leave that task to you. Send some of our men to visit the towns around the High Barracks to see if they have any insight into the incident."

"Of course, sir. Do we leave the ritual site?"

"We can gather nothing more from here. Come. Let's return to the barracks."

"What's our next step?" Smyth asked while the two turned to return to their steeds.

"We will see what we can find out from the surrounding villages and wait for the king's orders when he hears the news."

"It shouldn't be much longer before the message arrives," said Smyth. "We sent a courier that very night."

"Excellent. For now, we wait."

"What of Krista? She is the only piece of the puzzle we have."

"She is. I'm going to guess she isn't a message from the vazelead people. At least not from their military."

"Why is that?" Smyth asked when they reached their horses.

Paladin began to untie his horse from the tree. "Again, her cut marks were deliberate to avoid excessive bleeding. She told us she joined a cult to take shelter. I am thinking this cult had the knowledge to perform the necromantic ritual."

"So? They could have shared this information with the rest of their people."

"Unlikely. She used the word cult, often a derogatory term for an organized faith. They could be outcasts of the vazeleads."

"That's just a theory, though. Performing the ritual—now they could prove to their people that they are free, regaining their trust."

"That is true." Paladin nodded in the direction of the High Barracks.

"We need more answers, and the only one who can provide them is Krista."

"Will she talk?" Smyth asked while untying his horse from the tree. "She isn't the easiest one to deal with."

"She is in shock. I can only pray she will open up to me. Dr. Alsroc will want to examine the marks on her hand and neck. It will only add to her confusion."

"The Mental Damnation he is obsessed with? That has little importance compared to what *she* actually is."

"Maybe, maybe not. Why would she have the mark, then? I want to try to extract more information from her before the king makes a decision—and before Dr. Alsroc treats her as another test toy to study the Mental Damnation disease." Paladin tugged on his horse's muzzle, forcing it to walk into the thick foliage whence they came.

"How do you plan to do that?" Smyth asked, following behind.

Paladin turned back to face his comrade and said, "I'll make an offer that she cannot refuse."

CHAPTER XI

Everyone Has A Secret

Child.
Laughter flows with games.
Games flow with rules.
Rules flow with crime.
Do you amuse yourself?

Child.
Patience requires discipline.
Discipline requires teaching.
Teaching requires patience.
I'm out of the loop.

Child.
Will needs passion.
Passion needs strength.
Strength needs training.
Therefore I need you.

olling around on the cot, unsettled both physically and mentally, Krista groaned. Her headache escalated to a level of pain she didn't think was possible. Thoughts filled her mind: *Why does my head hurt so much? What are these words I keep hearing when I sleep? Is this going to get worse?* She had an awful feeling it was because of Ast'Bala's and Danil's marks.

It wasn't just the headaches; the rest of her body was no better. She could feel her heart beat at unstable rates. Blood rushed to her head with each pulse, making her limbs feel numb. Her innards felt like it was burning, yet her skin was chilled.

A voice echoed in her mind, the same voice, speaking nonsense to her for the past three nights. Every time the voice spoke, it felt as if the energy from her body was being sucked out.

Through the discomfort, Krista was unaware of her surroundings and accidentally rolled off the bed, falling onto the cold floor. She landed on her back and scurried to her feet. The rush to stand up shifted the blood flow from her head, offsetting her balance.

"Shit." Krista clutched the sides of her head in pain while swaying to keep upright.

She didn't feel safe in the small room Paladin had left her in. She felt claustrophobic. Even though small spaces had never bothered her before, it felt like she was trapped. Through the window on the opposite side of the room, Krista could see the sky was clear and dark. It was nighttime, with hundreds of stars sprinkling the midnight blue.

Focus on something else. I'm on the surface world—that's exciting! But the thoughts did no good; her body's turmoil overpowered her will.

She hissed. "I need fresh air." Krista wobbled over to the door and tried to open it but it was locked. *Right . . .*

Lightly, she knocked on the wooden door to see if anyone would hear her.

"What do you want?" came a man's muffled voice.

"Hi." She sniffed the door, trying to pick up the scent of the man behind it. It was the guard from the night before—the one who guarded her previous room.

"What?" the guard asked again.

"I'd like out; I want to take a walk."

The guard sighed. "Paladin ordered that your door remain shut unless he says otherwise."

Krista's headache flared again. "Bring him here, then!" She pounded on the door. *I don't have time for this.*

The guard did not respond.

Krista weakly hit the door once more and slid to her knees. "Open the door . . ."

Child!

The voices won't go away. Krista groaned and lay down on the stone floor, still clutching her head.

It was obvious that the guard couldn't care less about her pleading. She was just as displeased with the night as the day; the temperature had dropped, making the room feel subzero. The surface of her body was cool, yet her forehead burned.

Child! Listen . . .

"Go away!" Krista cried out.

She didn't think she would reply to the voice; she was certain it was only in her mind. But the closer she listened, the less the harsh voice seemed to be her imagination.

Girl, listen . . .

Slowly Krista rose from the ground, keeping her hands on the door for support. She brushed her scalp-feathers aside and looked around the room; where was the voice coming from?

Closer . . .

At first the voice seemed frightening, but the more attention she gave it, the more soothing it sounded and the clearer it became.

Yes, child. . .

As she focused on the voice her headache began to subside and her heart rate returned to normal.

Closer . . .

Krista pinpointed the voice; it was coming from the window and she slowly walked from the doorway to the window frame. She didn't know why she listened to its command, but it made her headache go away and that was worth it. Her body was exhausted and the voice seemed so welcoming.

She reached the window and saw nothing, so she leaned against the bricks and looked outside. Her eyes were used to the darkness and she could see clearly compared to the daytime. Now she could scan the whole barracks; in the distance there were stables, a garden surrounded by a crisscrossed fence, and various other buildings all surrounded by massive red brick walls.

Here, child!

The voice didn't originate from outside after all, but from the cracks within the metal window frame.

Krista squinted. "Hello?"

Wake up, child!

She shook her head. "But I am awake."

Black smoke slowly began to rise out of the crack and into the air.

Krista backed away from it and took a sniff, trying to pick up on the scent. It was odourless.

More smoke began to fill the room and swirled around in the air. It continued to grow outward, still staying in a compressed lump. The more smoke that came out, the more it began to take shape. At first there were two lumps: one on top and another bigger one on the bottom. The bottom lump stretched out and the shape of arms began to form, while the top lump began to mold into a head with an extended muzzle.

Bright blue smoke with a soft glow emerged from the crack, funneling inside the black smoke. It channeled through the black shape, and bore a striking resemblance to a creature known as a shade Krista had encountered in the underworld. Shades were intelligent lizard-shaped creatures that were highly tuned to presences that could not be detected with the five senses. Their bodies were made up of a translucent outer layer with a darker, black core inside, like an inverse version of the black and blue smoke. A shade's inner essence was said to be its spiritual portion—the one that could detect the feelings, thoughts and motives of those around them—while the exterior was its physical existence. Combined, the two shapes gave shades two unique bodies in a single bundle of existence.

The scary part about shades is they can read thoughts. Krista swallowed heavily, recalling the time she and Darkwing had broken into a potion shop and she'd been attacked by the shopkeeper's pet shade, which went wild at sensing her fear. *But shades are smooth, not all smoky.*

The black and blue smoke formed bright eyes, razor teeth and long, matted, tentacle-like hair. The wispy arms were thin but looked strong, and the hands had one thumb and two fingers each with extended claws.

The smoke began to compress and take on the texture of a smooth surface, almost like Krista's skin. The moonlight highlighted portions of the ethereal body.

Around the neck was a golden collar with hieroglyphics painted around it, much like the glyphs she'd seen in the Eyes of Eternal Life. The being did not grow legs; its torso merged into the smoke, which remained attached to the crack in the window.

Krista's jaw dropped. She was unsure whether she should be afraid or amazed. Either way, her headache was gone and her body stopped working in overdrive.

The being folded its arms and let out a deep growl. Its eyes locked on Krista. "So it appears you remain in this realm, child." The gravelly voice, that of a male, was followed by a close echo, almost sounding like two beings were talking simultaneously.

Krista scratched her head, uncertain what he meant. She was too distracted by his appearance. "What are you?"

"I am a ghoul. You've not heard of such?"

Krista shook her head.

"First sighting always horrifies mortals, knowing that we consume flesh, yet you remain calm. Why do you not fear me?"

"I didn't see anything to be afraid of." She massaged the side of her head. "Your voice is quite soothing," she said as a compliment.

The ghoul hissed. "What's your name, child?"

"Krista." She walked back and took a seat on her bed. "Yours?"

"I am Malpherities." He looked down at the scar on her arm. "That's a deep wound. How are you not dead?"

"Paladin saved me."

The ghoul's white eyes widened and he let out a satanic screech, his vocal cords vibrating at rapid speeds. The sound was like a thousand cries erupting from the depths of his throat.

Krista covered her ears to block out the shocking sound. She glanced back at the door to see if the guard would open it, but it remained closed.

Malpherities snorted. "Paladins cause nothing but chaos and havoc. They shove words of lies into your ears and poison your mind with false promises."

He really doesn't like paladins. Krista uncovered her ears. "You're a ghoul, you said?"

"Yes. Therefore, paladins are not my allies."

"Why?"

"We feast on the dead."

"But not the living?"

"No, not while the spirit is still in the body. A body with a spirit keeps it holy, and anything holy will burn me."

"Paladins are holy, and you are not. So that's why they're not your allies. That makes sense."

"You're a quick learner, child."

Krista wasn't sure if he was being genuine or sarcastic, but she figured she would brush the comment aside. "Are you from the underworld? I've seen something like you there; it's called a shade."

"Shades? No, child. Those diminutive creatures are trapped between this world and the afterlife. Their physical bodies here are of a beast, and their spirit is capable of so much more." The ghoul put on a wicked grin, showing the army of razor sharp teeth across his jaws. "If anything, I feel sorry for shades. Such brilliance locked inside a limiting existence." Malpherities moved closer to Krista and ran his claw from the mark on her neck, trailing down to the second mark on her palm with one long claw. "I come from Dreadweave Pass, child."

Malpherities's words flashed Krista back to guardian Danil, him holding her captive in the Eyes of Eternal Life, chaining her on the stone altar and carving the large gash into her arm.

So Danil did infect me. I do have Mental Damnation!

Krista gasped and got up from the bed, rushing to the door. "Don't take me to Dreadweave Pass! I don't want to go!" She pounded on the door. "Help!"

"Silence, child! Hush and let me explain. If the humans hear you, your life will become very complicated."

Krista stopped pounding and looked over her shoulder; she felt sick to her stomach. She had seen Ast'Bala and Danil, protectors of her people, change completely from this Mental Damnation. What could the disease do to her?

"I don't want to end up like my guardians." Krista turned around. "What's going to happen to me?" She hugged her arms around her.

"I'm not to bring you to Dreadweave Pass, child. Gatekeeper Danil has already accepted you into the realm."

"He hasn't taken me there yet, though. He only gave me this scar and this mark on my hand." She pointed at her arm.

"Danil is sophisticated. The scar on your arm has nothing to do with Dreadweave Pass or the Weaver—it was his free doing. Its meaning or purpose, I do not know. But the mark on your palm is your acceptance into Dreadweave Pass; his touch on your skin was enough. The first mark you got—the one on your neck—was just a flag to show Danil you were chosen. The other gatekeeper could not give you the full mark himself."

"Why couldn't he?" Krista asked.

"He has been given other duties from the Weaver." He looked around the tiny room. "I have been trying to contact you in your sleep, to find you before the Weaver does."

"Who is the Weaver?" Krista walked over to her bed, feeling a cold breeze enter the room.

"The Weaver rules Dreadweave Pass, and chooses the gatekeepers."

"So you were talking to me in my dreams?"

"If I did, you would have known my name already."

Krista felt her stomach turn upside down. "Someone has been talking to me in my sleep. Is it the Weaver?"

"Possibly."

"Why did you want to find me? Are you going to help me get away from him?"

"No one can escape the Weaver's realm."

Krista frowned, confused.

Malpherities looked to the ground. "Your dreams will only get worse, child, and turn into nightmares."

"Can you stop them?"

"No, I cannot; they're only images of Dreadweave Pass. Your visions will grow stronger until they become real. The feelings you feel during the night, the headaches, will grow stronger until you finally cross realms."

"Why have you been trying to contact me if you can't even help me?"

"I can't prevent the inevitable, but when you reach Dreadweave Pass, there is a world of opportunity if you have the right guide."

"I don't want to go. I don't want opportunity. I can't go!"

"You will go, child! Then I'll teach you to master realm-crossing at will. Just because you're in the Weaver's realm doesn't mean you cannot evade him. There is value in having you in the afterlife and in the mortal realm—there is a much larger issue at hand."

"Realm-crossing? To Dreadweave Pass? What larger issue?"

The locks to the room twisted and the door flung open.

Krista turned to see Paladin enter her room. She gasped and brought her arms to her chest. "Hi."

Paladin eyed Krista's messy scalp-feathers and wide-eyed expression. "The guard heard you yelling to yourself," he said.

She turned to Malpherities only to see an empty room. He was gone. "Who was I yelling at?" Krista asked, looking back at Paladin.

"Are you sure you're fine, Krista?" Paladin asked.

Krista nodded. "I just need to get some rest."

"All right, the doctor should be returning to the barracks soon. I think he'll help you greatly," Paladin said, leaving the room.

"Good night," Krista called out.

The door closed and the locks snapped together.

She looked around the room again, but she was alone. There was no sign that Malpherities had ever visited.

CHAPTER XII

Equals

Freedom.
My master demands.
As do I,
yet our vision does not align.
I must form my own plan.

Disloyalty.
My master punishes by death.
Obey his madness,
it would be nothing less.
I must act in stealth.

Plotting my escape.
Building relations,
Of whom I assign their stations.
All while holding in the ever-pressing hate.

Here I am,

In the land of the damned.

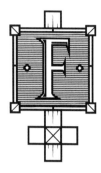ear: the root of all negative sensations. It extends further into emotions such as hate, jealousy, and resentment, to name a few. It is often an overlooked emotion because of these secondary terms. Not to Dievourse, though. He knows of his desires to express his anger and it certainly has little to do with fear. He is critical enough to understand that there intelligent fear and the fear provoked by conscious thought. Conscious fear is brewed by one's weak mind, toying with the endless possibilities of what could happen. Dievourse was certain in his thoughts and his actions. He only knew of practical fears, like his master's wrath.

I only fear the rational. The types of scenarios that are one hundred percent plausible and would harm me or end my life, like if the Weaver learns of my desire to stall his freedom, he thought to himself, keeping his gaze forward toward the wide-open mountain space.

Rational fear is something that every being needs to learn. It is not a sign of weakness. This type of fear will keep you alive. It is why I would not leap off this mountain, knowing the outcome would be catastrophic to my wellbeing. Intelligent fear is a sign of strength.

His black-and-red armour clanged with each step he took on the dark red granite ground, casually walking toward the end of the large plateau. He was well above the base level of Dreadweave Pass's nightmarish realm, making it impossible to see the terrain below the mountain. Only bright red sky with an orange horizon surrounded him and black swirling clouds just below the plateau. On each side of him, black stone blocks stacked to form columns on each side, making a pathway leading to the edge. Each block had minimalistic glyphs carved into it and was complete with a carved triangle on top. Dievourse had seen these symbols countless times before: they were the glyphs used by the Weaver in his necromantic rituals and the same glyphs he had seen in the Weaver's chamber.

The path led straight toward dozens of smooth black stone cylinder pillars aligned in concentric circles, the centre formation surrounding a black curved archway. The archway was nearly three times taller than Dievourse. It was complete with black spikes lined up along the top. Additional glyphs were carved onto the frame of the rift, these ones animated—glowing bright red—with smokeless flame burning from the outlines. Inside the archway was a spiraling vortex of glowing red lights and a subtle view of a frozen landscape; a gatekeeper's rift.

"You would think Ast'Bala would be waiting for us, considering this is his rift," came a raspy voice to Dievourse's side.

He glanced over to see his lieutenant who stared directly at the rift ahead of them. The puppet was dressed head to toe in studded leather armour. He had a mask covering his face, only revealing his stitched-on lips. His eyes were concealed by goggles, making them unreadable. He kept his hands firmly gripped on the sheathed daggers that draped on each side of his ribs, held up by leather straps across his chest and shoulders.

It seems just like yesterday I was with the surgeon building him, Dievourse thought, recalling when he first had the intelligence unit installed into the lieutenant's mind. *Although, with the time distortion of the Weaver's rifts, it is rather difficult to recall the exact time of an event.* He was grateful for his master giving him a loyal servant. It was one of the few things he could be thankful for. *I suppose he gave us life after death, but this wasn't quite the life I had expected.*

Dievourse puffed out his chest and nodded at his comrade. "He's occupied with more than just reaping innocence. The Weaver keeps him busy trying to convert his people's leaders into gatekeepers. We still need to arrange a squadron to guard the gate when he is absent," Dievourse replied, returning his gaze to the rift ahead.

"Can he be trusted?"

"I have spoken with him before and it is quite obvious he and Danil battle the Weaver's will. They want to do right by their people and we can use that to our advantage. Hence why he has not converted their two remaining leaders into gatekeepers."

"What if the Weaver were to find out, or El Aguro? They are keen on freeing him as soon as possible. The Weaver would lose all faith in you and possibly do much worse."

"Yes, this is why we must form allegiances with those who are not fully consumed by the Weaver's will."

"Like how we tried with Cursman?"

Dievourse ground his teeth. Hearing the name only irritated him. *The betrayer.* "That arrogant fool wishes for redemption in the eyes of the gods. He didn't share the same vision as you and I. Wherever he is, he'll rot away before he is redeemed. There is no redemption for our kind. This is why we must be the masters of our own destiny."

"That, I am willing to fight for."

"Danil and Ast'Bala also have a reason to fight: their people. As long as we remain resilient, the Weaver will not find out."

"His will flows through all of us. How is it possible for us to resist him sensing our plan to sabotage his freedom?"

"Cursman did," said Dievourse. "Unlike most puppets, we still possess free will. We can resist him."

"Sir, I fear it is a risk. His power is beyond ours."

"I will not deny that, lieutenant. He trusts me and I will ease his paranoia. In the end, the Weaver and I have the same objectives. This is all he can sense in my mind, and that is the only thought you should focus on when he speaks to you.."

"You talk as if you are equals with him."

Dievourse stopped in his tracks, turning to face his comrade. "Yes, the Weaver may be of heavenly origins, but he is drowned in his own power. This makes him childish. My history in the mortal realm and limited abilities have made me far more able than he ever will be." Dievourse scowled, staring at his ally.

The Lieutenant said nothing. He stared at him for several moments before a crackling noise erupted from the rift which was now only about a hundred paces away.

The two turned to see that an invisible force was pushing the vortex inside the rift forward, towards the two. The shape warped the frozen landscape, stretching it in the mold of the object. As it continued to push through, it formed a humanoid face, exposing more details as it continued to move. Eventually the central point of the vortex on the shape tore, causing red smoke to seep from the edges of the fresh tear.

The rip continued to grow bigger as a red reptilian face ripped through the bulge, exposing a black blindfold wrapped around his face. The blindfold and pointed features of the head were covered in ice and snow as gusts of ice-cold wind blew from the ripped vortex and past Dievourse and the lieutenant.

"Here he is." Dievourse straightened his posture while watching the gatekeeper continue to push through the seam. Thick red smoke took up the entirety of the rift until his massive, muscular form stepped into Dreadweave Pass. His tail swayed side to side, shaking off bits of snow and ice.

"General Dievourse." Ast'Bala's deep, booming voice echoed throughout the mountainscape as he folded his bat-like wings against his back. He stepped forward while brushing some snow off the black, sleeveless stola he wore.

"Gatekeeper Ast'Bala. Good to see you have not forgotten our gathering."

Ast'Bala stopped in his tracks, mere steps away from Dievourse and the lieutenant. He stood about twice as tall as the two before him. "Of course. As you mentioned, general, my options are limited."

Dievourse grinned. "That I did. Where is Gatekeeper Danil?"

"He is not my responsibility, you summoned us here."

Dievourse put his hands behind his back. "Aren't you and he leaders of your people? I thought you'd have some communication."

"Not after what I have done, or, what the Weaver made me do to our kind. It is unforgivable."

"Right, he made you free the prisoners, corrupting the city from within. Our master craves chaos. He much prefers destroying something and building anew. It is why he torments your mind: he wants to crush it."

Ast'Bala clutched his head. "I feel his pressure daily. It is difficult to resist. I thought you were going to convince him to stop this torture."

"I can only persuade him so much, Ast'Bala. In his eyes you serve him."

The lieutenant pointed to the red sky. "Sir, look."

Dievourse turned to look at the red sky, seeing a humanoid figure in the distance with wide bat-like wings spread, soaring toward them. "Perhaps Danil will be joining us after all."

Ast'Bala took a step back and growled. "He will not be pleased to see me."

"Don't try to solve this confrontation with violence. If we want to achieve anything we have to put our egos aside."

"Yes, Danil has been battling the Weaver's will on his own. He must know I still fight for our people, as he does."

"What he must know is he mustn't reap any more innocence. The Weaver must stay imprisoned."

The flying figure flapped his wings several more times, soaring closer to the plateau. Within minutes, the sound of whooshing air bounced against the mountainsides as the tailed reptilian being came into view. The long, tattered toga, scarred face, and long, black scalp-feathers were easily identifiable as Danil's.

He tilted his wings up to slow his speed and flapped a few times to gradually land in front of the three. His large two-toed claws hit the earth with a heavy thud, causing the ground to shake. His eyes stared directly at Ast'Bala, the fire around the sockets flickering intensely.

"You . . ." Danil sneered his high-pitched voice. He took a step forward, pointing viciously at Ast'Bala. "You caused all of this!"

Ast'Bala sized himself up with Danil while exposing his teeth. "I had no choice."

"You corrupted our people and destroyed the Five Guardians!"

Dievourse took a step forward, extending his hands toward each of the gatekeepers. "Enough! I didn't summon you two here to battle out your differences."

Danil relaxed his posture. "General Dievourse, I have heard much about you from the Weaver. You report directly to him. What do you want from us?"

"I do speak to our master, but that isn't why we are here."

Ast'Bala motioned at the general. "Hear him out, Danil."

Danil hissed and said, "Why should I listen to the likes of you?"

Dievourse nodded at Ast'Bala. "You should listen to your fellow gatekeeper because you two are in the same position."

"How so?"

"Gatekeeper El Aguro found your people and brought Ast'Bala and Cae to meet with the Weaver."

"Then this traitor killed Cae, freed our prisoners and destroyed the Five Guardians!"

"And now you both strive to resist the Weaver's will."

Danil folded his arms, eying the three of them.

"Now that I have your attention. I know the two of you are loyal to your people, yet your assignments from the Weaver have made this difficult, if not impossible. Ast'Bala has been ordered to convert the remaining guardians into gatekeepers, which is why you are here now, Danil." Dievourse pointed to the rift ahead of them. "The Weaver desires freedom. It makes him blind and unaware of the problems at hand."

"Which are?"

"He had you reap the innocence of a child, bringing it to Dreadweave Pass. That is not going to be the only child he wants you to reap. He needs more to be free."

"Yes, the Weaver went into detail about the necromantic ritual of blood he must perform to be free." Danil looked at Ast'Bala. "In fact, I was able to replicate this ritual."

Ast'Bala raised his spiked brow. "What do you mean?"

"The chaos you have caused allowed me to discover a way to free our people from the underworld, and I have. The Weaver spoke to me after you infected me. He told me of his need for the blood of the innocent to break the binds around him. I had a vision of the ritual that he projected into my mind so I would know why he needs the blood. I memorized the ritual and was able to perform it.

"You used the blood of children? Why?" demanded Ast'Bala.

"The Paladins of Zeal that shackled us use the same holy words that bound the Weaver. The ritual worked!"

Ast'Bala's jaw dropped. "You freed our people?"

"Yes, we can finally escape the underworld. I know brothers Demontochai and Zeveal will learn of the shackles being broken and bring our people to the surface world once again."

"How?"

"I informed Demontochai before I performed it," said Danil. "He will see the aftermath."

"What then?"

Dievourse cleared his throat. "I care little of your people, Danil. What you are telling me is you are familiar with the Weaver's ritual?"

"Yes, I am."

"Then the Weaver must have told you why it is so dangerous."

"Yes, the infectious touch Ast'Bala and I have on souls forces them to bypass the Heavenly Kingdom's sacred judgment where the soul will rest after death in the mortal realm."

Dievourse folded his arms. "Every soul since the creation of existence has been judged at the golden gates of the Heavenly Kingdoms, where they are to live in eternal peace beyond the gates or descend into one of the three hells of Dega'Mostikas's Triangle—one being Dreadweave Pass. The Heavenly Kingdoms would rain havoc and destruction upon the Weaver and his army if they discovered this pattern is broken."

"How would they do this?"

"A few souls here and there being brought to Dreadweave Pass can go unnoticed, especially thanks to the angel the Weaver has allied with in the Heavenly Kingdoms. If we start rapidly reaping souls . . . this will cause disruption. It will trigger a war between the Weaver and the Heavenly Kingdoms far too soon. The gods and angels will come to us." Dievourse pointed skyward. "We want the war up *there*, on *our* terms."

Danil glanced at Ast'Bala, then back at Dievourse. "How does this concern me?"

Ast'Bala stepped forward. "We must form unity, Danil. There may be bad blood between us, but we are still guardians!"

Dievourse shook his head. "Beside the point. You two have little to go on and no allies. Work with me to keep the Weaver imprisoned, for now."

Danil scowled. "What is in it for you, general?"

Dievourse's eyes scanned the three of the beings around him, staring from the lieutenant, to Ast'Bala and ending with Danil. "I want freedom, as do you all. On our terms."

Ast'Bala extended his claws. "We are enslaved to the Weaver's will. This is no way to live."

The lieutenant tightened his grip on his weapons and said, "We did not ask for this."

Danil nodded. "All right, say we are to form an allegiance. How do you plan to free us?"

Dievourse grinned. "I am glad you asked. There is a fifth ally who is key to our strategy . . ."

CHAPTER XIII

Replay

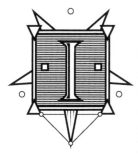 *lost her, it's my fault.* The words repeated in Darkwing's mind countless times. He was left to his thoughts during the night, exhausted from their travels and unable to get any sleep. He ran the mistakes he made with Krista over in his head numerous times.

Somehow I cannot help but think it's my fault.

He felt like a failure; he had failed not only himself but also his dear Krista. It had been just over a day, but it seemed like weeks since he'd last seen her. Darkwing was not used to the feeling of missing someone. It was a peculiar emotion that struck his heart heavy as he remembered her smell, her touch, and her smile—the smile that he rarely saw because he'd failed her more times than he'd pleased her.

It had taken until now for him to realize that Krista was so important to him. He tried to keep his life as simple as he could to make hers better, but he always managed to mess up and she was left to deal with the consequences. Like his attempt to join the Blood Hounds—and him thinking that hiding in a cult temple was a good idea.

In the past, Darkwing had always assumed Krista just whined and complained because she was a girl, and that's what girls did. But now he knew he was wrong; Krista deserved to be cherished. She'd stayed with him through his whole life, the few good times and the countless bad times.

His mind relapsed to memories of Krista; again, her smile, and then the sound of her crying out for him while Saulaph dragged her away.

I can't leave her ever again, Darkwing concluded after hours of dwelling in self-pity. He would pursue rescuing her no matter the risk. She was the one good thing in his life and he was not going to let that go.

I've made mistakes with her but that is going to change now.

Darkwing curled against a wall under a dusty blanket in the Blood Hound hideout for the night. The dirt floor was cold and the sheet provided some warmth, but he missed Krista's natural heat.

He sighed. Anything he thought about led his mind back to Krista.

Darkwing scanned the room for his comrades, Alistind and Draegust, finding them sleeping against opposite walls. Draegust remained where Darkwing had first found him. Alistind slept closer to Darkwing; she was obviously uncomfortable around Draegust. It made sense; as usual, the Blood Hound leader had spoken and acted like a pig.

Darkwing watched Alistind sleep; her breathing was steady and slow. Her eyes were closed tightly. He gazed at her vibrant red scalp-feathers, about two-thirds the length of Krista's. She was much closer to his age. He found it comforting to meet someone at about the same maturity level as him. He cared for Krista, but he often had to filter his thoughts around her so she would not worry so much. Perhaps with Alistind, he could speak his mind more; with their similar ages, they might relate to each other well.

He was curious about Alistind's past and her beliefs, but he also had a hard time grasping the idea of being interested in another female when Krista was gone because of his mistake. He had a close bond to Krista, but he was uncertain what that meant. Alistind, her appearance and her figure, drew him in.

But it feels wrong when I know Krista is in pain and alone and I can't comfort her.

It crossed his mind several times that Krista may be no longer alive. That the cultists had killed her. The thought was terrifying, and he pushed it aside. She was alive; he knew it. He could still feel her presence. Darkwing was never spiritual and could rarely quiet his mind to listen and feel his surroundings. However, tonight was different. Darkwing could feel a tingling through his body, the kind of vibe he felt when Krista was near him.

"She's still okay," he mumbled.

The sound of footsteps from above broke the silence. The noise over their heads was enough to rouse Alistind from her sleep.

She lifted her head and looked at Darkwing. He looked away, realizing he'd been staring at her.

"What was that noise?" she whispered.

It was nice to hear her voice. Her pitch, a high tone, was similar to Krista's.

"Nothing to worry about," Darkwing said. "Only the surface of the city. The hideout expands below an old tailor's shop out into the streets."

Alistind nodded. "Thank goodness. I suppose I'm still shaken up from the Renascence Guard."

"Same here." He paused. "Well, I mean more so that I cannot sleep."

"How come?" Alistind asked, leaning on her arm.

"It's Krista." He sighed.

"You loved her?"

Darkwing felt his heart stop for a moment. He was uncertain how to respond to the question, unsure if she meant *love* or friendship. Even then, he was hesitant about his true feelings.

"It's hard to explain," Darkwing started.

Alistind smiled. "Try."

Darkwing nodded. "I've protected her for so long. Since we were kids. We lived in the same village."

"Before the banishment?"

"Yep, I actually saved her when her family was slaughtered by the humans. From there, I protected her during our people's savage mutations."

"Did she ever show signs of becoming a Corrupt?"

Darkwing shook his head and looked down. "She did not, but I did. The memories are still clear to me and the urges still occur."

Alistind's eyes widened.

Darkwing scratched his head; it was clear she wanted to know. "It was odd. I never harmed her during these frenzies. I was most certain in the back of my mind I was going to be consumed by it and become a Corrupt. But Krista's presence always helped me resist the rage that boiled deep inside." He sighed. "Anyway, from there, we lived in the city and survived off of scraps. We couldn't get jobs. As you probably recall, everyone was desperate for work and there was only so much the Five Guardians could offer the people as the city developed. If you couldn't farm or offer trade skills, what could you bring to the city? So we were forced live as a pair of scum."

Alistind nodded. "Doesn't sound much different from me." She scooted over to Darkwing and sat beside him, their shoulders touching.

She turned her head and leaned closer so their noses were millimeters apart. "But you avoided my question," she whispered. "Do you love her?"

Darkwing stared blankly at Alistind. Her aroma was pleasing, her warmth welcoming, and her red eyes had a slow, waving flame, almost reminding him of the smoke of Magma Falls. They were far different from Krista's, whose eyes were always glimmering with life and flickered at a rapid pace.

"Well?" she asked, tilting her head.

Darkwing shook his head and looked to the ground. He felt his scales tingle on his back being so close to a female; he knew so few and Alistind was stunning. It was hard to think about his answer with her near. He couldn't focus on how he felt about Krista.

"She was like a sister to me," he said, looking back up into her eyes. They were like an addictive drug. "That's all."

She smiled. "Good." Saying no more, Alistind brought her arm to the back of his head and pulled him closer to her until their lips met. He could feel her soft-scaled lips press against his own and her tongue move into his mouth, coiling around his. Darkwing felt his tense muscles relax and he embraced her touch. Their kiss seemed to last forever but in reality it was only a few seconds. Alistind gently tugged on his bottom lip with her sharp teeth before their lips parted.

Darkwing was stunned for a moment, his mouth hanging open. He could still taste Alistind's tongue and his bottom lip buzzed.

A wide grin spread across Alistind's face as she began to coil the end of her tail around her hand. "I can't believe I just did that."

"Yeah." Darkwing nodded.

"Since we left the temple, I've been getting these thoughts and these feelings of freedom. I'm thinking on my own and it's thrilling. For so long I've let the Risen One lead me to happiness." She licked her lips. "I believed that the Risen One's teachings of patience and acceptance would lead me to happiness, but it only led to a state of simply existing." She looked back at Darkwing. "Then you came along and offered to take me away, which seemed scary at the time. But now, I've only scraped the surface of a whole new life filled with excitement."

Darkwing was unsure what to say to her; he had no idea that she'd thought so deeply about this. He'd figured she was just an airhead.

She brought her hand to his jawline and stroked his face. "I kissed you to thank you."

It was obvious that there was more to the kiss, and Darkwing felt it. He could still feel the tickle from her lips. His mind was empty; her kiss had shattered all thoughts he had of Krista, and it was just what he needed in such a dark time.

The feeling was too good to let pass. Without warning, Darkwing leaned in and kissed her, wanting the same sensation that he got the first time.

At first, Alistind seemed to resist his persistency, but she relaxed her lips and the two brought their hands onto each other's body, holding each other, her hands slipping under his shirt and his under her tunic.

"Hey, lover boy!" A raspy voice broke the heated moment.

Darkwing lifted his head and looked around; he had tapped into another state of his mind being with Alistind, something more intuitive and less structural. Until Draegust spoke, he was unaware that his hands were halfway down her trousers.

Draegust got up from his resting spot and raised his arms. "I'm all for you getting some action, but come on! Do you have to do it with me here?"

Darkwing pulled his hands away from Alistind's body.

"That's better," Draegust said. "Come here."

Darkwing looked over at Alistind, who clutched her tunic closed with both hands. He got up from the ground and walked toward Draegust.

The former gang leader nodded. "All right, do I have your attention, Darkwing?"

"Yes." It wasn't entirely true. Darkwing's mind was flooded with an intense sensation that surged through his veins. He could only list a handful of times he'd experienced being physically close with a female. Sure, he had been with Krista for many years, but never in the way he'd just connected with Alistind.

"You said Krista was part of a ritual?" Draegust put his hands on his hips.

Darkwing nodded, glancing back to see Alistind now stood beside him.

"All right, I know of someone who can help out with this."

"Who would you know that has to deal with rituals?"

Draegust smiled. "You know of him."

Darkwing squinted and shook his head.

Draegust grinned, showing his razor-sharp teeth. "Come, let me refresh your memory."

The three walked out of the Blood Hound hideout, moving up the stairway with Draegust in the lead, followed by Darkwing and Alistind. She walked close beside Darkwing, still keeping her distance from Draegust. Darkwing was both excited and nervous about her walking beside him so closely. All he could think about now was kissing her again, feeling her delicate skin and embracing her body. He never expected to react so intensely to a simple kiss.

Draegust led them down the street Darkwing and Alistind had used in the Lower District, leading to the Great Road.

"You're not mad, are you?" Alistind spoke softly as they walked.

"For what?" Darkwing asked.

"That we kissed," she said.

He smiled, finding it amusing. "No, why would I be? I kissed you back because . . ." He paused.

"You're nice to me; you defend those who can't protect themselves. The proof of that is how much you care for Krista and how you protected me from Draegust. I like those characteristics in a person."

Darkwing felt awkward with her talking about his character; his thoughts related to nothing she spoke of. He was a resentful vazelead and a slave to his urges.

She pushed her scalp-feathers back and looked to the ground. "I told you the kiss was to thank you, but that wasn't true. I think I like you."

He remained silent as they walked, unsure what he should say. Darkwing barely knew her and already she was offering herself to him. Vazeleads were reactive beings, but this seemed rather instantaneous.

Alistind looked up at him. "Do you feel the same way?"

Their moment of passion earlier was mostly because he missed Krista. He was weak and her acceptance of him felt too good to resist. But still, Alistind was sweet, different, and he liked being with her.

His mind painted a vision of when they would find Krista. He was unsure if he would still feel the same for Alistind then. Maybe it was only an urge and nothing more; the magic would be lost and Alistind's heart would be crushed.

"You're quite beautiful and pleasant," Darkwing started, not knowing what to say next. "I have to be honest, I'm not sure if I kissed back because I miss Krista and I'm weak, or if there is more."

Alistind smiled. "You're honest. I like that." She reached out and took his hand. "I do hope it's more."

Hearing himself say the word 'Krista' brought her into his thoughts again, and reminded him of his mission to find her. Darkwing suddenly remembered why they were following Draegust through the streets. He had to focus. However, he didn't mind Alistind holding his hand; it was nice to feel someone close during a stressful time.

Draegust had thrown his Blood Hound cuff to the ground as they travelled, making the group inconspicuous. The last thing they needed was to attract attention from past rival gangs or the Renascence Guard. Darkwing followed his action and dropped his cuff too.

Guess the Blood Hounds are officially done, he thought. It was funny to him considering all the work he put into trying to join their cause. Now they were gone. In a way it was like they never existed.

Except Draegust is still here.

It was difficult for Darkwing to trust Draegust. He'd only served him because of the Blood Hounds, and the only thing he could base his views on was the fact that Draegust had attempted to rape Krista.

The three reached the Great Road and walked up to the Commoner's District. The road was just as busy as last time Darkwing was here, with crowds of homeless wandering about and looking for places to stay. Especially after the convicts had destroyed a large portion of the Commoner's District, civilians fled here to find shelter.

They walked in silence while approaching the gates that divided the two districts. The gates, along with the walls beside them, were reinforced with sharp spikes and barbed wire from bottom to top—a means of keeping street vermin from climbing the wall.

Draegust slowed his pace and whispered, "Looks like order is slowly being restored."

Darkwing looked ahead at the Lower District gates, where there were two guards watching with the gates still open.

"Took them long enough," Darkwing replied.

"Yeah, just don't do anything funny," Draegust said.

The three walked up to the gates and the guards held their spears out in a defensive stance.

"Halt, travelers!" one guard said. His age was heard through his croaky voice, and visible through the dried scales on his tail.

"You come from the Lower District. How do I know you're not of any gang?" the guard hissed.

Draegust held his hands in the air, allowing the guards to search him. Alistind and Darkwing followed his actions.

The second guard, a female, marched toward the three and quickly patted all of them down. "They're not hiding any gang markings," she said, voice younger and stronger than that of her companion.

The older guard eyed the weapons attached to Draegust and Darkwing's belts. He lowered his guard and nodded at them. "You may pass. I warn you, though: the Renascence Guard is very aggressive in the Commoner's District, and weapons in their sight won't be taken lightly."

Draegust smiled. "Of course." He continued to lead Darkwing and Alistind into the Commoner's District.

Darkwing scanned the road littered with splintered wood and empty bags, eyeing the dark alleyways and the flat rooftops of the dusty red-and-beige-painted buildings. Several Renascence Guards in suits of sharp-edged, gunmetal armour complete with black kilts, long steel spears, and cone-shaped three-pointed helmets rushed down the road ahead of him and disappeared once they passed the intersection. Their tails were perked straight up, ready for combat.

Darkwing relaxed his grip on the weapon, knowing the guards were not a threat to him right now. They obviously were too busy dealing with the havoc from several days ago, when the prisoners were released by Ast'Bala.

"Let's stay close together," Draegust said quietly. "This place is still a mess."

The former gang leader walked along the Great Road, guiding them past the large circular marketplace, where the merchants and commoners were busy repairing their stores and cleaning the streets. Many vazeleads stood by, crying, as the Renascence Guard filled several wagons with corpses.

Darkwing tried not to focus so much on the scenery and kept his eye on their path; he didn't want to be sidetracked from his mission again. Nevertheless, he still found himself thinking about Alistind. It was nice to daydream of her when he had thoughts of Krista and the ritual return to his mind. He decided that he would give her offer serious consideration when he got some answers about where Krista was.

Draegust pointed as they turned off the Great Road. "Right there."

The street seemed familiar and Darkwing realized that they had returned to the strange potion store where he'd stolen a bottle of elixir to gain acceptance to the Blood Hounds—and, he remembered with a pang of remorse, where he'd once left Krista behind.

It's my fault, Darkwing thought. He forced a laugh. "In there? You honestly think that old ruffled feather will let us in? After I robbed his shop?"

Draegust shrugged as they continued to walk, seeing that the store had been closed up with boxes and boarded up with planks of wood. "I never said anything about him letting us in. What I told you was I knew of someone who might understand the ritual."

"Great," Darkwing muttered.

They approached the door to see that the planks of wood had been nailed to the frame, sealing the entrance.

Draegust stepped closer to the door and lightly knocked on the planks.

Silence.

"Maybe he isn't home," Alistind suggested.

Both Draegust and Darkwing looked back at her.

Alistind folded her arms. "Perhaps he doesn't even live here and kept his shop safe during the prisoner escape."

Draegust shook his head. "Not likely."

"He lives here," Darkwing said while walking to the window, trying to see into the store. It was impossible. "Both times I was here, he came down from the loft. Besides, he has a shade on guard duty; I'm surprised we haven't heard it yet."

Draegust pounded on the door. "Open up, old scale-breath!"

No answer.

Alistind sat down while Draegust continued to yell at the door. Darkwing moved along the front and sides of the building, staying in sight of his companions to ensure safety. He tried to find another way in and remembered the back entrance where he'd been able to pick the lock, but decided he wouldn't mention it to Draegust. Intruding on the elder could prove fatal; the shade would not hesitate to kill. He also didn't think Alistind would be able to handle her emotions around a shade; fear would overrun her. He returned to the front of the store to see Draegust pounding on the door again.

"Open up!" He was aggravated this time and spat on the ground.

A muffled voice came from the store. "You despise the earth?"

Darkwing's and Alistind's attention spiked when the voice spoke and they moved closer to the door.

Draegust nodded and licked his lips. "Yeah, I do. The underworld is one big shit show."

"It's what we were given," the voice replied.

"We were forced to have it." Draegust folded his arms. "We don't belong here."

"God was kind enough to forge us to this land in payment for the humans' mistake."

"God? Give me a break. God is a human fairy tale. If there were such a thing, don't you think he'd break the 'Prayer of Power' that the paladins shackled us with?"

"The paladins are still mortal, and mortals have free will."

Draegust shook his head. "Will you let us in?" he asked.

"Why should I?"

Alistind spoke up, moving beside Draegust. "We need help."

Darkwing was surprised that she engaged with the elder; he still figured she was more passive. He knew she was willing to help him find Krista, and it was good to see. Plus, Darkwing had said 'she's like a sister'. It was possible that Alistind wanted to prove herself to him.

"Why would I help the three of you?"

Darkwing looked up to see that the window directly above the door had a crack in it. One fire-engulfed eye peeked through, looking down at the three of them. "He can see us." Darkwing pointed.

"Yes, I can." The voice paused. "Why do you return, Darkwing? I know not of where Krista is."

Draegust laughed. "Told you he was the one to go to. He knows what we want before we tell him."

Darkwing shook his head. "I was wrong to steal from your store. I was wrong to leave Krista behind." He sighed. "I found her again, and she accepted my apology."

"And your apology is not accepted by me. Krista is a girl—a child; therefore, a fool." The eye disappeared from the window.

Draegust pounded on the door again. "Hey! We're not done!" he shouted.

Darkwing glanced to the street behind him, seeing a couple passing Renascence Guards take notice of them.

"Try not to be too aggressive," Darkwing warned. "We don't want to attract unwanted attention."

Draegust bit his lip and kicked the door. "All right."

It was amazing that Draegust showed such eagerness in rescuing Krista. It occurred to Darkwing that he might truly have no interest in harming her, and only needed to keep his mind set on a goal, regardless of what it was. Besides, Draegust didn't have many allies now that the Blood Hounds were murdered. The intensity that radiated from Draegust's body, his voice, and his eyes made it quite clear that he wasn't going to give up on talking with the elder.

"Apology wasn't why you came to me, Darkwing." The elder's voice came back, this time louder, coming from directly behind the front door.

"That's what I said," Draegust added.

"You bring two friends. One shows aggression, yet that is in his nature. The other is confused with life. I know you mean no harm, yes?"

"Yes," Darkwing replied.

There were a couple seconds of silence.

"Come in, tell me why you are here." The sound of splintering wood came from inside the building and soon the door opened inward, revealing a frail elder behind the planks of wood.

"I'm old; help me take these off."

Draegust nodded and clutched a plank with both hands, tearing it free from the doorframe.

Darkwing helped with the remaining planks and soon the doorway was clear.

The three walked into the potion shop, keeping their heads low while following behind the elder as he led them through the candlelit store. The front half of the store hosted shelves and display counters for the different items he sold. There were bottles with liquids and jars with organs floating inside. The elder took them beyond the front of the shop and down a hall to the far left that led up a short staircase up to the second level. This floor was one large room, not divided by walls. The furniture was sectioned into quadrants, with the dining room to the left, kitchen and bedroom at the far end and the living room as the entrance to the second level.

The elder brought them to the kitchen area, where all four sat down on blackwood chairs at the blackwood table.

"Now tell me, why do the three of you come?" the elder asked.

"It's Krista," Darkwing quickly replied.

The elder nodded. "The speed in your response suggests to me she is in trouble."

Nodding, Darkwing explained to the elder what had happened, starting with the release of the prisoners from the citadel jail leading up to the Renascence Guard's slaughter of the cult. He described Ast'Bala, Krista's mark, Danil, and the guardians' fixation on her. The story took a long time to relate. After a while, Alistind and Draegust seemed to lose interest in the tale but the elder remained motionless with his eyes on Darkwing, watching every movement he made.

When Darkwing's story came to the ritual as described by the Renascence Guard captain, the elder leaned forward.

"The captain said he could not find her, but he believes she could be alive," Darkwing said. "So that is why I am here—to find out more about the ritual."

The elder nodded and smiled at Darkwing.

The three looked at one another, confused.

"She's very much alive," the elder said.

"How do you know?" Draegust replied, folding his arms.

The elder sat up straight. "Your mind is young, buzzing around. It is too busy looking and unable to calm itself and see. You would not understand."

"I think I understand." Darkwing swallowed. "Can you help us find her?" Darkwing felt out of place to ask. After all, he did steal from the store.

"So noble of you to find her," the elder remarked, standing up from his chair. "From your story, you tell me after you left her to the mercy of my shade, you returned to her—and wanted to show your loyalty."

Darkwing remained silent.

"Therefore, I accept your apology for the thievery of my potion."

Nodding, Darkwing replied, "Thank you." He could honestly not care less about the acceptance of his apology. All he wanted was answers.

"I can help you in your time of crisis. This news you bring me has a lot of questions that need answering."

A creaking sound came from the stairway. Darkwing, Alistind, and Draegust glanced over to see a reptilian creature crawling on all fours up to the second level. It was the shade. Darkwing had never seen a shade in the light before; it had an outer skin that was dark and translucent, allowing one to see the interior of its body. Inside the semitransparent membrane, a second black opaque cell floated in the centre, almost like a yolk in an egg. Its overall shape seemed lizard-like; the shade crawled on four legs and had a frilled neck made of the same translucent skin.

The shade's movements recalled those of a cat. It paused in its tracks, eyeing the three visitors. It growled and its voice echoed in

Darkwing's thoughts. *New flesh!*

Alistind fiddled with her tail and looked away as the shade crawled on the floor, examining them.

The elder waved his hand at the shade and shook his head. "Don't mind him. Tell me though, why do you all still sit here?"

The three exchanged looks with one another.

"What do you mean?" Alistind asked.

"Have you visited this ritual's aftermath?" he asked.

"The Renascence Guard swarmed the temple," Darkwing said.

"That was yesterday. Today, it's our turn."

Darkwing leapt to his feet. Finally they were taking action to find Krista.

The elder gestured with his hand toward the stairway. "Let us gather some supplies for the journey and you will take me to this temple. We will look for any clues left behind."

CHAPTER XIV

Abnormal

I see.

World of beauty,

Skies cannot touch me.

Hope for those who sinned mortally.

Kingdom of thee.

I was curious.

To end crisis.

They did not endorse.

There, I was made powerless.

I saw.

It was a moment of awe.

They saw me fit an outlaw.

My banishment, voila.

I am angered.

Therefore I suffered.

Drowned and despaired.

Naturally, vengeance flowered.

So I seek.

I have a technique.

Child, do not shriek.

It only proves you're weak.

Help me, for what I seek.

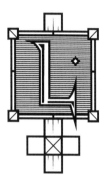ight shone into the room through a window, bouncing off the opposite wall and over the bedframe. Underneath the casted light, Krista lay on her mattress with a severe case of bedhead. The pillow was thrown to the ground and her sheets were kicked to the lower corners of the bed. The night seemed so short, yet so painful. Her head ached and she felt the pulsing of the veins in her skull with each beat of her heart. Her sleep was similar to the previous night's, but this time it was worse: there were more frightening poetic whispers and visions that flickered through her mind. The imagery flashed so fast she could barely make out what it was. She could only recall blood—lots of blood.

Krista sat up, cross-legged and hunched over, looking down at her mattress. After tonight, she was uncertain whether she ever wanted to sleep again; the increasingly haunting shuteye was causing her more stress than being awake during daylight. But she knew she didn't have much of a choice: her body would eventually tire and she'd pass out.

These nights are so intense. They're more exhausting than the daytime.

A light breeze blew into her room and brushed against her skin. The wind felt like little ice monsters biting her body and it caused her to shiver. The cool surface world was still unbearable.

Her stomach growled, making Krista realize she'd had nothing to eat since she first came to the surface. She didn't know if the humans planned on feeding her anytime soon, and she didn't want to wait to find out.

I could starve to death. Would they really do that? They are humans after all.

Krista gathered her strength, got up from the bed, and pushed her thoughts aside. She wobbled over to the closed door of her room and twisted the knob, finding—as expected—that it was locked.

She knocked on it. "Hello?"

The guard did not reply.

"I'd like out of my room."

"We already told you, girl, you're not to come out," the guard replied.

"Get Paladin!" she hissed, slamming both of her palms flat on the door. "I'm hungry."

Krista heard another voice speak up, but it was a whisper and she could not make it out.

The guard replied to the stranger, but he was also too quiet for her to hear.

She pressed her face against the splintered door, straining to listen. It was impossible to hear everything they were saying, but she was able to distinguish numerous words.

". . . said she's hungry . . . vazelead . . . plants . . . no . . . fangs . . ."

Frazzled, Krista moved back to her bed to keep warm. She pulled the sheets closer and felt them against her legs, noticing how soft they were compared to the underworld's rough cloth. She liked it.

It's the only warmth I have. The underworld was much warmer . . . and I had Darkwing. The thought of his name made her heart ache. Despite her physical discomfort, thinking of the boy was far more painful. How would she ever be able to see him again?

If I find a way back down there, Darkwing wouldn't believe me if I told him I made it to the surface.

She tightened the blanket around herself. The thought of having him hold her made her feel hollow. He was her safe place. *I could always go to him for comfort. Even if he was busy I could wait and he would come back to comfort me.* Her stomach gurgled and she let out a sigh. *He always found a way to get us food, too.*

Oddly enough, back in the City of Renascence just before Ast'Bala lost his sanity, Krista had become fixated on leaving the city life and the underworld entirely. The thought of trying to find a new home was madness since the Five Guardians had been trying for centuries.

Now here I am, away from the City of Renascence. She couldn't help but smirk. In a way she got what she wanted, but it didn't make her feel better. The fact that Darkwing was not with her made the accidental success empty.

Careful for what you wish for. Krista looked out the window to see that the blue sky was as vibrant as ever. There were also hints of orange and yellow near the horizon. It was a sight that would take her a while to get used to; it had been so long since she'd last seen the sky and its colours.

Krista unbuckled her boots and let the soft sheets slide between her two-toed feet. They were so luxurious it almost tickled her. She also unbuckled her belt and could feel the pressure it held on her body release, letting her skin relax. Clearly, she'd had it on too tight.

Her mind was busy thinking about how the human culture differed from her own. Their manners and traditions seemed so polite, unlike those of her own people. Even the High District civilians had no class compared to the humans in these barracks.

Now that I think of it, that ghoul who visited me had manners like my people.

Krista remembered Malpherities talking about Dreadweave Pass and recalled him mentioning that he came from there. He'd been vague about the details of his home, which was frustrating. Krista knew so little about Dreadweave Pass, but from what she knew about Mental Damnation, it was frightening, and it was information she'd need sooner or later. From what she saw on her hand, and what Malpherities mentioned, she was going to enter Dreadweave Pass whether she wanted to or not.

It is so outlandish, she thought, not fully grasping how she would be taken to Dreadweave Pass. How could she prepare herself for something she knew nothing about?

It seems like everyone knows more about Dreadweave Pass than me: the guardians, Abesun, and now this ghoul. I need answers.

She stood and walked over to the window, eyeing the crack where the ghoul had come from.

"Malpherities," she whispered.

Krista peeked into the crack, getting as close as she could to see inside, but the tiny hole was pitch black.

"Malpherities! I have a question."

Nothing.

Krista stood, slamming her fists against the window frame. The force of her blow against the solid bricks hurt her palms and she rubbed them afterward, turning back to face her room.

Krista was frazzled. "No one's listening to me!" She picked up her pillow from the floor and threw it at the door.

That was something Darkwing was getting better at: listening to me. She couldn't help but think back to the boy when she was in trouble, she relied on him for so long that any time she was threatened with any unknown scenario she used him as a crutch.

She went back and sat on her bed. "Even then, I have to fight for my own way . . ." She buried her head into her arms.

The locks to her door rattled. Seconds later, Paladin opened the door and barged into her room. He was dressed in light steel armour which covered his lower legs, forearms, and torso, with his red tunic underneath.

"The guards heard you talking to yourself again," he said, walking over to her bedside.

She paid little attention to his words because she noticed the tray in his hands. From what she could see, it held a glass of water and white bread. Her eyes widened, and she could feel her stomach growl relentlessly at the sight of the bread.

Paladin smiled at her wide eyes and sat down beside her, placing the tray between them. "They told me you were hungry, too."

Seeing the tray from above, Krista saw more food: an unfamiliar fruit that was red with seeds, a glass of milk, and several strips of red meat. She hadn't seen this kind of feast in many years. It almost seemed unfair for her to have it all to herself. The sudden rush of new scents, of flesh and sweet fruit, overwhelmed her and she stared blankly at the tray. The underworld smelled mostly stale and dry, and she could pick out each scent and identify it without a problem. But on the surface world, it was a different story. Everything had a fresh, strong smell that mixed with another, some overpowering others and, in the end, it made it all too difficult for Krista to concentrate.

"Go on. Eat. You must be famished," Paladin insisted, seeing her stare at the tray.

"Thank you." Krista snatched the bread; it was the most familiar to her.

Taking a tiny bite, Krista tasted it. The bread was light and fluffy and didn't have much flavour, yet it was pleasing. Krista devoured the rest of it in a couple bites and moved on to the meat.

There were three thin strips. She took one and tore half off with her teeth, chewing on the flesh to get a sense of the flavour.

"That's bacon," Paladin explained.

The mixture of hickory smoke and grease exploded in her mouth and Krista nodded happily. "It's delicious!" She grabbed the other two strips and devoured them as whole pieces.

Paladin watched her with a smile as she moved on to the water, downing it in several gulps.

Krista burped and wiped her face. "Thank you."

Paladin bowed his head in response.

Krista took one of the red fruits, feeling its bumpy texture. It was covered with tiny seeds. There were a few leaves growing from the top of the fruit, but it was still small enough to chew whole.

She popped the fruit in her mouth and bit down, letting the juicy sweetness overwhelm her taste buds.

Paladin chuckled. "You're not supposed to eat the top."

Krista swallowed. "Really? I'm sorry."

"Don't worry about it. It's not important."

"I like the fruit the best, I think. It is so sweet!" She took another one and was careful not to bite the whole fruit this time.

"It's called a strawberry," Paladin said. "We grow the fruit here in the garden."

"Do you grow other fruits?" Krista asked, excited that she might be able to taste more.

"Yes, we do. In time, I'm sure you'll be able to try them all."

Krista looked at the milk and took the glass into her hands. It felt cool as she lifted it and brought the liquid to her lips. She took a sip and quickly gagged but managed to swallow it.

Paladin's brow furrowed. "Is it spoiled?"

"No, sorry. All these tastes are new to me. This milk tastes very rich." She was not used to the flavour; the milk her own people got from the creatures in the underworld was far saltier.

"Your nights aren't getting any better, are they?" Paladin's face turned grim.

Krista sighed. "No."

"I want our relationship to remain honest, Krista. I do not want it to go sour. I know something is happening to you; I can't see anything physically wrong, but your mind must be suffering. The guards tell me they hear you chatter in your sleep, mumbling words."

"I'm not speaking them." She grabbed her tail and began to pick at the scales on it, seeing that they were a bit dry. "Someone is speaking to me, in my dreams."

"What is this 'someone' telling you?"

"I don't know. It's all like a poem. I don't understand poems."

"Can you repeat any of them to me?"

"They're all vague." Krista shook her head. "The one today was a little easier to remember."

"You wouldn't mind sharing, would you?"

Krista licked her lips before reciting. "*I see. World of beauty . . .*" She spoke the remainder of the poem from her dream during the night. "*. . . It only proves you're weak. Help me, for what I seek.*" Krista shrugged. "That's it."

Paladin nodded and rubbed his neck.

"They'll go away?" Krista asked, resting her chin on her knees.

"I'm sure they will. I'd like to move on, though."

"Okay."

"What did you do in the underworld?"

"Nothing. I was a street orphan; my people called us 'scum.'"

"Do you want to return to your home?"

Krista opened her mouth, but no words came out. The question replayed all the recent events through her mind: Draegust, the prison, the Five Guardians' corruption, and Darkwing—who was, in her opinion, the only good thing in the underworld. There were so many negatives and only one positive.

"You're unsure. But they're your people; why would you not want to go back?"

"It's not the same anymore," she replied, rubbing her shoulder. Her skin felt cold. "My people are in a horrible state. Our leaders have fallen." She paused. "Why do you care?"

"Krista, I need to know if your people are a threat to my kingdom's safety. Any information you can give me would be of great honour."

"Great honour?" She squinted. "I'd be betraying my people. Why would you ask such a thing?" Krista backed away in her bed, folding her arms.

Paladin leaned forward and poked her rib; it hurt and she grunted. Strangely enough, his jab hit the precise point where her body was still healing from being beaten by the Renascence Guard almost a week ago.

Leaning back, Paladin sighed. "It doesn't seem like they were nice to you."

Krista ignored Paladin and tried to think of Darkwing, but only hurtful memories—like when he abandoned her for the Blood Hounds—entered her mind.

"I'm willing to let you live in my barracks. I will make sure you're safe, Krista, as long as you're willing to tell me what I want to know."

Her head was frazzled; she was not good at making such critical decisions. "Can I think about it?"

Rising to his feet, Paladin clapped his hands together. "I'll show you my goodwill, Krista, to prove I am not your enemy."

I never thought he was my enemy; only that ghoul said paladins were bad.

"I'll let you think about the dilemma, and you'll be free to roam my barracks. I'll leave your door unlocked at night, as long as you tell me you'll keep out of trouble."

"That'd be nice."

"Promise me, though, that you'll greatly consider my offer, and remain out of trouble."

"Promise," Krista said with a smile.

With freedom now on her side, the boy she met earlier entered her mind. "Where can I find William?"

Paladin frowned. "As I said, stay out of trouble." He took the tray from her bed and left the room. The guard at the door glared at Krista and then followed behind Paladin.

Krista remained in her room. She didn't know what to do with the free time that Paladin blessed her with.

I want to find William. He's nice to me.

She figured the boy would be training outside, but it scared her to go out and face the sun again. The boiling sensation it caused under her skin was not worth it.

Where else could I find William? She began to play with her tail. *I remember Paladin said they could go eat lunch. They probably eat lunch indoors.*

Quickly, Krista strapped her boots and buckled her belt. She used her fingers to brush through her scalp-feathers, doing her best to clean up her appearance.

Paladin won't mind if I see William during lunch.

Krista walked out of her room and into the hall. She glanced down both ends of the hall to see if Paladin was still near, but he was nowhere to be seen.

Good.

She stepped out of the room and tried to recall where Paladin had taken her to find the training ground.

Paladin brought me to the second floor when I wasn't feeling good. So I need to find the staircase.

After what seemed like ten minutes, she found the stairway leading to the main floor. Once she reached ground level, she could see there was more activity on this level. Men marched down the halls. They ranged in age and size; some walked alone and others walked in pairs. The boys wore simple tunics much like William had and the men wore suits of armour, like the outfit Paladin was in today.

Krista kept walking down the halls, taking a right from the staircase and keeping to the corners to stay out of the humans' way. While she walked, several humans eyed her from head to toe. Their facial expressions ranged from shock to awe to disgust. It made her feel ashamed of her physical features. She couldn't hide her skin or her tail, but she kept her mouth closed to hide her fangs.

They don't seem to like me.

After several minutes of wandering, Krista walked past a crossroad where a large, closed, circular green door rested to her right. The smell of cooked meat—different than the bacon she'd eaten earlier—came through the cracks. It had to be the dining hall.

Opposite of the circular door was another door; this one was black and reinforced with metal bolts and had a window to its left. She walked to the window where she was able to peek outside. The sun blazed through and she could feel the intense light radiate on her skin.

I just want to look; I won't stay in the light for long. Maybe I can see the training ground. She looked out the window to see the bright green grass. She squinted her eyes to adjust to the lighting and scanned the terrain. She spotted the road Paladin had taken her down the day before. Her eyes trailed the path toward the training ground where there was a large group of boys, just like the day before. Krista leaned in closer, nose pressing on the glass until she spotted a blond boy in the crowd of humans.

William!

"Enough! Return after lunch." Paladin's muffled voice echoed in the distance.

The boys marched in Krista's direction, toward the keep, in pairs. Her eyes followed the road they walked up to see the door they'd come from—it was the one beside the window.

I can't have them all see me yet; I just want William's attention.

Krista glanced around to find a hiding spot, but found nothing. She rushed to the nearest corner back at the fork in the hall where she could be out of sight and still see William when he came through the door.

The boys slammed the door open, the noise echoing through the keep while the door rebounded, making the next boy push the door aside. They laughed and talked amongst one another, bragging about their swordsmanship. Their presence intimidated Krista; they walked confidently with loud voices that numbed her hearing.

Most of the boys had moved across the hall to the dining room without noticing Krista poking her head around the corner. At the tail end of the group, William walked in with two other boys—one with red hair and the other with black. The two boys with William twirled their wooden swords they used in practice, laughing and smiling at each other.

This is it. Krista felt a surge of fear rush through her body. She wasn't sure if it was because two other boys accompanied William, or if she was just shy. He'd been so nice her and she didn't want him to get the wrong impression. He reminded her of Darkwing.

"Hey, Will, you forgot your sword," one of the boys said.

"Oh, right," William replied.

"We'll meet up with you at lunch."

William turned around and rushed back outside.

Krista knew this was her chance to get the boy alone. She waited for William's friends to walk away and stepped out from the corner. She watched William run back for his sword from the window.

I'm so nervous. Krista could feel her scales stand up from the excitement. She knew Paladin had advised her to stay away from him, but she found it difficult to listen; the boy was friendly, and for a human, he was quite handsome.

She watched William jog back from the training ground up to the keep. This time, she was ready for him.

The blond boy entered the keep and Krista stepped in front of him. "Hi," she said.

William stepped back, seeming startled, but then relaxed his posture. "Krista!" He smiled.

Krista went in for a hug; she felt overly pleased to see him.

The boy was tense but he put his arms around her. She picked up his scent; it was not as strong as Darkwing's and smelled cleaner, almost like the cultists from the temple. Krista could feel his muscles underneath his shirt; they were tight, either from the training he was doing or out of nervousness.

He is kind of squishy. Humans feel so different from my people.

"What are you doing here?" he asked.

"I wanted to spend more time with you," Krista said with a light jump, breaking her hands free from him.

"I'd like to spend more time with you, too."

Heavy footsteps boomed in the distance, gradually growing louder. Someone was getting closer. Krista grabbed the boy's hand and pulled him into the corner she'd hid in earlier.

She coiled her tail around his ankle, preventing him from moving. "I want to know more about you." She felt her sense of adventure kick in. It was exciting not being allowed to see him; it made him more tempting. Plus, she enjoyed looking at him. She found him much easier on the eyes than her own people—or the other humans, for that matter. His features were far softer than other beings. "I'm sure you have all sorts of stories to share with me."

"Yeah." The boy seemed almost afraid of her tight grip on his leg. "I do have stories." He shook his head. "You seemed so ill yesterday, and so lively today."

"The sun doesn't like me, but I'm better now." She took his hand and tugged on it. "Let's go!"

William tried to pull free. "I can't."

Krista tilted her head and released her grasp on him. "Why?" She frowned.

"It's not like I can skip lunch; I'll have nothing to eat until sunset."

"Go get something to eat then and come back."

"I have to study the kingdom's history after."

"Can't you leave your training just once?"

William folded his arms. "I can't. I would be severely punished."

Krista could tell there was no convincing him and she sighed.

"I can meet you during the night, though. Our training ends when the sun sets and we can see each other after the evening meal."

Krista smiled and nodded. "I'll be waiting."

"I'll be waiting first." William winked and walked past her, back down the hall leading to the circular door.

Krista sighed and leaned against the bricks, squinting in the sunlight from the window. She had no idea what to do now.

I don't know why I got so excited about him, but he doesn't seem to judge me like the other humans do.

She still had the rest of the day to spend, but she felt intimidated by the men and didn't want to explore the rest of the keep.

Her attention was suddenly caught by her shadow, as black fog rose from the darkness. It began to shape itself. More dark fog followed, and eventually, blue fog funneled within the blackness, forming the shape of the ghoul Malpherities. He was closer to her this time and she could see he was about a head taller.

She backed up, unsettled by the ghoul so close to her.

"Rather an airheaded mortal, isn't he?" Malpherities asked.

"Where'd you come from?" Krista asked, looking down at her shadow. The smoke still trailed from it. "Don't say mean things about William; he's my friend."

"You barely know him."

She didn't want to argue with the ghoul about who her friends should be. William was nice and a human, while Malpherities was not so nice and a mysterious creature.

"Where'd you come from?" she repeated.

"Your mind has opened a seam between Dreadweave Pass and this realm, allowing me to cross over here and accompany you, my dear child."

"I don't understand what that means. What if I don't want you around? I'll just close the seam?"

The ghoul laughed. "No, girl, you can't. No one can. We talked of this last night, don't you remember? Once a gatekeeper reaps you, there is no going back." Malpherities fiddled with his claws. "Do not see William tonight. You must not waste your time with boys of inferior races."

"He's not inferior," Krista hissed.

"You defend someone who was so quick to leave you."

"He was in a hurry—I don't think his lunchtime is very long."

"Fear was in his eyes, not compassion."

"You're wrong."

"Don't be a fool!" Malpherities's dreadlocked hair shot to life as if electrically charged, standing straight up while he rose into the air, towering over her.

Krista looked up at him and covered herself with her arms, scared of the ghoul's dark, muscular figure; it reminded her of the Renascence Guard.

The ghoul brought himself down, his hair draping back down to his shoulders. "You are consumed with fear, child."

Krista lowered her arms and stroked her scalp-feathers. "Why can't

I see William?"

"You have greater problems that are soon to arise."

"Like what?"

"Oh, I don't know . . . perhaps something like crossing realms into Dreadweave Pass. Also, a doctor. He will be coming here soon."

"How did you know?" Krista asked. "Paladin told me, but you weren't here."

"We share a bond, girl, from the moment you were accepted into Dreadweave Pass. I see, know, hear, and feel what you embrace."

"Well, I don't like that."

Malpherities moved closer to her. She couldn't pick up on his smell, but she felt a creeping energy radiate from his body the closer she got, making her scales stand up and her skin tingle. "Listen, this doctor will tell you things. He'll say he is helping you. Don't believe him—his words are filthy lies. They'll sound convincing, but will only lead to your destruction. You must remain strong and stay close to me."

Krista shook her head. "Why are you helping me?"

"See you later," came a boy's voice.

Krista looked back to see William wave at her with a flatbread sandwich in his hand as he walked by with his two friends.

She smiled at him and looked back at Malpherities, only to see that he was gone again.

CHAPTER XV

The Bug

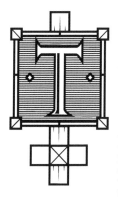

he sun seemed to never set. It mocked Krista from high in the sky with its bright glare, preventing her from enjoying the darkness of the night.

The beam of the sun wasn't as devastating to her skin inside the shaded keep; the shelter kept the bizarre tingling the sun sparked in her innards away. She could still feel the strange light that the sun radiated as she stared through the window, but only enough to keep the warmth in her body, reminding her of the underworld while she waited for the sun to disappear under the horizon.

Sighing, Krista rested her cheek against the frame of the window, her skin smudging against the cool glass. She was tired of waiting; questions about William chattered in her head and she knew the boy would soon answer them. How long had he been in the barracks, or had he lived here his whole life? Where was his family?

In the back of her mind she knew she should be concerned as to how she came to the surface world, but she hardly knew what to think. Paladin seemed to be interested in the scenario, but only to help the humans, not to aid her in finding her way back to Darkwing.

It's like I'm in a whole new world. A different reality where I do not belong. Heavy thoughts that entered her mind were daunting and the last thing she wanted to think about. Having someone like William provided an easy escape for her to forget about heavy topics, like returning home.

While she waited, she pondered where the boy was. It was possible that William's training had ended for the day because the sun was finally beginning to set. But she had no real guess as to when she would see him. Maybe William did not want to spend time with her; he very well could be afraid of her reptilian characteristics, like Malpherities had said.

She thought about the barracks and its lack of females. Most of the humans there seemed to be men. She had noticed a few women; they ranged in age, but none were interested in talking to Krista. She assumed they thought she was ugly.

She decided after meeting with William that she could try to explore the barracks more. The fruits from her breakfast had been so delicious and she'd love to find where the garden was so she could pick some more to eat later. She also wanted to learn what had changed on the surface world since her people's banishment. Who was the king of Zingalg? What other empires were there? Were the draconem still around?

Her mind was far more relaxed than it had been earlier in the day, letting her think clearer than when she first awoke on the surface. The memories from last night's sleep passed through her mind, but the voices that spoke to her only spilled random words that were incomprehensible. It irritated her that no one would give her answers to all the questions she had.

I want answers, now. Why I am even here and what will happen next are too mysterious.

The only being that had been kind enough to help her was Abesun. When Krista had met him, they'd been ambushed by a group of Corrupt. During the battle, Abesun had been overpowered and Krista was forced to make her first kill ever, giving Abesun the edge he needed to defeat the remaining Corrupt attackers.

She'd gone into shock committing murder for the first time, and it was in this state that Abesun saw the mark Ast'Bala had left on her.

Abesun revealed he had the strange mark on his palm too, and that he had been to Dreadweave Pass and survived.

He gave her a wealth of information about what was to come, telling her it was a path that she had to walk alone and that no one in the real world could help her. He'd explained, "Mental Damnation is a gateway into hell. At first it appears just as a vision in your dreams. But as the days go on, the visions become real."

As a reference, he'd shown her a pendant. The symbol matched the icon on his and her palms.

Abesun claimed he had ripped the pendant from inside a gatekeeper's ribcage, where it resided in place of their heart. If Krista wanted freedom from Mental Damnation, she had to obtain the pendant from the ribcage of the gatekeeper who'd infected her. It was, according to Abesun, the key to freeing her soul from Dreadweave Pass and being rid of the illness for good.

"It's not an illness. It is a gift," a voice hissed.

Krista saw the reflection of Malpherities in the black frame of the split window and spun around.

"Where did you go?" she asked, wanting to know why he'd left her earlier.

The ghoul growled. "I returned to Dreadweave Pass."

Krista folded her arms. *He's always so vague!* "Well, why did you leave?"

"I didn't leave, I'm here."

Squinting, Krista shook her head. "I meant when William walked by. He's a nice boy; I think he'd like you."

The ghoul laughed. "He's trained by a paladin, and he follows the humans' faith of God. I'm an atrocity to his beliefs."

"You avoided my original question again."

The ghoul stared at her blankly.

"You're always avoiding my questions with half-answers."

"I did not avoid; I simply didn't give the answer you were seeking."

"Well, can you be more clear?"

The ghoul shook his head. "We are bound to each other. What you see, I see. What I see, you see. When I left, I was here still."

Krista didn't like the idea of him knowing her thoughts. Her mind was supposed to be private, not shared with shady beings. "I don't want to be bound to you," she protested. "I didn't want to be marked by Ast'Bala or Danil. I didn't want any of this chaos to happen to me."

He hissed. "Do not drown in self-pity. It's your own fault they marked you for the reaping."

"What do you mean?"

"If you'd simply grown up quicker, you wouldn't have had to deal with this."

"It wasn't my fault! I don't want to grow up, either." She slid to the floor. The thought of growing up brought back memories of Darkwing: his scent, his touch. "It's easier to make friends when you're a kid."

"On the contrary, Krista, maturing mentally and physically opens a whole new window of understanding and opportunity. When you're grown, you are less prone to loneliness."

"How so?"

The ghoul seeped down to her level, his tail fog hovering in the air. "Conquest and conquering your fears, your desires, your weaknesses . . . things a child cannot comprehend. Once you defeat them, you realize they only existed in your thoughts from the beginning. Like the concept of loneliness."

"I don't think I can do any of that." Malpherities's words seemed so big, and they overwhelmed her.

"Of course not, you're only a child! Yet I see you maturing slowly." The ghoul paused. "You recently murdered a mortal, didn't you?"

"It wasn't murder! I didn't kill him!" She folded her arms.

The ghoul laughed and shook his head. "No, that wasn't murder, was it? Please, don't be a fool! You killed the Corrupt vazeleads. Deal with it."

"I didn't mean to kill him."

"Of course not."

Krista, so full of questions earlier, didn't know what to ask the ghoul. But he was all she had for help with Dreadweave Pass right now.

The ghoul looked up. "The sun is almost set. Are you really about to meet this William?"

"Yes. He's nice. I'd like to make some friends here."

"He is a waste of your time. Friends only result in greater foes."

"I suppose you've never had a real friend, then, have you?"

"I've lived for over a thousand centuries, girl. I've had my share of friendships and I'm doing you a favour in letting you know: don't ever trust them."

"Are you my friend?" Krista asked with a mischievous grin.

The ghoul smiled back at her with a mouth full of teeth. "I can be whatever you wish me to be."

She nodded and scratched her arm. "A thousand centuries? Were you always a ghoul, floating around with no legs?"

"Unimportant stories, girl. Would only fill your mind with nonsense."

"Okay." Krista thought of another question she had. "You said a doctor was coming here?"

"Yes." Malpherities spoke quickly; the question clearly grabbed his interest. "The doctor will tell you that Mental Damnation is only your imagination, an illness that toys with your mind. He'll tell you that it's not real."

"How do I know it isn't real?"

"It very much is, girl."

"I don't smell you. I smell everything. So how do I know you're real? As far as I know—"

The ghoul brought his hand slowly to Krista's clavicle. He pressed one claw into her skin until it poked through the surface and he dragged it down, ripping her flesh open.

"That hurts!" Krista yelped, slapping his claw away.

"Krista!"

She got to her feet and shot her gaze to the entrance to see William waving at her. Krista spun to the window to see that the sun was gone and the stars were beginning to shine.

"William!" She smiled at him.

Glancing to the ground where she sat, Krista realized that once again, Malpherities had vanished.

William ran toward her with a smile, eying her collarbone where the new scratch was. He shifted his gaze to her eyes. "What were you doing?"

Krista hugged her arms and shook her head. "Nothing." She smiled back at him. "I was beginning to think you weren't going to come."

William chuckled. "Of course I'd come. Why would I leave a girl like you alone?" he smoothly replied.

Krista giggled. She liked his charming personality, so unlike what she'd seen during his lunch.

"So, now that it's just us, where would you like to go?"

Krista shrugged. "Paladin told me that there aren't many places we can go, with the night guard."

William shook his head. "Paladin says a lot of things, and the night guard isn't anything to worry about. He only tells us that they are to keep order in the barracks. We can go anywhere you'd like."

Krista looked out the window, noticing the strange tingle under her skin was no longer present. "Well, I'd like to talk . . . and I'd like to be outside."

Nodding, William smiled. "I've already got a few ideas of where we could go." He turned to leave. "Stay close to me. The night watch have good eyes, but they're easy to avoid."

Krista took the boy's hand. It seemed to startle William, the way she was so persistent with her touch. "I'll just hold your hand." She smiled.

William smiled back and the two snuck out of the keep through the black door, moving across the field and straying away from the dirt path. Wind blew past their faces and their legs brushed against every blade of grass, sending a chill through Krista's body.

On the bright side, Krista's vision during the night was much better. She could make out the true size of the garrison, and saw that it stretched far and wide. Along the distant walls, silhouette figures—the night watch—could be seen patrolling the outer rims of the barracks.

The two rushed past the stables to the far left of the barracks, keeping away from the open fields to stay out of sight. It was difficult to stop and observe the details of the buildings they passed. Krista locked her eyes on the horses in the stables; their scent was strong and she loved the manes that ran down their necks.

"They're just horses," William told her. "Let's keep going."

Nodding, Krista continued to move with the boy. *I haven't seen any of this in about two centuries.*

Away from the stables, she brought her attention to the texture of William's hand. It was far bumpier and rougher than the hand of a vazelead. She wasn't sure if she liked the feel of it, so unfamiliar. She preferred the smooth stiffness of her people's skin.

Between the noise of the wind and daydreaming about William's touch, Krista paid little attention to where they were going. William led her across various paths and over a large hill until they reached a crystal-clear river where a wooden bridge arched overtop. William took her down the hill and underneath the bridge, where it was sheltered.

She sat down on the sandy dirt. "This is a pretty place."

William nodded. "I often come here when we're not training. It's nice to get away from all the people. Plus, this bridge isn't often used, so it's not like there are many disruptions." He sat down beside her and the two stared into the water.

"It's been so long since I've been on the surface." She looked into the boy's eyes. "What's it like living up here?"

William seemed confused by her question. "What do you mean?"

"I mean what it is like living here . . . I'm from the underworld, so I'm curious."

"The underworld?" William repeated.

Krista nodded with a smile. "It's very different from here. Less smells. Darker—and warmer." A wind blew under the bridge and Krista shivered from the coolness as it flowed over her.

William bit his lip. "You're cold?"

"A little," she said with a weak smile.

William shook his head. "I don't have a coat to offer you." He paused, thinking of his words. "I could hold you."

"Sure!" Krista said quickly, scooting closer to him. She felt no awkwardness in snuggling up to the boy. He smelled good and he felt good. She could see in William's eyes that he was nervous. She figured that humans weren't as much of a physical race as the vazeleads were; Krista could recall plenty of scenarios where her people preferred to use physical actions rather than words, whether it was expressing joy, violence, sadness, or intimacy.

She placed her head against his chest as she huddled against his warm body. Krista was grateful for his warmth. "Thanks, I don't think I knew how cold I was," she said with a smile.

"I don't want you to freeze," William said with a shaky voice.

She smiled and remembered her question. "So what's it like on the surface world?"

Rising from the dark shadows of the water, Malpherities sprung out in front of them. His familiar fog didn't penetrate the ripples but appeared from the reflection of the sky. "The surface world is only filled with hairy mortals like the one you're pressed against!"

Krista looked up to see William was staring off into the opposite direction, thinking about her question.

She quickly sat up and pointed at the ghoul. "Look!" Krista exclaimed.

William and Krista both stared at the river, seeing only the reflection of the sky and no Malpherities.

"What is it?" he asked.

Krista was silent, unsure what to say.

A deep aggravated growl erupted behind her, and she felt the vibrations of the sound tingle along her backside. "You tried to expose me, girl!"

Krista spun around to see the ghoul beside them.

William turned around and shook his head. "What do you see?"

"You see nothing," Malpherities said.

What? Krista thought, confused that William could not see the ghoul. Yet Malpherities was plainly in front of them. "I think the cold is just getting to me," she lied.

"Good. You lie," Malpherities added.

William stood with Krista and took her hand. "We'll go inside, then." The two began strolling from under the bridge and back up the hill.

"I still want to know about you," Krista repeated as they walked.

She glanced behind them to see that Malpherities remained at the bridge, watching her walk away. Krista didn't get why he was acting so hostile to her when he said he was going to help her. Why was he bothering her now? She didn't like that he decided when he would visit, and could physically harm her, yet no one else could see him. He had full advantage over her.

William took her back inside the keep then through the circular door into the dining room. She remembered seeing the boys, including William, enter the room during their midday meal. She hadn't been inside before but, seeing the layout, realized it was similar to the dining room of the cult she'd temporarily been a part of. Many tables were lined up and down the long hallway. But here, the tables were wooden, shorter, and slightly distanced from one another allowing people to move around.

William took Krista deep into the narrow brick room. She could feel the heat rise the further they went, warming her body. He sat her down at one of the benches attached to the table and moved around to face her.

"That better?" he asked.

Krista glanced around and her eye was caught by a bright room with an oven inside. It was visible through a cutout in a wall. She squinted to see there was a sink, a rack of knives, and a cutting board on a counter. The wall had a doorway to the far right leading into the kitchen. She smiled. "Much better."

She noticed the dining room was exceptionally dark; only the fire from the oven beamed an orange hue through the window into the dining hall.

"Why is the fire on?" she asked.

"The cooks often bake bread during the night," William said.

Krista sniffed the air and could smell the fresh baking. She inhaled slowly, soaking in the scents.

"It's not too bad," William said. "The surface world. It would be bright, compared to a place called the underworld."

Krista nodded. "I've noticed that."

"In the underworld, how dark is it?"

"Like it is here now: the same warmth and brightness," she said, looking around the room. "Yep," she added.

William wiped his forehead. "Too warm for me," he said with a smile.

She grinned. "Trust me, I don't think you'd be able to live down there. You'd roast alive."

William nodded, unsettled by the words.

She leaned forward, looking deep into his irises. "Any stories to share with me?" Her eyes twinkled. "I'd like to know what it's like growing up in the Kingdom of Zingalg."

William shrugged. "It's fairly basic. We bring loyalty to our kingdom—do as our king wants. My father wanted me to be here. I barely remember him; he sent me off when I was only four. Even when I was at my old home, it's not like he was around often."

Krista shook her head. She wasn't sure how a human's age compared to a vazelead's "Four?" She knew she would still be in her mother's arms at that age. "I know humans age faster than me. At least that's what my parents said."

William measured with his hand to demonstrate the size to the floor. "That big," he said.

Krista giggled. "You were tiny."

William nodded. "That was a long time ago. What about you? What's your world like?"

"Well, it's been a real mess." She began to play with the tip of her tail with her index finger. Krista was unsure how much she should even tell the boy about her life. *Where's the line between too much information and being cold?*

The thought ran through her mind while she stared at the boy's genuine smile. He remained motionless while she thought about his question, leaving several moments of silence.

I don't think he even knows what race I am, she thought, realizing that she had a blank canvas to tell her story from.

"Well, to start, the underworld is a very hot environment with a lot of wind and sand."

"Oh?" William leaned forward, eyes wide.

"Our people managed to survive through protective clothing. We built a unified city for our people. Being far from perfect, it did manage to keep us together so we wouldn't stray."

"Why would that happen?"

Krista looked to the ground. "Oh, well, it is the way of our people before things changed."

"What changed?"

Krista swallowed heavily. She felt awkward discussing her people's past with William. It was clearer than ever that he had no clue about the vazelead banishment. Now that she had Paladin apologize for her entire race's exile to the underworld, she wondered if there was more to the banishment than she realized.

"Well?" William asked.

Krista blinked twice before returning to the present. "Our people went through a lot," Krista stated, hoping to avoid the question.

I have to be careful, she thought. Despite being interested in the boy, she remembered that she was on the surface world, with humans. Was William her enemy? *Or am I being paranoid?* she thought.

Shaking her head, she replied, "Our people have had a hard time identifying ourselves. Most of us thought unification was the best method. We made one massive city."

William leaned back in surprise and replied, "for a whole race?"

"Yeah, it's pretty impressive in size."

"Tell me more!"

Krista smiled, relieved that she didn't have to get into details about her people's banishment. She could easily go on about the adventures as a street scum.

William remained wide-eyed with interest in her adventures of thievery, gangs, and escaping from the Renascence Guard. The boy didn't speak much about the surface world, leaving Krista to do most of the talking. She was careful not to tell him of any of the more recent episodes from her life, with the Five Guardians, Abesun, or the Eyes of Eternal Life, though. *All this stuff about Mental Damnation is creepy. I don't want him to think I'm a freak or anything.* Footsteps from the kitchen interrupted their conversation. A man appeared, wearing an apron. He was bald, wore grey slacks, and was fairly tubby.

"That you, William?" he called out.

"Well met, Chef Doyel!" William replied.

"Boy, what have I told you about mooching fresh bread? Not happening anymore. You're older than that now," he shouted.

"I'm not here for any bread," William said with a smile.

The chef glanced at Krista. "You with the new girl?"

Krista waved at him, seeing that he was a friendly man.

"I made your meal this morning."

"It was tasty. Thank you."

Nodding, the chef walked into the kitchen and pulled the bread from the oven behind the wall. He placed the steaming loaves along the window frame dividing the rooms to let them cool. "You two best get yourselves to bed now, all right? It's rather late and Paladin wouldn't like to hear that the night watch found you."

"All right," William said, getting up from his seat.

"Bye." Krista waved at the chef as they left the dining room.

She walked beside William while they moved down the halls. "He was a nice man," she said.

William nodded. "Yeah."

The two stopped when they reached a fork in the hallway. William was to walk down one way, while Krista had to return to her room on the second floor.

"It was fun to spend the evening with you." Krista said, holding her forearm with the opposite hand.

"Nice to talk to someone who's from an entirely new world," William said. "You have so many stories!"

Krista giggled. "I suppose."

It was just my life. Crazy times trying to survive with Darkwing. His name didn't seem to have as much effect on her as it did earlier in the day. Being in a new world with someone to help show her around made it easier to cope with the scenario. Despite missing Darkwing, she felt excited for what the future held for her in the barracks and on the surface.

William smiled while rubbing the back of his neck and said, "I'd better get some rest. Paladin wakes us pretty early."

Krista waved goodbye. She watched the boy quietly walk away, not wanting to wake anyone as he passed the green-painted doors on each side of the hall.

As for herself, Krista headed back to the stairs, returning to her room for the night and thinking of evening—William's smile, his smell, and their exchange of stories and culture.

CHAPTER XVI

Sign of Trust

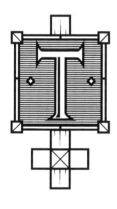

rust: when one lets down their guard and allows a person to perform or an event to occur without interfering. To gain one's trust can be a challenging task and once you gain that trust, it should be treasured. If all beings in a society had this ideology, it would create an underlying mutual understanding in the civilization. Everyone has been given free will to hold another's trust, or break it for their own desires.

Some may even argue that as long as the person whose trust is broken is unaware of the event, it does not matter at all. If you betray one's trust and the truster does not discover the exploitation, then what is there to worry about? The truster still believes that nothing has changed.

It is a simple concept, and it is flawless except for the one aspect that will cause distress when one breaks trust but isn't caught: morality. If you can live without having decency, then gaining people's trust and manipulating them for your own advantage becomes a regular way of being.

But everyone has some idea of morality, even the most untrustworthy individuals. Even the ones that have been trampled on and defeated by life have morality somewhere deep inside—it just happens to be twisted to fit their needs. Does that make it wrong? As far as they are concerned, their untrustworthy actions are justified by their trust in their own moral beliefs.

Not all beings that have been through the challenges of life have flawed senses of morality; some know their actions are unjustifiable. They simply have no other choice if they wish to survive, and they live with the burden.

He won't find out, Krista told herself silently while climbing the stairway leading to her room. Paladin won't know that I spent time with William; the only person who saw us was the chef. He was nice.

Moonlight shone through the barred windows into the keep. The light was more radiant than during the other nights Krista had spent on the surface. There were no clouds in sight, which allowed the moon to shine at its fullest.

It's so pretty on the surface, she thought while walking down the hall toward her room.

Krista did her best to keep quiet while passing closed doors, assuming that humans were sleeping on the other side. She did not want anyone to discover her wandering the halls.

This was a good night. William and I had fun. Krista reached her room and slowly turned the handle of the door to push it open. The hinges must have been oiled because it opened without a sound. Once Krista stepped inside the room, she carefully closed the door, eyeing the door's edge until it lined up with the frame, then released her grip on the knob.

I don't want to slam it shut—that's just asking for trouble.

She released the handle and let out a deep sigh. Finally, she was alone. Krista turned to face her bed and was startled to see Malpherities floating by the window, his essence projecting from the crack in the window frame.

Krista gasped at the sight of him and brushed her scalp-feathers out of her face. "You scared me."

The ghoul slammed his fist into the wall, cracking the stone. "What is wrong with you, girl?"

Krista remained stiff, afraid of his hostility.

"You thought the boy could see me?"

"I was confused."

"No one can see me! They're not gifted!" The ghoul swooped closer to Krista, his essence nearly pressing against her face. His black fog disintegrated from the window and began to funnel from the numerous small cracks in the ground. "You were given a gift; your sixth sense has been heightened!"

Krista stepped back. "Stop talking nonsense to me! I don't understand what you're saying. What's a sixth sense?"

Malpherities hissed. "You're naïve. You don't pay attention to what I tell you. My information is valuable."

"I don't want a sixth sense."

"We all have a sixth sense, Krista. Yours is just better."

"Tell me—what is a sixth sense?"

The ghoul hovered over to her right. "Your sixth sense picks up on the energies in the world, auras projected by all objects that can't be seen, smelled, or heard. They can be felt—and everyone feels them."

Krista looked up at him. "You mean vibes?"

"Yes, you could call it that, and yours are far beyond any other mortal. It allows you to see me and to feel me with your mind."

"Am I going to see others like you?"

"Possibly. I have a strong sense myself, which puts us on equal levels and makes it easier for us to communicate compared to other beings."

"I don't want a strong sixth sense. It isn't fun."

"Life isn't fun, girl! It is about stabilizing the chaos known as your existence to achieve what you desire."

Krista shook her head and walked toward her window, arms folded. "A doctor is coming though; he can make me all better."

"The doctor won't make you better. I warned you of him to protect you: the more you neglect the reality that is in front of you, the greater it will rebound."

"Is that a threat?" She turned to face Malpherities.

"I am not your foe, but I come from a world that will tear all the flesh from the body," he said while floating over to her bedside.

"I won't go there, then."

"The gatekeeper willed it so, and you'll be brought to the Weaver's realm!"

"Abesun beat the gatekeeper, and I will too."

Malpherities roared and grabbed her bedframe. With one tug from his lean, muscular arms, the bed tipped over and landed upside down. The mattress and sheets flipped over onto the floor. "You can't beat the Weaver! Who is to say that this Abesun isn't simply a part of the Weaver's plan? Just because he told you something doesn't make it true. You trust blindly."

"Why would the Weaver kill his gatekeeper and then set Abesun free?"

"The Weaver flows through his minions. His minions cross realms; they are his eyes and ears. His plan is great, far beyond your comprehension. I guarantee you, your friend did not escape the Weaver."

"He did, I saw him. He tore a pendant from the previous gatekeeper's chest."

"Don't be stupid. Your friend did not escape. When his death comes, he'll be judged by the gods and placed in the Weaver's realm again."

"He'll escape then, too."

"Not when death overrules. Then he'll become another one of the Weaver's minions. Even the heavenly angels cannot escape Dreadweave Pass"

Krista shook her head. "You're only trying to scare me. I don't want to talk to you anymore." She rushed to the door. She wanted to find Paladin. Maybe he could help her with the Weaver.

The ghoul grabbed her tail and pulled her back, hard. She screamed as she was thrown to the floor, chest first.

"Running will do you no good! You cannot prevent what has been decided by the gatekeepers. You *will* enter Dreadweave Pass."

"Let me go!" She squirmed, trying to break free of his claws.

"Promise me you won't run."

"Okay." Krista calmed down and nodded.

Malpherities released his grip on her tail and sighed. "I don't understand why you run, girl. I have yet to hurt you."

"You cut me." She pointed at her collarbone.

"If you call that pain, you truly will not survive Dreadweave Pass."

Krista bit her lip. "Well, yeah, it's just a scratch."

"If I had let you run down the halls to Paladin, he would simply have assumed you're insane. He would lock you in your room."

"Why?"

"He wouldn't want to risk any harm to the humans of this barracks."

Krista nodded. She feared the ghoul still, but she knew he was right. He'd only been trying to warn her, but she kept acting childish and it made the ghoul angry.

"Tell me, why do you help me?"

"I saved you, when you were marked. I bound my essence to you, so when you cross into Dreadweave Pass we can escape before the Weaver finds you. Then we can focus on the larger issues at hand."

"But you just said no one can beat the Weaver. How can you beat him at something big?"

The ghoul folded his arms. "Alone, maybe not. But with you still being alive while in the afterlife, things may be different."

"I don't follow."

Malpherities glanced over to the bedframe, still laying on its side; he swooped over and flipped it right-side up, gently placing the sheets back on the mattress. "In time, you will understand."

Krista examined the metal, which was now bent and folded inward from Malpherities's strength.

"They won't be pleased with this," Malpherities commented, looking at the bed. He then gazed over to the new crack in the wall where he had punched the stone.

"No." Krista folded her arms, worried. *What am I going to say happened?* They'd never believe her if she told them Malpherities did it.

"I'm sorry." The ghoul looked down to the floor.

She stood and walked toward him. "Earlier, you told me that friends betray one another."

"Yes, I did."

"Can you tell me of a relationship between two people that can have a permanent trust?"

The ghoul remained silent, staring at the ground.

"Can you?"

He shook his head. "I know of none."

Slowly Krista lifted the ghoul's head, fingers on his smooth jawline. She wanted to see his eyes—which weren't glowing as brightly anymore. They were slanted and full of sorrow.

"I can teach you," Krista said.

He broke free of her hand and growled. "I told you before, girl, I've been in existence for so long, and I have yet to see one life that I can trust."

"Do you know why you saved me?"

Malpherities ground his teeth.

Krista smiled. "I think you pitied me."

"Pity is for the weak."

"It's the only explanation I can see."

"Not everything needs explaining."

I get him now. He's not so mysterious after all; he's just lonely. Krista smiled. "I'll be your friend."

The ghoul snickered. "I told you. I need no friends."

"I think you do. I also think you need a new definition of a friend."

The ghoul shook his head.

Krista brought out her hand. "Can we start over?" As farfetched as it seemed, if these dreams she was having during the night were to become more of a reality, she would have to have a friend. Malpherities was ancient and claimed to have seen many things in his time; he would be a good guide.

The ghoul squinted while eyeing her hand.

"It's a sign of trust."

The ghoul smiled. "Of course." He extended his claws and shook Krista's small hand. "Trust."

CHAPTER XVII

Day Walker

PATIENT: KRISTALANTICE SCALEBANE

AGE: UNKNOWN
DAY: ONE
ENTRY: ONE

My travels were long to the High Barracks, which is now my sanctum. I do prefer the quarters I had in King Loathsan's castle, but the central location of the barracks is far more effective to travel from. I did not plan on returning to the High Barracks so soon; however, it's impossible to predict when this will take another victim's life. Mental Damnation—just when it seems I am closer to understanding the disease, it shows yet another new facet. It was painful to me to leave Mrs. Soulstone to bury her boy in the dirt and then bring the news to his father. However, there was nothing that I could do for the family. The illness seems to prove greater than anyone, no matter their willpower.

It is interesting to me to see this disease's high favour of children. I have heard stories of mature patients conquering this sickness of the mind. If they can remain grounded and truly do not believe in the hallucinations, their body can fight off the disease. However, these are stories from other doctors, not from my own experience. Doctors are people—and people lie.

It has occurred to me that the disease knows children do not understand the difference between reality and stories. Perhaps this is why children have been its main victims; the disease may be able to sense an undeveloped mind.

This brings me to my current state of events. I was rather displeased that the death of Mrs. Soulstone's son occurred so quickly and I would be returning to the barracks so soon. The High Barracks of Zingalg offers diminutive work, tending wounded soldiers and mending broken bones while I await news of another diagnosed victim.

But thankfully it seems this return trip will prove to be more. I received word from Paladin regarding a development in his barracks. This issue isn't physical but psychological. His letter told of a girl not of this world who too suffers from Mental Damnation.

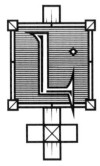ight invaded the room as the clouds cleared in the distance and the sun peeked from the horizon. Krista squinted and raised her hand to block the light. The brightness was overwhelming, causing her head to ache. *I really didn't expect the light to be so intense. Guess I still have to get used to it.* She rolled over on her bed to face the wall, turning her back to the sun.

Krista stretched, feeling the sheets of her bed run against her bare legs.

The night before, Malpherities had left her after they shook hands, leaving her alone in her room. She was happy that she was alone; it allowed her to finally relax. It was nice to be free of Malpherities blabbering on doom and darkness nonsense, and have no Paladin around telling her how to behave.

But her rest wasn't as peaceful as she had hoped. *The same visions haunted my mind—blood, but this time I saw more. There were pools of blood for miles around. But it seems like a vague memory and I can't remember all the details.* Krista had removed her clothes, trying to relax in her slumber. But even the soft sheets on her body could not help soothe the headache she now woke up to.

Her eyes were half open and she lifted her hands to rub the gunk from her eyelids. She brought her knuckles an inch away from her face to see smeared, dried blood covering her skin. Her eyes widened and her heart stopped momentarily at the sight.

Krista screamed and sprang from her bed, falling to the ground and landing on her wounded arm.

Quickly, she scurried up and looked around the room. Blood was spread on the floor, the walls, and all over her sheets. There was also dried blood caked on the bent bedframe. Her clothes were scattered on the ground.

A knock came at her door.

Krista gasped. "Just a moment!" She dashed around the room gathering her clothing. *Shit, this isn't good.*

Wasting no time, Krista got dressed. It hurt to use her hands and she glanced at her knuckles, which were swollen, bruised, and cut. While pulling on her boots, Krista looked over to the wall that Malpherities had smashed, seeing that it was still cracked, but now was also covered in blood. She fixed her scalp-feathers as best as she could, but without a mirror she was practically helpless.

It'll have to do, as long as it is out of my face.

She buttoned the front of her black dress and took one last look around the room, realizing there was nothing else she could do to conceal the mayhem. *It's as good as it's going to get.* Krista cleared her throat. "Come in."

The door opened before she finished speaking and Paladin marched in. His mouth dropped as he looked around, eyeing the chaos.

He spotted her wounded hands. "Krista, what happened here?"

She hid her hands behind her back while staring at the ground. "Nothing."

Paladin walked over and kneeled before her, taking hold of her shoulders. "Lies aren't tolerated here." He pulled her right arm from her back and examined the bruises. "What were you doing last night?"

Krista grunted when Paladin held her hand; his touch made the wounds sting. She tried to pull free, but he kept a firm grip on her. "It's nothing, really."

Paladin glanced back and pointed at the crack in the wall. "These walls are built to withstand armies. You're just a girl who spent one night in a room alone and now there are cracks in the stone." He shook his head. "How long were you hitting it for? Your hands are in terrible condition."

Krista pushed her scalp-feathers aside with her free hand. It felt like sandpaper while she ran her sensitive, cut fingers through it.

"I don't know." She could feel a tear fall down her cheek. It was true—Krista could not remember hurting herself. What if Malpherities had injured her hands during the night? She was certain she would have awakened if he did, but even that didn't make sense. *What is happening to me?*

Paladin shook his head again. "Come with me, and we'll take care of your hands."

Krista sniffled as Paladin stood. "Okay."

Paladin walked out of the room, assuming she was following. Krista stayed close behind him and kept her bloody hands close to her body, hiding them from sight. The two walked from her room and down to the first level of the keep. Paladin did not look back at her once; he kept his eyes keen on the path he walked.

What happened last night? Is this what Mental Damnation does to you? Is this the kind of experiences Abesun had talked about? With an eerie feeling, Krista remembered Abesun's words. *'Things happen in Dreadweave Pass that I cannot explain to you. When you are infected with Mental Damnation, you take a journey you must travel alone to understand.'* It worried her that eventually Dreadweave Pass would become more real like Malpherities had said. Abesun never explained what he saw in Dreadweave Pass, which worried her even more. She feared the unknown.

Paladin led her through the keep for a couple of minutes until they reached an office door. Krista recognized the hallway by the polished suits of armour on each side; they were at the office where she'd first awakened.

Paladin opened the door and held his hand out for her to proceed.

"Thanks," she said, stepping into the room.

The room had not changed since she'd last left: the operating table was still where she recalled it being, and the shelves were still to the far side. Krista walked to the operating table and tried to climb onto it. She found it difficult to get onto the bed without putting her weight on her hands, but she managed to gather her strength and get on top of it using her forearms.

Paladin walked over to the far right of the room where he picked up a rag and a tin bucket of fresh water. Krista was unsure where the rag and bucket had come from; her mind was too flustered with all the blood.

"Here, let me wash your hands," Paladin volunteered, approaching.

He placed the bucket on the table and Krista held out her right hand for Paladin to wash.

Paladin took the rag from the bucket and placed it gently on her hand. The cool water stung as it seeped into the cuts and bruises; eventually she got used to the pain and Paladin cleaned the blood and rock chips that were stuck to her skin. After the wash, Paladin wrapped her hand in strips of linen cloth from the cupboards on the far left of the room.

"That should be enough," Paladin said. "You'd better rest. Give your hands some time to heal."

Krista nodded and got up from the table, ready to leave when another man walked into the office. It was Smyth, the curly-haired man from her first day at the keep. He scowled at her as he entered, then looked at Paladin.

The man bowed. "Paladin."

"Smyth."

"Dr. Alsroc has arrived."

Nodding, Paladin began to leave. Krista leaped from the operating table and tried to follow behind him, but he was faster than her and closed the office door behind him.

"Wait here, Krista, so the doctor can assist you further with your wounds." His instructions were muffled through the door. Locks rattled on the other side before Paladin's footsteps faded down the hall.

Krista sat herself on the operating table again. She tried to scratch her hands; the linen was itchy and she wanted it off. Paladin had tied it too tight and she could feel the circulation cut off in her fingers, which were quickly losing sensation.

Her mind was frazzled. The blood, Malpherities, Dreadweave Pass— all things she knew little of and was caught in the middle of.

What about Darkwing? She shook her head. *Where is that boy?*

On top of that, now she was going to meet this doctor everyone kept talking about.

Krista had never liked seeing doctors of any kind. She only had vague memories from being a child on the surface world, of stern voices and bad-tasting medicines.

A hissing sound caught her attention, like a kettle would make, coming from below her legs. She leaned over the table to look underneath. Black fog was rising from the shadow underneath the table.

Oh great, him again.

Malpherities's fog came out from under the table and the ghoul took shape beside her. "The doctor is coming."

Krista lifted her hands for Malpherities to see her wounds.

The ghoul raised an eyebrow. "What did you do?"

"Go see my room . . . It's covered in blood. Even the wall you punched—my blood is there too."

Malpherities folded his arms. "That is most bizarre."

It was difficult for Krista to tell if the ghoul was lying. They did shake hands, though, showing that they trusted one another. *I have to trust him, so that means he is speaking the truth.* "Paladin wasn't happy about the disaster in my room."

"I'm sorry for the mess, Krista."

"How did it happen? Is this what Mental Damnation does?"

"Your body could have reacted to your mind trying to cross realms. Like sleepwalking during a bad dream. It is hard to say."

"I'm scared. Is this going to get worse?"

"At first, yes, but once you're in Dreadweave Pass, you will adapt."

"What about the doctor?"

"He's a fool. He thinks that Mental Damnation is a disease—an illness that can be cured with worldly medicine. He has no grasp of what it really is."

Krista didn't care what it really was, or about anything to do with Mental Damnation for that matter. She never asked to be infected and nothing about it interested her. *All I wanted was to try to gather myself together in the barracks with the humans, then figure out if I want to stay or go home to Darkwing.* But now the doctor was here, Malpherities was here, and things had the potential to become far worse for her.

Doctors always make things worse.

"When he comes in here, act normal; tell him you don't remember anything." Malpherities moved closer to her. "Most importantly, don't tell him of me."

Krista nodded. *It's not like the doctor would understand what I see, feel, or hear, anyway.* The doctor could declare she was crazy and everyone would believe him. *Because he is a doctor.* She sighed. "I'm scared."

"You said that already."

"Can we run away?"

Malpherities snorted. "Where to?"

"I don't want to be here anymore. I thought this was a friendly place but now they are trying to imprison me like my own people did."

"Don't be absurd. Your home was a disaster, and here they have order. The only place that will be worse than your homeland is Dreadweave Pass."

Krista shook her head and stared to the ground.

The ghoul licked his lips. "It isn't going to be easy for you to explain your damaged hands—or the room."

"No . . ." Krista looked to the ground. She swung her legs in the air, watching her boots.

"I'm sorry, again."

Krista shook her head. "It's fine. Whatever made me damage the room and injure myself . . . Malpherities, can you just not touch anything anymore?"

"Agreed. You don't need any more trouble. As long as you'll listen to my advice. We are friends, Krista, remember? Friends listen."

"Okay."

The locks to the door began to rattle and Krista looked up, watching the handle twist. She glanced over to Malpherities but he had vanished.

The door creaked open and Paladin entered the room with an older, pale man. He had a tired expression on his wrinkly face. His grey hair was brushed back, revealing the distinctive lines across his forehead. The saggy bags underneath his eyes were discoloured and a shaggy beard surrounded his frowning lips.

Paladin waved his hand to Krista. "Here she is, Dr. Alsroc."

The old man's eyes moved back and forth while staring at Krista. "Poor girl, I didn't think the metamorphosis fumes of the underworld would cause such a shift in their appearance. It's remarkable in a way."

Krista kept her head low. She didn't like looking at the old man; when he stared at her it was like he was examining her like an object. *Makes me feel like I'm not living.*

"Does she have the mark?" the doctor asked.

Paladin stepped toward Krista and she looked up at him. Gently he brushed her scalp-feathers aside, revealing the mark on her neck. He kept his hand firmly on her shoulder, preventing her from moving.

The doctor stroked his beard. "Interesting spot for the mark. It is exceptionally faded, too."

"She has one here, too, and it's more intense." Paladin lifted her hand. "Unfortunately, she's wounded and we had to wrap her hands."

"That's where the mark normally is." The doctor walked over to the office table to the left of the room and grabbed a wooden stool that rested behind. He dragged the stool over, the legs of it scraping against the stone floor. He brought it over to the operating table and sat down. He was now eye-level with Krista and he smiled. "Hello, my name is Dr. Alsroc. What is your name?"

Krista looked down to see he also had a notebook with a pen. The book was open and had words scribbled on it. *I can't read them, but I bet it's about me.* She didn't like the idea that he would be writing about things she said.

Paladin poked her shoulder.

"Krista," she mumbled.

"Is that your real name?"

Sighing, she replied, "Scalebane. Kristalantice Scalebane." She watched as the doctor wrote on the paper before continuing to his next question.

"Okay, Kristalantice, I'd like you to feel comfortable with talking to me. I'm your friend." He paused, making sure he had her attention. "What's your favourite colour?"

Krista smirked at the question. She glanced up at the Paladin, who stared down at her with a grim face. Krista realized that they were both serious and they wanted to know about her favourite colour.

It seemed odd to her that the doctor wasn't looking at her physical condition.

She scratched her head lightly. "I don't really have one."

"Do you have a favourite animal?"

She shook her head. "Why are you asking me these questions? Paladin told me you were going to fix me."

The doctor scribbled more words on his paper before responding. "I'm here to help you. As for 'fixing' you, I don't think it is possible for me to do. From what I've seen in the past, only you can fix yourself. This goes for anyone who wants a change."

She slouched down. *This guy is just as useless as anyone else that knows about Mental Damnation. It is all up to me—they all say that.*

Alsroc crossed his legs. "If you don't wish to talk about simple things to get to know each other, I'll just move onto more serious matters."

"Please, I don't want to sit here anymore."

"How did you get the mark?" he asked, pointing at her neck with his pen.

"Another vazelead gave it to me," she mumbled.

"Do you recall how he gave it to you?"

"Yes."

Alsroc shook his head. "Can you clarify? Was it transferred by touch, breath, or in a sexual manner?"

These questions seem so personal. Krista was unsure how she should reply to it. "He burned me with his palm." She coiled her tail around her index finger, fidgeting with the tip of it. "By touch, I guess."

Dr. Alsroc wrote on his paper again. "Tell me, have you been having any headaches since you got this mark?"

Krista remembered what Malpherities told her to do: tell the doctor nothing. "No," she lied.

"Patients do not often recall how they get the puncture mark. I've always hypothesized it to be from a bite, with the shape coming from the swelling."

"It wasn't a bite. My people's bites don't make that shape—it was his palm that touched me."

"Most interesting. Have you had any hallucinations?"

"No."

"Do you hear any voices during the day, or night?"

"No."

"How about nightmares?"

"No." Krista glanced up at the Paladin, whose gaze remained on Krista. He obviously knew she had lied, as she had talked to him about the dreams before.

"Okay." The doctor stood and finished jotting down notes on the paper.

"Well?" Paladin asked, releasing his hand from Krista's shoulder.

Krista resisted the urge to rub her shoulder and remained still. She had not realized how strong his grip was until he let go. She realized that he'd intentionally squeezed after she lied to the doctor.

"It's definitely a case of Mental Damnation—the mark is a clear sign," Alsroc said as he moved to the desk, placing the notebook on the surface. "She hasn't shown any symptoms of the early stages of the illness, though."

"Is it contagious?"

The doctor let out a soft chuckle. "No, she can't infect anyone with it. Very few cases will you see a person be a carrier of the disease; those are hostile and will try to infect anyone young with it."

He must mean gatekeepers, like Ast'Bala and Danil.

"Most are just the victims and cannot pass it on." He sat on the chair behind the desk, fingertips touching one another, legs crossed.

Nodding, Paladin folded his arms. "Her hands were badly wounded during the night and her room is a disaster. She claims not to remember anything." He sighed. "I don't think she has the physical strength to do the damage that she did."

Leaning back in his chair, Alsroc replied, "During their sleep, patients who suffer Mental Damnation have shown spontaneous bursts of strength and have done extraordinary things while sleepwalking."

"Sleepwalking?"

"Sometimes they'll sleepwalk and, as I said, they gain strength. Other times they have internal bleeding or rapid muscle growth. In odd cases, their bones break, yet they are exposed to no pressure that could make the bones snap. My theory is the stress the disease puts on the body causes the muscles to tighten too much and they crush the bones between."

Krista didn't care about the information; she remembered Malpherities told her that the doctor would try to put logic where there was none to be found. He didn't have Mental Damnation and therefore could never understand it. The ghoul told her that her sixth sense was enhanced, and it would tell her much more than what the doctor was saying.

I should trust my friends. It is all I have, she thought while sliding from the table. Krista adjusted the bottom of her dress, which had slid up. "Can I leave now?"

Alsroc nodded. "Of course. Thank you for your time, Kristalantice."

Smiling, Krista walked out of the room. She didn't care what else they had to say. She wanted to spend some time alone; perhaps find a way to clean her room. *I need to think. How long will this doctor be here? I don't want another person telling me what to do. What will Mental Damnation do to me next and can Malpherities help?*

She exited the office to see Malpherities waiting by the doorframe.

"Wait!" he demanded.

The ghoul grabbed Krista's mouth as she gasped.

"It is important that we hear what they say," he said, pulling Krista to the side beside the door.

Paladin sighed. "You think this sleepwalking will get worse?"

"Most likely," Alsroc replied.

"Should she be restrained during the night?"

"No, not yet, that wouldn't be fair. The disease is still in its early stages and has plenty of time to evolve. Chances are the sleepwalking won't be as dangerous as time passes." Alsroc paused. "She's a vazelead.

How did she get to the surface? Did she tell you anything else?"

"She lied to you. Krista has had several nightmares and inside these nightmares she said a poetic voice speaks to her."

"I'm not surprised she lied, as this is probably quite frightening for her. Victims often have a poetic voice speak to them in the early stages of the disease, yes."

"I know you strongly believe this is a disease, Dr. Alsroc, but I'll ask again: have you ever considered an exorcism on a patient with Mental Damnation?"

"I have attempted with a number of priests, including Father Isaac here in the High Barracks. It has never given any positive results. We have even tried during the patients' nightmares and they only ignore the priest's words."

"It seems odd to me that this disease is immune to the holy words of God. There are only a handful of events in history that have defied God, and they have all been related to the Book of Consulo. The histories describe events much like the scene where I first found Krista."

Alsroc chuckled. "Book of Consulo? I assure you, this is not the work of anything supernatural. I've dissected infected brains firsthand; it is an oversized physical entity that attaches itself to the brain tissue."

"Yes, so you have told me. As much as I would enjoy another debate over what Mental Damnation really is, I have some ungrateful children that I need to bring in here for medical attention."

"That's our cue," Malpherities said.

Krista picked up her pace down the hall. As she walked, Krista noticed that the ghoul moved with her, his black fog linked to her own shadow.

Malpherities scowled. "The doctor only sees you as another experiment to study Mental Damnation on—another toy to play with."

"Great," Krista mumbled.

The two walked up to the second floor and back into her room in silence. She was unsure what she was supposed to say to Malpherities; she did not know the doctor and he seemed friendly. *Often friendly people are nice because they want something,* she reminded herself.

Once they entered her room, Krista sighed. "You seem to know a bit about this doctor. Have you dealt with him before?"

"Yes, and he is nothing but trouble."

Krista sat down on her bed and stared out her window with the sun beating down on her skin. She liked the strange tingle she felt from it, but only for short spurts.

Before it starts to make me bleed, the warmth is soothing. If only I could be out in the sun all day. The night was so cold.

Malpherities floated over to the edge of her bed. "Mental Damnation can't be beaten by the doctor's psychological games."

Krista nodded while staring at the sun. *It's so mesmerizing.*

Malpherities gazed at the bright light. "The sun isn't good for you."

"I like it, though."

"It'll melt your innards."

"How do you know what the sun does to me?"

"I can sense what you feel, girl. Remember?"

"Yeah." Krista scratched her nose. "I noticed something." She lightly rubbed her stomach, feeling her soft dress. "Every time the sunbeams hit me, my bare skin seems to be affected by the rays more than my parts that are covered up."

"Yes, because it is exposed."

"What if I cover up my skin?"

"There's no telling if it would even help. Don't put our minds in useless places."

"You got a better idea on how to spend my time? I want to walk in the day, not be trapped in here. Besides, then I can see William again."

The ghoul shook his head.

"Do you think it would work? If we found enough material to cover all my skin?"

Malpherities stared at the sky with his arms crossed.

"Do you?"

The ghoul growled before answering, "Yes . . . it's possible it could work."

Krista smiled.

"We'd need thick material, to prevent any rays of sun from touching your skin."

"These brick walls protect me from the sun, so I don't see why tightly woven material wouldn't."

"The sun is a mysterious being, filled with light, wrath, anger, and joy. It is uncertain what it will do."

Krista rolled her eyes. "Sure." She stood from her bed and glanced around her room. "Maybe the blankets will work if I wrap them around me."

"The blankets are light materials. We need some thick fabric."

"Then I guess we should go look for some."

She led the way out of her room and ghoul followed behind her. The two walked down the halls with the idea of asking someone for help. Any human they passed kept to themselves; even when she waved at them they ignored her.

"Should we ask Paladin?" she questioned.

"No, he wouldn't let you risk walking in the daylight. We'd even be better off to talk to the doctor, or anyone else."

The two travelled down the stairway to the first floor and took a turn to the right. They were brought to a halt when they crossed paths with Smyth.

"Hi," Krista said, slightly startled to see him.

The man seemed calm, and was walking slowly. He squinted when he noticed her hands. "What happened to your hands?"

"You came in the office earlier, didn't you see the blood in the bucket?"

He shook his head. "My mind was elsewhere. Must have slipped by me."

"Well, it's a long story."

Malpherities sighed. "Ask him about cloth!"

Krista glanced to see the ghoul was still beside her. She shifted her eyes between the man and the ghoul, and realized that the man didn't see Malpherities. *I can't get over that no one even senses him.*

"Where are you going in such a hurry, anyway?"

"I need clothes." She brushed her scalp-feathers back, "Paladin wouldn't understand, but the sun hurts me and I need to cover my skin better. Can you help me?"

The man looked around. "I heard about your incident outside. What do you think will help?"

"If I had more heavy clothing, the sun wouldn't touch me."

"It's not a bad theory." He smirked. "I didn't take you for a thinker, but I have to say, I am impressed."

"Thanks."

"We do have spare clothes. Come with me." He turned around and began walking down the hall he came from.

Krista walked beside him. "Thank you."

"What does the sun do to you?"

"The rays from the sun, do you feel them?"

The man shook his head. "You mean the heat?"

"That, and a tingling. It feels good at first. I found out the hard way, though, that it starts to melt me from inside. That's what made me bleed: blood came from my mouth, from my nose, and I got dizzy."

"That's a shame." The man stopped midway through the hall at a black door and twisted the bronze handle, pushing the door open. Inside was a storage room with stacks of wooden boxes. Some were clamped shut and others left open with clothes dangling out. Krista followed Smyth into the room and peeked inside the boxes to see all sorts of items ranging from shoes and coats to tools and jars.

The man opened a box and brought out a long coat. He unfolded it and eyed it from top to bottom. "This one should fit you perfectly. It belonged to one of the boys, but he was sent home recently." He handed the jacket to Krista.

"Why was he sent home?" she asked, putting the jacket on.

"He was weak."

Slipping the coat on, Krista felt the material: linen with leather lining along the shoulders, elbows, and edges of the coat. It draped over her heavily. *I'll get used to the weight.*

Smyth nodded. "Fits well."

She glanced at her feet, seeing that the coat was only a couple inches from the floor.

"That should keep the sun off your skin."

Krista smiled. "Thank you."

Malpherities shook his head. "Not enough coverage."

"I think I need more, though."

Smyth walked out of the room. "Take what you need. No one ever comes in here. I don't think they'll miss anything."

"Okay, I won't take too much," Krista replied. "Thanks again for helping me."

He took a slight bow. "I don't mind helping one with an idea. If no one helped another with their theories, we wouldn't be where we are today."

Krista nodded slowly. "You're right."

"Of course I am. Close the door when you're done."

"Bye."

Krista heard the man's footsteps echo away, leaving her and Malpherities to look through the crates.

"He has a bit of a stale personality, doesn't he?" Malpherities grinned.

"I guess. He helped us, at least."

"Indeed. That coat is a good start," Malpherities said, lifting a pair of trousers from a box and then chucking them to the ground. "But your skimpy dress isn't enough to cover your neck and legs."

"This is a pretty dress. I was happy when I found it." *Or stole it, for that matter.*

The two spent at least an hour looking through the boxes. It hurt Krista to use her hands and she asked Malpherities to look through the clothes for her. She didn't want to strain her fingers; the pain was too much for to deal with.

They had found several scarves and rags for her face, along with buckles and various cloth scraps to wrap around her legs and cover what her dress left exposed. She found a pair of leather gloves that would fit well on her hands after they healed and the linen wraps came off.

Malpherities backed up to take a look at her. They were able to cover most areas of her skin with the trench coat and two dark brown scarves wrapped around her face. Underneath the long coat she wore a lighter, shorter red jacket with a heavy, baggy hood that rested on top of her scalp-feathers and most of her face. Scraps of what used to be to shirts and pants wrapped around her legs and were secured with buckles.

She smiled and posed for the ghoul. "How do I look?"

"Several parts of your skin are still exposed, but your coat should cover them." He moved closer to her. "I suppose you're set."

"Perfect." Krista smiled.

The two exited the room and closed the door behind them.

"Let's test it out," she said, walking down the hall until they came across an exit that led into the sunlight. Krista pointed. "That door will do."

"If you still feel the tingle, don't hesitate to come back inside. Being a creature of the darkness is nothing to fear," Malpherities said.

She nodded at him as the ghoul buttoned up her coat for her. "Okay, let's try it out." She let out a heavy sigh.

Malpherities moved aside, leaving Krista to face the door.

She took each step toward the door slowly, getting closer to the door until she could touch the handle. Carefully, Krista pulled it open and stepped outside into the blinding light, a vazelead walking underneath the sun.

CHAPTER XVIII

Mental Obesity

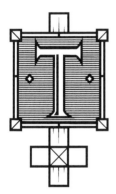he aftermath of a raid: once-spotless hallways furnished with hand-painted wall scrolls were now paintings of genocide with blood-smeared walls, corpses pushed to the sides of the floor, and the stench of the dead permeating the underground building.

It was once a place of peace and meditation— now a graveyard for those that could not escape death. The corpses were covered in slashes and stab wounds, several of them with skulls penetrated or crushed by the brute force of boots and blunt objects.

The Eyes of Eternal Life had been raided by the Renascence Guard, who showed no mercy against the defenseless devotees of the cult.

The adventurers that wandered into the abandoned temple knew of the massacre, but had not realized the extent of the brutality until seeing the aftermath with their own eyes. The sheer number of bodies, pools of blood, vandalized wall paintings, splintered shelves, and broken candle stands would make anyone realize there wasn't anything here worth salvaging. But not for this group: they were looking for clues. They were led by a young, bold vazelead who strove to fix the mistakes he had made in the past.

"Darkwing!" a voice shouted.

The vazelead responded to his name, realizing it was his ally, Draegust, who called him.

"What is it?" he called back.

"You really wore one of these?" Draegust asked with a crooked smirk, lifting a corpse from the ground.

Darkwing nodded, seeing that he was referring to the red robe wrapped around the dead cultist's body.

Draegust laughed. "You really didn't care where you went, as long as she was safe."

"Obviously this was the wrong place."

Returning to the temple brought back memories of Krista to Darkwing. Despite the little time they'd spent here, it reminded him of her being taken away from him. It made him sick to his stomach.

Keep it together, he thought. Darkwing knew his mind was getting the better of him because of their long travel. The group had hiked hastily out of the City of Renascence and out into the sand dunes of the underworld to reach the temple. They didn't stop to rest during their travel since it would only add more time, with no answers, to Krista's disappearance.

"Where was this ritual?" their frail elder comrade asked, scratching his light-toned, dry, scaly neck.

A hiss erupted from the elder's pet shade, which crawled on all fours close to its master. Its smooth translucent outer layer was barely visible in the dark space, but the inner black core could be seen clearly. *Bodies mastered by no souls. No feast.* It spoke to Darkwing's mind—and possibly his other comrades, too.

Darkwing never fully understood how shades could communicate telepathically. He had been told that it was because of being partly here and partly in the afterlife, but he wasn't much of a spiritual person and didn't ask beyond that.

He led his group down a hallway to the right of the entrance, trying to remember where his quarters were. Without the dim light, the carpets, or the paintings on the walls it was difficult to get his bearings. The bare stone halls all looked the same.

Alistind walked close beside him, eyes wide in awe. "Where did they take the rugs? The inscriptions?" she asked.

Draegust spat on a corpse as he walked by. "The Renascence Guard probably took everything from the temple to burn. Cults aren't welcomed in the City of Renascence as they show no loyalty to the Five Guardians."

"Neither do you," Alistind hissed. "At least the temple brought peace to those who followed."

"At least I'm not stupid enough to raise attention to myself."

"Is that why you got the rest of your gang killed?"

Draegust growled and locked eyes with Alistind, his jaw clenched.

"Here." Darkwing tapped the frame of a doorway marked 206. "This was our room."

"Kinda small," Draegust said as he peeked through the doorframe.

Darkwing pointed down the hallway. "That's where they dragged her away; I lost track of her then."

The old vazelead casually walked down the hallway, moving past his three companions. "And where's the ritual?"

"The elders lived on the lower level—that's where they held the high council," Alistind replied. "I've never been down there, but I'm sure it isn't as large as the upper level. We only had twelve elders."

"Do you happen to possess anything of Krista's?" the elder asked Darkwing.

The question sparked his memory, and he remembered that he had Krista's necklace. "I do!" Darkwing took the orange necklace he'd given Krista from his pocket and handed it to the elder.

Taking it gently, the elder kneeled and allowed his shade to examine it. "Track her."

Little scent, the shade snorted.

"It may be difficult, but you must," the elder insisted.

The shade growled again and scurried down the hall, turning the corner Krista had been taken around.

The elder handed the necklace back to Darkwing. "Let us continue."

Darkwing took the necklace carefully and put it in his pocket. The four followed the shade.

"It's a nice necklace," Alistind commented. She walked close to

Darkwing, their shoulders nearly touching, while she played with the tip of her tail.

"She liked it; it matched her eye colour."

It was difficult to follow the shade because he rushed through the halls faster than they could keep up, even if they were to run. At one point, the group lost the shade entirely but he showed up again from behind, indicating he had circled the entire temple. Darkwing didn't know if the shade would be able to find the site of the ritual, but the elder insisted that the shade would succeed.

"Look!" Alistind exclaimed and pointed off to their right where a small hall ended with a linear stairway leading deeper into the temple.

The shade picked up on her shout and buzzed past the four, running down the stairway.

"They managed to clear this place quickly," Draegust noted. "You'd think the Renascence Guard would be busy with the escaped prisoners."

"They hate those that show no loyalty to the Five Guardians far more than petty vermin," the elder replied.

"One thing is unclear to me," Draegust said. "What's your name, wrinkle scale?"

The elder chuckled. "You call me by Wrinkle Scale, therefore that is my name."

"No, your birth name."

"The concept of birth can be misleading, Draegust. It confines our minds to age and the past, limiting us from what we are capable of thinking. Simply accepting ourselves as we are now sets us free from what has happened and the worries of tomorrow. A name is backed by the history behind it."

Draegust shook his head. "Whatever, Wrinkles. You're the one who talks about human fairy tales of God."

"God?" Alistind asked.

"God is the one who gave us life. It's something I learned while with the humans during the Drac Age. I prayed, and he gave our people freedom from the humans through the Drac Lord Fongoxent."

Alistind looked to the ground. "But I thought the Risen One was the one who was going to free us."

"We all make mistakes, but God is forgiving."

Draegust snorted. "You don't need forgiveness or praying. You've got yourself, sweetie; that's all we have. Make peace with that."

Wrinkle Scale spoke. "We're never alone. God is within all of us. No matter how hard you push him away."

Darkwing gestured forward. "Can we stay focused?" He was ill at ease coming back to the temple and hearing their debate about philosophical concepts bored him.

The four moved in rows of two, walking to the linear staircase and following it down to the second level. The corpses and bloody walls ceased, becoming just a vacant hallway. The shade was several paces ahead, dashing down the narrow hall. Darkwing noticed that the creature's nose was never on the ground or in the air, so it wasn't clear what scent he was using to detect Krista.

Maybe shades picked up on otherworldly sensations that I can't, he thought.

"How is the shade finding where the ritual was?" Alistind asked.

"Dead skin," Wrinkle Scale replied. "It is guaranteed the necklace had dead skin of Krista's on it, even a tiny piece. Shades can see what the skin is willing to share."

Alistind squinted. "You're saying our skin has its own mind?"

"No, it's a part of us. Once it separates from us, it carries an encrypted essence of our past, essentially a vision of where that being had been. One with an open mind is able to see these visions—taste and hear them to find the answers one is looking for."

"I still don't follow," she mumbled.

"It's not for us to understand. We'd be blessed with the shade's gift if we were meant to have it."

The shade scurried back to the four. *Located.*

"Where?" Darkwing asked. He felt his scales stand up from the excitement, craving to know where Krista was.

Here. The shade moved slower, at a speed that the four could follow. He led them to the end of the hall where a large circular door was left wide open. The lock had been blasted out and lay a couple feet from the door. Beyond the door was a room with four pillars and a blood-drenched altar in the middle. It was difficult to see the details from a distance, but Darkwing could make out the gist of the scene. He rushed past his three companions and into the empty room, stopping dead-centre. Blood soaked the altar and most of the floor, still sticky.

Alistind squealed when she entered the room. To the corner of one of the columns, a pure white vazelead corpse lay flat, face-down. The tail flopped to one side and the head had been dismembered; only muscle tissue and torn skin remained on the neck.

Darkwing looked around the floor. The head was just a few feet away from the body in a pool of semi-dried blood. The red eyes rolled halfway back in their sockets, mouth open and tongue sticking out to one side.

Alistind leaned down to the corpse, touching the shoulder. "Poor dear Saulaph," she sniffled.

"A pale face." Draegust glared at the corpse. "Rare breed."

"He was a caring soul. His physical looks did not matter."

Darkwing scratched his head. "This doesn't make sense. The Renascence Guard captain said the door was shut when his men came down here."

"My guess is the ritual had something to do with it," Wrinkle Scale replied.

"Or maybe whoever did all this opened the door when they were done?" Draegust said.

"So where would Krista be, then?" Darkwing asked.

Alistind walked up to Darkwing and gently placed herself in his arms. "We'll find her," she mumbled into his chest while clutching his shirt.

The shade jumped onto the altar and snorted while staring at the blood. His movements were fluent and fast while analyzing the scene with his white eyes scanning back and forth. He scurried off the altar and around it. On the opposite side of the altar, the shade pulled out a scrap of cloth. *It speaks; she was here.*

Wrinkle Scale took the cloth. "It's drenched in blood, mostly dried out," he said, handing it to Darkwing. "Keep it. We may need it."

Darkwing took the cloth. The blood was caked into every seam and it was still slightly damp to the touch. Sniffing the cloth, Darkwing could pick up the weak scent of Krista, even over the rotting stench of Saulaph.

"This isn't an ordinary ritual," Wrinkle Scale announced while circling around the altar, hands behind his back. He gradually brought his gaze to the ceiling. "Something far greater than a bloodbath took place."

Alistind looked up and gasped. "What is that?"

The brick ceiling was smeared in more blood, painting a circle of glyphs that looked identical to the ones found throughout the temple. A smaller blood circle was daubed inside the outer glyphs, and inside that, an outline of dots formed another circle. The dots were inconsistent in size, with visible fingerprint impressions. The three blood-painted circles were incomplete and their ends branched outward into opposite directions, forming straight lines.

Inside the open space of the circle was a wide, thick splatter of black blood, forming two triangles, one stretching longer than the other. In the centre of the triangles was the outline of an eyeball. Some of the thicker clumps of blood drooped from the ceiling and had dried out like stalactites.

Darkwing tilted his head to the side to get a better look at the face inside the circles. The painting reminded him of something; suddenly, his heart clenched. The mark Krista had on her neck.

"I recognize this." Darkwing stood and walked to the centre of the room. "Krista had the same marking on her neck."

Wrinkle Scale nodded. "I think I may know what has happened here."

"What? Where's Krista?" Darkwing moved closer to the elder, feeling his heart race.

"A necromantic ritual of blood."

Silence filled the room. Darkwing wasn't sure what the elder meant. "Krista's blood?" he asked, horrified.

Draegust sighed. "As if any of us would know what a necromantic ritual of blood is."

"How old was Krista?" Wrinkle Scale asked.

Darkwing shook his head, not completely sure of the answer. "Three hundred . . . maybe three-fifty."

Wrinkle Scale nodded while rubbing his chin. "What of Saulaph? What was he like?"

Alistind shook her head. "I didn't know him well; we were simply together under the protection of the temple."

"To my best guess, this ritual used the blood of innocent minds.

It required a lot of blood for the ritual to succeed, hence Saulaph being murdered to make up the extra blood Krista could not. With that blood, the ritual shattered any holy chains that surrounded this place."

"Chains?"

Wrinkle Scale stood straight up, eyeing the group. "Yes, chains. The holy shackles the paladins placed on us are broken. If my hypothesis is correct, we are no longer bound to the underworld."

Darkwing's mouth fell open. This was big news.

Draegust rubbed his face. "This changes everything for us. What makes you so sure?"

"There are two reasons why I've put this theory together: The first clue is from what the Renascence Guard heard down here, yet Krista and Danil are nowhere to be found. Second is the knowledge I have of this symbol. I've seen it before, on my nephew."

Darkwing squinted. "Your nephew had that mark? Like Krista?"

Wrinkle Scale looked to the ground and sighed. "Yes, I lost him to it."

Alistind's eyes slanted. "I'm so sorry."

Wrinkle Scale nodded. "It's all right, life is a gift and you must remember it can easily be taken away. I do know though that this mark consumes the minds of those that have it. I have witnessed this symbol from the humans while I was in slavery too. They often took a group of us vazeleads to their temple in an attempt to convert us to their beliefs and keep the building tidy. In this temple, I observed a group of paladins confine a man to a room—a man they deemed to be possessed by evil, after he had received a mark on his palm."

Darkwing pointed up to the ceiling and spoke. "That mark?"

"Yes. The mark drove him mad. From what we've seen of our guardians, it may have been a case of Mental Damnation. The man was shackled much like how our people are to the underworld; he couldn't leave the room. He tried to run out, but the invisible chains pulled him back. He would shout how he would impale every last paladin who bound him with stalactites. One night, I was at the temple cleaning the halls in preparation for the morning ceremony, and the man stopped shouting. Shortly after, I heard a mouse squeak and shrill. It must have made its way into the room because I peeked through the small window in the door to see the mouse snatched by the man with his teeth, tearing it to shreds. With the blood, he began to smear small dots to form a circle and glyphs similar to the ones in this very room." Wrinkle Scale pointed at the ceiling. "He then charged the door, breaking it open and knocking me out cold from the force. When I awoke, the humans had found me and the man was nowhere to be seen."

"How did your nephew get it?" Darkwing asked.

"I do not know. He was always a wanderer. He traveled beyond Magma Falls. He could have gotten it from anywhere."

Draegust let out a deep breath. "So this ritual we're standing on is like what that human did in that church?"

"Yes, only that our shackles around the underworld are on a much larger scale and needed more blood from sentient beings rather than animals to release them."

"Damn," Draegust muttered.

"That's my theory. Whoever performed this ritual knew of great arts and of a language only mastered by the most evil of souls. It requires a greater state of mind than you or I are in . . . one that is able to trick the gods using the innocence of a child as a mask."

"Did Krista die? How much of this is her blood?" Alistind asked.

"I am uncertain how strong the shackles of the underworld are—or were." Wrinkle Scale pointed at Saulaph's corpse. "The blood in this room appears to be mostly his. Coupled with the fact that there is only one body, I'm assuming Krista survived this ritual."

"Then where is she?" Darkwing asked.

Wrinkle Scale smiled. "By my reckoning, she is alive and she is the first vazelead to walk on the surface world for nearly two hundred years."

Darkwing glanced around at his companions, taken aback. "Krista is on the surface? Well, can we find her? Can we reach the surface world?"

"It's possible."

"Where's the entrance, then? We need to go, now!" Darkwing exclaimed. The vision of Krista alone on the surface world worried him; what if she was discovered by humans? How would they react? How would they treat her? What type of humans would find her?

Knights? Bandits? Simple folk?

I can't leave her alone.

"I know not of the way," Wrinkle Scale admitted. "But I know of a shaman who may be able to assist us."

"Shaman? I have not heard that word in a century." Draegust squinted. "Who practices such arts in our city?"

"She's not of our city," Wrinkle Scale replied. "Come. She lives not far from here: beyond Magma Falls."

"Let's go." Darkwing placed the bloody cloth in his pocket and rushed out of the room. He didn't like stepping in the sticky blood on the floor, knowing some of it was Krista's.

I can't believe this. The scene was surreal to him, still unable to fully grasp that it was Krista's blood.

"What the hell did we get ourselves into, Darkwing?" Draegust let out a deep breath. "Danil obviously is the mastermind; I told you those guardians were always up to something."

Alistind rushed behind Darkwing. "I'm tired. Can we rest first?" she whispered.

The words reminded him of Krista. She'd complained to him often about how she was tired or hungry. In fact, being tired and hungry was all Krista complained about. He did his best to block her out of his mind, but hearing the words come from Alistind brought an ache to his heart.

Stop. Focus, he thought while rubbing his chin. "Um, we'll rest soon, but we can't waste time. Wrinkle Scale is willing to help us find Krista and we should take full advantage of this," Darkwing replied.

"Why is he helping us?"

"I don't know. It seems to me that he is interested in the ritual more than he is in finding Krista."

Draegust shrugged. "Can you blame him? Finding your girl just got a whole lot more interesting if we're returning to the surface world." He let out a chuckle. "Can any of you even remember what the sun feels like?"

Alistind's eyes widened. "Or what the moon looks like? What about feeling grass between our feet?" She smiled and laughed, imagining.

Darkwing shook his head. "But we don't even know how to get there. Our freedom does us no good until we meet this shaman."

Alistind smirked. "A shaman. I thought only primal species had shamanistic beliefs, like trolls on the surface world. We get to see trolls!"

"Apparently we're primitive, too," Draegust replied.

Alistind sighed dreamily. "It will be good to see those creatures again; I only have faint memories of trolls."

Wrinkle Scale turned his head, looking back at the three. "We're all primitive in a way. Yet we think living in a city we are civilized—which is why you have that opinion, Alistind. Because of vazeleads that share your thoughts, Fleerew the shaman has had to live far beyond civilization to conceal her practices."

Draegust nodded. "This is a perfect example of why the Five Guardians have made our lives wretched. Anyone who didn't believe in them, they discarded."

Darkwing couldn't care less about the surface world, or the trolls, or the humans, or even the underworld. To him, it was all the same: both were filled with mortals—mortals that embraced anger, greed, and revenge. It was all he'd ever seen in any civilization. Beauty didn't exist when mass numbers of people were involved. It only boosted their primal behaviours of survival.

The search party left the second level and made its way out of the temple, following Wrinkle Scale.

The group exited the temple through the spiral staircase leading up to the ground level, out of the cavern, and into the sand dunes of the underground.

Draegust remained silent on their travels, keeping to himself at the rear of the party to ensure that they weren't being followed by anyone or stalked by nearby beasts. The shade and Wrinkle Scale kept the lead, followed by Darkwing and Alistind.

While they travelled, Wrinkle Scale informed the group, "We will walk slow. We are best to save our energy for when we meet the shaman. She could easily influence the minds of weak-willed beings."

"Shamans can do that?" Alistind asked. "I thought they just collected bugs and put plants into boiling water and danced around it, claiming to see visions."

"That is a common misunderstanding, Alistind. Often races that practice shamanism don't speak a common tongue and when they are discovered by beings that do, shamans are mistaken as being primeval or savage. When these shamans sense thoughts; they usually cannot explain it in a language that is comprehensible and are mistaken for being unintelligent. Fleerew, on the other hand, can speak English perfectly fine and she will tell you what she senses."

In the core of his gut, Darkwing didn't want to meet the shaman. He didn't feel like dealing with the head games or the optical illusions shamans were known to perform to get what they wanted. But he was desperate and willing to go to any extent to find Krista. He was simply grateful that they could get a lead on her whereabouts. Not too long ago, he was left overwhelmed with nowhere to look after the raid on the temple.

I've got to take what I can get to find Krista, he concluded.

The group travelled up and down the sandy hills of the underworld leading to Magma Falls. The large mountain could be seen in the near distance, the top disappearing into the black sky. Steam rose from the ground near the bottom of the waterfall, where a large pool of lava rested.

Wrinkle Scale did not tire, unlike the other three who panted and were wearing out quickly from all the walking they had already done that day.

"What can this shaman do for us?" Darkwing asked while exhaling heavily.

"She can see great visions that may assist us in finding Krista." He pointed at Darkwing's pouch containing the bloody cloth. "That's what the cloth is for; she'll need the blood."

"Can't your shade just do it?"

"Probably, but he would not know how to get to the surface world."

"And the shaman will?"

"Yes. She personally knows the half-breed, the only being that can cross freely from the underworld to the surface."

"Half-breed?" Alistind asked.

"He's a myth, ain't he?" Draegust added.

"Oh no, he's very much alive." Wrinkle Scale sighed.

"What can he do?" Darkwing asked.

"Because he is half-human and half-vazelead, he is able to pass between the surface and underworld as he pleases. He can show us the way."

"Why didn't the shackles drag him back down like they would drag us?"

"It is believed that the holy shackles were unsure what to do with him because of his mixed ancestry, so they let him pass."

"Sounds like an aldrif shit story to me," Draegust murmured.

The group travelled up the last sand dune that led them right to Magma Falls; the path had become rockier and began to gradually climb upward. The waterfall poured off into several streams that flowed down to the massive lava pool. The group's path led them further off to the right side of the mountain, far away from the farmers.

They stopped by a stream to refresh themselves, but only for a few moments. The taste of cool water on the tongue and the freshness of water splashed on the face were just what the group needed after the long walk.

Wrinkle Scale looked up the mountain. "I suggest we keep moving. The day is well over and the farmers have gone home. When the farmers are gone, the Corrupt come from their caves to drink and hunt."

"How does he know what time of day it is?" Alistind whispered.

Darkwing shrugged. "He's rather mysterious."

Draegust moved close to Darkwing. "The old scale breath is taking us through the Corrupt's land. He's going to get us killed!"

Darkwing glanced at the old vazelead, who wasn't listening. "No, I doubt it." Darkwing knew that the Corrupt's cannibalistic and barbaric behaviour was feared by all vazelead, even Draegust.

Draegust squinted. "Why? He doesn't need us; this is all just a game to him. Why did he even help us?"

"He wants to see the surface world again," said Alistind, "and the ritual interests him. Besides, no one is stupid enough to endanger themselves by the Corrupt."

Draegust shook his head. "Well, he has the information from us, so he has no need to help now. I bet he'll kill us with this shaman. It's what I'd do."

Darkwing turned to look Draegust in the eyes and said, "Or perhaps you're paranoid because you're you. Not everyone is diabolical; some beings value loyalty."

Draegust growled. "Loyalty . . ."

"Maybe he needs our protection from the dangers out here," Darkwing added.

Wrinkle Scale moved effortlessly up the rough path, demonstrating surprising physical fitness as they climbed the mountains. Draegust followed close behind him; he too was very fit and had no troubles climbing the rocks of Magma Falls. Darkwing was forced to lag behind and assist Alistind in her climb.

"I'm sorry," she apologized when the incline leveled out and they moved onto a more even surface. "I've never climbed this high before."

"It's fine." Darkwing kept hold of her arm as they walked.

He examined their surroundings: they were at the entrance to the same cave he'd spent the night in with Krista before they joined the cult. "I brought Krista here when we were hiding from Danil."

Wrinkle Scale looked back at Darkwing as he entered the wide cave entrance. "And here you are again."

The five moved in single file through the cave's stale air. The entrance started off large, but was shaped like a funnel and soon became cramped. The walls were covered with jagged rocks that would pierce through skin if someone were to fall on them.

Wrinkle Scale did not seem alarmed and guided the group through the winding cavern.

As they ventured further into the cave, a fresh breeze began to blow past them. Wrinkle Scale was taking them out onto the other side of the mountain.

"Stay close," Draegust warned. "There's no telling if there are Corrupt around us."

The five reached the end of the cave and emerged on the opposite side of Magma Falls. All they could see was a vast emptiness of black sky. Not even a single pool of molten lava glowed in the distance – only charcoal-coloured fog that blocked their view of the scenery, fading into the black sky. This back side of Magma Falls was steeper and less friendly to walk down.

"What is this?" Alistind asked.

"This is the underworld..." Draegust folded his arms. "This is where the guardians failed in their quest to find us new hope. Our people were grateful to find the land that we have when we were banished to the underworld. The rest of this plane is dark, uninhabitable, and unforgiving."

"Here." Wrinkle Scale pointed at another cave just down the ridged pathway to the left.

Darkwing found it odd that there was a path here, even if it was extremely steep. It was unnatural—it seemed to be worn out by many years of trampling feet. This part of the underworld was supposed to be uninhabited—except for the Corrupt, but they tended to run rampant like animals and rarely stuck to a path twice. Regardless, Darkwing stared at the cave ahead and made out a dim light from inside that flickered. The light of a fire.

"She's home," said Wrinkle Scale.

The path was steep and it took several minutes to walk to the bottom and across to reach the cave. Draegust kept his eyes above them and below, watching to see if any Corrupt were creeping amongst the rocks.

Once they got closer to the cavern, animal skulls and beads could be seen hanging from the jagged rocks on the cave ceiling. Poles made of blackwood were pierced into the ground with vazelead skulls forced through them.

"Looks welcoming," Draegust commented.

Alistind forced her hand around Darkwing's arm. It was obvious she was scared. She was pressed close against his body and he could hear her soft pants of exhaustion and fear.

As for himself, Darkwing felt no fear. He was far too deep in his thoughts of achieving his goal: finding Krista. It was more important than a fear of skulls.

Wrinkle Scale led the group, followed by the shade, Darkwing, Alistind, and Draegust. The cave was small, and the entrance was just large enough for one to enter at a time.

The group went in one by one, slowly. The cave interior was a sparse, open space with a couple blackwood shelves holding glass jars filled with organs and roots. Two cauldrons were visible in the room, one off to the corner and another dead-centre in the room, boiling with water over a fire underneath a steel frame. More beads and skulls dangled from the ceiling of the cave. A small doorway could be seen covered by a sheet of brown and black beads. The room reminded Darkwing of Wrinkle Scale's store, which was filled with the same voodoo materials.

"Who's there?" a deep-toned feminine voice demanded.

"Fleerew! It is I," Wrinkle Scale announced.

A female vazelead emerged from the bead-covered doorway. She wore only leather straps that covered her torso, wrists, and ankles, with strips tied to a band around her waist to form a long skirt. She had floral and skull tattoos covering her arms, neck, and chest—something that would cause the Renascence Guard to lose their mind for expressing individuality.

"What do you want?" she asked, clutching a blackwood staff with skulls dangling from ropes near the top; they rattled from the beads inside them. Her glassy, fire-engulfed eyes had no pupils but she stared at Wrinkle Scale anyway.

Draegust cursed. "She's a Corrupt!" he shouted.

Darkwing shot his gaze to the shaman's eyes, seeing the lack of pupils that was a hallmark of the Corrupt. Darkwing felt an empty feeling hit his stomach and he pushed Alistind behind him. He scanned the rest of the shaman's face, noticing a single bone pierced through her nostrils. Her spiked brows had painted designs that matched her flower tattoos. She was no normal Corrupt; they didn't take that much care into their appearance.

The shaman chuckled. "I see that you bring new blood to me," she said with a sly grin, showing her crooked, sharp teeth. "What brings you here?" Her black scalp-feathers swayed side to side while eyeing Wrinkle Scale. The beads and bones attached to them jingled as her head moved.

"I bring news that will interest you greatly," Wrinkle Scale said.

Folding her arms, Fleerew leaned against the doorframe and raised an eyebrow. "Yet you don't tell me: what do'ya want?"

Darkwing stood close to Draegust, keeping Alistind behind them both to ensure her safety. The Corrupt were known to be unpredictable. He found it difficult to keep his gaze off the shaman's eyes; their emptiness was like a vortex consuming his better senses.

He found it odd that the shaman paid little attention to the three of them and only acknowledged Wrinkle Scale. He looked away from her eyes and felt his senses perk. He didn't feel safe with the Corrupt shaman or Wrinkle Scale—both were very mysterious.

"I'm up for dashing out of here. I'll back you up," Draegust whispered to Darkwing.

"What for?" the shaman's voice boomed, bouncing off the cavern walls.

Draegust's eyes widened and he locked gazes with her empty eyes.

"You the one who came looking for me. Why do you run so easily?" Draegust did not respond.

"We came for answers," Darkwing replied.

The shaman smiled with an open mouth, revealing a silver piercing through her tongue. "Ah, you want answers from me? Yet I'm told you bring something I wish to know."

"Shall we exchange?" Wrinkle Scale offered.

Fleerew nodded. "All right, tell me your questions."

"Darkwing." Wrinkle Scale pointed at Darkwing's pouch.

Darkwing took out the bloody cloth from his pocket and stepped forward to hand it over to the shaman.

"We need your assistance in telling us where the blood's originator is currently located," Wrinkle Scale said. "We also need a guide . . . to the surface world."

Fleerew cackled manically. "You can't leave to the surface. No one can. Only the sun walker, Abesun! You of all should know that!"

"You, Fleerew, know I am no longer in contact with him."

"That I do. Regardless, the surface world is not accessible to us."

Wrinkle Scale's nostrils flared while he kept his stare on the shaman.

Fleerew leaned forward. "Or is that no longer the case?"

"Not anymore," Wrinkle Scale replied.

She furrowed her brow and nodded. "All right, I'll see what I can do with this." The shaman stepped forward, taking the cloth from Darkwing's hand then gradually moving to the centre cauldron.

Fleerew dipped the cloth in the pot and pulled it out, wringing out the blood. The cloth was soaked with a strange, bright green liquid from the cauldron. She waved it back and forth in her hands at a slow pace, chanting in a language they could not understand.

"I still say this is bad news," Draegust whispered.

"Let's just wait. I think we might be getting somewhere with this," Darkwing replied.

The shaman rolled the cloth into a ball, crushing it with her hands for a few seconds. Then she set it free, throwing it to the ground with a surprising amount of force.

"Speak to me," she whispered.

The black cloth sprung to life by unfolding on its own. The green liquid on the cloth moved to the centre of the fabric, the colour becoming more vibrant. The liquid then began to vibrate and spread across the cloth, drizzling in different directions as if it were painting a picture.

"Show us what ya hide," Fleerew said.

The green liquid spread and compacted together to form lines, eventually showing a detailed picture of a girl in a short dress, boots, and a tail on the floor. The liquid droplets moved around making the image animate the girl, who was twitching violently.

Darkwing was the only one to notice that the girl in the image was Krista. He recognized her boots and dress, but not the location.

"Krista!" he exclaimed moving toward the cloth.

Wrinkle Scale brought him to a halt with a steady hand. "Wait."

"What's wrong with her?" Darkwing asked.

The image of Krista kicked viciously and rolled on the ground, flailing.

Fleerew shook her head. "Take us back." She waved her hands around.

As Fleerew moved her fingers, Darkwing realized that the green liquid was synchronized with her hands and each movement she made caused the liquid to come to life.

The liquid fused together in the centre then spread outward again to draw a new image, showing great walls surrounding a group of buildings.

"What is that?" Alistind's jaw dropped.

"Human structures," Draegust hissed. "Only they build their castles and keeps with those types of shingles."

"The owner of this blood is kept inside these barracks," Fleerew said, lifting her arms in the air, breaking the channel of liquid and causing it to sink back into the fabric, losing its brightness.

"We have to go there," Darkwing said. He feared what possible torture Krista was going through, seeing her image in such pain. She was in the hands of humans and it angered him.

Fleerew shrugged. "I wish you luck."

"Won't you take us?" Darkwing asked.

"Why should I? I have yet to see what you have to offer me."

Wrinkle Scale stood tall. "We offer you this knowledge: we are no longer bound here. The vazeleads may now leave the underworld."

Fleerew chuckled. "That is all? Why should I show you how to get to the surface? That knowledge would have fallen into my hands eventually." She folded her arms. "You must do better."

Draegust flared his nostrils and charged at the shaman, grabbing her by the neck. "How about your life?"

The group watched the confrontation in shock; only the sound of the cauldron bubbling filled the room.

Fleerew's neck tightened while she smiled at Draegust, eyeing him up and down as he clutched harder, his claws puncturing her skin.

Alistind buried her head into Darkwing's arm. "I can't watch."

Darkwing raised his hand. "Don't kill her." Draegust would be capable of doing something so stupid.

"Why?" Draegust argued. "She'll need to breathe eventually."

"Keep squeezing, fool," Fleerew chuckled, choking out the words.

"I don't think she'll care if she can't breathe," said Darkwing. "Her death won't solve anything for us. We need her."

Draegust gave her one last glare and growled. He broke his grasp on her with a shove, pushing her back against the cave wall. Draegust stomped back to stand beside Darkwing, shaking his head and muttering curses.

Darkwing folded his arms. "If the knowledge of the surface world isn't enough, what do you want?"

Fleerew rubbed her neck and her face twisted into an evil smile. "I've got someone who I want you to pay a visit to."

CHAPTER XIX

Fool's Curiosity

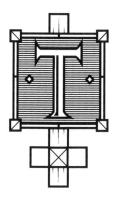here was not a single cloud in sight; only the blazing sun was visible in the clear blue sky. The beams from the sun bounced off the blades of grass, intensifying the exposure of the view. Still, despite the light and the heat, Krista ventured out from the keep and into the outdoors. She could feel the waves from the sun radiate across her body. The heavy clothing that she wore kept her skin hidden from even a sliver of direct sunlight, and already, she could feel the difference. Her innards did not tingle and her body felt comfortable in the heat.

Malpherities followed beside her sharply cast shadow, his eyes examining her gait. "How do you feel?"

She looked at the ghoul and shrugged. "I feel fine, no tingle at all—only warmth."

He grinned. "Perhaps your plan worked after all. Congratulations, Krista, you might be the first of your people to walk under the sun for more than two centuries."

It felt like a big accomplishment for her; she was no longer limited to just the night. Krista knew she would have to get used to seeing in the brightness of the day, but her eyes would adapt over time.

Now I can actually explore this place without worrying about the night watch. Krista didn't feel so constrained anymore. Even with having Mental Damnation to worry about, she could only deal with one problem at a time. The challenge to walk in the sunlight was an easier dilemma to tackle and the taste of victory helped motivate her, giving her the confidence to solve her own problems.

I have to—Darkwing is not here to help me, I am actually on my own.

"So now that you can walk amongst the day, what do you plan to do?" Malpherities asked.

Krista scratched her head as they walked. *Ouch.* Her hands still hurt from the bruises. "I wanted to spend more time with William."

The ghoul sighed. "I told you not to see the boy. He'll only hold you back."

Krista ignored his comment and glanced around the open fields to see if William was nearby. "One victory at a time."

William's regular training ground was empty; not even Paladin was in sight.

The two were silent while they came to a fork in the brown dirt road. They took the path off to the left, leading away from the training fields. This brought them to where the grass was longer and the hills were steeper. It was still harder to see in the day than it was the night she'd been wandering the hills with William. *It's like everything is glowing.* Her head slightly ached in the front but it was tough to tell if it was from the sun or from Mental Damnation.

Krista looked to the far side of the keep where the stables were. *At least there's something I recognize.*

The red roof of the stables was more vibrant in the daylight and the splinters in the wood were easier to distinguish. She stepped to the side of the road toward the stables, scanning the stalls to see two horses inside. They poked their heads out of the open windows. The animals stared at Krista, who happened to be the only one near them.

"I wonder if they think I'm weird-looking like the humans do," she said.

Malpherities stroked his jawline. "You're new to them—you have a different smell and appearance. They might befriend you or they might be fearful—it depends on their nature."

Krista approached the two hazel-brown animals with slow, gradual steps. Once she was several footsteps away, she could see how large they really were.

Their heads are like three times the size of mine! Their smell was strong and she could hear the sound of each exhale they made.

The horse to Krista's left, the darker of the two, flicked its ears and lowered its head while she brought out her hand to pet its thick, dark mane.

"They're beautiful."

"The dark one is named Windspear," Malpherities said.

The horse to the right let out a shriek and kicked the wall of the stable, startling the darker horse, which thrust its head forward and knocked Krista's hand aside.

"Easy!" Krista stepped back, realizing Malpherities was now beside her.

The animals snorted a couple times and retreated deeper into their shelter until only the click of their trotting hooves could be heard.

Krista looked at Malpherities. "You startled them."

"They can't see me, remember?"

"Well, they were fine before you came. Maybe they sense you like I can."

"So it would appear."

"It just seems odd." *Maybe there's more to Mental Damnation than Dr. Alsroc knows.* "How did you know its name, anyway?"

Malpherities pointed at the stable wall where two signs were mounted on the walls.

Krista squinted at the words. "I can't read it. You know how to read English?"

"I know many languages. When you're as old as I am, you learn as new languages are developed."

I wish I could read. Krista bit her lip and walked back to the road, following the path William had taken her down. She wanted to look at the water during the daylight. It would be good to familiarize herself with the High Barracks.

This time, she stayed on the road instead of cutting off into the grass. *I shouldn't take shortcuts. Everyone has such good manners here.*

While she walked, Krista paid extra attention to how her body felt. Her innards seemed normal, she felt warm, and there were no severe headaches or dizziness. The clothing truly did work against the sun.

Krista walked up a small hill where she noticed a large oak tree just over the other side. The trunk of the tree spiraled upward and split into countless twisted branches that grew lush green leaves and cast a wide shadow below. Down at the base of the tree, three boys were fighting in the shade with their training swords. The boys were dwarfed by the size of the tree—they looked like pebbles in comparison.

"Wait a minute." Krista squinted and looked closer at the boys. One of them had blond hair—William.

She smiled and ran down the hill toward them. Krista was a bit shy to talk to the other boys and she was uncertain how they would react to her. Thankfully, her vazelead features were hidden by the extra clothing. *They won't have to judge my body.*

"William!" Krista waved at them from about two dozen paces away.

The boys stopped fighting and glanced at William.

"Krista? Is that you?" William looked at his friends then began to walk toward her.

"Hey." Krista smiled. *He can't see my smile, but that's okay . . . that means he can't see my fangs.*

"Who's that?" a red-haired boy asked.

William glanced at the boy. "A friend." He looked back at Krista with his sharp blue eyes, the eyes Krista found all too mesmerizing. "You should go inside, in case you start to bleed again."

"I fixed the sun problem." Krista raised her arms, revealing the various scraps of clothing tied over her body.

"What do you mean?"

Krista sighed and pointed at her jacket. "All of this clothing."

"Who is she?" the redhead asked again.

William lightly took Krista's arm and guided her closer to the boys under the shade. "This is Krista. Krista, this is Jeuth and Talif." He pointed at the redhead, then the black-haired boy, whose eyes were hidden beneath his bangs.

Now that Krista was closer, she sniffed the air and could pick up on the boys' scents. They were sweaty and covered in dirt, which made it difficult to track their unique smell. She could still pick out William's scent because she had spent time with him previously. She liked the aroma of his body; it was strong but not overwhelming.

The two boys exchanged looks and shrugged. "What is she?" they whispered.

Krista felt a surge of anger channel through her body and put her hands on her hips. "You could just ask me." *There's no need to talk about me like I'm not even here.*

Jeuth folded his arms. "Okay, what are you?"

"Vazelead." She boldly stated. The quick response surprised her, especially how she was insecure to share her people's name with William the previous night.

Perhaps I'm gaining more confidence from my victory over the sun.

The boys shook their heads while staring at her.

Krista sighed. "From the underworld? The paladins banished us there." She realized it was possible that they had not even heard of the place. For all she knew, the events that took place on Mount Kuzuchi weren't taught as history.

"Only bad creatures live in the underworld. How'd you even get up here?" Talif asked.

Malpherities appeared from her shadow and sized himself up to the boys. "Don't give them any information; they'll simply use it against you."

Krista glanced at Malpherities. "Why?"

The three boys exchanged looks, unsure what to say.

Talif put his hands in his pockets. "Just curious."

"Don't talk to me when other mortals are around; it'll prove fatal," Malpherities murmured.

"You sure are weird-looking," Talif said. "What's with your eyes? They look like they're on fire."

Krista felt her heart crush inward and she looked down to the ground. Even with the amount of clothing she had on, the humans still judged her and it made her uncomfortable in her own skin. *Perhaps my confidence is fake.* "I tried to be nice to them, but they only care about how I look." She mumbled, hoping Malpherities would catch her venting.

"Guys, back off. She's had a rough couple of days," William said protectively.

"Why? What happened?" Talif asked.

Krista did her best to roll up her right sleeve, exposing the long scar down her arm.

The boys gasped.

Slowly she brought the sleeve back down. "Paladin said there was a necromantic ritual, and I was the victim."

"What kind of ritual?" Jeuth asked.

"I don't know," Krista shrugged.

The boys remained silent and stared off into the distance.

Malpherities waved his hand at them. "That was more information than what these pathetic humans need to know."

Talif smirked and pointed at her hand. "What about your hand, why is it wrapped up?"

"Yeah, and why are your eyes on fire?" Jeuth added.

Malpherities roared. "Little pricks. Tell them your hands got crushed during the ritual, and fire is a part of your physical makeup."

Krista didn't hesitate and quickly repeated Malpherities's words. She spoke fast, acting as if the questions had been asked plenty of times before.

The boys nodded. Jeuth and Talif sat down on the grass, seeming to prefer staring at her over continuing their training.

"What exactly is a vazelead?" Jeuth questioned.

"We're reptilian," she replied, sitting down on the grass.

William sat himself beside her.

Jeuth folded his arms. "But aren't vazeleads supposed to be all scaly? That's how they look in our textbook."

"We used to be, but we didn't need rough scales in the underworld like we did on the surface. Less winds and sharp elements to worry about down there, so most of the scales fell off." Krista brought her tail out from under her coat and rested it on her legs. She examined its condition to see if she had any dry or loose scales. Her tail was mostly smooth and the scales were a dark charcoal—a sign of good health. There was one scale that was slightly dried up and she plucked it free.

"Here," she said, handing it over to William. "This one is a little dry;

normally they're kind of leathery."

The three boys scooted close to one another to inspect the scale.

She felt awkward sitting outside of the group. "They run along my backside, too."

"Hey!" a man shouted from the distance.

The four spun their heads back to the hill to see a tall red-bearded man marching toward them.

"Jelly John . . ." William mumbled.

Krista glanced at the boys as they hurried to their feet, training swords in hand.

She bit her lip. *Should I stand or stay sitting?*

"Stand," Malpherities ordered.

Krista stood and brushed the grass from her clothes.

"What were you boys doing?" the red-bearded man asked.

I know him, that's Captain John. Krista recognized the red beard and long hair. He was there the day she first woke inside the barracks.

"Nothing," William said quickly.

"Indeed. Punishment is needed for this." John glanced at Krista. "I thought you couldn't walk during the day?"

"I can now." She pointed at her jacket. *How does everyone know about me?*

Malpherities folded his arms. "Word spreads fast here."

"Don't disrupt the boys' training; come back inside." Lightly, John put his arm around Krista's back, forcing her to come with him. "I'll walk you back to the keep," he said and glanced at the other three. "Boys, remain standing until I return."

Krista looked back at them; they were staring at her. She felt guilty—after all, it was her fault that they were in trouble. If she had obeyed Paladin and never came to bother them, they wouldn't be getting punished.

Gently, Krista pulled her scarf down past her chin. She mouthed the word 'sorry' to the boys as she walked away.

"Keep moving." John tapped her back.

She pulled her scarf up again and kept her head low as the man walked her back to the keep.

"It's nice to see you're getting better," he said. "But it also causes trouble for us." The man's tone wasn't as aggressive as it was for the boys. He sounded tired, like he needed a good rest.

"Sorry," Krista replied.

Krista looked around her shadow to try and place Malpherities, but he was nowhere to be seen. *Of course he is gone. He always leaves me.*

John brought her back to the same entrance she had left from the keep. When they entered the door, he kept his arm around her, guiding her down the long hallway. Krista took off her scarf and pulled down her hood. It was nice to feel the fresh air on her scalp.

"Don't be sorry, you're only a girl in a strange world. It is natural for you to be curious. But as I have said, it causes trouble for me. Would you be more comfortable with another girl?"

"What do you mean?"

"Paladin and I would like someone to keep an eye on you, and we want you to feel safe here."

She smiled. "I'd prefer nobody. I promise I'll be better next time."

"We don't want a next time."

The man took Krista off to their first right where the hall ended a couple paces forward with a stone spiraling staircase leading to the lower level. The open doorframe was finished with green-painted wood.

"You'll like her, she's about your age."

Krista nodded. *I doubt she's my age.*

He led her down the stairs. It was a long walk, but the staircase was wide which made it easier to go down compared to some of the stairs back in the City of Renascence. They reached the bottom of the stairway to discover it took them into a cool narrow hall; the walls were made with jagged stone and were inconsistent in spacing. There were black metal torches mounted on each wall, spread evenly apart. The floor looked dirty and it was hard to tell if it was dust or if the floor was just naturally brown.

The man stepped ahead of her and guided her down the hall. "I'm sure you've heard what the boys call me—Jelly John."

Krista giggled.

"Address me as John, all right?" he requested.

Her smile faded. "Yes, sir—I mean, John."

"I think you'll like her, she's named Marilyn and is the youngest maid of the barracks."

"It's a big barracks, how many more maids are there?"

"There are about five other maids and the boys help them as punishment from time to time. There's a lot to take care of in here and Madam Marilyn always appreciates the help."

"Am I being punished?"

The man laughed. "No, we just want to keep track of you."

"Paladin said he gave me freedom."

"Yes, you do have freedom—he also said to stay out of trouble. Madam Marilyn will just ensure that you do."

Krista was unsure if she liked this supervision they were setting her up with. *It'll make it really difficult to do anything I'd like.*

They approached the end of the hall where a rounded closed door waited. John stopped before they entered.

"Be sure to address her as Madam," he whispered. He twisted the handle and pushed the door forward while walking inside. Krista followed close behind him to see beyond the door there was an open room made of symmetrical light grey stones that sloped toward a centre drain. There was a large pile of clothes and sheets off to the left nearly touching the short ceiling, ranging from shirts to curtains to trousers. Several buckets of water were scattered around the room. There were also several ropes mounted from wall to wall, heavy with clothing hanging to dry. The room smelt of damp soap, with the addition of a strange funk—a mixture of human sweat, maybe cheese, and dirt—coming from the piles of clothes. A woman wearing a black bandana around her forehead was sitting on a stool, vigorously scrubbing a shirt in a tub filled with soapy water.

"Madam Marilyn," John called out.

The woman looked up and her blonde hair fell aside, revealing her emerald green eyes, narrow pale face, and youthful skin. She was only a girl—possibly no more mature than Krista.

Marilyn got up from her stool, lifting her black dress and white apron as she approached the two. She glanced at Krista for a split second then quickly brought her gaze to John. "Captain John?" she took a curtsy.

John patted Krista's back. "She's yours."

The girl glared at Krista, and her scowl made it obvious she was not happy with the arrangement.

Krista recognized the blonde hair and green eyes; she was the same maid who'd helped her when Krista had a bath.

"Keep an eye on her, we don't want her to get in any trouble," John added. He bowed and exited the room, closing the door as he left, leaving Krista alone with the maid.

Krista smiled at her.

Marilyn wasn't any taller than Krista, and just as thin. However, her presence was intimidating and she stood straight with more confidence. She eyed Krista from head to toe, the same displeased scowl on her face.

"Hi." Krista began to wrap her tail around her finger; she felt ill at ease being alone with the girl.

The maid sighed. "Hi," she said, and spun around, hurrying over to the tub where she was previously cleaning.

Krista followed behind her. "You're supposed to keep track of me." She sat down on the floor, watching Marilyn sit on the stool.

"So I hear," Marilyn replied as she began to run the shirt against a scrub board in the tub. The soapy water splashed out of the tub, leaving water spots on the floor.

Does she have a problem with me too? Krista bit her lip. It seemed like everyone she met had issues with her.

"They told me your name was Madam Marilyn." Krista scratched her neck.

"Yes, it is."

"I'm Krista."

The maid did not reply.

Krista clenched her teeth before speaking. "Can I help you?"

The maid chuckled and stopped scrubbing the shirt. "I haven't heard that in a long time." She took the shirt from the tub and began to wring the water out. "Any of the boys sent here as punishment slack in their work." She took one free hand and pointed at the large pile. "Grab something and start cleaning it in this tub."

Krista got to her feet immediately and walked over to the pile of clothes. She looked at the range of colours, materials, and sizes in the pile. There were so many to choose from and she did not know what to start with.

I have to start somewhere, I suppose. She stuck her hands into the pile and began sifting through the tangled mess. Krista picked up a couple of shirts and walked back to the tub. The smell of the clothes was much stronger while holding them close and Krista gagged.

"What?" the maid asked.

"Sorry, these clothes reek."

"They're boys. They sweat a lot."

Krista dropped the pile by the tub, only keeping a deep red shirt in her hand. Krista placed it in the dented metal tub and quickly noticed her hands stinging. She suddenly remembered that they were injured and it caused her to grunt.

"What's wrong?" Marilyn eyed her.

Krista raised her wrists. "I hurt my hands."

Marilyn pushed her hair back and pressed her lips together. She nodded her head, acknowledging the table behind Krista. "Take the things I've got to my side and pin them on the ropes to dry."

"Okay." Krista walked over to the maid's side and took several of the wet shirts that rested on the edge of the tub. She swung them over her shoulder and walked over to the ropes behind the maid. There were dozens of clips off to the far left end of the rope, and she went over to take one of the wooden clips. She plucked it open with one hand; the pressure she used to open the clamp was also painful. But she did her best to ignore the pain and hang the clothes to dry.

The two worked in silence, cleaning the textiles for several hours. Marilyn scrubbed the clothes ruthlessly in the tub then squeezed the excess water out. From there, Krista hung them to dry on the series of ropes. As the time passed, Krista's hands grew more tired and sore from the repetitive motion. It surprised her how Marilyn showed no exhaustion performing the hard work.

Eventually, Marilyn spoke. "Done! Plenty of clothes left to wash, but that is all we need for now." The maid wrung out one last pair of trousers. "Much quicker with a helper, especially with one that doesn't slack around," she said with a smile.

Krista took the trousers and hung them up. "Glad to be of help." Her fingers felt raw from the work she'd put them through. *Finally we're done.*

"What did you say your name was?"

"Krista."

"What are you, Krista?"

"Vazelead."

Marilyn inspected Krista's tail that poked out from under her coat. "You know, John often sends plenty of people to me for punishment . . . You're different, though, as you only need supervision. Correct?"

"Yes."

"Are you hungry?"

Krista nodded. With such a hectic day, she had completely forgotten about her stomach.

"Vazeleads are from the underworld, aren't they? You must not be familiar with surface fruit."

"I had some the other day, strawberries I think they were called." *So she knows something about my people. Guess she has studied more than those boys.*

A genuine smile spread across Marilyn's face. "My favourite! Would you like some?"

"Yes, please."

"Come with me, then," she waved.

Madam Marilyn led Krista out of the basement level of the keep and back up to the main floor. The sun was now setting and there was an orange hue cast on the interior of the keep. The maid walked quickly and Krista did her best to keep up through the halls. Marilyn took Krista down a hallway where she had not been before; this one had several gold-framed portrait paintings of men dressed in puffy tunics and crowns. The hall eventually led her to an exit with a black wooden door that had metal bolts on it.

"This way is quicker to the garden," Marilyn said while pushing the door open.

Krista wrapped her scarf around her face and lifted her hood as they entered the sunlight. Seeing Marilyn in the light of the day, Krista realized how pale her skin was. Her hair was so blonde it could almost pass as white. Marilyn didn't seem to pay much attention to Krista's stare and continued to lead her down the gravel road. They passed the stables and Krista could see that the two brown horses had their heads peeking out from the windows again.

I wish Malpherities hadn't scared them away.

"Are any of the horses yours?" Krista asked.

"No, they are only for the warriors of the barracks like Paladin and John. There are more horses too, but often the men take them in their travels."

"Where do they travel?"

"Sometimes to our kingdom capital, sometimes on a quest . . . Honestly, I wouldn't know. I simply clean their clothes."

The two walked past the stables and another building with a staircase leading to the tall front doors. It was made of white brick and the shingles were the same red as the stables. Atop the roof was a tower with a large golden bell. On the roof of the tower, a white cross was mounted.

"Come on, let's go." Marilyn waved at Krista. The maid was gaining distance on her and Krista had to jog to catch up.

The two crossed a warped wooden bridge—the same one Krista and William had visited the night before. She gazed down at the river as they passed, looking into the crystal-clear water. Once they were across, Krista looked ahead to see that the road led to a white wooden gate surrounded by a hedge that was as tall as she was. The gate swung outward and Marilyn led Krista through. Krista staggered a bit behind from Marilyn, mesmerized by the lush greenery on both sides of the path. The garden had side paths with vegetation planted in rows. The plants varied in size; some were supported with sticks that were tied to the plants by rope and other plants had sturdy stems and could stand on their own. Some of the vegetation was short and stubby, like the vegetables Krista remembered growing in the garden behind her childhood home. The taller plants had a range of colourful fruits dangling from their branches.

"This place is beautiful," Krista said, looking at the richness of the vegetation. *My mom sure would have appreciated this garden.*

"This is our orchard," Marilyn explained, waving her hand at the scene. "Move quickly, we don't want the gardeners to spot us."

Krista felt a rush of excitement. "What if we get caught?"

Marilyn led her through the thick garden, passing high bushes.

"They caught me once and were most unpleasant." Marilyn looked back at her and lifted her sleeve, revealing a scabbed scar.

"It's quite recent." Krista spoke before thinking.

Nodding, Marilyn stopped walking and kneeled beside a patch of shrubs half Krista's size, complete with pointed leaves and dozens of red berries. "Here they are."

Krista stared at the plump, bright red fruit covered in seeds—the strawberries.

"Take as much as you'd like."

"Won't they know it was us?"

Marilyn smiled and shook her head. "They can't prove it," she said as she plucked some of the berries. "Go on, take them—a thank-you gift from me to you. I would have been busy with those clothes well into the night if it wasn't for you."

Krista started picking a few, making sure she grabbed the best ones.

"Go on! Take a bunch!" Marilyn encouraged.

Krista smiled and began to pluck the berries faster, filling her hands with as many as she could hold, even placing some in her pockets.

Marilyn held hers with the apron around her waist. "All right, let's find some shade."

The maid led Krista out of the garden and back onto the road.

"We'll go to the Twisted Hermit," Marilyn decided while they walked back over the bridge.

"What's that?" Krista asked.

"It's a large tree near the centre of the barracks. The boys often go there when they're not training. But this late into the evening, I think they will all be inside eating dinner."

The two cut off the road and walked up a hill, and she noticed the same spiraling oak tree from earlier in the day.

"Oh yeah, I have been here," she said.

"Neat, isn't it?"

"It really is. How old is it?"

Marilyn brought Krista close to the trunk of the tree and sat down, leaning against the wood. "I'm not sure; it's got to be hundreds of years, though."

Krista took her scarf off and sat cross-legged on the grass beside Marilyn. She tossed one berry at a time into her mouth and bit down on the sweet, juicy fruit.

Marilyn ate the berries slowly, taking tiny nibbles and chewing graciously.

Krista noticed the difference in their eating habits and felt ashamed.

Maybe it's my manners that make the humans not like me. She tried to slow down her consumption of the berries, mimicking Marilyn.

The wind picked up, blowing Krista's scalp-feathers into her face. She brushed it aside. "Thank you, Madam Marilyn."

The girl's eyes stared off into the sky and she shook her head. "No need to thank me," she sighed. "You don't need to call me Madam, either."

"John told me to."

"Yes, well, John is a polite man." Her voice softened at the mention of John.

Krista took a small bite of a strawberry. "Is he your husband?"

The maid laughed heavily. "Heavens, no! I don't have a husband."

"Do you plan to have one?"

"I don't think so—it is truly up to Paladin. I highly doubt he will want me to."

"Why do you need him to decide?"

"It's a complicated situation."

Krista smiled. "I know of complicated situations." She devoured another berry before speaking. "I was a street vermin in my home."

Marilyn looked at Krista as her mouth dropped. "You didn't have a family?"

"No, they died before we were banished to the underworld."

Marilyn nodded. "Mine were murdered. My mother wasn't allowed to have children. She was supposed to be pure, like Paladin teaches me to be."

"Did they live in the High Barracks?"

"No, this was elsewhere. Thankfully Paladin found me and he brought me back here."

"So he's like your father?"

"I suppose." Marilyn ate her last strawberry. "Paladin still teaches me of his holy art and ensures that I follow the path of God."

"Can you use a sword?" Krista asked excitedly.

"No, he wants to keep me away from violence, away from anything related to the Seven Deadly Sins. He said he wants to keep me pure."

"Seven Deadly Sins?" Krista took some berries from her pocket and continued to eat.

"They are the seven mortal actions that are sins in the eyes of God,"

Marilyn explained.

"Oh, what are they?"

"Well, there is the sin of lust, where you desire another's body. Then there is gluttony, consuming more than you need. There's also greed, another excess sin but falls in line with a desire for wealth and fame. The fourth sin is sloth, meaning you're dirty or lazy. Another is pride, thinking you're more important than you really are. Envy is when you desire to be different or have what others have. The last of the seven sins is wrath, an angry sin of vengeance and self-destruction." Marilyn brushed her hair aside. "Paladin wants me to be everything opposite of these, which are the Seven Heavenly Virtues, everything pure."

Krista stared at the grass bellow her. "Wow, by the sounds of it I can't ever be pure."

"But you're just a girl, no older than me?"

"My people are corrupt compared to the people of on the surface. Those sins happen a lot where I come from. I've murdered, stolen . . . been raped." She looked up at the maid.

The statement changed Marilyn's posture and she slouched down. "I'm so sorry," Marilyn softly replied.

Krista finished her final berry and shrugged. "It's no big deal. We come from different cultures and I think I'm doing pretty well."

"What was it like?" Marilyn asked leaning forward.

"What part?"

"The murder. Paladin has been on many crusades, slain many. He won't talk of it to me. I want to know."

Krista remembered clearly what she felt when she assisted the half-breed Abesun in killing a Corrupt vazelead, but she wasn't sure how it could be placed into words. She hadn't wanted to do it; it just happened that way. The feeling of the spear pressing into flesh, warm blood spewing against her face, and the look of a dying creature's eyes as their life seeped from reality.

"It's hard to explain." She began to pluck some of the blades of grass. "It was truly an accident; I didn't mean to kill him."

"Well, how did it happen? How did it feel?" Marilyn's voice was filled with excitement.

"I was saving a friend; another vazelead was trying to eat him.

There are some bad vazeleads in the underworld who live outside the city and eat their own kind. I only wanted to wound him so my friend could escape." Krista fiddled with the grass below her, trying to recall how the spear penetrated through the Corrupt's throat. "I must have tripped or lost my balance because the spear didn't jab him but ran right into his throat."

"Poked right through?"

"I don't remember. It was shocking to me: blood sprayed, and he yelped. After I realized what I had done, I felt as if something was ripped out of me or something. I knew I had killed him. I can't explain the feeling. I was silent, in complete shock."

Marilyn nodded. "It's something you have to go through, I guess."

"It was fear, with maybe a hint of excitement," Krista added.

The maid's eyes widened. "Must have been thrilling . . ." She brushed her hair aside. "You said you felt something was taken from you?"

Krista nodded. "I felt I lost something . . ."

"Innocence." Malpherities rose from his smoke from her shadow. "The murder stripped the purity from your soul."

Krista frowned and brushed her scalp-feathers aside, too, as the wind blew stronger and she looked into Marilyn's wide green eyes. "It was the loss of innocence."

CHAPTER XX

Realm Crosser

Child!
The headaches of passing.
Place you in pain.
Pain that is pushing.
How can you handle?
Something so straining.

Child!
I am most excited.
You are scared, I see.
Don't be, the worst is rapid.
Then you'll see why.
Why we must drain blood.

Child!
Focus your thoughts.
Time is irrelative.

Resistance will make you rot.

Listen to the teacher.

For words of wise,

Is what he has taught.

Child!

Upon entrance.

I will meet you.

Enter your trance.

Don't dare be scared.

Take a chance.

Please.

So we may dance.

 ords that were rambles ceased their babble and started transforming into comprehensible statements. These whispering words told of a spiritual passing into another world—whispering words from the ruler of this new land.

The transition into the realm as told by the whispering lord was difficult; proof of this was seen in the realm-crosser's feathers. They were tattered and spread out wildly over the mattress, still stained with blood from previous tortured nights. The sheets were kicked off the bedframe, crumpled in a pile across the room.

The moon cast a dim light into the brick chamber, spreading a faint blue hue across the rough brick foundation. The realm-crosser's back was highlighted by the glow, reflecting from the leathery scales running down her spine. The girl's long tail lashed out vigorously into the air as she buried her face into the pillow. The sharp claws of her hands dug into the back of her scalp, causing enough pressure to puncture the skin and draw black blood from her head. The droplets seeped out into her scalp-feathers.

Despite the pain, Krista—the realm-crosser—ignored her body's cries for her to stop. She continued to clutch her head.

She rolled onto her back and dragged her hands to the front of her face, smearing the blood across her soft skin. The headache ran from the front of her head over the sides, veins throbbing as if something was trying to break free from her skull.

Her eyes opened and she spread her arms across her bed, realizing that someone was speaking to her in a poetic voice again.

"The whispers in my dream . . ." she mumbled. "Merging blood? That wasn't Malpherities."

Shaking her head, Krista sat up and noticed she hadn't taken her clothes off—even her coat was still on. It was difficult to remember what had happened during the night. She recalled talking to Marilyn about murder, Malpherities helping her articulate her thoughts, and returning to her room once the sun had set. Now she was here, with a swelling headache that compelled her to clutch her head.

"I must have passed out," she said aloud.

The sound surprised her, and she realized that for once, no one was there to reply.

Krista felt a chill crawl up from her spine to the puncture wounds in her scalp. She had an overwhelming fear that these whispers were about Dreadweave Pass and may not be Malpherities, but the Weaver. She decided to shake the thoughts away, but the more she tried, the stronger the pain in her head was.

Krista had been unaware of the headache until she woke up and was able to think clearer. She'd had plenty of headaches since being on the surface world, but this one was different—far stronger and most unbearable.

A sharp pain rushed to the front of her head, as if she had fallen from a rooftop and hit the pavement below. The surge caused Krista to roll to her side and tumble onto the floor, screeching. She clutched the front of her head and landed on her elbows.

She didn't think it was physically possible to feel such levels of agony and retain consciousness. The pain felt as if an army of hammers were plummeting ruthless blows onto her skull in synchronized motion.

Krista rolled back and forth on the floor as the headache continued to escalate. She felt no control of her movements; her body curled inward and sprung out sporadically. She tried to move her hands as her fingers clawed into her scalp again, peeling back the skin like clay.

The sound of hissing erupted in the room, like a high-pitched wind in the forest. She lashed her eyes to the crack in the window frame where black fog seeped from the hole.

"Mal—!" Krista started but burst into tears before finishing his name. "Make it stop!"

The ghoul emerged from the fog and stared at her with open arms, his face emotionless while he watched her.

"Please!" she continued to cry.

"The time has come, Krista," Malpherities said.

A gush of pressure rocketed against Krista's skull, throwing the back of her head against the stone floor, violent enough to knock her silly.

Her vision was blurry and the scene of the ceiling began to sway up and down in a wave motion; the blow knocked her thoughts clear as she watched Malpherities hover over her.

"Relax your mind. Let go of this world," he whispered.

Through the pain, Krista lost connection with her body and began to feel numb. Her hearing faded and all she had left was her sight.

The stone floor around her began to twist and crumble, breaking down into a charcoal liquid. The furniture around her sunk into the mystery fluid. The liquid picked up speed as if it were an ocean, pushing her body up and down against the violent tide. The walls collapsed from the floor's movement and they disappeared below the liquid. The ceiling above her spiraled inward like a maelstrom—devouring the roofing and then sky—leaving nothing but blackness and an endless sea of charcoal fluid surrounding her.

The vortex in the pitch-black sky continued engulfing reality and began to suck the liquid upward around her. The fluid ran into the sky like droplets of water rolling down a leaf in reverse. The remnants of the liquid flowing upward began to slow in speed, eventually hardening and changing shape, mutating in colours, forming dark rotting trees and steep dirt hills in the distance. The remaining droplets spread outward and faded to form fog which darkened the scenery. The sky stopped swirling, lightening from charcoal into a blood-red hue with varying shades of black spiral-shaped clouds.

Krista regained her senses; the pain disappeared and control of her body returned. As soon as she realized she was a couple feet in the air, she fell onto moist dirt, tumbling down the slippery ground, screaming with what breath she had left.

Krista reached the bottom of the slope and fell into a pool filled with a thick, dark liquid.

She squirmed in the pond, trying to find which way was up. Eventually she surfaced, gasping for air. Panting, Krista looked around. She got to her feet in the pool, which reached to just above her waist.

"Malpherities!" Krista cried, droplets of liquid pouring down her face into her open mouth.

She spat it out and licked her lips, recognizing the salty tang of blood. She hissed and quickly waded through the thick pool, walking out and onto the moist dirt. Krista shook her body, trying to remove the clotted blood from her scalp-feathers and clothes but it was too thick and gooey to fling off.

"Krista!" Malpherities buzzed from the top of the mud hill she'd rolled down, soaring down to her level.

"What is this?" she exclaimed while raising her arms, blood dripping from her limbs.

The ghoul stopped when they were eye-level. Krista's eyebrows were slanted back, eyes wide with fear while Malpherities's were wide with joy.

He spread his arms toward the scenery. "This is Dreadweave Pass. Welcome to my home."

Krista felt her stomach shrivel up at his words. "So Abesun really was telling the truth." She spun around several times examining her surroundings: the pool of blood she'd fallen into was one of hundreds that spread for miles around, fading into the distant fog. Her eyes latched onto one of the trees nearby; the bark bulged out, forming what appeared to be a nose, a mouth, and thick eyebrows. Below the bulging bark, the trunk expanded and contracted as if it were breathing.

She pointed at it. "It's alive!"

"Yes, aren't your world's trees alive, too?"

Krista smeared some blood from her face. "I . . . I don't know." She was barely able to grasp the situation. "I never thought that they were this much alive. These trees are breathing!" Krista glanced around at the blood pools again and shook her head. "I don't want to be here; take me back."

"I can't."

"Take me back!" she hissed at the ghoul, sizing up to him. The aggression surprised her; rarely did she act in such a hostile manner. She lowered herself and brushed her blood-drenched scalp-feathers aside. "Please, Mal." She didn't intentionally start shortening Malpherities's name, but found it easier to say.

The ghoul stared at her with a blank expression. "I can't, Krista."

Her mouth trembled and she felt a tear fall from her cheek. She was horrified and only wanted to go back to her world.

"Only you can take yourself back."

"How?"

"You must relax your mind. Calm your active thoughts, and then you'll be able to focus on crossing realms. It's like using a muscle; there's no thought expressed in a muscle's movement, yet you can control it."

"Then how did I come here to begin with? I was far from relaxed last night."

The ghoul shrugged. "You must have been in your sleep at one point—even the slightest moment of peace will activate your third eye's ability to pass into this realm."

"Third eye?"

"Yes, every creature under the heavens is gifted with a third eye found deep inside your subconscious. Some beings are naturally more gifted with it than others, but all living things with the third eye are capable of seeing the unseeable, hearing the unheard, and feeling what cannot be felt with your primitive senses."

"So a third eye is like the sixth sense you mentioned earlier?"

"Correct; the third eye is linked to your soul. When you fell asleep, you activated your newfound gift of realm-crossing because your mind was not focused on building thoughts through words, but through feelings."

Krista squatted on the ground and her limbs shook as she lowered herself. "Okay, so sleeping is the key?"

"It can be."

She lay down on the mud. It felt cool as her body sunk a couple millimeters into it. "Then I'll sleep, and I'll wake up in the real world."

Malpherities shook his head. "Don't be a fool. You're not going to have a restful sleep."

"Why not? Apparently the skull-splitting headaches are relaxing enough to put me here!" she shouted.

The ghoul growled and folded his arms.

She closed her eyes and ignored Malpherities. Krista didn't like Dreadweave Pass; it was frightening and the strong smell of blood clouded her ability to pick up on any other scent. It oddly reminded her of her encounter with Saulaph and Danil with the immense amount of blood.

This can't be happening. It's too surreal.

Time inched little by little and she found it impossible to sleep. There was not a single sound in the distance, only silence. Trying to sleep in unfamiliar territory was stressful enough, let alone in another world.

This can't be another realm. Malpherities must have taken me from the keep and into the forest.

"This is pointless," Malpherities growled.

Krista sat up. "I can't fall asleep."

"You won't. Even if you do, you're in shock and can't calm your mind."

She frowned. *I know he's right.*

"Get up, we should leave this place."

"Where are we?"

"The Blood Swamp."

"Where does the blood come from? Why doesn't it dry up?"

"The blood of mortals, from your realm."

"What?"

"Where did you think all the blood went when you washed it away? Leave it to dry then scrape it off? It rains from the sky and ends up here—it gives the trees nourishment."

"Icky," she mumbled while returning to her feet. Krista found the mud too slippery and she fell onto the dirt. Rolling backward into the blood pool, her body curled up as she dunked into the liquid.

She scurried up and out of the blood, hissing and spitting some from her mouth. "This is disgusting!" she cried, crawling back onto the mud.

"That's why I said we should leave."

"Where?" Krista got back to her feet. *Watch my step . . .*

"Mortals have built a number of towns here; we can find one where you will be safe. The Weaver can't keep watch of everything that happens in every corner at every moment in the realm. Besides, the wild of Dreadweave Pass is not forgiving."

"Fine. Help me up," she demanded.

The ghoul offered his claws. They were sharp and uncomfortable to touch, but they acted as support so she could walk up the hill.

"Follow me. We'll reach the main road soon."

I don't understand why Danil would want to infect me with Mental Damnation. Why would he make me come here? How could he do this to his own kind? As frightened as she was, she was also in awe at the fact she was in Dreadweave Pass. Just like Ast'Bala, Abesun, Danil, and Malpherities had all talked about.

Krista found it difficult to follow Malpherities up the hill because he didn't walk on the muddy ground like she did and left no footsteps behind. She realized there was a slight red hue in the mud, like on her clothes.

Is the dirt moist from blood and not water? The thought disgusted her and she tried not to think about it as her boots pressed into the soil.

They reached the top of the hill and walked on a flatter, narrow dirt path. Her attention was brought to Malpherities again, as his smoke was not fused with her shadow like it was in her realm. It only floated and disintegrated in the air, as if he were a ghost.

"How can you live here, Mal?" Krista asked, hoping the small talk would calm her nerves; her heart raced as they passed near a couple of the breathing trees, with their scratchy elderly voices inhaling and exhaling.

"It is my home."

"But it's horrible."

Malpherities chuckled. "To you it is, but from my perspective, it is comfortable. I am attuned to it. Give it time and you'll be just as friendly to it as I am."

"But how will I have time to adjust to it? Isn't the Weaver after me?" She licked her lips, tasting the blood again. "Is he after me now? Now that I am here . . . in his realm?"

"Yes, he is."

"I want to go home," she whined.

"You have no home."

Krista squinted her eyes. "What? Yes I do."

"Where?"

"The barracks, the underworld."

"You're despised by your own people, the humans hate you—is that what you call a home?"

"I call home a place to live in."

"Home should be safe, and your places are not safe. Therefore, you have no home."

"Dreadweave Pass is safe for you?"

"Yes. As far as I am aware, I am safe."

The two travelled in silence up and down the slippery dirt. Krista was unsure what else to ask the ghoul. He was blunt and showed little interest in her words or sympathy to her reaction to Dreadweave Pass—it was as if he'd dealt with this situation a million times before.

We had agreed to be honest with each other, so I have to trust him. What else can I do? But it doesn't mean he is telling me everything, just enough to make what he says honest. She found his answers vague, and knew he knew more than he wanted to share.

"The road is just up here." Malpherities announced.

"Where? I don't see it." She looked back and could only see an endless sea of fog and breathing trees.

Silence.

"Mal?" Krista spun back to see he was nowhere to be found. "Mal?" she called out. "This isn't funny." She twirled around over and over trying to find the ghoul, but he had vanished.

Thoughts buzzed in her mind. *Where did he go? Did he fall? Did he intentionally leave me? Or did someone capture him?*

An ear-shattering shriek reverberated through the swamp. The initial sound was close, and then it echoed for miles around her, making it difficult to pinpoint the origin.

She froze in her spot, eyes wide as she breathed heavily. *I don't want to know where that came from . . . The road!*

She dashed in the direction Malpherities was guiding her before he disappeared, hoping to find the road or the ghoul. It was possible he was waiting for her.

Another screech roared through the swamp. Even the trees seemed to catch their breath at the horrific sound.

Fear chilled Krista's spine, her heart pounded, and her legs sprinted faster than she'd ever ran before. She was careful not to slip on the mud and avoided the blood pools on the side of the dirt path. As she ran, a slight echo of her steps was heard in the distance, gradually getting faster and louder.

Dare I look back? Her heart pounded as the footsteps began to multiply.

One quick glance, and Krista saw nothing over her shoulder. Just more woods. She brought her head forward to see her path was now blocked by a humanoid several footsteps ahead.

Krista skidded to a stop and gasped, realizing the humanoid was human-flesh-toned and naked. Much of its skin was peeling off, revealing muscle tissues and organs exposed in its flat torso. Metal staples kept its limbs and various sections of the skin attached. Its genitals had been torn off, leaving remnants of rotting flesh and veins dangling between its legs.

Her boot slipped in the mud and she landed on her rear, inches away from the naked humanoid.

The bald, hairless being opened its mouth while hissing, revealing a second set of small sharp teeth inside its mouth, with one long slimy tongue slithering out. Its irises were red and the eyelids peeled away, keeping the bloodshot eyes wide open and locked on her.

Krista backed up and leaped to her feet. The being took one step forward, its entire body shaking from the motion. Then it took another step, moving like a string puppet, yet with no strings. It continued to step toward her, raising its arms and exposing the long, three-fingered, suction-cupped tentacles it had for hands.

This cannot be real. At first the thin frame of the humanoid reminded her of the Corrupt from the underworld but now she saw how much more terrifying this creature was.

Her instinct was to run. She turned around to dash in the opposite direction but behind her stood five more disfigured humanoids.

One flesh-toned creature looked like it was stapled together from two bodies. It stood on four hands, head staring into the sky in a crab-like position with the second body's torso growing from the stretched-out mouth. The whole creature had no legs, only arms and hands held together by metal staples.

Several of the other beings had multiple arms, razor-sharp teeth and extended jaws. Some had hands that were replaced with boney spikes stained with blood. All the beings were mutated far beyond anything natural.

One being had four legs in pairs that were stapled together to form thicker legs. It was at least two heads taller than the others and stepped forward with one rumbling roar, showing its extended twin sabre teeth and brawny arms—ready to crush her.

Krista's legs trembled and she fell to her knees in shock of the monsters. From both sides, they began to close in on her, moving like automatons.

Krista couldn't see any way to escape; the dirt path was blocked and the sides were so steep and slippery that she would surely break her neck from the fall.

"Don't kill me," she wept.

As the creatures closed in on her, she looked up to see Malpherities diving from the air.

I knew he'd come back!

He crashed into the crowd of humanoids, screaming, knocking several of them down to the muddy ground.

That doesn't look good. From the mechanics of his crash, Krista wondered whether he'd really dove from the sky, or was thrown.

When Malpherities tried to get up, he sunk back down. There was a spear piercing his arm, pinning him into the mud. Black smoke seeped from the wound and evaporated into the air.

The humanoids ran past Krista to one another, losing their interest in her. They stood in a defensive position, prepared for combat while glancing around the swamp. They hissed, screeched and made clicking noises amongst one another.

"Mal!" Krista began crawling toward him.

"I'm stuck!" he growled.

"Can't you poof out?"

Malpherities shook his head. "What?"

"Like how you vanish in my realm all the time."

"I'm only a spectator of your realm, only seen by those willing to see me—like you," he grunted. "Here, I am real."

Krista swallowed heavily at his words; they were in trouble.

The humanoids began to shrill as a newcomer emerged from further up the path, dashing out of the fog. It was difficult to make out who or what it was, but the silhouette showed a feminine figure with slim legs, an armoured skirt, and a long ponytail, holding a curved claymore ignited with white flame.

The intruder leaped into the scene and landed with a heavy thud, splashing spots of soil onto Krista and several of the humanoids.

Krista wiped the mud from her eyes and examined the newcomer. She was a human with bright red hair and pale white skin. Light bronze armour covered her body and was held together with leather straps. Her lean muscles were exposed. Her hands gripped around the leather handle of her weapon, just below the guard, which was carved to resemble flames. The bright, white burning blade ended in a sharp hook.

Krista's gaze was brought to the figure's chest: dangling from her breastplate was a pendant, the same icon she had seen on Paladin.

"A paladin!" she exclaimed.

Malpherities shrieked. His scream that was strikingly similar to those of the humanoids.

The paladin charged the four-legged humanoid, twirling her heavy blade as if it were merely a stick. Her speed was too great for the humanoid to react and she leaped several feet into the air, lashing the claymore down on the large being. The blade cut into its scalp and sliced through the flesh and bone like it was a rotten tomato. The white flame from the sword expanded onto the humanoid, causing it to ignite into a bright white flame, burning it to a crisp.

Three of the humanoids assembled as one and rushed the paladin, thinking they could strike while she was recovering from her last attack. Without a moment's hesitation, the human swung the blade around, throwing several of the monsters back. The blow knocked them hard against the trees, splintering the trunks and leaving the humanoids with wide gashes across their chests. Gargles came from the trees as thick red sap began to ooze from the broken bark.

The being that ran on four hands tightened its throat and let out a tense roar from both heads as it charged toward the paladin, trying to lash at her with its long single-clawed hands and snapping its razor-sharp teeth.

Without effort, the paladin dodged the attack, rolling on the dirt and back onto her feet. She closed her eyes, whispering, her voice rapidly growing louder. ". . . lead us not into temptation but deliver us from the evil one . . ." Her eyes flung open and her pendant began to glow bright white.

The humanoid skidded to a stop and turned around, kicking the dirt back several times.

". . . the Beast that you saw was, and soon not, born of destruction and forged from unholy ground . . ." The light channeled through the paladin's pendant and up the necklace, surging into her skin and lighting up the veins leading directly to the palm of her free hand.

The humanoid on four hands rushed toward the paladin again, crossing its clawed arms across its chest, preparing to slice her throat.

". . . commence the holy spirit to rain destruction and cast you back to the earth whence you came!"

Inches away from the humanoid, the paladin thrust her free hand forward, slamming her open palm against its torso before it could spread its claws. The white flame seeped from her veins and fused into the creature's body, moving into the bloodstream and lighting the humanoid up with white fire. Within seconds, the creature combusted and stumbled to the ground, screaming and burning.

Krista watched as the two remaining creatures got to their feet and rushed after the paladin. But the paladin was prepared and charged first, holding her claymore back, ready for an upper strike.

The creatures' eyes lit up with fear. Her blade hurled at them with a single swoop, slicing into their deformed flesh and making them burst into flames.

They screamed in agony, their voices like a crowd of beings screeching at once. The white fire was quick and relentless, lasting only several seconds before it annihilated the creatures, leaving them in charred black chunks.

Unbelievable. Krista sat staring in awe at the battle scene. She'd thought the Five Guardians were impressive, but this human was beyond anything she could comprehend.

The paladin did not sheathe her sword and marched toward Krista and Malpherities.

"Thank you!" Krista exclaimed.

She walked past Krista and approached the ghoul, pulling the spear clean from his arm. Malpherities attempted to scurry away but she tossed the spear aside and snatched his neck, lifting him with one arm.

"Wait!" Krista shouted. "Don't kill him!"

Malpherities tried to squirm free, but it was no use: her grasp was too strong.

"In the name of our Father in Heaven, this land will be cleansed of the Beast and all who blindly follow!" the paladin shouted. Her voice booming as she extended her sword back, ready to strike.

CHAPTER XXI

In Reality

PATIENT: KRISTALANTICE SCALEBANE

DAY: ONE
ENTRY: TWO

I was quite intrigued to meet Kristalantice earlier today. While I was staying at Mrs. Soulstone's farm I received a letter from Paladin about a child who was not human, infected with Mental Damnation. Many unanswerable questions ran through my mind in the moment. Paladin noted that the child was a vazelead, a species I had only read about through textbooks because they were banished to the underworld almost two hundred years ago.

The textbook described the vazelead people as peaceful creatures with slow learning abilities. So how would a vazelead diagnosed with Mental Damnation behave with their naturally stagnant processing mental state? I am aware that vazeleads were unable to return to the surface, so it is a mystery as to why this one was found. That is a much larger issue Paladin is investigating. Mental Damnation started plaguing the Kingdom of Zingalg about a decade ago, which is when I caught wind of it. Through my studies I have learned that the disease has been lurking through the known world for far longer, but an exact root time is difficult to trace.

So my question would be, how would a vazelead also contract this human disease? Does it in fact originate in the underworld? If so, how did it originally come to the surface? These are difficult questions that will take time to answer. Every time I attempt to trace the origins of the disease to learn more, my research takes me around an endless circle of traveling and misinformed knowledge. Can't anyone keep their information clear?

At first when I met Krista, I wondered whether she was a carrier of the disease due to her mutated appearance, which is common with carriers. I also had knowledge of the metamorphosis fumes that cloud the underworld. After being introduced to her and seeing her behaviour patterns, I could determine that her strange appearance was in fact simply from the mutations from the fumes and deduced that all her people must have gone through similar transformations. Krista is not a carrier—thank God. The aggression of carriers makes them nearly impossible to work with.

Even though this is the first time I have met Krista, I am eager to learn more about her. Her social skills and nature will likely differ greatly from other patients; the humans with this disease tend to be fairly predictable. Is Krista going to react the same as them? Victims have all been consistent with symptoms in the past. Krista comes from the underworld, a dark, frightening place. Will this give her an advantage against the hallucinations of the disease? Only time will tell, and for now all I can do is talk with her and have her open her thoughts to me. She was resistant to basic questions; something more is on her mind and I hope to understand what that is. Whether she is simply scared of the disease she has, or if there is something else bothering her, it will play a critical role in the way she reacts to Mental Damnation. The disease is known to take its victims' surroundings and convince the infected that the environment is harmful to them.

For the time being, all I can do is wait, observe, and gradually have her speak with me more. In the meantime, Paladin always has other tasks that I need to keep up with: mending wounded trainees and his spiritual student, Marilyn. I'm pleased that we will be able to catch up.

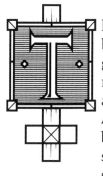

he air was cool, with a soft warm breeze blowing over the trees, shrubs and tall grass growing on each side of the gravel road. The light on the path was dimming as the sun began to set for the day. Dr. Alsroc kept his hands cupped behind his back, breathing in through his nose to savour the fresh air in the High Barracks garden. He enjoyed the wind that swept between his feet, wrapped in leather sandals. His red robe—the Kingdom of Zingalg's distinct deep-red royal colour—reached down to his ankles, collecting some of the dust that rose from each step he took.

To his right was Paladin, who wore his full uniform, complete with a breastplate, shin and wrist guards, and chainmail shirt. Alsroc often reflected that the man never knew when to take off his suit and lower his guard. He kept his gaze straight ahead, mouth closed tight and eyes squinted; there must be many thoughts boiling through his mind.

Dr. Alsroc specialized in understanding the expression of emotions in the body, and the critical role it played in studying Mental

Damnation. Being able to decode a subject's physical language could reveal so much more than the words they used, which could easily be twisted to tell lies or half-truths. The body is much more difficult to control and will reflect emotions.

"Something on your mind, Paladin?" Dr. Alsroc asked, turning to look at the leaves on the trees blowing with each breeze.

Paladin sighed. "Indeed you are right, Dr. Alsroc."

"You never hide it well."

"I do not, but no one asks. They simply assume it's my age and write it off as such."

Dr. Alsroc smirked. "Even in your age you still behave and look the same as the day I met you."

"Back when you were an upstart youth—much like some of these boys," Paladin replied, pausing. "I owe my clarity to God and the strength he gives."

"I wish I could say the same for myself. However, I don't think God has been too kind to me. I'm getting old and the constant traveling is beginning to wear on me."

"You always have a place at the High Barracks of Zingalg; perhaps it is your calling. Not chasing around after mentally troubled youth to learn more about an incurable disease."

"This incurable disease is becoming more rampant as time goes by. If I do not investigate, who will? And when?"

"Rampant? Or is it simply the few bizarre cases that have happened and they are being talked about more frequently?"

"No, it is truly more prominent now. I've been studying cases of it for over five years and all of them hold striking similarities with symptoms and lifespan expectancies after being diagnosed with the disease."

"Again, it all seems too structured to be something that nature could conjure."

"I know your theory on Mental Damnation being a spiritual experience. I have been down this road before."

"Not far enough, clearly."

Alsroc exhaled heavily. It was frustrating to talk with Paladin about this topic; they always differed in opinion on what exactly the disease was and Paladin refused to see his side of the argument. They had spent hours debating before, hypothesizing and criticizing the other's stance on the subject.

"Yes, well, if my studies take me down that path again I am not going to rule it out. But for now, my best results have been through medicine and alchemy which, for me, supports the idea of it being a disease, not otherworldly."

Paladin shrugged. "Suit yourself."

"Change of topic: how are the boys doing with their training? I've only seen a couple of them in my office with wounds since I have come back."

"They're the same as before. Immature, childish, and stupid."

"That's a little bit of a harsh statement, don't you think?" said Alsroc.

Paladin folded his arms. "It's a fact. Every day is like pulling teeth to keep their attention. They have warm food, a roof over their head, yet they are ungrateful for what they have been given."

"They train long hours every day, with little to no downtime. They're exhausted."

"Paladins were able to endure far more practical and aggressive training. These boys' abilities to learn are lagging so much that I haven't even been able to introduce them to their real training."

"Which is?" Alsroc asked.

"Field training; leaving the barracks to go onto missions where they will experience their first kill."

"They are simply boys."

Paladin relaxed his arms. "Yes, and with that they are bothered."

"Any in particular?"

"William. He started talking to Krista."

"Oh? I was certain the boys would be discouraged to talk with her because of her appearance."

"Most of the men and women in the High Barracks are," said Paladin. "William is different, though; he has difficulties keeping focus. His mind is constantly wandering in directions that aren't relevant to his training."

Alsroc shook his head. "He is a boy; their minds aren't developed."

"Exactly why it is crucial that he focuses: so his mind will develop properly. So he shines best in the eyes of the kingdom and to God."

"Ideally. Does Krista take interest in him as well?"

"They both seem to want to get to know each other more," said Paladin.

"How old is she exactly?"

"She says she is three hundred. Vazeleads are a slow-aging race and their minds develop equally as slowly. I'd say based on her maturity level, mentally she can't be older than 15 or 16. William's age."

Alsroc stroked his beard. "Quite interesting. Krista is much older than most of the cases I have dealt with Mental Damnation. The majority are ages six to twelve. I have had a couple cases with older patients."

"What were the results with the older cases?"

Alsroc looked to the ground. "Never ended well. They did have stronger resistances to the disease, though. It took them far longer to buy into the hallucinations that are projected by Mental Damnation. The schizophrenic behaviours were almost non-existent in some. Regardless, they still perished."

"Through internal bleeding? Like the others?" Paladin asked.

"Yes, it always ends that way. If they manage to survive with the disease for a couple weeks, they mention the sighting of the Weaver in the fictional hell of Dreadweave Pass."

"Again, strikingly similar to the history of the Heavenly Kingdoms and Dega'Mostikas's Triangle."

"But not exactly familiar. Does anyone actually know details of Dega'Mostikas's Triangle?"

"No, we don't. It has always just been known as the three hells."

"Exactly. Dreadweave Pass and the Weaver are fictional characters. Something seen in every case," said Alsroc.

"Is that not odd to you?"

"It is unexplained. Which doesn't mean I will start calling to the Heavens for answers. I hypothesize that the original Mental Damnation disease could have come from one victim's mind, who had the original thought of Dreadweave Pass and the Weaver. From there, the memory was permanently transcribed into each disease."

"You think the disease changes, then?" Paladin asked. "Why wouldn't it bring in other thoughts from new victims?"

"I believe the disease can alter with each carrier that passes Mental

Damnation onto a new victim, who will then experience some of the thoughts from the carrier. Mental Damnation feeds on energy, or thoughts, in the mind—so it would only make sense it holds on to some of those thoughts when it infects a new body. Similar to a phantom limb syndrome, it projects these visions and feelings into one's mind. But because carriers are so rare, I don't think the disease mutates often and the thoughts of the Weaver and Dreadweave Pass from the original carrier are consistent."

"Another theory," said Paladin.

Alsroc shrugged. "It's better than nothing. With something so unexplained I must remain optimistic. Especially seeing how many lives Mental Damnation destroys."

"How did it go with your last patient, by the way?"

Alsroc stopped in his tracks and shook his head. "Not good. I was there for fifteen days and on the last night Frenan got increasingly worse. He died in my arms that very evening; there was no remedy that could aid him."

Paladin nodded and looked up to the sky. "Heartbreaking."

"His mother was devastated. It was her only son and her husband had been away from the farm that day to trade some of their goods. She had to bring the crushing news to him when he returned."

"Were you able to learn something from the experience?"

"I did get to study the disease at an earlier state. A lot of the patients I discover require a lot of traveling through the kingdom and I don't see them until the later stages of the disease. So I took a lot of notes about the early development of Mental Damnation."

"What stage is Krista in, then?"

"She hasn't shown any of the symptoms yet, so I am guessing it has only been a day or two since she has gotten the mark."

"Krista had it the day I found her, which was about that time."

"Let's keep a close watch on her, then. Her case could be critical toward the cure of this disease."

"We will. I have her working with Madam Marilyn during the day to keep her out of trouble. Otherwise she spends too much time with William and his friends. I do not want her distracting them from their studies."

"Understandable. How is she getting along with Marilyn?"

"Well, I presume. They spent some time together after their day's work, chatting under the Twisted Hermit. I think having a girl of similar maturity will be good for Krista."

"Do you know much about Krista's past?"

The two stepped forward, continuing their stroll down the garden.

"No, I don't; we haven't talked much. She is still new to the surface and it is taking time for her to adjust. I had proposed an offer to her: safekeeping here in the High Barracks in exchange for crucial knowledge about her people. I am hoping she accepts and I can learn more about her then."

"What if she doesn't accept this offer?"

"I will have to take her to the kingdom's capital, where they will not treat her as kindly as I have."

"Indeed. I assume you have sent word to the king about her being a vazelead on the surface?"

"Of course. He will be expecting further details about the vazelead people soon. I am eager to know how they got here too. If I do not provide this information to the king, he will demand Krista be turned over to him so the information can be extracted from her by other means."

"Is there any way you can stall them? I'd like to keep Krista in our hands for as long as we can. There's much to learn from her."

"I agree; It would pain me to send a child to such a place. I can stall the king for a short time if Krista doesn't accept my offer. But I am hoping that her working alongside Marilyn will warm her up to us and she'll willingly offer the information. The potential of her people being free from the underworld is a risk to the kingdom."

"That would be preferable, wouldn't it? I have to add: since I have been gone for a number of weeks—and with the excitement surrounding Krista—I haven't been up to date with Marilyn. How is she managing?"

"Same as before. She is disturbed greatly. I worry about her faith in God."

"Nothing has improved since you've taken her under your wing?"

"I have always kept watch on her since she has grown up in the High Barracks, but now that I have taken a more active role in her life, teaching her the ways of God, I have only seen little improvements.

She expresses a lot of curiosity in dark, unholy topics and holds in so much anger toward her surroundings. Things someone so young shouldn't be engaged with."

"We could put her on some medication to help calm her temper."

"I would prefer we didn't. I fear there is more going on in her life than she wishes to share with me. She seems to be in pain. I regret not spending more one-on-one time with her to strengthen her spirit. My days are consumed by the boys and most evenings involve the management of the High Barracks, the security of the kingdom, and being roped into the politics of Zingalg and the eastern empires."

"You are spread thin, Paladin; there's little more you can take on."

"It angers me to spend more time consulting than delivering the word of God."

"That was another era. We're at a time of peace more than ever, and your other skills are being utilized now. Let me help with Marilyn; her situation has similarities to Mental Damnation and I can provide her with herbs that will help reduce her anger."

"I appreciate your offer, Dr. Alsroc, but I would rather keep her away from worldly medicine for her internal spiritual conflict. If anything, I'll have her spend more time with Father Isaac in the church. You are here to help mend my soldiers and study Krista. Focus on her."

"Then let me make the calls on how we treat Krista. She is clinically ill, not spiritually haunted."

"Fair enough, you are in charge of her wellbeing."

Alsroc nodded. "Good. I will begin mixing a new herbal potion that will keep her emotions at bay, before Mental Damnation consumes her and she loses control."

ENCYCLOPEDIA

Characters

Abesun (abe-son) – Half human and half vazelead, his name translates to 'obscene' in Draconic. Abesun wanders both the underworld and surface world, able to move between the two undetected by the holy shackles created by the Paladins of Zeal. He is unaccepted by both humans and vazeleads due to their racial dispute toward each other. He is a known survivor of Mental Damnation, bearing the mark on his hand.

Alistind – A red-scalp-feathered vazelead who was a missionary for the Eyes of Eternal Life.

Alsroc, Doctor – Physician at the High Barracks who often journeys throughout Zingalg to investigate the mysterious disease known as Mental Damnation. He has a long-running history with Paladin and the two remain in disagreement over the disease. Doctor Alsroc is certain that it is a worldly issue and not spiritual.

Ast'Bala – One of the Five Guardians of the vazelead, Ast'Bala is the only of his kind with red skin. He is the second of the guardians to become corrupt with Mental Damnation and to be chosen as a gatekeeper by the Weaver. He hand-picked Krista to be reaped by a gatekeeper of their world, which ends up being Danil.

Cae Norphyl (say nor-fill) – The youngest of the Five Guardians, he is easily identifiable from his smoky-grey skin and blue-flamed eyes. Ast'Bala said Cae was the first to become infected with Mental Damnation and he was forced to kill him.

Creator, the – Known as God amongst the humans. The being who created the Heavenly Kingdoms, the mortal realm, and Dega'Mostikas's Triangle.

Cursman (curse-man) – Known as 'the betrayer' according to General Dievourse, Cursman was a puppet in the Weaver's army that escaped the fallen god's grasp.

Danil – One of the Five Guardians, and the older brother of Demontochai. He becomes consumed by Mental Damnation, becoming a gatekeeper, from Ast'Bala's touch during a battle in the marketplace in the City of Renascence. He mysteriously uses Krista in a ritual that brings them both to the surface world.

Das – A well-profited vazelead in the High District who is known for lavish parties. Krista had gone to his party in hopes of obtaining food, only to be discovered and ultimately banned from the High District.

Darkwing Lashback – Krista's closest friend who has known her since before their people's banishment to the underworld. His intentions are good-natured but his actions are no proof of it. He once had interest in the Blood Hounds before the Guardians Ast'Bala and Danil became obsessed with finding Krista.

Demontochai (dee-mon-toe-kai) – One of the Five Guardians, Demontochai is the younger brother of Danil. He shrouds his identity under a steel mask, keeping a cloak and plated armour on at all times. He remains the only guardian to maintain order in the City of Renascence after Ast'Bala's corruption.

Dievourse, General (die-vorsse) – The Weaver's primary general in his army. He answers directly to his master and is tormented by his own thoughts and desires. He is one of the few puppets of the Weaver to be blessed with free will.

Draegust Bronzefeather (dray-gust) – The leader of the former gang known as the Blood Hounds. His plucked feathers create a shaved undercut hairstyle that makes him easily identifiable among his people.

Doyel – Chef at the High Barracks, he makes most of the food for the boys and soldiers in the barracks, aided by several assistants.

El Aguro (el-a-gooro) – One of the Weaver's gatekeepers who guards an unknown world. He was the one who initially found the vazelead people and the Five Guardians.

Father Isaac – Priest of the High Barracks church.

Fanlos – One of the original Blood Hound members, presumed dead after their attempt to assault Demontochai.

Fleerew – A half-Corrupt found on the far side of Magma Falls. She is known for her shamanistic practices, giving her supernatural powers.

Fongoxent (fong-oh-zent) – Draconem of gold. He discovered that the vazelead people and the draconem shared a common ancestry during the Drac Age.

Forrlash (for-lash) – A Renascence Guard who patrols the Lower District in search of gangs and scum. He captured Krista and Darkwing in one of his purges, losing his partner in the process before the prisoners were set free.

Franch – One of the paladins on Mount Kuzuchi, close friend of Zalphium. He perished during the ice storm caused by Drac Lord Karazickle.

Fythem (fi-them) – The citadel prison's head torturer. He decides where prisoners go and when they should be interrogated for information.

Hazuel (has-you'll) – One of the Weaver's previous gatekeepers. His key was torn from his rib cage by Abesun, killing him in the process so the half-breed could escape from Dreadweave Pass.

Jeuth – A redheaded boy who is training at the High Barracks of Zingalg. He is friends with William.

John, Captain – Serves directly under Paladin at the High Barracks, carrying out his commands. He is also responsible for the soldiers at the barracks, sending them on tasks and maintaining order within the barracks walls.

Karazickle (cara-zic-el) – Also known as Drac Lord of the Night. The last of the drac lords and the most dangerous of his kind. A paladin named Zalphium accuses Saule, the leader of the Paladins of Zeal, of being the Drac Lord in disguise through a formula of transmogrification. His current location remains unknown.

Kristalantice Scalebane (Krista) – A young vazelead who struggles with her own identity after her family is killed during their people's banishment. She has a habit of latching onto those stronger than her for protection opposed to growing as her own being. After reaching the surface world and being infected with Mental Damnation, she now struggles with her own mental wellbeing.

Lieutenant, the – General Dievourse's loyal servant. He executes any command given to him by Dievourse without question. Built from various flesh parts—like all the Weaver's puppets—he remains silent awaiting a command.

Malpherities – A ghoul who resides in Dreadweave Pass. He takes an interest in saving Krista and her case of Mental Damnation. The two have a lot of friction in their relationship because only Krista can see him in the real world. Eventually the two of them learn to work together.

Marilyn – Maid at the High Barracks of Zingalg. She is one of the few maids there, which causes her a lot of work. She is standoffish and does not warm up to people easily. Paladin rescued her from her mother and father at a young age and now he tries to teach her the ways of God.

Muluve Scalebane (muh-love) – Krista's mother who was murdered by the Knight's Union during the vazelead banishment.

Necktelantelx (neck-tah-lan-tell-ex) – One of the drac lords of the drac age. Current status remains unknown.

Paladin – The last of the Paladins. He assumed the name 'Paladin' so the world would remember what they once were. He is first in command of the High Barracks where his responsibilities include training the boys and managing the soldiers and staff. He is lost in his past and longs for the days of crusades.

Risen One, the – The mysterious being that the Eyes of Eternal Life worships. They believe he is in a state of limbo and needs his followers to awaken him.

Salanth Scalebane (sall-an-th) – Krista's ill-fated little brother who was killed during the vazelead banishment.

Saulaph (sah-ool-af) – An albino vazelead who could only find shelter through the Eyes of Eternal Life. He worked as a missionary to recruit more members into the temple. Danil managed to control his mind with his dark powers as a gatekeeper and sacrificed the albino's life to complete a necromantic ritual of blood.

Saule (sah-ool) – Founder and leader of the Paladins of Zeal. Responsible for the order of banishing the vazelead people to the underworld. He is accused of being Karazickle, Drac Lord of the Night, by a young paladin named Zalphium during the banishment of the vazelead people.

Scalius Scalebane (scale-yes) – Krista's father, a carpenter who taught Krista about self-defense and morals. He perished by the Knight's Union during the banishment of the vazelead people.

Shoth – Co-founder of the Blood Hounds. He left the gang finding himself unable to commit fully. Still working as a for-hire killer for the Blood Hounds, he was eventually caught by the Renascence Guard. He escaped during the prisoner release caused by Ast'Bala.

Smyth – At equal place in the High Barracks with Captain John, answering directly to Paladin.

Snog – Blood Hound member who followed Draegust closely. He is presumed dead after their attempt to attack guardian Demontochai.

Sporathun (spore-wrath-son) – A fallen angel who was banished to Dreadweave Pass. He caused immense destruction in anger of his expulsion before General Dievourse could intervene.

Talif – A black-haired boy training at the High Barracks of Zingalg. Friends with William.

Weaver, The – Ruler of Dreadweave Pass. Victims of Mental Damnation see him just before they perish. He is said to be a fallen god banished from the heavens for his unholy practices of fusing souls against their will.

William – One of the boys training at the High Barracks. Krista is charmed by his blonde hair, blue eyes, and warm personality. The two of them continue to try to spend time together which causes him to lose focus on his training.

Wrinkle Scale – The elder vazelead who runs a potion shop that Krista and Darkwing broke into. He had informed Krista that he is the uncle of Abesun.

Zalphium (zal-fee-um) – A young paladin who had discovered the truth about the Paladins of Zeal leader,

Saule. Exposed Saule to his brethren during the banishment of the vazeleads. He is presumed dead after Karazickle summoned an ice storm.

Zeveal – One of the Five Guardians of the vazelead people. Battled Ast'Bala just after he corrupted Danil. His current status remains unknown.

Factions/Groups

Blood Hounds – One of many gangs found in the City of Renascence, led by Draegust. Also the gang Darkwing was infatuated with and ultimately joined. They strongly believed in anarchy, attempting to bring the downfall of the Renascence Guard and the Five Guardians. The group was massacred by Demontochai when they attempted to overthrow him and claim the City of Renascence for themselves.

Corrupt, the – A group of vazeleads whose bodies reacted poorly to the metamorphosis fumes of the underworld. Their physical forms and minds degenerated, making them behave like rabid animals, craving anarchy. They stray from civilization and resort to cannibalism for food.

Council of Just – The overruling group of the brave and bold heroes who led humanity out of the dark times of the Drac Age. They have been entrusted with making critical decisions for the best of all humanity.

Drac Lords – The leaders of the draconem. They hold higher intelligence and otherworldly powers than their lesser kin; this gives them the rightful place as rulers of their kind. All except for Karazickle are believed to have died during the Drac Age, defeated by the humans.

Eyes of Eternal Life – A vazelead cult that resides in the underworld desert not far from Magma Falls. They worship the being known as the Risen One who promises them freedom from the humans' banishment if awakened. They believe they offer the vazelead people an alternative to living under the Five Guardians and Renascence Guard.

Five Guardians, the – The leaders of the vazelead people who united their race under a single civilization. They were able to achieve this because their bodies reacted uniquely to the metamorphosis fumes from most of their kind, giving them super strength, size, and draconic wings. They had recently fallen apart after Ast'Bala and Cae had come into contact with Mental Damnation.

Gatekeepers, the – Privileged beings chosen by the Weaver to guard the rifts to various worlds in the mortal realm. They personally hunt souls for the Weaver to complete the harvest. There had always been two gatekeepers until El Aguro discovered the vazelead people. This convinced the Weaver to maximize his efforts in reaping souls. He converted three of the Five Guardians into gatekeepers: Cae, Ast'Bala, and Danil.

High Council – The high council of the Eyes of Eternal Life oversaw the temple members' efforts in freeing the Risen One. They spoke with him directly to free him from his slumber.

Knight's Union – Brave men from around the world who spent their entire lives training in battle. They allied with the Paladins of Zeal to end the Drac Age and to banish the vazelead people from the surface world.

Paladins of Zeal – Holy men who devoted their existence to the church of God and mystical rites. They allied with the Knight's Union to end the Drac Age and to banish the vazelead people.

Renascence Guard – The military of the vazelead people created by the Five Guardians to lead their people back to a righteous path. They are committed to ridding their people of gangs and those who follow false faiths. Their sole purpose is to unify their people as a single entity with the Five Guardians. The Renascence Guard captains wear bronze armour compared to their brethren. The gate guards wear less armour than those sent on execution missions.

Savage Claw – One of the gangs that reside in the Lower District. The second largest gang next to the Blood Hounds.

Places

Blood Hound Hideout – Located near the southern outskirts of the City of Renascence.

City of Renascence – The unified efforts of the banished vazeleads to bring their people together. The city was built against a mountainside and sectioned into three areas: The Lower District, the Commoner's District, and the High District.

Citadel – The large castle that resides in the High District. It functions as the home of the Five Guardians and training grounds of the Renascence Guard. The far-right wing extends into the Commoner's District, functioning as the city's prisons where they keep convicts and gang members of the city.

Citadel Bell – The only indicator of time in the City of Renascence. Its workings remain a mystery to the common vazelead people. They only know that one ring indicates midday, two rings means midnight, and three rings means morning.

Commoner's District, the – One of the three districts in the City of Renascence, it is home to middle-class vazeleads. Situated between the other two districts, it is also home of the marketplace—where commoners trade their goods amongst one another.

Dega'Mostikas's Triangle (deh-gah-moss-ti-cas) – The triangular shape that forms the three hells of the afterlife.

Dreadweave Pass – The nightmarish hell victims of Mental Damnation find themselves in. It is said to be one of the three hells in Dega'Mostikas's Triangle. Ruled by the Weaver and his army of puppets. The Heavenly Kingdoms use it as a state of purgatory where souls can redeem themselves from their mortal life of sin.

Eyes of Eternal Life Temple – Located near Magma Falls, it is home for the cult Eyes of Eternal Life.

Heavenly Kingdoms – The ideal place a soul resides in the afterlife. The gods, angels, and souls deemed worthy live eternally in the kingdoms.

High Barracks of Zingalg – The barracks designated to

train the mightiest warriors in the kingdom. It is run by Paladin, the sole remaining member of the Paladins of Zeal. The barracks often takes boys at a young age to start their training early, so they can be resilient and ready to serve their king as soon as they become men.

High District, the – One of the three districts of the City of Renascence. It is the smallest of the three and only home to the upper class of vazeleads. The streets are scattered with art installations, sculptures, and unique architectural designs.

Kingdom of Zingalg (zin-gal-g) – A country comprising the continent of Zingalg in the South Atlantic. It is home to the largest mountain in the world, Mount Kuzuchi. Currently ruled by King Loathsan.

Kuzuchi Forest (cu-zu-chi) – The forest area at the base of Mount Kuzuchi. Krista's home village was not far from the mountain; her and her father used to pick berries from the shrubs located in the forest.

Lower District, the – The largest of the three districts in the City of Renascence, it is where the gangs and scum reside. Most of the buildings are built from clay, blackwood trees, and stone. The upper half is where the Savage Claw reside while the lower half is the Blood Hounds' territory.

Magma Falls – The only water source in the underworld comes from this large mountain—or presumed pillar—with a pathway leading to the surface world, as directed by Abesun. The water runs down the mountainside and into a large lava pool creating immense amounts of steam. Vazelead farmers harvest water to bring to the City of Renascence on the near side of the mountain whereas the far side is littered with Corrupt.

Mortal realm – The realm of the living as defined by the Heavenly Kingdoms. There are numerous worlds found in this realm; the exact number remains unknown.

Mount Kuzuchi (cu-zu-chi) – The tallest mountain in the world. Its height extends beyond the clouds—high enough that when you reached the peak, you could hear angels sing. It is also the only known gateway into the underworld.

Slum Tower – Located in the South Lower District. It has become one of the primary locations for the city's homeless population. It provides shelter from the harsh winds, gangs, and Renascence Guard.

Temple of Zeal – The Paladins of Zeal's primary headquarters, reserved for serving God and training. Its current state remains unknown since the paladins were destroyed by the Drac Lord Karazickle.

Twisted Hermit, the – A large tree in the centre of the High Barracks of Zingalg. It is often used as a gathering spot for the boys due to the shelter it provides.

Underworld, the – An incredibly dark place beneath the surface, lit only by the molten lava that surrounds the landscape. Most of the land remains uncharted and uninhabitable from the darkness, harsh winds, and heat, except for by beings who mutated adaptations from the metamorphosis fumes. The underworld is also native to the giant beasts and bugs who roam the vast sand dunes.

Zingalg – A continent in the South Atlantic. Ruled by a single kingdom.

Items

Aldrif cheese (al-drif) – A dairy product made by vazelead farmers from their aldrif cattle.

Dracoins (drah-coins) – The currency used by vazelead people in the City of Renascence.

Races

Angels – Servants of the gods in the Heavenly Kingdoms. Their chanting can be heard by mortals atop Mount Kuzuchi.

Draconem (drah-co-nem) – A large flying reptilian kind with several subspecies. The older, wiser draconem such as the Drac Lords rule over their lesser kin. A notable Drac Lord is Karazickle, Drac Lord of the Night.

Ghouls – Spectral beings that are quite like shades with the exception of mobility. A notable ghoul is Malpherities, who takes an interest in Krista.

Gods – Powerful beings who reside in the Heavenly Kingdoms. They dictate what happens in the mortal realm and in the afterlife.

Humans – The most dominant race throughout the known world. They have been able to advance their technologies and reproduce their kind quicker than any of the other sentient races. Two of their factions, the Paladins of Zeal and the Knight's Union, are responsible for ending the Drac Age through allegiances with the nymphs.

Nymphs – Supernatural beings that have knowledge of words of power that can manipulate simple minds. The nymphs and humans formed a union to end the Drac Age, utilizing their respective strengths.

Puppets – Beings created by the Weaver through means of necromancy. They are his sentient servants constructed from body parts of various souls while maintaining each body's consciousness.

Troll – A tribal race with the ability to manipulate the weather.

Vazelead (vayse-lead) – Meaning 'Drac Men' in Draconic, they are a reptilian race originating in the South Atlantic and the Kingdom of Zingalg. Naturally their lifespans last for hundreds of years, bodies and minds maturing slowly.

They were banished from the surface by humans to live in the underworld because the humans believed they served the Drac Lord Karazickle. This has yet to be proven true or false.

In the underworld, the harsh living conditions mutated their appearance to have dark smooth skin and scales running down their backs. Their eyes glow with fire, believed to be caused by their desire for vengeance upon mankind.

Creatures

Aldrifs – Cattle of the vazelead farmers, they are used to produce dairy products.

Desert Crawlers – Creatures that live throughout the deserts of the underworld, they feast on any flesh they can find. When found young, they can be tamed and used as watch dogs. They are commonly used by farmers to guard their fungus fields.

Dune Diggers – Large, bulky creatures used by the vazelead people as cavalry and as a source of meat. Their faces are often covered with a muzzle to protect civilians from their sharp teeth.

Dune Worms – Large worms that live in the desert of the underworld. They are hunted by the vazelead people for their meat.

Shades – Difficult to tame, shades are mysterious reptilian creatures of the underworld that have many rumours surrounding their ethereal form. Their appearance remains as mysterious as their telepathic abilities, able to send complete sentences into people's thoughts.

Eras

Drac Age – A time when powerful drac lords ruled the world. It was eventually brought to an end when the humans learned words of power from the nymphs.

Vazelead Banishment – After the Drac Age, humans became the dominant race throughout the globe. They grew paranoid of other races gaining power and were willing to punish any being that posed a threat. Saule, the leader of the Paladins of Zeal, accused the vazelead people of being loyal servants to the Drac Lords. Because of this, they were banished to the underworld where they could no longer be a threat.

Languages

Draconic (drah-con-ick) – Language of the draconem. Vazeleads also spoke a weak version of it when they were initially discovered by humans.

English – The common tongue amongst the humans, in Europe and the Kingdom of Zingalg. They forced the vazelead people to learn the language when they enslaved them.

Disorders

Mental Damnation – A brain disease that causes horrific hallucinations, hostile dreams, psychosis, and paranoia. The afflicted believe that they cross into hell during their sleep. The physical effects include self-inflicted trauma, barbaric behavior, sporadic muscle growth, and decaying of flesh.

Plants

Blackwood Trees – Whether a root or an actual tree, it is a type of plant that grows rapidly in the underworld. It is commonly used to build structures in the City of Renascence and by farmers for their water harvests.

Alron Mushrooms – Commonly found in the underworld, this fungus is cultivated and eaten by the vazelead people.

Misc

Day Cycle – Eyes of Eternal Life designation for days dedicated to attempting to free the Risen One.

Law of Unity – Created by the Five Guardians, the basic law includes modest concepts such as outlawing murder and theft. A further 'unity law' under development would trump all other laws: when in public, vazeleads are to conceal all skin, including their faces, under clothing.

Metamorphosis Fumes – A natural element in the air of the underworld. Anyone who inhales the fumes will have their body's evolutionary process drastically increased, quickly mutating them to adapt to the underworld's harsh environment.

Necromantic Ritual of Blood – A powerful blood ritual that requires a sacrifice of the innocent. Their blood is used to trick the holy power of the subject's imprisoner into thinking they detained an innocent being. The shackles then break, freeing the ritual performer.

Prayer of Power – An ability performed by paladins, capable of many different feats depending on what they desired to achieve.

Scum/Street Runner – Homeless in the City of Renascence. Name given by commoners and the Renascence Guard to identify those who are not contributing to their civilization.

Silent Day – Eyes of Eternal Life designation for resting days where the temple members are free to do as they please.

Poem References

Thank you for reading Dream, would you consider giving it a review?

Reviewing an author's book on primary book sites such as Amazon, Kobo and Goodreads drastically help authors promote their novels and it becomes a case study for them when pursuing new endeavors. A review can be as short as a couple of sentences or up to several paragraphs, it's up to you. You can find review options on Goodreads or your preferred online distributor such as Amazon or Kobo.

Additional Work by Konn Lavery

Mental Damnation Series | Seed Me Horror Novel | YEGman Thriller Novel

S.O.S. - YEGman Novel Soundtrack | World Mother: Seed Me Novel Score.

Find *Seed Me, YEGman, S.O.S - YEGman Novel Soundtrack* and the *World Mother: Seed Me Novel Score* at:
www.konnlavery.com

About the Author

Konn Lavery is a Canadian horror, thriller and fantasy writer who is known for his Mental Damnation series. The second book, Dream, reached the Edmonton Journal's top five selling fictional books list. He started writing fantasy stories at a very young age while being home schooled. It wasn't until graduating college that he began professionally pursuing his work with his first release, Reality. Since then he has continued to write works of fiction, expanding his

interest in the horror, thriller and fantasy genres.

His literary work is done in the long hours of the night. By day, Konn runs his own graphic design and website development business under the title Reveal Design (www.revealdesign.ca). These skills have been transcribed into the formatting and artwork found within his publications supporting his fascination of transmedia storytelling.

67500926R00217

Made in the USA
Middletown, DE
11 September 2019